EASY MONEY is the fast-moving story of Lex Parlane, a flamboyant Glaswegian self-made millionaire, bookmaker and gambler. Self-proclaimed "the most famous Scotsman since Rabbie Burns", Lex is driven by his love of the turf, of the lure of a bet, of fast horses and even faster women. Few can keep up with his pace. One of them is James Richmond, an incorrigible young spendthrift and hedonist who happens to be the youngest son of racing's premier Duke, the Senior Steward of the Jockey Club. Lex oversees and contributes to his initiation and gradual descent into the compelling but addictive world of gambling and horse racing, alcohol and drugs.

The story takes Parlane, Richmond and Parlane's tame journalist friend Jack McQueen — sports reporter and another compulsive punter — on a vivid, detailed and often extremely funny journey through the racetracks, betting offices, restaurants and night-clubs of Glasgow, Dublin and London. It also paints a wickedly comic, larger-than-life picture of the English upper class's horsey establishment. And all the time Lex is trying to keep one swift step ahead of the authorities.

About the Author

Jamie Reid was born in Dingwall and educated at University College, Oxford and Stanford University, California. He has been a passionate follower of horse-racing all his life; he had his first bet on a horse at the age of six.

He used to be an actor and worked at the Crucible Theatre in Sheffield in 1977-8. At the age of nineteen he wrote his first play which later won a First Fringe Award at the Edinburgh Festival in 1974. He then became a playwright, with his first professionally produced play being *The Bozo*, performed at the Young Vic in 1978. He was resident writer at the Young Vic from 1979-80. The most recent of his five major stage plays was the highly acclaimed adaptation of *The Night They Raided Minsky's*, which was on national tour in 1982-3. *Easy Money* is Jamie Reid's first novel.

For Mel and David

Copyright © Jamie Reid, 1985

First published in Great Britain in 1985 by
Mainstream Publishing Company (Edinburgh) Ltd

Coronet edition 1987

Printed and bound in Great Britain for
Hodder and Stoughton Paperbacks, a
division of Hodder and Stoughton Ltd.,
Mill Road, Dunton Green, Sevenoaks,
Kent (Editorial Office: 47 Bedford
Square, London, WC1B 3DP) by
Cox & Wyman Ltd., Reading.

British Library Cataloguing in Publication Data

Reid, Jamie
 Easy money.
 I. Title
 823'.914 [F]   PR6068.E45

 ISBN 0–340–40412–4

EASY MONEY

Jamie Reid

CORONET BOOKS
Hodder and Stoughton

1

Lex Parlane. Eyes like a shark in a face of puff pastry. That afternoon Lex and the boys had taken nearly three hundred thousand out of the ring on the winner of the big four-mile Amateur Riders' steeplechase. The champagne had been flowing ever since. First on the racecourse. Then in their helicopters. Then in their hotel suites. The gold and turquoise private dining room of their luxury modern Cotswold hotel was now littered with the fragmented remains of their specially selected dinner menu. Avocado Crab Mexicaine. Salmon Pancakes Portugaise. Then a choice of Guinea Fowl Chartreuse or Venison in Hunter Sauce followed by Chocolat au Pot Delicieuse served with whipped cream and Cointreau.

The mostly Irish company of more than twenty men but no women included an expatriate ice cream baron from Newark, New Jersey, two priests, two brothers – both cattle rustlers – from Belfast, several prominent Dublin horse dealers and the now tuxedoed figure of Lex Parlane. Lex was flushed and beaming hugely, little folds of fat popping out over his shirt collar. He was the Scot who'd got the money on for this particular Irish coup. And from the look of their suits you could tell there was nothing cheap about this gathering. Nothing cheap about the bottles of vintage armagnac and vintage port. Nothing cheap about the cut of the huge Romeo and Juliet cigars in their hands. To the more senior of the three Italian waiters present the large oval table of increasingly expansive diners appeared to be completely shrouded in a thick blue pall of rich and aromatic smoke. The waiter, silverhaired and sleekly uniformed in blue velvet and black brocade, smiled to himself and nodded imperceptibly.

This was not how it used to be, he thought. In the old days. At the Metropole. And the Savoy.

The hundredth champagne bottle had just been passed. To commemorate the occasion a couple of puffing and pink-faced junior waiters – local boys in hired bow ties – were rolling a pair of grand pianos into the dining room. Several sweet trolleys were swept away along with a standard lamp and a canteen of cutlery. One wing of the table was then collapsed and the chairs moved round so that the two pianos could be moved into the now empty space of swirling Cyril Lord luxury. Lex took the chair at one while a rubicund Country and Western star from Blackrock, County Dublin, jumped up on top of the other and launched into the obligatory rendition of *Rose of Tralee*. He followed this up with a quick medley comprising *Tie a Yellow Ribbon Round The Old Oak Tree*, *Ramona* and *Sailing*, which included a special extra verse about wadfuls of conquering Irish punts sailing across the Irish Sea. It was all respectable Ryan's Hotel-Bray seafront stuff, but when Lex took over the level of audience interest and concentration rose audibly. Lex took the tone upmarket. All the way up to his favourite recording star, Frankie Sinatra. Starting with *Chicago* and then moving on confidently into *High Hopes* and *New York, New York*, Lex played 'Blue Eyes' to his Irish Dean Martin. His piano playing had been tuneful, rhythmic, even mellifluous. His singing was even better. His deep well-soaked West of Scotland bass voice boomed out around the room with considerable assurance. He paused just once, turning on his stool to wink across the room at the three Italian waiters who were still standing there beneath the fluted crenellations of the dining room doorway.

"There's an old saying from my schooldays," said Lex. "Coat your lungs and pass the brandy." They all laughed. Lex inhaled deeply on his cigar, held the tobacco in his lungs for several seconds and then exhaled the smoke luxuriously. The eldest Italian responded spontaneously by snatching up the bottle of armagnac nearest to him and throwing it across the room at Lex who saw it coming and caught it dextrously with one hand above his head. "Thanks, pal," said Lex, uncorking the bottle and holding it up to the Italian as if in a salute. He took a large gulp, replaced the stopper and slammed the bottle back down on the top of the piano. He turned back to the gathering.

"Alright, my chinas," he said. "This next number is dedicated to the maestro himself. Mr Lester Piggott!" With a bravura flourish he swung back round to the piano keys and launched into *Who wants to be a millionaire?* "I do," chorused the table, roaring their approval and banging on the table top with their hands and glasses. Lex carried on singing.

He was still singing five hours later when he finally opened the door of his gold and turquoise bedroom suite, number 509. Some of the other guests heard him. Some of them waved at him irritably from their bedroom doorways with rolled-up copies of *Horse and Hound*. Lex couldn't have cared less that night. As he was often fond of saying to his pet journalist on the *Citizen*, he never spared a thought for his rivals, detractors or better-bred critics. Parkhead, he would say, wasn't Perthshire and they didn't wear tweeds on the Rutherglen Road or brown trilby hats in the Gallowgate. That was where Lex's status was still that of a folk hero, a legend who'd put one over on the London-based Tescoland bookies with their executive suits and their accountancy minds. It was a legend that had crossed the Irish Sea too and Lex enjoyed similar canonisation in Dublin, Belfast and Cork.

Lex might well have reflected on these things that night. He often reflected on Glasgow. He was always careful about how and with whom he criticised Scotland. He hated the place but it was still his native habitat, his natural environment and constituency, and he used it to explain at least a part of his much-cherished 'Jack the Lad' identity. It had given him a role in life, a way through, an automatic image and response that he could assume at will

whenever a place or a situation required it. Lex understood these things and that understanding made him
strong.

Ripping off his smartly buckled shoes and his tailored
suit trousers, the blue silk shirt and black bow tie, he
fumbled his way into the gold and turquoise Queensize
Regency bed. He had to push past the half-eaten club
sandwiches, the *Timeform* black books and the empty
bottles of Scotch and American beer. Waiting for him was
the warm and sleeping figure of a Chinese hooker from
West Bromwich whom he'd picked up in a bar on the
racecourse about twelve hours earlier. The girl rolled
drowsily into his arms, her head nestling on his chest so
that her hair tickled his cheek and nose. But Lex didn't
mind. He luxuriated in its tousled newly shampooed
softness and enjoyed feeling the agreeable weight of her
nicotine-coloured leg pressing against his groin. He shut
his eyes and started to think.

Sleep never came easy for Lex Parlane. He needed little
and even when he was in bed his mind was always racing,
both literally and figuratively speaking. He was happy that
night. Happy, confident and strong. This was his favourite
racing bonanza of the whole year. Cheltenham. For the
rest of the time the place was a ludicrous joke. An absurd
mixture of bath buns and bath chairs, of elderly colonels
and even older Regency squares, many of them hideously
repainted in blood-chilling shades of mango chutney and
aquamarine. Lex adored it. The place was so easy for him.
It had even less steel than Weybridge. At least there was a
kind of callous charm about Weybridge, a glint of rugged
aftershave between the conifers. Cheltenham had street
names like Montpellier and Lansdowne. The once proud
addresses of retired civil servants home from the empire.
Now their homes were all divided up into private flats for
penniless widows, offices for estate agents, private nursing
homes, private schools and colleges for independent tuition. This was true of almost all the town. Except the
racecourse.

For three days in the third week in March Cheltenham racecourse became the home, the life-blood and the anointed crowning place of National Hunt Racing. And for three exhausting, raucous and alcoholic days Cheltenham the racecourse transformed Cheltenham the town. Whether it wanted to be transformed or not. The winners were exultant. The losers commiserated themselves with the thought that they should've won anyway. Only the non-players tended to look on bleakly from the sidelines. The hotel owners had a great week. They were all winners.

Lex loved hotels. He loved their convenience. Their room service. Their functional impersonality. And most of all he loved their expense. He was a winner that night. And as always when he won it was easy to feel that it was always this way. He'd win again tomorrow when his long-term selection took the Tote Cheltenham Gold Cup and then he could plan confidently for his next major business venture. The next stage of the spectacular entrepreneurial career that had carried him triumphantly from Bedford Street, Glasgow, to stockbroker Surrey inside eleven vivid and glorious years.

He looked around the room. His things were all in place. His three-hundred-guinea black tuxedo suit jacket lay sprawled across the back of a chair while three newly cleaned racecourse suits in black, blue and grey were hanging up neatly in the cupboard. Lying over each pair of suit trousers was a flamboyantly coloured wide pattern American tie purchased the previous summer on a business trip to Las Vegas. His narcotics packets were all stowed away safely in the chest of drawers. The box of cigars and the bottle of armagnac stood conveniently close to hand on the bedside table. His Rolex watch was still on his wrist. The signet rings were still on his fingers and the black tinted shades were lying on the floor by his side.

The Chinese girl shifted her weight slightly, pressing her body even more firmly against his inner thigh. Lex was in Laredo. Lex Parlane was especially fond of the Wild West

of America. His favourite fantasy was that of an outlaw on
the run. Inimitable. Unstoppable. And most important of
all, seemingly indestructible. The presence in his bed each
night of a dance-hall floosie seemed to make that image
complete right down to the last detail. He felt a tingling
sense of anticipation as if he was being dried with a
current of warm air all the way up his naked body, from
the tip of his toes to the top of his scalp. His nose was still
full of cocaine but his mind was not blurred in spite of the
alcohol. He could sense its keenness. Its clarity and edge.
Like cutting butter with a laser. He was alive. He was
Butch Cassidy if he was anyone. He felt a million dollars.
The Chinese girl opened her eyes, looked up and smiled.

When the chambermaid slipped his *Sporting Life* under
the bedroom door only a few hours later Lex was inevitably centre page three in Festival Diary. An all-action
photo of grinning connections after the four-mile chaser's
spectacular success. Even in the grainy black and white
tones of the Press Association's syndicated photograph
Lex's shades seemed to glint with victory in the late March
sun. Further back in the half-moon of onlooking pressmen
a presentation party of Hermès women and parade
ground men waited hesitantly for their moment, hovering
unstared at, awkward on the edges of the action. The
older women were all in velveteen Robin Hood hats and
elderly overcoats from Harrods or the main department
store of their local county town. The camera had not been
kind to them and they all seemed to be standing either legs
astride or balanced birdlike on one knee-booted foot,
their eyes arrested in a childish expression of upward
motion. Their mostly trilby-hatted husbands, except for
one wet-haired man who'd left his in the Range Rover,
gaped wanly at the camera, blank-faced and open-
mouthed.

When Lex saw the picture he smiled, sipped on his early
morning vodka and made a quick mental note of the nine
or ten phone calls that he needed to make before dressing,
five of them to check on his winnings of the previous day,

the rest to make plans for the coming action. Then he went into his bathroom, turned on the shower and sang.

> *Come fly with me*
> *Come fly*
> *Come fly away*

Life was sweet at the top.

2

"Tell me something, Washy," said the Duke shooting his cuff like a thirties star. "Would you say . . . I was an eccentric sort of chap?"

Lieutenant Colonel G.A.W. 'Washy' Cleveland farted, frowned and scratched the back of his neck. "Well, Johnny," he said, "a bit over imaginative maybe. A bit . . . over serious at times. But eccentric? Lord no. Never!"

The Duke nodded gravely and lit another cigarette from the silver box in his inside jacket pocket. He was a tall and not unhandsome looking man of about sixty with a trim moustache, an aquiline nose and a profile like Basil Rathbone. His companion's was the pudgier, pink-faced look of the more overtly inbred English landowner. The two men were walking slowly and alone up the long, wide expanse of turf known as the Rowley Mile. For more than three hundred years the home and headquarters of British thoroughbred flat racing. It was just after half past five, the end of a warm and drowsy October afternoon. Each man wore a suit and hat but no overcoat. Washy's hat was worn with the brim turned up at the front like a nineteenth-century American cavalry officer. This was thought by his friends to make him a 'character' and he was invariably referred to as such by the racing press. He also carried a shooting stick. They had just passed the one mile starting gate and somewhere up above them a skylark was singing. Other than the sound of the skylark the heath was silent and still.

"Marvellous weather, eh Johnny?" said Washy beaming happily. "And the light . . . it's sort of gold . . . and yet it's sort of blue at the same time." He chuckled to himself like a schoolboy. "Extraordinary really."

The Duke was not thinking about the weather. The following afternoon would see the official opening of Newmarket's first October meeting. The Duke's homebred and unbeaten two-year-old filly would start a hot favourite for the Group One Cheveley Park Stakes. On the Saturday evening he would be in Paris, making the official speech of reply as Senior Steward of the Jockey Club at the Société d'Encouragement's annual eve of Arc de Triomphe dinner at Maxim's. About seventeen hours later, at Longchamp racecourse on the southern edges of the Bois de Boulogne, his Derby runner-up would carry his colours into battle in the richest horse race in Europe. And the following Friday was his birthday. Yet, in spite of these things, the Duke was not a happy man.

"You know, Washy," he said ". . . it was my grandfather, the fourteenth Duke, who first introduced the practice of playing music to his horses. That was at his old Thorpe Lodge Stud. Up near Sandringham."

"I remember it well. We shot there last Christmas."

"At about six o'clock each morning and again at six each night, a senior stud groom would walk out into the courtyard with a wind-up gramophone, a folding table and a His Master's Voice recording of some major classical masterpiece. A few moments later . . . and out over the heads of the most majestic creatures known to man would flow the rippling cadences and sonorous tones of Beethoven, Handel, Schubert and Brahms. Debussy sometimes. Mahler never." He paused for one moment, pushing his hands down firmly into his suit trouser pockets. Were it not for the hat he could well have been a member of the England selectors or more likely the chairman of the MCC inspecting the square at Lords before the opening of a Test Match. "The thing is, Washy," he continued, "no one has yet proved that music can affect a stallion's potency. On the other hand, if you had seen as I have seen the erect member of the male horse after prolonged exposure to Beethoven's *Eroïca* then you would know that such a theory was no horse shit!" The two men laughed. Then the Duke frowned, his mouth tightening visibly. "But for this . . . harmless . . . and innocent practice . . . I am now castigated in the annals of Fleet Street as the 'eccentric' even 'senile' head of 'racing's ruling élite'. You saw them this morning." He had the cuttings in his waistcoat pocket. " 'Jockey Club Capers'. 'Delusion reigns at Portman Square'. 'The Stewards: Five Men Who Came Too Late And Stayed Too Long!' " His moustache began to twitch in a martial manner, his lower and his stiff upper lip mashing away furiously together. "It won't do, Washy," he said, shaking his head in a determined fashion. "It won't do at all."

Washy sighed, looked at the sky and tut-tutted generally in his best nanny-like manner. "Now look here, Johnny . . ." he said, opening up his shooting stick, forcing the point into the hallowed ground and then sinking his large well-trousered bottom down gratefully onto the open seat provided, ". . . you don't want to worry your head about the blasted gutter press. They can't even write for a start off. And as for the other lot, well, they're not our type at all. Left-wingers mainly. Beards and *Guardian* readers and all that sort of thing. And you know as well as I do, the left-wing never go racing."

"I would hardly call *The Times* left-wing, Washy," said the Duke, aiming a sudden violent kick at a clump of blue ragwort. "We shouldn't have to be worrying about this sort of tripe! We should be fighting the American-breds. The goddamned tyranny of the almighty dollar. Commercial breeders? Hah!" He waved his fist at the distant grandstand. "Exploiters! You've read the latest stuff from Ireland? 'Nervous disposition means premature retirement for dual classic winner. "We couldn't afford to keep him in training," say sporting owners.' Couldn't afford to? Who the hell do they think they are? This is Horse Racing not Association Football." The Duke's voice which had risen dramatically in the last few moments calmed down a few semitones but the passion remained. "Our fathers and their fathers before them bred the best to the best but they also let them run! They didn't just pack them off to stud at barely three years of age after one major race and a couple of private gallops. You know what they got for this one, Washy? Forty million dollars. Forty million! Where would that leave Hyperion? Blue Peter? Dante or Eclipse? What with the Arabs on the one hand and these syndicates on the other there will soon be nothing left of our beautiful, proud and noble sport. Take this week. The Middle Park and the Cheveley. Historic contests! We should be watching the natural descendants of our own English-bred winners of the great English thoroughbred races. Instead we'll probably see some little chestnut pony who goes six furlongs like a bullet and packs up after one season." He sighed deeply. "We should be fighting these things, Washy. Fighting them! With all our might and main. But before we can do that . . ." he paused deliberately, ". . . we must put our own house in order first." He turned back round and looked Washy in the eye. "You know what I'm referring to?"

Washy blinked. "Something rotten in the state of Denmark?"

The Duke nodded. "Precisely. Something called Lex Parlane."

"Not again surely?"

"I'm afraid so, Washy."

"He's not still going on about that Cheltenham business?"

"He is, you know."

"But that's nearly seven months ago now."

"I know, Washy, I know. This morning I got a call from our man on the *Telegraph*. It seems Parlane's been talking again. To the newspapers. Television. The lot. Hills have finally paid their last remaining debts on the race. Mecca too. Goldline won't budge."

"Bloody Weiss!"

"The Scotsman apparently says that until he gets paid in

full he intends to organise a 'Campaign to Democratise Horse Racing'. He confessed all this on *Newsnight* if you please."

"That's the BBC for you. They've never loved racing. Can't our people do anything?"

"I'm seeing Tom Bottomore in London on my way back from the Arc. But . . ." he made a face, ". . . his influence is strictly limited. We kicked up such a hell of a stink on *Sportsnight* after that Hexham stipendiary steward fiasco. And then when the bugger turned out to be drunk after all we were made to look damned fools in front of the whole television viewing nation. Oh no, Washy. The Jockey Club are not exactly flavour of the month at Broadcasting House."

"So what will this 'Campaign' involve?"

"Making us look like fools and buffoons. Not exactly hard, you might say. And generally making life very hot for Goldline and Louis Weiss. Of course he's bound to make hay with these music stories too. Probably leaked them to the press himself." Crossing his arms the Duke walked slowly over to the newly-painted white running rail and gazed out pensively at the heath. It had been a dry summer and he saw that there were patches of brown grass along the edges of the gallops known as Racecourse Side. The gallops were sprinkled with chalk and marked out neatly with small clumps of birch twigs. On the racecourse itself however the Duke observed that the turf was still thick, green and fresh-looking thanks to constant watering.

Washy looked up. "About Weiss, Johnny," he said. "Can't you have him in for a private chat? See what a little bit of quiet persuasion will do?"

"He's coming to the hall tomorrow morning after breakfast," said the Duke, without turning round. "He's involved with this pitch battle business too."

"Pitch battle?"

"Parlane wants to bet from a pitch in the ring on the southern circuit. Goldline want to stop him. Through the

National Bookmakers Association of course. But Parlane knows they're behind it. The trouble is, the more they carry on the more he stirs it up for them. Rebounds on their heads in the end. Ours too."

"Bloody man."

"Clever man."

"Well, I don't know . . . the unacceptable face of racing. That's what I'd call him." As if to emphasise the strength of his feelings Washy punched his fist into the open crown of his brown trilby hat.

"He may be unacceptable, Washy," said the Duke, stroking his left earlobe patiently. "He is also an extremely astute self-publicist. He wants an enquiry."

"Does he, by Jove?"

"He'll have to have one too. But discreet. Give that fellow half a chance and he'd broadcast the entire proceedings from the rooftop of the Churchill Hotel."

"That's a bookmaker for you."

"Committees, Washy, committees. There's a Tatts' all-purposes a fortnight today. See if you can get them to change things around. They owe us a favour. Will you do that for me?"

"I'll get on to Ticker and Brigade tomorrow morning. They can talk to GHQ and we should be able to send around a memo by clubrooms tea."

"See to it, Washy. See to it. We must handle these matters most carefully. If we can't see off this Scotsman our authority could be heading for the rocks."

"That bad? He'd hardly be the first bad egg."

"This time it's different, Washy. The hounds are baying at our heels too. Witness these articles." He still had the cuttings in his hand. "And if racing's administration becomes discredited who's going to be left to protect the sport? Oh, no. We owe it something better than to sell it all off to a bunch of showmen, spivs and cheapjack commercial operators." An American Air Force jet roared by overhead on its way back to Mildenhall. "Some chance then of stemming the American tide."

The Duke stepped back and signalled imperiously with his right arm towards the Running Gap, the gap in the Devil's Dyke around which the horses swing on their way into the straight from the Cesarewitch start. A waiting Land Rover parked discreetly close to the running rail by the ten-furlong gate moved obediently towards them. Washy put on his hat and packed up his shooting stick and the two men waited in silence. Just before they boarded the Land Rover the Duke looked down at his watch. Eighteen fifteen hours precisely. Waterloo, thought Washy.

The Duke stepped back and signalled imperiously with his right arm towards the Running Gap, the gap in the Devil's Dyke around which the horses swing on their way into the straight from the Cesarewitch start. A waiting Land Rover parked discreetly close to the running rail by the ten-furlong gate obediently towards them. Washy put on his hat and packed up his shooting stick and the two men waited in silence. Just before they boarded the Land Rover the Duke looked down at his watch. Eighteen fifteen hours precisely. Waterloo, thought Washy.

Driving off the heath towards the Birdcage Walk the Land Rover was passed by an aggressively self-made young Newmarket trainer on a chestnut cob. The trainer was followed by two colts, the first a lead horse for the second, a strong musclebound American-bred fancy for Thursday's Middle Park Stakes. As the Duke drove past him the trainer saluted with his whip. The Duke made no acknowledgement. The three horsemen then turned and galloped away on past the edges of the car park and up towards the rim of the heath. The trainer paused suddenly at the top, a theatrical figure, silhouetted strikingly against the skyline.

A moment later he was gone. The heath was empty once again.

3

Breakfast was thick creamy porridge followed by devilled kidneys, sausages, mushrooms, grilled bacon, grilled tomatoes, fried bread, toast, marmalade and coffee. The coffee was poured by the butler Bennett from an elegantly inlaid Limoges coffee pot that had once been a present from the Grand Hotel des Anglais in Trouville to commemorate twenty-one summers of ducal visits. The Duke enjoyed his coffee and his tea and he drank both beverages in copious amounts in spite of the fact that his doctor warned him that they inflamed his bladder and were bad for his health.

"So what Doc?" the Duke would say over an Assam Finest or a pot of freshly brewed Kenyan Blue Mountain. "Life is an almost constant wait between visits to the lavatory. It just so happens that my days are more eventful than the other fellow's."

For the Duke this day had begun like any other. Bennett had woken him at six with a large pot of Fortnum's Breakfast Special and his copy of *The Sporting Life*. While sitting up in bed the Duke had drunk two cups of tea, eaten three digestive biscuits and conducted his first casual scrutiny of the day's racing headlines. He'd then dressed quickly in his morning outdoor gallops wear and strode down the front stairs and out through the hall, the morning room, the office, the breakfast room, the kitchen, the laundry, the back kitchen and the drying room and on into the main courtyard at the rear of the building. It was not such a long walk as it would have been in the old days. In the big house.

The autumnal brilliance of the previous day had not

entirely disappeared but as yet the morning was misty and cold with a heavy dew. As the Duke walked across the gravel and set off down the rhododendron walk that led to his private paddocks he could feel the cold acutely. It attacked his lungs and chilled his blood. The two Jack Russells, Wallet and Tripe, lolloped along in front of him. Theirs were privileged lives, cosseted existences that mostly took place in milieus far removed from the trades-man's entrance. Consequently they rarely enjoyed those certain essential satisfactions of the canine world common to most other dogs: namely, a postman to savage and a milkman to chase.

"Wallet. Tripe. Come here!" shouted the Duke. Wallet and Tripe took no notice whatsoever. This was how it always was. "Damned dogs," growled the Duke happily. Some people felt that the Duke's own voice sounded disconcertingly similar to the bark of his Jack Russells, especially in his more staccato moments when brisk on the telephone, gruff in committee or wagging with pleasure at the end of a race. Suffice it to say that the Duke was not aware of these associations.

A few moments later, this irascible trio, scowling collectively at the early morning sky, rounded the end of the rhododendron walk and came upon the main stabling area of the Duke's stud. They were greeted by the soothing sounds of Mozart's concerto for clarinet in A major, this week's choice of 'morning music' for the stud's equine residents. The Duke inspected his resident complement of nine stallions as they were given their oats and breakfast feed and looked on proudly as the star attraction of his bloodstock empire, his 2,000 Guineas and Champion Stakes winner, beaten only once in a twelve-race career that had spanned three seasons, was led out of his box for his morning constitutional. The stallion's chestnut coat gleamed with muscle and conditioning and he walked like royalty past the onlooking Duke and his beaming stud manager. Even the Jack Russells were suitably cowed, keeping themselves to the background and their mouths shut. The Duke too said nothing. No words could possibly describe his feelings as the stallion, ears pricked and head cocked slightly to one side, returned his gaze unflinchingly.

"He's a Christian of a horse, your Grace," said the stud manager unnecessarily. "Super. Really super." The Duke winced. Although an excellent horsemaster the stud manager had always been a woefully unimaginative fellow when it came to the resources of the English language and 'super' in no way did justice to the splendour of the thoroughbred on view. The Duke resolved to buy the man a special Open University Literature and Language course for his next Christmas present.

At seven twenty the Duke's Range Rover was waiting to drive him on the short but pleasant journey through Babraham and Six Mile Bottom to Newmarket Heath, where he was joined on the gallops by his urbanely unruffled private trainer, cigarette holder at the ready. Miles De Berry had once been the heavyweight boxing champion at Eton and with his lugubrious face and voluminous bulk cut a droll figure as he stalked the daybreak gallops clouded in rich scents. Other than horses, De Berry's chief compulsions were exotic shirts, exotic Asiatic house boys and exotic foreign tobaccos of which the French make Boyard, a particularly head-spinning lungful, was his undisputed favourite. There were those who suggested that the makings of these pungent smokes contained more than the normal lawfully permitted substances but the Duke, as an habitual magistrate and upholder of the law, considered it none of his business to have an intimate knowledge of the flavour and effect of a marijuana cigarette.

"Morning, Johnny," said De Berry, coughing and gasping in his usual way. "You see the Red God?" He pointed out a feisty little two-year-old with a jet black coat and homicidal eyes. "What a shit! He nearly took a stable lad's head off last week. Mind you, he almost did the same at the Highflyer Sales. Gordon Richards and Scobie Breas-

ley were walking just behind him at the time. As I said to
Lester afterwards, 'If he'd taken those two out at least
he'd have been famous for something!' " The Duke
chuckled appreciatively. "There's the Bustino," said De
Berry. Another line of horses had started cantering slowly
towards them, the Duke's son of the 1974 St Leger winner
moving freely in the lead. The horses' breath streamed out
against the hillside. "He could be a Cup horse next year,"
said De Berry. "It just depends on how much of a shit he
is." The Duke nodded. As the stocky-looking chestnut
reached the top of the hill his lad gently eased him down
to a trot and then swung back down to the foot of the
hill.

The Duke gazed down the long dolled-out gallops and
out across the trees and rooftops of the town towards the
distant buildings of the Rowley Mile. A wind was blowing
in from the North Sea and the sky was beginning to clear.
Clouds were chasing away the mist and some first glim-
mers of sunshine were beginning to pick out the russet and
gold colours amongst the trees around the town. The
exercising horses and their lads were a colourful scene.
Many of the lads had checked lumberjack jackets and
multicoloured hats which they wore pulled down low over
their compulsory safety helmets. Some of the 'lads' must
undoubtedly have been grandfathers while others looked
scarcely old enough to shave.

"Isn't that the Jago boy?" asked the Duke, peering
sternly at a middle-aged, sullen and ill-looking man who
was smoking a cigarette while slumped astride a scrawny
looking two-year-old from another trainer's string.

"That's right," said De Berry. "He was the one in the
Captain Banbury-Transport and General Workers' Union
horsewhipping incident."

"I remember it well," said the Duke. "I thought he'd
been given his marching orders."

"He wouldn't smoke while he rode out for me," said De
Berry.

They walked across to the Limekilns and watched as the

Duke's Nassau Stakes winner did her final bit of serious
work before the Sun Chariot on Saturday. She was
followed a quarter of an hour later by the two-year-old
apple of the Duke's eye. With the Cheveley Park now
only hours away she was given just an exercise canter. She
looked in perfect health. The gallops over, the Duke's
eyes wandered down to the long lines of horses and men
that were beginning to move up the Bury Road. The
Cambridge rush hour traffic was steering its usual hesitant
course between them, also on the way to its daily work.
Were it not for the presence of the Eastern Counties
Omnibus Company's garage on the far side of the road the
scene could have been a picture of 1914 cavalry man-
oeuvres on the Russian front just before the Battle of
Tannenberg, thought the Duke.

The Duke's reverie was broken by the annoying attentions of the new Secretary to the Jockey Club, an impossibly smarmy man in a flat cap and well-polished lime green
wellingtons which the Duke had always felt were just a
little too flashy for their own good. The Secretary was
followed by a handful of owners and trainers nodding
cordial greetings and the inevitable posse of obsequious
pressmen hoping to curry favour with the authorities of
the turf. At least this lot were better than the types you
met on the way down the hill, said De Berry. The former
had actually bothered to get up early and walk to the top
of the gallops in an effort to learn something interesting.
The latter just stumbled out of bed at the last minute,
still red-eyed and drunk from the night before. And
then they expected automatically to partake of the
serious information that their more dedicated
colleagues had been diligently cultivating for the past
two hours.

By half past eight the Duke had had enough.

"Refreshments at Rye House Lodge, Johnny?" asked
De Berry. "Won Loc will be waiting. And you know what
his breakfasts are like on Newmarket race days. Lavish."
His eyes twinkled with the seasoned relish of a man who

has drunk Polynesian fried chicken's blood in Hong Kong clip joints while watching teenage Chinese rent boys wrestle naked in the street.

"Not today, Miles," said the Duke. "Got a few appointments of my own." He got back to Dereham Hall and walked straight into the large, dark, mahogany and olive green breakfast room where the morning papers were laid out neatly for his inspection. After a quick cursory glance at *The Times*, *Financial Times*, and *Telegraph*, the Duke moved on for a second longer look at his *Sporting Life*, especially the form for the Cheveley Park Stakes, which he consumed as eagerly as his breakfast.

"Bennett," he shouted, reading something he didn't like, "what the hell's this Canadian-bred beast doing here?"

"I'm sure I don't know, your Grace," said Bennett, arriving tactfully with a copy of the *North American Stallion Review*. The Duke looked up his rival filly's breeding and discovered that the sire had never run but that the dam had been the ranking winner of four stakes races including the Del Gato Country Club Arkansas TV Oaks.

"Parvenu," said the Duke, chucking the book inadvertently into the marmalade. "Do you know, Bennett, we're 5-2 with Hills. I think I ought to get a piece of that." Helping himself to his third cup of coffee the Duke sat back in his chair and lit a cigarette. Through the window at his back he could see one of the stallions taking his leisure in a paddock of lush grass. Behind the paddock was a field of cows and behind that a line of elm trees. The images seemed a perfect complement to the collection of famous racing oil colours that adorned the walls of the Duke's home. Frith, Gainsborough, Stubbs of course and, most important of all, the Duke's favourite, Sawrey Gilpin. Gilpin's 'Brood Mares And Colts In A Landscape' hung over the breakfast room fireplace, its russet and green colours blending in harmoniously with the colours of the room. Adequate testimony, one might think, to the

Duke's power and security, to his abundance, content-ment and ease.

The paintings lied.

4

Letherby, the Duke's private secretary, had placed a selection of the more important letters, memos and other documents on the top of the Duke's desk for his immediate attention. First though, he summarised their contents with his usual brisk efficiency.

"Tickets for Longchamp, your Grace," said Letherby, pointing out an official French Jockey Club envelope. "Press conference times and briefings, dinner reservations, the usual thing. I called Maxim's. The fricassée de homard will be on the menu again this year."

"Well done, Letherby."

"As to the Cambridgeshire, M. Romanet will be arriving at Cambridge airport at eleven thirty on Saturday morning. Oh, and there'll be an extra party at luncheon. From the Irish Turf Club. They rang and I said okay." The Duke nodded. "The Home Secretary's meeting has been fixed for Friday week at the Carlton. In connection with that there's a party of three Conservative backbench MPs turning up at teatime today. They're hollow vessels. Shouldn't do us any harm." The Duke nodded again. "The pink and yellow slips contain your final unofficial tally from the sales . . ." The Duke had a quick glance. The sums looked encouraging. ". . . And Mr Weiss is waiting in the billiard room."

"Well done, Letherby!" The Duke liked Letherby. He was an intelligent young man not much older than his own boy James but there the comparison ended. Letherby was responsible, organised and devoted to horse riding. Not to gambling. But to the sensible administration of the turf's affairs.

On his way into the billiard room the Duke passed a photograph of himself, his late wife and both his sons, Rowland and James, sitting at a table in the open air restaurant at Deauville racecourse in 1979. Even then Rowland had the look, his mother's look, of a miniature Führer. An SAS socialite in miniature. The younger boy, in white fedora and black dark glasses, was being served from a plate of glistening seafood by a bow-tied monsieur. The Duke's thoughts were immediately if momentarily torn between fricassée de homard and the prodigality of youth. Rowland might wear dark glasses. In some Falangist nightmare of the future. But somehow he couldn't ever imagine young Letherby wearing a pair of black shades. Then he opened the door of the billiard room and saw Louis Weiss.

Weiss was the Chairman of Goldline Investments Limited, one of the leading nationwide bookmaking companies. Goldline was a creature of many parts, all of them profitable. Weiss detested racehorses but he was a genius at keeping the books. At this moment he was standing at the window and staring out across the mottled lawn towards the kitchen garden. An abandoned croquet mallet was lying on the lawn beneath the wall.

The Duke could only surmise as to whether the passing of the seasons caused any great wave of melancholy in the bookmaker's heart. He supposed that losers were losers just as surely over the sticks as ever they were on the flat. He glanced at his watch. Weiss had been waiting for almost half an hour. "Good morning, Louis," he said breezily, closing the door behind him.

Weiss turned round. "Your Grace." His normally sharp features and demeanour were marred by a certain sourness, part tiredness and part irritation. The latest copy of *The European Racehorse* lay unopened on the table by his side.

"Didn't keep you, I hope?"

"When the Jockey Club summon one to a private meeting, I can only assume that they intend to proceed in a prompt and business-like manner. That is how my business is run. If others think differently . . ." he shrugged, ". . . that's their lookout." He stood there stiffly at the far end of the table feeling up a red with his right hand. The Duke ran his eyes over the sharply cut blue cashmere coat, the sharp grey suit and the pearl grey tie and the trim black Gucci shoes, their buckles glinting like mousetraps.

"Now then, Louis," said the Duke. "This blasted betting coup. What's the latest situation?"

"Extensive and malicious copy in today's racing press. Abusive remarks by Parlane himself on Breakfast Television. It's criminal. And from now on I want the police to handle it."

"That would be bad for racing. And bad for you. None of us can benefit from the increasing glare of public attention." A gardener had appeared outside and was beginning to sweep the wormcasts off the lawn. There was bonfire smoke from beyond the hedge. "Can't you find some way to settle with them, Louis?" asked the Duke. "Behind the scenes? After all . . . it has been going on now for almost seven months and it's getting awfully tedious."

Louis Weiss was in immediately. "These men planned a conspiracy to defraud. To defraud my company and the betting public. And you know as well as I do that without the levy taken from bookmaking racing in this country would be in a pretty parlous state. People must be assured that every horse race is a true and honest contest! Run on its own merits! And that, the Cheltenham staying chase most blatantly was not."

"Uhm," said the Duke as a second gardener walked past them wheeling a barrow full of weeds and old leaves. "The thing is, Louis. . ." he reached for his cigarette case and offered one to Weiss who refused as usual, ". . . the public have read too many detective stories . . . the bookmaker always the villain, loud checked suits and fat cigars, that sort of thing." The Duke was like an aged but still cunning snooker professional deliberately attempting to slow down the pace of the game. "And these Cheltenham fellows . . . it's not as if anyone was actually physically hurt . . . so the public, well, they feel a lot of sympathy. If you take them to court you'll win a Pyrrhic victory maybe . . . but little else."

"We're not talking Dick Francis here, you know," said Weiss. The Duke said nothing. "Alright . . . we take risks. But we'd warned this lot before. Everyone knew they'd been cooking that horse for at least three months. There should've been an immediate steward's enquiry and a proper official disqualification. And I would have expected that the Senior Steward of the Jockey Club would believe in upholding the full letter of the racing law."

"Of course I do, Louis," said the Duke calmly. "Of course I do. But there are ways in which these things can be done. In order to achieve the best possible results." He ran his hand over the pleasantly svelte green baize covering of the billiard table. "My father, Louis, always used to say that a good bookmaker ought to be like a good mistress. Accommodating . . . but discreet."

Weiss stared at him. "When my father was owed fifty thousand pounds by the old Aly Khan he summoned him round to his Mayfair flat to explain himself. "Be a good man," he said. "Grow up and pay up." The Duke's eyes flickered. "My business now employs more than seven thousand people in the bookmaking industry alone and we invest more than two hundred thousand pounds in racing prize money per annum. I think most people . . . especially the racetracks . . . are pretty grateful for our patronage these days. You see we're not in the backroom of the pub any more, your Grace. We're High Street. Next door to McDonald's and W.H. Smith's. We have a holiday business, a leisure and hotel business and we subsidise productions at Covent Garden and the National Theatre. I and my directors sit at the same table as the Chancellor of the Exchequer and members of the Government. We don't need any lessons on etiquette and manners from the Stewards of the Jockey Club."

The Duke frowned and looked down at the coffee table. He picked up *The European Racehorse*. "Did you see the paintings in the hall on your way in, Louis?" he asked. "Stubbs. Every one of them. There's twenty-five more in the National Gallery. I let them hang there at least half the year." He was reading an article on Italian stud fees. The author was a Viscount, a distant cousin of the late Duchess. "The legal word is, Louis . . . that even if you did take it all the way . . . in terms of hard evidence you haven't got a leg to stand on. There's no proof. Remember Gay Future. If you do go to court . . . you'll only make a fool of yourself. And what's more . . . we'll have to disown you."

"They are criminals."

"And must be punished, I agree," said the Duke, tossing the magazine onto the billiard table. "They don't belong in racing and never will. But we must choose the right moment." The bookmaker looked sick. "What about Lex Parlane?"

Weiss sighed. "We think he got the money on but he used so many accounts. . ."

"I don't mean Cheltenham. I mean this pitch battle business. Sounds like he's got a good case to me."

"And it sounds like you're going soft to me. Do you take orders from a bully boy?"

"Choose your time, Louis," said the Duke soothingly. "Choose your time. Lex Parlane has been on the rails for, what, five, six, seven or eight years? Big time stuff. Now we both know that at many southern race meetings, especially evenings in summer, the Tattersalls pitches are often half empty. He wants to move in. Why not let him?"

"He's not on the list."

"Then put him on the list."

"There are other people waiting."

"Then speed up the process."

"He's a crook! He insults me up and down the country.

He cheapens the sport."

"I agree, Louis, I agree. But don't give him the ammunition to start sniping at the rest of us." Weiss sank back into a chair. The Duke moved closer. If this had been an arm wrestling contest then Weiss's wrist would now be hovering only inches above the table. "I'll fix Lex Parlane," said the Duke. "You settle the coup. We'll have them all into Portman Square. Discreetly. No one need know."

"I object."

"Otherwise the media will roast us all. At the moment we must be patient."

"You don't trade with a blackmailer!" Weiss shook with rage. "He's called me a coward. And a thief!"

"When you're in a club, Louis," said the Duke softly, "you play it by the rules. He wants to join? Let him. Then when he's safely inside . . . then we'll get him!"

Weiss gazed at the brown wooden panelling, at the long racks of snooker and billiard cues on the wall and at the dusty boxes of white chalk and he reflected on the gentle mafia-like charms of the English aristocracy. "Very well," he said quietly, pulling on his black leather driving gloves and getting to his feet. "We'll play it your way."

"Well done, Louis," said the Duke cheerily. "We'll take care of it."

"I have to go," said Weiss.

"Off to the racecourse already? It's not even drinks before lunchtime."

"I'm not going racing today. I have to drive to Brighton. I'm making a speech at the Conservative Party Conference."

"Are you really? Well, I never. Do give my best to the Prime Minister. If you see her."

"Good morning." Weiss started for the door.

"Oh, by the way, Louis," called the Duke. "What odds are you offering on mine today?"

"Fifteen to eight," said Weiss, not bothering to turn.

"Fifteen to eight? But Hills go five to two."

Weiss paused momentarily, one hand on the door handle. "I don't stand on a box in the rain, your Grace," he said coldly, "wearing a cheap suit and a silly hat and drinking tea from a paper cup. I run a profitable business and I aim to keep it that way. If that's not accommodating enough for you . . . then I suggest you try Lex Parlane. Thank you for the coffee."

On his way out Weiss was passed by the bustling figure of Letherby who'd been summoned a few moments earlier by the Duke's discreet pressing of a button underneath the billiard room table. Letherby had been intended to escort Weiss to the door but the bookmaker's rapid departure had made his role redundant.

"I say," he said. "Fast car." Weiss's Jaguar receded loudly up the drive.

"The trouble with chaps like that," said the Duke, "is that no matter how much money they make they've still got these two enormous wooden blocks, one on each shoulder."

"Pretty tricky customer, eh, your Grace?"

"It's not him that I'm worried about."

5

James Richmond paused for one moment to flick his hair back off his forehead and then tipped the large bag of dirty laundry out onto the drawing room floor. A gold cufflink rolled across the Persian carpet, followed by one half of a used airline ticket to Paris and a half-empty bottle of Eau Sauvage, the rest of which he'd thrust into the heap some three weeks earlier in an effort to keep down the smell.

He sniffed his way gingerly through the soiled piles of shirts, underpants and socks, eventually selecting the least offensive combination he could muster. The blue silk shirt from Turnbull and Asser went well with the pink and yellow socks and the bottom half of his brother's green tweed suit. He decided to do without pants.

There was a stirring from the bedroom next door. The girl in his bed had stretched, yawned, and gone back to sleep. The girl on the floor was wriggling uncomfortably. Her left foot had somehow managed to get stuck inside her copious handbag and she was struggling to pull it free.

James strolled into the large and comfortably run-down Scottish kitchen, made himself a coffee and lit another joint. While he was waiting for the kettle to boil, he gazed out at the Highland scene beyond the window. A pair of lugubrious looking longhorn cattle were mooching about between the garden and the loch. Unsurprisingly it was raining once again. James sighed. Only the previous evening he'd been talking on the telephone to his father and complaining that while they may have been having an Indian summer down in Newmarket every day of his three-week Scottish incarceration had seemed to be accompanied by shivering winds, steady drizzle and slate grey skies.

There was a cakestand set up for tea in the walk-in larder. He put a couple of scones and a jam sponge into his trouser pockets, swept up *The Sporting Life* from the kitchen table and sauntered back across the living room and into the library where he collapsed heavily into a large and leatherbound Edwardian sofa from which the stuffing was beginning to emerge at both ends. He picked up a pair of dark glasses from off the carpet and put them on. He checked through the *TV Times*. Less than half an hour to the televised racing. He ran his eyes back down the York card, mentally approving his earlier selections of three crossed doubles and a treble, tax paid. Then, dextrously switching on the stereo with his big right toe, he settled back happily to enjoy his breakfast. A large pile of worn-out books waited on the floor by his side. He disregarded the more serious looking volumes of Engels, Marx and J.M. Keynes and opted instead for Percy F. Westerman's *In the Clutches of the Dyaks*, a rattling good yarn set in a land of fiendish peril where natives and chaps fought hourly for their honour beneath the hot tropical sun. It was not quite five past two.

Lex killed the music only a matter of seconds after walking in the room.

"Indulgent undergraduate nonsense," he said, taking out a cassette tape of his own from his suit pocket. It was *Little Old Wine Drinker Me* by Dean Martin. "I tried knocking but the noise was deafening. So I came by the back door. The dog didn't mind. He was cuddling up with these at the time." He plucked a pair of James's boxer shorts out of his jacket pocket and tossed them across the room. James groaned. He'd been midway through the jam sponge and a ferocious battle with the Gorilla Men on the Bongo River. Lex's smart black suit, his shades and black fedora were a rude interruption. "Nice little place you've got here," said Lex, taking a jaundiced look at the elderly furniture, the faded carpet and the murky paintings of misty glens and stags at bay. "Remind me. What year is this again, 1896? Or have we leapt into the twentieth century? 1951?" James groaned even louder and buried his head beneath a chair cushion. "Signs of life," said Lex, sensing triumph. "Good afternoon. Or exactly what time of day do you call this?"

"You fat crook," said James, chucking his cushion at the big Glaswegian.

"Haha! Compliments from the quality. Anyone would guess you were a Duke's son. It's the natural grace and charm. The expensive apparel. The elegant Knightsbridge style."

"Your gall, my friend, amazes me. It really. . ."

" 'Fucking amazes me'. I can read your mind! Just think. That's why you'll need an adviser like me. If you ever make it with the highups like your dad. And you'll be lucky too. If they ever knew the extent of your degeneracy they'd bar the doors. But. . ." he winked, ". . . I'll see you alright."

"How's that?" asked James, sweeping the crumbs from his shirt.

"If the likes of you were ever to take up your rightful place in society, you could be eaten alive. There's no telling what they might write about you in Jennifer's Diary. But with me to protect you. . ." he grinned, "things will be different." James looked sceptical. "There's nothing society figures like better than the presence in their midst of a genuine gangster. The little ladies get their orgasms from just brushing on the sleeves of your chalk stripe suit. It makes every party an instant success." He doffed his hat. "Meet Mr Lex Parlane. Well-known partygoer and business financier. You'll do fine."

"Has it ever occurred to you, Lex," said James, pushing the empty cassette box off the end of the sofa with his foot, "that just because I spend my untutored youth in the company of a thug like yourself. . ."

"Too kind."

". . . if I was ever to take up my 'rightful place in society', as you put it . . . the likes of you could be out with the dirty washing." He flung his shorts back in Lex's face. Lex didn't move. His eyes were indistinguishable behind the darkness of his own dark glasses. "I . . . am a nineteen-year-old Duke's son," said James, settling back comfortably. "It is generally agreed that I am a man without a sense of direction. Diffident. Easy going. Lazy. An incorrigible gambler. And *that* is why I consort with a bookmaker."

"I'm the only one who'll tolerate you. You and your fucking debts."

"One day . . ." James had his eye on a cobweb on the ceiling, ". . . I may be surrounded by peers of the realm. Millionaires. Captains of Commerce and Industry."

"And then?"

"And then . . . I shall do as they do."

"Just like Al Capone."

"No, Lex. Not like Al Capone. Town and Country. The City. England."

Lex shrugged. "Who needs Chicago? I can get you the best muscle on the Clyde. One day you'll need it too. And that's a fact!" He swung round cheerily and turned up the volume on the stereo. "This was terrific music. In those days . . . they really understood rhythm. Sexy. Really sexy." He started to do a rumba round the room, waving his hands like a Black and White Minstrel. "So," he said, snapping his fingers in time to the beat. "You invited me to lunch. Where is it?"

"Oh shit!"

"What?"

"I forgot! Sorry, Lex. But there's bound to be loads in the fridge. The housekeeper. . ."

"You forgot?" He spoke to a stag's head on the wall. "He forgot. My lunch. He forgot my lunch!" He banged his head against the little wooden plaque with the stag's name on it and its date of death. "And there's me . . . driven all the way up from Glasgow. And just hoping for a wee bite to eat and a refreshing soft drink!"

"You didn't drive up especially. Not to see me. No way,
Lex, no way!"

"True. I stopped at Crianlarich on the way. To see the
Honourable Mr Wishart."

"James Wishart?"

Lex nodded. "He owed me fifteen hundred. From last
month's poker game at the castle. I've got his cash." He
patted his suit top pocket. "Nice boy, Mr Wishart. Very
good manners."

"James Wishart couldn't play a game of patience let
alone beat you at poker."

"He thinks he's the Cincinnati Kid. You know, Jimmy
. . . I'm having a spot of trouble with your old man and his
friends. About my Tattersalls plans. And they still owe me
a few from our Cheltenham job."

"That's nothing to do with my father surely? Just the
other bookies?"

"Don't you believe it, son. They're all mixed up in it
somewhere. You see the London boys don't like my face.
Neither Goldline nor the Jockey Club. But when I move
south for good I'm going to need those decent pitches.
I've done my time round Musselburgh and Hamilton
Park. I want Ascot and Newmarket. I mean, the rails are
okay but a good pitch on a southern course, well, that's a
whole new meal ticket. I know that it's Weiss who's
holding me up. He distrusts all Scots. Especially us
bookies like himself. He thinks we're all Mick McGahey
with a loud suit."

"I'm sure you'll get what you want."

"You're damned right I will. Restraint of trade, that's
what I call it. Bad sport and sour grapes. I've had to
embarrass them all accordingly. TV, press, the usual
thing." He smiled. "It's worked too. I've had my sum-
mons to Portman Square. It came last week. Your old
man and the senior beaks. I'm sending my fucking solici-
tor."

"They do have a nasty habit of catching up with you."

"Not with me they don't. Not for a long time yet, son. And besides, who's worrying who? My life's here and now."

"I wish I could feel the same."

"You will one day. Now how about a fucking drink? I feel as if I've been here an hour already."

"There's a bottle of Bacardi in the cupboard there behind you."

Lex found the bottle, along with two glasses, both of which he polished ostentatiously on the arm of his jacket before pouring in the rum. He knocked back his drink, refilled his glass and then sat down at a table in the corner. Out of his suit pockets came his little white packet, his credit card and a crisp new fifty pound note. James smiled. "Well, Lord James," said Lex, proceeding to chop out two enormous tramlines of cocaine. "How is the catering round here? Does nanny . . . sorry, 'the house-keeper', keep a good eye on you?"

"Mrs McLavity? Pretty well, actually. She would make my breakfast . . . if I got up on time."

"Hah-ha! Of course us working-class boys are used to cooking our own breakfasts. And before dawn too." James scornfully ignored this remark while Lex hoovered up a line of cocaine and then gestured him expansively towards the table.

"Mrs McLavity's really very decent," said James, picking up the rolled-up fifty pound note. "She does the shopping in Oban once or twice a week. And she's always putting homemade pies and puddings into the fridge. Along with enormous platefuls of cakes and scones and homemade sponge with jam and. . ."

"Get on with it."

"The only trouble is . . ." he finished off his line, ". . . she won't do the washing. My father's forbidden it."

"So I noticed." Lex started chopping out more white granules.

James stood up. He was sniffing busily. "I seem to remember there's a bottle of brandy behind this chair," he said, flicking the switch on the television set. "By the way, Lex. . ." – he'd found the bottle – ". . . I really fancy that bottom weight in the third. Especially with the apprentice riding. He's been in cracking form these last few weeks."

"It's not off an inch. And that's official." Lex hoovered up line number two.

James looked crestfallen. "But I rang up this morning. . ."

"Then ring up again. You want Dubai Prince or Millstream in that race. Dubai's best."

"But I've got a hundred quid on that fucking horse. It's part of my treble."

"Then put it on something else."

"Oh, shit!"

"Listen. You can lay off the bet with me if you want. Through the office. No sweat."

"Fucking horse. Fucking crooks!"

Lex shook his head. "Will you just look at the state of you? A young man. Background. Education. And here you are sitting on a horsehair sofa with a bottle of Remy and a crumpled up copy of *The Sporting Life*. Screaming blue murder because some poor wee pony won't pay your dope bills for the coming month." He downed his rum and reached for the brandy. "I ask you. What are you doing?"

"I'm revising," said James, heading back for more cocaine.

"For what?"

"For an exam."

"You failed it once already."

"I'm supposed to try again. Otherwise. . ." he sighed, ". . . Oxford will throw me out. And my father will cut off my allowance. Or send me to the Gold Coast. Or both."

"It still might be better than moping about in some dingy old dump in the Highlands," said Lex, picking up one of James's books off the floor. "You should be pursuing the Sweet Bird of Youth!"

James said nothing. He sniffed up his line of white

powder and rubbed what was left of the drug round his
gums with the forefinger of his right hand. The midweek
racing theme tune started up on the television.

"And what the hell's this?" asked Lex, looking at the
book. "*Coral Island* by R.M. Ballantyne? That's *Boy's
Own Paper* stuff."

"It's PPE."

"What?"

"Politics, Philosophy and Economics." Lex looked confused. "I'm meant to be writing a special essay. On the
'Colonial Literature of the late nineteenth and early
twentieth century'."

"You should be reading that Ross MacDonald. Or Ed
McBain. That's a cracker."

"Some people say it's not 'Literature'."

"Well it's better than this kid's stuff, that's for sure."

Brough Scott's boyish face appeared from the York
grandstand. While James finished rolling a joint Lex
picked up his brandy glass and paced across the room to
the window with the broken sash cord. He stared out
bleakly at the loch. A gust of wind rippled across the
surface of the water. The water was cold and grey looking
and a solid covering of grey cloud still sat along the hills
above the wood. Lex shivered. "So this all belongs to your
old man, eh?"

James nodded. "You should see it when they're shooting. Lots of wet tweed and cigar smoke."

"All these pictures and dead animals. They give me the
creeps." James handed him the joint.

"It's traditional. Deer. Grouse. And someone to shoot
them. Without the shoot there'd probably be no birds left
in three years' time. They depend on each other."

Lex scowled. "I'm hungry." He started for the kitchen.
"That man has serious problems," he muttered, as he
walked past the television set. James looked round. Some
fat man with sticking-up hair was standing on a box on the
rails waving his arms around wildly and shouting a lot
about betting.

"He's alright," said James. "People like to know about the odds."

"Put another record on for Christ's sake," shouted Lex from the kitchen.

"Just a minute," said James. He turned down the volume and looked at the odds. The apprentice-ridden lightweight had been backed down heavily from three to one to seven to four favourite. Lex's two selections were easy to back at sixes and ten to one respectively. James picked up the telephone and got through to the Mecca Bookmakers office in Glasgow. He gave them his name and number and was about to ask for two hundred and fifty pounds each way on the ten to one shot, Millstream. Then he hesitated for a moment and changed his mind. He asked for five hundred pounds to win. On the nose. Tax paid. There was a brief pause on the other end of the line while someone went away and checked his credit. A different voice came back, a managerial voice, polite but firm. They wanted to know if he'd received his last month's bills and when he was going to pay them. James stalled about cheques in the post. There was another pause while they went away again and checked out the horse. James looked up at the television. The field were down at the start. He started drumming nervously on the table with his fingers. The voice came back. They would accept the bet. James slammed down the phone, killed off the stereo and turned up the volume on the television set. There was good late money for Dubai Prince, fours from six to one. Millstream had drifted. It was now out to twelves. James poured more brandy. They were going behind.

Lex re-entered from the kitchen. "Who are the women?" he asked, attacking a plate of cold sausages and a hefty slice of game pie.

"Yesterday evening . . . I was bored with work. So I rang up Camilla in Callander. And summoned her over! Lucy, her anorexic friend, came too. I was just about to kick them both out, actually, when you arrived."

"Sexy?"

"I can't speak for Lucy. Camilla's okay. Terrific legs."
Lex grinned. "Classy!"

"Yeah. But demanding too." Lex was intrigued. James
was concentrating on the starting stalls. The handlers were
having problems with a reluctant filly. They tried the
blindfold.

"How long are you here for?" asked Lex.

"Term begins in about ten days' time. So do my exams.
But I'm in no hurry."

"Who needs exams . . . when there's life?" The stalls
crashed open and they were off. The top weight made the
running. A Newmarket trained five-year-old, he was the
class horse in a competitive handicap and the jockey tried
to make it from the front. He nearly succeeded too. By
subtly quickening, then slowing, then quickening the
pace, he had them all in trouble with more than a quarter
of a mile to go. A twenty to one outsider trained by a
Yorkshire pig farmer more renowned for his point-to-
point horses than his flat racers suddenly shot out of the
pack at the distance. He was followed by Dubai Prince
and the apprentice-ridden lightweight. The favourite had
been held up in the rear throughout and given an almost
impossible task. The top weight manfully resisted the
outsider's late challenge but was eventually run out of it in
the final dying yards by Dubai Prince who won in the end
by a short looking neck. Five lengths back in third came
Millstream, James's bet, who made a lot of late ground up
in the closing stages and just managed to pip the outsider
on the line, though only by a head. The favourite was
fifth. James sat there, his mouth opening and shutting like
a fish.

"What did I tell you?" said Lex, getting up to change
around the tape. "We'll have made a killing on the track.
They had their instructions. Hit that favourite hard!" He
grinned. "I hope we got the Goldline boys along the way."
James was just sighing and shaking his head. Lex offered
him a sausage. "Yours did alright. He just needs further."

"Alright? What's alright? Why didn't he ride him from the front? He's obviously a stayer."

"George rode a really fine race. He just couldn't go the pace, that's all. He already needs further. That's all there is to it."

"That's all?"

"Yeah. You were stupid. If you'd done it each way. . .? But that's racing."

"Fuck off, Lex!"

"Don't be a fool, son. That result is what this game is all about." He started chopping out more cocaine.

James hit the sofa with his fist. "But I really fancied that Pulborough thing in the last. The two-year-old. Now I'm stuffed."

"You can have what you want with me."

"Oh, fuck." James slumped back miserably against the wall.

"Listen. We could, er, maybe have a bit of fun later on. I'm calling up this geyser from the South. It seems there's a job on today and he's got something for me. It's in the five forty-five at Newton Abbot. Jump race. If we left now. . ." he picked up the fifty pound note, ". . . we could go down to Glasgow."

"Glasgow?"

"Yeah." Lex cleaned away line number three. "We can go to my office for the business. Get nice and comfy. Get in a few bottles. Some more charlie. Life could be grand. I'll see you get a piece of the action. That way you'll pay off your bills. And you can still back the two-year-old with me." He proffered the re-rolled note. "Later on tonight there's an Old Firm game at Parkhead Celtic and Rangers. I bet you've never seen one of them. I've got some, er, business in the directors' box . . . but you can savour the atmosphere! Spot of dinner later on. My flat. A game of cards. We could call up one of those well-heeled friends of yours. Like Mr Wishart. I could do with a spot of pocket money. What do you say?"

James sighed. "I don't know, Lex. I still haven't recovered from last weekend."

Lex grinned. "What did you think of my Bella? Ain't she something?"

"She's beautiful. And she sure can drink."

"Men would pay money for her. The price of a weekend at the Albany Four Seasons. I give her love . . . and protection. She needs the security. You understand?"

James nodded. "I understand."

"Good." Lex lit up a large cigar. What did you think of my club?"

"The casino?"

Lex shook his head. "No! 'The Tartan Cavalier'. I won it off the Greek playing brag. That was last New Year's and just look at the improvements that I've made since then."

"It's a dive."

"Are you kidding? That 'dive' is the best fucking nightspot in the whole of Scotland. And you know what it used to be called? 'Venus Loves You'." He wrinkled up his nose with a look of intense distaste. "I mean, I ask you? That's cheap."

"Do you know what I'd really love right now?" said James, gazing wistfully into the middle distance. "A five hundred guinea Cerutti brothers Italian-cut suit. In dark brown. Or black for winter."

Lex stared at him and frowned. "What have I got to do with your suits?"

"What have I got to do with you and your fucking clubs?"

"Alright, alright. You don't have to shout. You've been to my place enough times, don't forget."

"And treated you pretty well too."

"I'll agree to that."

"Yeah. And elsewhere where my money would stretch. And where it wouldn't stretch . . . I've used credit."

"You've used it like the heir apparent, there's no denying it. Just don't forget who your friends are, Jimmy. Especially when you're older and a nob."

"How could I ever forget my friends, Lex?" said James,

starting up again for the cocaine table. "Five hundred pounds is a cheap price to pay for an afternoon in your company!"

"Ooh! Next thing I know you'll be bringing me out in a right Scots melancholy."

"You're only melancholy, Lex, when your conscience tells you that somehow you could've made even more money out of all those losing five-bob yankee punters in Motherwell and Perth."

"I have no shops in Perth."

"You're like a Mississippi card shop so dreadfully upset that the steamboat journey's been unavoidably prolonged by an extra two hours. 'Never mind everybody,' you say, your eyes glinting with good cheer. 'How about whiling away the time with a quick game of chance?' You fat crook!"

All of a sudden there was silence. Lex got calmly to his feet and switched off the stereo. He was standing there just across the room and looking the nineteen-year-old right in the eye. James felt elated yet depressed. He could hear the rapid beat of his heart and he could feel the blood rushing round his body from his head to his toes and from his eyes to his jaw. His jaw was clicking and his mouth was quickly drying up.

Lex spoke softly. "You . . . are a rascally young toff. Your similes are most unsavoury." He was looking at James' shirt, at his brother's green tweed trousers only held up by a frayed old pyjama cord and at the two-tone socks on his feet. He shook his head. "No more vanity. I too would like a new suit of clothes. I wouldn't mind a good name to go with it."

"You love the one you've got."

"You know, a highup from the Jockey Club stopped me on the track the other day about you. He said I was a bad influence. He said your father was worried. He said you were behaving like a useless young layabout. I denied it all, of course."

"Who said that?"

"Cleveland."

"Washy Cleveland?" Lex nodded. "Hah! The fat buffoon! I'll bet he was sweating at the time." James started pacing round the room, warming to his theme as he went. "Washy Cleveland is the kind of man who sweats a lot about everything. Over his son's slow progress at Sandhurst. Over the content and punctuation of his annual entry in Debrett's. Over talking to a hood like you, you name it. He's got less brains than a stuffed fox!"

Lex was smiling. "My God, you've got a way with words. You've corrupted me. There were things I didn't know about till I met you. And that's the truth."

"Bollocks!"

"Not this thing, maybe. . ." He put away his credit card and his little white packets and picked up his fifty pound note. "But if I am a 'villain', it's all down to you."

"Then how about doing something villainous," said James, rolling his glass along the carpet.

"Now that's the attitude! This job this afternoon, well . . ." – a cynical smile flashed across Lex's face – ". . . it wouldn't exactly be Jockey Club Rules! I've got another scam on too. Ayr this weekend. An on course job. You'll like that."

"A coup, eh? Who's that going to fleece? The favourite backers in your own shops? And there's you, the friend of the working class."

Lex cuffed him hard around the head. "You know when Colonel Cleveland was complaining to me about you I was really very decent. I said you were a bright, intelligent young man whose best years were all ahead of you. You loved the horses, sure, but you had the guts and the character to take your losses without whining. I didn't tell him about the delay I'd negotiated over your four thousand pound unpaid William Hills bill. Nor did I mention the one or two other on course layers about the country who are down by the odd monkey or two. And I certainly didn't mention the two and a half grand that you still owe me. Now wasn't that decent of me?" James said nothing. Lex put his arm around James's neck, hugged him tight and ruffled his hair with his hand. "We all have our natural vocation in life, son. . ." he said, almost whispering in James's ear, ". . . and just now . . . yours is called making me money." He laughed loudly and kissed him on the top of his forehead. Then he pushed him roughly away. "Come on! Glasgow!"

An extremely pretty but cross-looking blonde girl about James's height and age suddenly wandered into the room wrapped in a sheet. She had a sulky sort of face with short, straight hair and a tiny *retroussé* nose. As she stood there looking accusingly at James, Lex noticed her legs beneath the sheet. They were long, suntanned and definitely sexy, he thought.

"You might've told me you were here," said Camilla, pouting hard. "And you might at least have offered me a bloody cup of coffee. Lucy keeps being sick and I have to listen."

Lex winced. When Camilla spoke she had a voice like a well-bred chainsaw.

6

Pulling away from the lodge gates Lex's immaculate blue
Rolls almost collided with a battered old Land Rover
which had a brace of guns in the back. The Land Rover
had been attempting to reverse out of a muddy track near
the edges of the loch but it had managed to get its left rear
wheel stuck in a narrow ditch that ran by the side of the
road.

"Fucking Scots peasant!" Lex shouted, banging his car
horn ill-temperedly. "Move yourself." The fucking Scots
peasant turned out to be none other than Mr McLavity,
the gamekeeper, and he was not pleased. He had been
about to set off up through the forest to find the stalking
ponies on the moor above. The sound of raised voices, car
horns and skidding tyres brought a crescendo of crazed
barking from the dog pound behind his house. James
caught a glimpse of the cottage between the trees. Grey
granite and redbrick with a thin trickle of blue and grey
smoke drifting up towards the sky. The dogs ran round to
the front of the dog pound and hurled themselves hyster-
ically against the wire mesh fence. Finally the gamekeeper
succeeded in extricating the Land Rover from the ditch
and struggled crossly on past the Rolls. James gave him an
embarrassed nod while Lex called him a squarehead.
Then the Rolls accelerated swiftly away up the narrow
road, across General Wade's bridge and on past the hotel
and the cluster of yellow and red campers' tents that were
pitched in the fields by the river. James saw a heron swoop
down low over the loch and land in the lilac bushes behind
the hotel garden. The sky had lightened since Lex's arrival
but the bracken and fir trees were still damp and dark

looking, thanks to the endless rain. As they drew towards
the bend in the road James gazed back at the gaunt outline
of the greystone house across the water. He saw a lone
walker striding out purposefully along a mountain path
some two or three hundred feet above them and he
attempted to draw the attention of the others in the car to
the figure of the walker and to the general lonely beauty
of the West Highland landscape.

"D'you want to have a carpet on the two-year-old?"
asked Lex, looking straight ahead. Then they rounded the
turning in the road and the loch disappeared from view.

Camilla's anorexic friend was dropped off at Bridge of
Orchy railway station so that she could catch her connection up to Mallaig for the ferry back to Skye where her
uncle lived. No one seemed greatly to lament her leaving.
Further down the road they passed the long blue and
white Inter City Express train snaking its way around the
contours of the hillside on its way up to Fort William and
the North. Then at Crianlarich the Rolls was passed by a
little red GPO Postbus scuttling back cheerfully up to
Inveroran and the Bridge.

James looked round at Camilla who was sitting in the
back seat wearing Lex's headphones. It had been impossible just to leave her behind so Lex had finally agreed to
take her with them providing she kept her mouth shut all
the way between Loch Tulla and the city. He'd even
offered her fifty pounds when they got to Glasgow so long
as she kept her promise. The car stereo continued to
thunder out all the way down the Loch Lomond road and
at Arrochar Lex gave Camilla the cocaine packet and told
her to chop out three more lines while he continued
driving. He snorted his line up effortlessly, one hand still
on the driving wheel. At Luss he stopped the Rolls by an
elderly looking waterfront hotel where he made a few
warning phone calls to friends in the city and bought two
bottles of vintage Bollinger from the reluctant hotel
keeper who'd been planning to keep them on ice as part of
the catering facilities for a wedding reception the follow-

ing Saturday. Lex tipped him twenty-five pounds and
signed autographs for the bewildered hotel staff. The
intake of yet more alcohol compelled James to call for a
stop by Balloch pierhead where he bought himself a
greasy hamburger from a van parked in a lay-by. The
hamburger smelled disgusting and Lex made him eat it in
the road. It went some way to filling the gap in his
stomach but it did little to dispel the nervous tension. The
trouble with trips like this was that you could never be
quite sure where or when the day or evening or night
would end or what state you would be in when it did. One
thing was certain – however sumptuous Lex's generosity,
there was also something calculated and slightly callous
about it. If he wanted you around all he had to do was buy
you. His personality intimidated you into submission with
its extraordinary mixture of excitement, enthusiasm,
affection and contempt. And for every wonderful, wild
and freeloading hour in Lex's company you could never
quite foretell when a moment would strike when you'd be
left reeling, aghast at the scale and extent of your own
uncontrollable profligacy and sick in your heart with the
knowledge of just how appallingly far you were living
beyond your means.

   James's guilt was not confined to his financial excesses,
although they were bad enough. Indeed the thought of all
those mounting bills, debts and overdrafts ticking away in
the roots of his and his father's relationship was rather like
envisaging a cell of sleeping foreign agents, planted,
secure and terminally threatening. What made things even
worse was the knowledge that if his university career was
to have any chance of a decent prolongation, it was
absolutely vital that he should continue to work and revise
steadily and calmly in the quiet and undisturbed atmosphere of the Loch Tulla Shooting Lodge. The thought of
being thrown out of Oxford was one he could cope with.
Although the experience was a not enjoyable one, the
prospect of expulsion from any institution had always
appealed to him as bestowing a certain incendiary lustre.

What he did dread was the thought of the final dramatic confrontations, first with a suavely stern-faced college master and then with his abjectly hurt and disappointed father. For several years now James had sought to minimise as far as possible all emotional contact with his father, especially on matters of his educational progress. Now, the imminent commencement of the Michaelmas Term and of the exam he would have to succeed in if his survival was to be ensured, seemed certain to bring with it the seed of some eventual, unavoidable collision.

He looked back across at the road signs on Lex's side of the car. Milton, Bowling, Duntocher and Dalmuir. Outer suburbs of Glasgow. Names and places that he'd never even heard of. Lex was smiling. He'd just changed the tape on the car stereo, from Count Basie to Sammy Davis, Jr, live at Toots Shors.

> *You're the top!*
> *You're the Coliseum.*

As the music began to quicken, gaining perceptibly in tempo and panache, it lifted James's mood and spirits with it. His stomach seemed to settle and his mind began to rest again, at last anchored by some rudder of partial sobriety and clarity. He started to beat out a rhythm with his hand on the car dashboard. He opened his window with the automatic switch. The air outside was hardly clean but it was cool. They were passing Clydebank. Lex had said Clydebank was a mortuary. An ageing necropolis of ugly people and ugly buildings. Tired, grey and sick looking.

The bookmaker offered him the two-thirds empty champagne bottle that was sitting on the floor by his feet. James drank from it far too quickly, burning his chest and sending the bubbles back up his nose. He laughed and began to sing out loud in time to the tape. Here they were bowling along past the miserable granite doorways of a wicked old Victorian Scottish city as if it was Chicago, Miami or downtown LA. That was the special magic of Lex Parlane. Whoever was with him and wherever they

were he could somehow make them feel as if even their
dreariest surroundings were transformed in his company
into landscapes of glamour and excitement, possibility and
mystique.

What James didn't know was that Lex knew and
understood precisely this effect that he had on people. It
was an important part of his power and control. Especially
over other Scotsmen. For Lex Parlane was not like other
Glaswegians. He was not forever caught up in some
twisted and introverted past. Bound by the legends of
stoical suffering, of violence, guilt and pain. Some men,
hard men you'd think them, unwittingly connived at the
soul-breaking old images of their native city. They
boasted of its violence. Bragged that the roughneck grit of
their town was what gave them their stomach and heart.
Secretly they feared its ugly old Victorian monoliths and
its bleak jail-like modern housing projects, but their
relationship with that landscape was a deeply masochistic
one. It scared them but they couldn't keep away from it.
They were like frightened children drawn back again and
again to a familiar ghost story that they know will keep
them awake all night. But Lex Parlane was not afraid.
What was Scotland to him anyway? Calvin, Calvary and
tea and hats at four. Something to jeer at, not fear. One
wave of his champagne bottle and it was gone. Trans-
cended by the power of his imagination and through the
force of his character and personality into Vegas, Florida
and Lakeside Illinois. What the others didn't know was
that Lex would only use these Clydeside settings as
prototypes for his fantastic recreations as long as he
needed to. For Lex Parlane was equally determined that
they would never be the outermost limit of his growth and
career, his final or enduring horizons. His ultimate destiny
lay elsewhere.

"Good day to you, sir. Good old Lexie!" called a man
from a rusting Dodge van as it toiled and spluttered in the
neighbouring lane. The man had a Zapata moustache and
he was wearing a huge tartan cowboy hat. His girlfriend

grinned and waved too from beneath the mass of her blonde, beehive hairdo.

"Just a few of my friends and admirers," said Lex, nodding and smiling his modest smile. The Rolls swept on towards the city.

7

The betting shop on the ground floor of the head office building was one of only three in the whole city with a special executive lounge where, for a minimum five pound bet, punters could enjoy the comfort of leatherette black armchairs along with free cups of coffee and tea while they followed the fortunes of their selections. It also boasted a regular daily copy of just about every page of published racing form in the British Isles.

But it was the main room next door that formed the bread-and-butter basis of Lex's business and this held good for every office in his organisation. And these almost always crowded rooms were filled with more than just cheap cigarette smoke. They were filled with every kind of modern technical equipment. Two parallel lines of five Japanese computerised information systems flashing up continuous details of odds, runners and riders, betting shows, results, starting prices and place dividends on not only all the major betting races but also on all the major sporting events throughout the year from the first division championship to grand prix motor racing, and from the results of each year's Oscar ceremonies to the outcome of next week's *Dallas* episode. And then there were the regular free copies of the monthly firm newsletter, *The Lex Parlane Suggestion*, the free 50p bets for old-age pensioners on Wednesday and Friday afternoons, the free ice creams on summer weekdays and the special Lex Raceday presentations to the most successful Lex Parlane Connection punter of the month.

Most of the faces in Lex's offices – the same kind of faces as in the betting shops of most of the other big firms in the city, except that in Lex's shops there were more of them – were not winning ones. The floors of the Blyths-wood Street shop, like the floors of the hundred-and-twenty-five other shops in Glasgow, Scotland and the North of England, well-polished though they regularly were, were almost always marked and worn-looking, thanks to all the scuffed shoe prints and the dragged stools and the cigarette butts and the faded pen and pencil marks of a thousand losing betting slips. Yankees, Doubles, Trebles, Accumulators, Canadians, Heinz's and Super Yankees. 50p doubles and trebles, one pound each way doubles, five, ten, fifteen, twenty and twenty-five pound win bets and fifty pound win bets and a hundred pound win doubles and tricasts and triellas and forecasts and ITV sevens.

Lex was fond of joking that the extra thick and deep pile of his office carpeting did in fact come from the special thick underlay of more than five hundred losing five, ten and fifty pound ante-post betting vouchers. And his office was certainly not lacking in comfort. There was a giant-size television console, the American-style cocktail cabinet that ran right down the length of one wall and there were the framed photographs around the room of Lex's more successful racehorses. Then there was the huge pine desk flown in from Bloomingdale's in New York City and the black leather and leopardskin executive's chair to go with it. The desk featured five separate telephones and two of them, those nearest Lex's right and left hands respectively, were framed in gold. Also on the desk was Lex's favourite logo. 'Lex Parlane. Most famous Scotsman since Rabbie Burns.'

The sofas and chairs were mostly steel, leather and more leopardskin, a kind of cross between Conran's High-Tech and Macey's Low Imperial. James Richmond was seated on the sofa in the window while Lex was at his desk and on the telephone. Reema Donachie, one of Lex's favourite secretaries, was ministering to their every need. Reema was a big-breasted, curvaceous redhead with big lips and twinkling eyes. Reema understood Lex. Lex said she reminded him of everything that was best about his ex-wife. She was terrific on the telephone and great with the big credit customers, unfriendly Glasgow authorities and the contents of the cocktail cabinet. She could make any drink, book any restaurant, club or plane, always send the right card, present or bunch of flowers and always make the right excuse without query or complaint.

Just now James was learning about the contents and effectiveness of a Reema Donachie whisky sour. He had two glasses still unfinished on the carpet by his side. For the moment though, he was nursing a large cup of hot strong black coffee made for him by Reema. He looked out of the window down towards St Vincent Street, where the rush hour traffic was beginning to roar, and out across the rooftops of the city towards the distant vista of Pollockshields and Mount Florida on the other side of the river. James had only a sketchy knowledge of Glasgow. His explorations of it to date had mostly been conducted from the inside of Lex's Mercedes or Rolls, speeding on their way towards some restaurant, night club or race-track. Initially the solid black granite tenement buildings and the cold white concrete and breezeblock modern estates had repelled and depressed him with their monstrous dourness. There was too, though, a definite sense of possibility, a feeling of latent energy and excitement that couldn't entirely be explained by the explosive nature of Lex's own personality.

A woman reporter from a Scottish weekly magazine arrived in the office to do a quick interview with Lex. She was accompanied by a scruffy-looking photographer who'd just finished taking pictures of Lena Zavaroni leaving Glasgow Airport for a holiday engagement in Tenerife. Lex charmed the woman reporter with ridiculous ease. He gave her the usual line about there being only two men in racing, him and Lester Piggott, and he boasted of the generous aid that he gave to numerous

West of Scotland charities and sporting organisations. Was it true, she asked him, that he'd once said he'd take the last few bob off a dying man?

"Of course it's true," said Lex. "What use would it be to him if he was really dying? But it might help me to make my next million!" He grinned cheerfully at the camera, waving the teacup that Reema had suddenly slipped into his hand in an effort to counteract the otherwise somewhat excessively alcoholic image.

Then Camilla walked in carrying a boxful of oranges and lemons and two bottles of Old Harper that Lex had sent out for to replenish the dwindling cocktail supplies. She'd been given her fifty pounds and she was beginning to enjoy herself. As soon as she saw the photographer her eyes lit up and she needed no invitation from Lex to sprawl herself seductively across his desk top, one arm looped around his shoulder. Reema moved in on the other side and the tableau was complete. 'Lex Parlane and his lovely ladies', the photographer's caption would eventually read. 'Glasgow's ever popular racing personality enjoys the flattering attentions of redheaded Reema and the glamorous and honourable Camilla Forbes-Sempill, one of Lex's prominent social acquaintances.' James caught Camilla's eye, shook his head and smiled. Camilla stuck her tongue out at him. Then, with five o'clock rapidly approaching, the woman reporter and the photographer were bundled back out of the office and down the stairs in to the street. The two women made another pitcher of bourbon whisky sours and then Reema went next door into the manager's office to check on the results of the day's business so far. Camilla was sent down into the basement flat to watch a video.

At two minutes past five Lex's phone call came through from London. The conversation was terse and strictly to the point. When Lex put the phone down he looked up at James and winked.

"It's an each way job. The Bugler. Could start as far out as twelves." James looked confused. Lex tossed him a copy of *The Sporting Life*, the page turned open at Newton Abbot. "Look at the last race," he said. "There's a short priced favourite who's a certainty but the next two horses in the market are both moderate maidens from big stables, each ridden by a leading jockey. Well, one of them is not going to finish in the first three! That lets The Bugler into the frame at a very nice price. Betting each way it's money for old rope!"

"I see." James's mind was spinning with the thought of all the other cosy little races that might have been fixed in this way.

"How much shall I put you down for?" asked Lex, his pen poised at the ready. "I've got about eight grand to get on for the man. All each way of course."

"A hundred each way?"

"Make it two. The two-year-old won, by the way."

James swopped his coffee for a whisky sour. Lex lit a cigar and started to make a list of his various account numbers along with each telephone number by their side and the sum of money that he intended to invest. The time passed quickly. Just after five fifteen a man walked into the office. He was tall and broad-shouldered with a receding hairline and an aggressive but cherubic sort of face. James put him down as around forty-five and a heavy drinker. He was wearing a rather tattered old gaberdine raincoat that looked like the kind of mac an American private detective might wear when his first choice was at the cleaners. He had an evening newspaper in one hand and he was smoking an obnoxious smelling cheroot.

"Where have you been?" asked Lex, without looking up. "I called the desk five times."

"Playing snooker with my sub-editor. He owes me three weeks' wages."

"James Richmond meet Jack McQueen, 'the voice of sport'. Jack's my star reporter on the *Citizen*. Official biographer too."

"His Lordship, eh?" McQueen looked James up and down contemptuously.

"The Lord Strathfillan to you," said Lex grinning.

"Fuck off, Lex."

"Is this your idea of getting in with the upper classes?" asked McQueen, sitting down heavily in the chair by Lex's desk.

"He's alright. He's a good boy. A friend. And he likes a punt too, eh, Jimmy?" Lex looked back at his list. "It's The Bugler. Each way. Bolger wants eight thousand."

"Bloody crooks."

"How much can you take?"

"Two or three hundred?"

"Do me a favour, Jack. Three fifty each way."

McQueen breathed out noisily through his nose. "I'll do it with Corals."

"Good man. I have to get on first." He picked up one of the gold telephone receivers and started dialling. "You can use the other gold phone, Jack. James, you use the red one." James moved closer to the desk. Lex got through to the Hills office in the city, gave them his name and number and asked for the odds on The Bugler in the five forty-five at Newton Abbot. A girl's voice came back to him. Eight to one. Lex threw a look at the others. Someone obviously suspected something. Still, Lex had to get on Michael Bolger's money. That was their agreement and there was a commission in it for him too so he asked for eight hundred pounds each way at eight to one. There was a pause. Then the girl came back. They'd accept the money. Lex made a note of the bet on his special piece of paper and then rang Mecca and Ward Hill placing four hundred and fifty and five hundred pounds each way respectively. Then he rang a prearranged contact in Govanhill, a shebeen manager and ex-bank robber called Willie Smith. He told Willie to put two hundred and fifty pounds on each way for Bolger and then added a further two thousand pounds each way for him personally on Willie's account with Louis Weiss. That gave him a special

sense of pleasure. But once again he did stress that the bet
was for each way money only. Then James rang Hills and
had his two hundred pounds each way and McQueen rang
Corals and had his three fifty each way. Then Lex rang
Corals himself and asked for a thousand pounds each way
at the new odds of seven to one. There was a lengthy
pause. Lex looked anxiously at his watch. The time had
moved on to five thirty-seven. Then the Corals voice came
back. They were adamant. They would accept absolutely
no more bets on the The Bugler in the five forty-five at
Newton Abbot. Lex looked up again. There had definitely
been a serious leakage of information. He rang off
abruptly and started to dial the office number of his
special oncourse man at Newton Abbot races. The
oncourse man was in fact just another bookmaker trading
under his own name on a pitch in Tattersalls. None of
Lex's rivals and enemies yet knew of this special relationship. The oncourse man carried a little bleeper in his
right suit pocket and when the bleeper sounded he knew
to pick up the blower on the rails and dial into his own
main office.

"The trouble with Benny," said Lex to McQueen in a
low voice, ". . . is he can probably only take about fifteen
hundred." He made the connection and although the line
was bad succeeded in sending back seven hundred pounds
each way spread over several different prices. It was now
just three minutes to the off.

"You're still a grand and a half short," said McQueen.

"I know," said Lex.

"How about the Greek? He owes us a few."

"I'll try him."

Lex dialled Marcos Investments, a burgeoning property
development company with its own suite of private penthouse offices on the top floor of the Stakis Pond Hotel. A
private phone rang in a private bedroom and a suavely
un-Scottish voice came on the line.

"George? Lex. I'll come straight to the point. I want
you to put some money on a horse for me. It's seven

hundred and fifty pounds each way on The Bugler in the five forty-five at Newton Abbot. It's off in about a minute, George, so you've gotta hurry. O.K.?" The suave well-oiled voice acceded swiftly to Lex's demands. "Good man, George. I'll call you back." He slammed the phone down. "Done it!" McQueen allowed himself a smile. James gulped another drink down nervously. Lex dialled London.

"Hello? Mickey? Lex. I got your money on. Here it is." He proceeded to read out the list of bets and prices obtained. James tried to imagine the mysterious person-age on the other end of the telephone. An inspired playboy professional? A gangster? Or just a disaffected bookmaker? James favoured the latter.

When Bolger had rung off, Lex, James and McQueen each picked up a red telephone again to be connected to the Exchange Telegraph Commentary from the shop down below. The race was off three minutes late. There was fog at Newton Abbot and the going was on the soft side of good. One of the two 'suspect' horses led on the first circuit, closely followed by the short priced favourite. There was no mention yet of The Bugler. It almost made James want to laugh, sitting in the palatial surroundings of Lex's office and listening to the clipped and nasal tones of the Extel commentator, a voice so much associated with the one-star sleaze of the betting offices. With two flights of hurdles left to jump the same two horses were in the lead. Then there was the inevitable dogs show from Monmore and another dogs result from somewhere else. When the commentary came back to Newton Abbot it transpired that the first suspect horse was dropping back as the result of an 'unfortunate blunder' at the last. The favourite was scrambling away towards the line, closely pursued by suspect horse number two and that was the way they finished. But then there was an agonising pause while the three men waited for the commentator to call out third place. Another dogs commentary intervened, followed by a tote dividend at York. At last they got the full list of starting prices from Newton Abbot and sure enough, third at thirteen to two, was number fourteen, The Bugler. James was thrilled to bits and showed it. McQueen jumped up and went across to the cocktail cabinet, coming back with a chilled bottle of Veuve Clicquot and three glasses.

"You can all have dinner on my bill at the hotel," said Lex, beaming. "I'll get two grand as commission. Plus Willie's money. And all for half an hour's work on a wet Thursday afternoon." They all laughed loudly. "You can see what I mean now, Jimmy. I've got this game in my pocket. And that's gonna help you one day too!"

McQueen shook his head. "If that lot ever get caught they'll end up being warned off for life."

"If, if, if!" said Lex sipping his champagne happily. "Lex is your boy and he'll never get caught." One of the gold telephones started to ring as if on cue. "That should be London now," said Lex, picking the receiver up briskly. "Hello, Mickey?"

But it wasn't Mickey it was Willie Smith and Willie had bad news, at least for Lex. "I'm sorry, Lex," he started mumbling apologetically. "I couldn't get the money on each way. Not with Corals. They'd only take it to win."

Lex's face went white. Very calmly he tightened his grip on the telephone. "So what are you saying, Willie? You didn't put it on?"

"No, Lex. That's just the point. I put it all on. To win."

"You did what?"

"I put on the whole forty-five hundred. But to win only."

"Are you fucking deaf? I told you. That horse was each way money only."

"I know, Lex. But I was worried. I thought you had to get it on. For a face."

Lex paused. His icy rage seemed to permeate the whole room, chilling the already cold glass of champagne in James's hand down to freezing point. "It's alright, Willie," he said in a flat voice. "Innocent mistake. I'll be in touch." Willie started to continue with his apologies but Lex put the phone down on him. "The little turd," he said to the others. "He's been helping himself to the scam and then putting it all on my cheque."

"What are you going to do?" asked McQueen, lighting another cheroot.

"When useless little runts like Willie Smith start losing me money I lose them." He picked up his cigar cutter and sliced viciously through the neck of a fresh Havana.

"How much will your friend have made?" asked James tentatively. "The one in London?"

"Bolger's no friend. I just deal with him commercially on an occasional basis."

"How much money?" asked McQueen.

"All in all about ten thousand pounds profit on an outlay of twenty-five grand."

James looked confused. "But he doesn't put the money down himself?"

"He can't. He's been warned off. So I do it for him."

"It seems a lot of money to put at risk for such a small return."

"Bollocks! Bolger's got a tie-up with the jockeys. Garvin, Nicholson and Fry. And I've done jobs with Garvin myself. If it all goes according to plan it's the easiest money you can ever earn. It should have been easy for me today."

"Let's go to the game," said McQueen.

8

Lex left the Rolls in the garage. His white Mercedes was parked three blocks away. He drove them down Sauchiehall Street past the now closed shops and the cinema queues and the thriving bars and the Indian restaurants. They passed Queen Street Station and nearby George Square with its 'Glasgow's Miles Better' signs and headed down the High Street towards Glasgow Cross.

"Here we go," said Lex, snorting some more cocaine off his key ring. "Across the Great Divide."

James soon saw what he meant. East of Glasgow Cross was a world and a landscape far removed from the flashy prosperity of Lex's West End headquarters offices. Their route took them down along the Gallowgate. They parked the car by a bar called Jimmy Mac's. The bar and its rear garage were the only two buildings left standing on a patch of waste ground about fifty yards square that stood between a modern housing estate and a row of derelict black brick factories with padlocks and security patrol signs on their front doors. Grass and weeds were growing up between the flagstones.

James looked on in disbelief as a pair of burly young minders with denim jackets, green-and-white scarves and flared suit trousers came out of the bar, got into the Mercedes and drove it back round to the garage at the rear.

"I know what you're thinking," said McQueen. "It's all a part of the Parlane football ritual. Those two boys are both members of his own private supporters club. And it's just the same whether he's at Parkhead or Ibrox. I mean he's not even a fucking Catholic but round here they all think he's a national hero. I believe it's what's known as a personality cult.''

Jimmy Mac's had wire mesh bars across the doors and windows. Inside it was packed with Celtic football supporters and the atmosphere was formidable. Big men and boys in tartan and denim all swathed in the green and white.

Lex bought a round. Many of the men in the bar seemed to know Lex personally and many of them laid bets with him on the outcome of the match. There were no women. Up above the bar there were three signed photographs. The Pope, John F Kennedy and Danny McGrain.

From Jimmy Mac's they had to walk the rest of the way to the stadium. Over more tangled patches of waste ground, past more razed tenements and modern precincts and stuttering highrise blocks. Hundreds of other people were all heading in the same direction. The further they went, the more the crowd swelled and across a wider front it seemed to be marching. Cars and taxis were not allowed beyond this point but James could see them in the background, all stacked up in rows beneath the railway bridges or beside the whisky hoardings or behind the supporters club coaches and double decker buses that had come in from not just the rest of Glasgow but from all over Scotland. And watching them from all sides were the tight and serried ranks of Glasgow's finest, their peaked caps pulled down hard over their eyes. Emphatic. Intimidating. Their uniforms neat and shining, their faces glaring or just impassive.

Then the floodlights of the ground came into view and the crowd started to be channelled down a narrower path. The air was thick with the sound of singing and chanting and the rancid smells of a dozen hot dog vans and hamburger kiosks. Whisky breathing vendors pressed their way towards them selling flags and rosettes and Celtic mascots. Lex continued to behave as if he was on a royal progression. The film star returned. Seve Ballesteros striding up the eighteenth fairway towards the final green at St Andrews. Only just before the crowd swung left into a tight alleyway behind the stand, Lex neatly separated himself from the crush so that he and James and McQueen could cut round by Kerrydale Street and the primary school and make their entrance into the ground by the more prestigious front gateway. Lex flashed a few words and a few notes in the direction of the gateman, McQueen flashed his press pass and a moment or so later the three men found themselves standing in the main hallway of the Celtic ground.

Lex undid a few buttons on his sleek camel hair coat and breathed cigar smoke out over their heads. They were still surrounded by a large crowd of people but these were different kinds of people to the fans outside. It was not just the obvious air of greater prosperity, the better cut clothes and the superior brands of strong whisky. As they stood there in the hall and all looked up at the famous green-and-white team portraits on the wall above them they shared a general feeling of importance and exclusivity, of being on the inside, of enjoying a special privileged access to players and management that the boys on the street would never quite know.

Across the other side of the hallway was the glittering Celtic trophy room containing the 1967 European Cup, along with countless Scottish FA Cups, League Cups and First Division championship shields.

The atmosphere was still spartan. Scottish. Not luxurious. Vinyl-covered floors. Dark brown wooden panelling around the walls. And a whiff of lubricant and massage oil from down the corridor. Bare wooden tables and white shower room tiles. Inside the boardroom it was different.

Lex moved in easily through the open doorway and was quickly engaged in animated conversation by other hearty and hardfaced men. More bets were struck on the side as discussion sprang up about share prices and country clubs, the outcome of that day's horse racing and prospects for the match ahead.

"When do we go outside?" James asked McQueen. "I'm beginning to get excited."

"When your man's all finished with the business."

"What business?"

McQueen grinned and pointed to a corner of the room where Lex was busy in close consultation with a fat and porcine-featured man with blood-red skin and thick black Brylcreemed hair. The man wore a black, well-cut suit with a wide leather belt and a shiny gold buckle.

"That's Fat Jimmy," said McQueen. "Fat Jimmy's a director of another old Glasgow Club and a very big player – and I don't mean football!"

"So?"

"So he and one of the leading players in the Scottish game are into Lex for a great deal of money. About a quarter of a million at the latest estimate. Well, Lex is trying to work out a meaningful accommodation."

"What's he going to do?"

"They're going to transfer the player in question to one of the leading English clubs. Liverpool. Manchester United. Spurs. Then Fat Jimmy can start paying off his debts to Lex through his share of the transfer fee."

"What?"

"They've done it before. Household names."

"But he can't do that."

"Lex can do anything he wants. That's why he's Lex Parlane. A few years ago he even fixed the results of the Grand National."

"He did what?"

"You heard me. He fixed the Grand National."

"But the Grand National's unique. It's a legend!" He was spluttering. "An heroic event for the Corinthian sportsman!"

"Lex fixed it just the same."

At that moment Lex and Fat Jimmy started moving out of the room and across the hallway towards the stairs. McQueen followed and James followed McQueen.

They had seats in the Directors' Box. With more than

fifteen minutes to go before kick off time the stadium was
already comfortably heading towards its 53,000 plus
capacity. McQueen reached out and put a hand on the
nineteen-year-old's shoulder. "Not quite the Varsity, eh?
Celtic and Rangers." McQueen grinned unkindly. "The
incognito English aristocrat's son hoping to pass himself
off as one of the lads."

"I can look after myself," said James, taking his seat.

"If you wanna get the best atmosphere . . . you
shouldn't be up here. This is for the oldies."

"Shouldn't you be in the Press Box?"

"I'm not a cub reporter, son. I'm freelance."

Thousands of fans were still pouring into the ground at
the Celtic end, jamming together so tightly that they could
hardly move either forward or back. And up at the
opposite end of the ground thousands of the other fans
were still arriving too. The blue-and-white boys of Govan
and Ibrox and the Copland Road. The Loyalist supporting
army of Glasgow Rangers. Massed ranks of police and
stewards kept the two sides well apart. As the public
address system blared out a tape of loud, old and emotional pop music and as the police cordons began their first
measured clockwise patrol around the edges of the touchline, the Rangers players came out on to the pitch to warm
up. Ten minutes later it was the turn of the Celtic team
and in each instance the reaction was the same. In fact the
air was soon so thick with chants and choruses, that the
tape of sixties pop songs became rapidly inaudible. Then
the tannoy announced the final composition of the two
sides to more screams of rage and approbation. They
played *You'll Never Walk Alone*. Up went the Celtic
scarves and all of a sudden the Rangers end of the ground
broke into a counter chorus of 'No Pope of Rome' to the
tune of *Home, Home on the Range*. James could feel the
hair standing up on the nape of his neck. He turned the
collar up on the black trenchcoat Lex had lent him and
adjusted his dark glasses. He was willing himself to blend
in with the Directors' Box. He had to look like an

acceptable Lex Parlane Connection rails man or sidekick. The singing got louder and more diversified and emotional. McQueen was singing. Lex wasn't singing but he was smiling alright. Then the teams ran out on to the pitch and the game began.

As a football match it was no great contest. Celtic completed a comprehensive three-nil drubbing of their old enemy and as usual in an Old Firm game the tackling was hard and there were a high number of bookings. The result though was not what Richmond would remember. He'd remember the moment when the floodlights came on raking the crowd and the blue night sky and illuminating the rooftops of the city away across the London Road towards the South. He'd remember the crowd jumping high and jubilantly into the air after each Celtic goal and McQueen and Fat Jimmy pummelling and slapping him on his back and shoulders and neck. And probably most acutely of all he'd remember the set piece exchanges between the fans of the two sides. At one point a group of young Rangers boys came down to the edge of the touchline and unfurled a huge Union Jack. Seen from the Directors' Box they were like a party of Zulu warriors dancing tauntingly in front of the main Impi at Rorkes Drift. The response from the Celtic end was immediate. Two tall and redheaded boys hoisted the Irish tricolour and the Republican songs and slogans started to fly through the air, thick and fast.

The blue-and-white boys responded with *The Sash* and *God Save The Queen* and then a smoke bomb exploded over the Rangers end. The police started rushing towards the hole in the fencing. As the smoke began to drift across the ground, tickling the eyes and burning the throat, the sound of the songs and the sight of the tricolour and the running policemen began to evoke in James a feeling of anarchy and sedition like a school uprising turned prison riot. These then were the symbols and catchphrases of anarchic resistance to imposed authority. And the thrill was all the greater and all the easier for being part of a shared and mass group reaction in which the name or face of the individual enemy could be safely and necessarily ignored. Only James wasn't down there on the terraces, behind the Celtic goal or up at the Rangers end. He was sitting with Fat Jimmy and McQueen and Lex Parlane high up in the Directors' Box. Snug amidst the silk ties and the fur collars and the other directors' wives. Watching Lex viewing one of his native city's most passionate rituals while buying and selling its frenzied emotion with all the dispassionate calm of a stockbroker selling off British North Sea oil to the Gulf Sheikhs.

On their way out of the ground James and McQueen were nearly crushed by the great press of people. The first and second floor windows of the flats nearby were all open and the women were leaning out on the window ledges looking down at the chanting celebratory crowds below.

They went back to Jimmy Mac's bar.

In spite of the Celtic victory Lex was still collecting large sums of money from losing punters, most of whom had wagered incorrectly on the size of the winning margin or the identity of the individual goal scorers. Then back in the smooth comfort of the Mercedes, James saw Fat Jimmy give Lex a large manilla envelope filled, he presumed, with a healthy number of crisp, fifty pound notes. Driving back up the Gallowgate they passed a battered old Corporation double decker bus lurching its way home to Shettleston and Tollcross. Two boys had opened the emergency exit on the top deck and they were sitting drunkenly astride the roof waving a Celtic banner. Then the Mercedes passed Glasgow Cross and they were back in their own country.

The rest of the evening unfolded in typical Lex fashion. They had dinner at the Holiday Inn and the champagne flowed throughout. Lex paid for everybody and chose all the richest and most expensive dishes on the menu such as double cream Lobster Thermidor followed by grouse roasted on a thick bed of paté, shallots, asparagus, Pernod, white wine, cream and brandy. He followed this up with a special jam and Cointreau pancake basted in malt whisky and flamed individually at the waiter's table. Then they went on to the "Tartan Cavalier" where the champagne and white powder continued to be consumed in great abundance. They were met at the club by Reema, a blonde-haired hostess girl called Patti – Fat Jimmy's 'escort' for the night – Camilla and two rich but rash young friends of hers and James's. They had been contacted earlier on as part of Lex's pre-arranged plan for a projected and hopefully remunerative poker game later that night. The party were entertained from the stage by Frank Carson, Bonnie Langford and an ex-Falkirk High School Girl Strippers Band. They all danced. Lex danced with Reema. James danced with Camilla. Then Lex danced with Camilla.

When they got back to Lex's flat on the top floor of the head office building they drank more champagne and then brandy. James put his arms around Camilla but she was more interested in watching Lex and the way he played his cards. Half an hour into the poker game James was already down by several hundred pounds and beginning to experience considerable difficulties in talking, thinking and focusing correctly on the other people round the table. By half past five that morning Lex had won over a thousand pounds from Fat Jimmy alone. McQueen had won too. Rory McAlpine and Alan McAllister-Hall were each down by about seven hundred and fifty pounds. James's losses were officially near six hundred pounds but he knew that Lex would probably allow him much of that back again for introducing the two new players. The others started to go. Reema and the hostess girl – who had fallen asleep hours before – each kissed James as they went. Camilla and Lex were now smooching in the corner. Lex winked. James tried to reach out and touch Camilla's ankle with his hand but failed. That's when he really passed out.

When he awoke he had a crunching headache. His face
and body felt as if it had been wrapped in warm flannel
and it seemed as if somebody was trying to shove a
mixture of flannel and dry sand into his mouth and down
his throat. His nose felt heavy and blocked and when he
tried to touch the roof of his mouth with his tongue he
discovered that it was burned dry and rasping.

He'd been sleeping in a squashed-up heap on Lex's
black leather sofa, a leopardskin rug sprawled over his
body and an embroidered cushion stuffed over his head.
Stumbling uncertainly to his feet he discovered a hundred
and one stiff aches and pains in his shoulders, ribs and
neck. The room was still in total disarray. Records lay out
of their sleeves everywhere. Glasses and bottles were all
over the floor and coffee table, mingling with the trays full
of cigar ash and roaches and cigarette ends. A bottle of
port had spilled all over one of Lex's Dean Martin albums,
while the glass surface of the coffee table betrayed the
tell-tale marks of numerous large lines of cocaine. James's
heart was beating fast. He weaved his way uncertainly
towards the kitchen, filled a pint milk bottle full of water,
drank it, refilled it and then somehow just managed to
make it to the bathroom before he was sick. He reap-
peared fifteen minutes later, clutching onto a towel and a
large tube of toothpaste, some of which he'd succeeded in
smearing around his lips and mouth. He drank from his
water bottle once again and walked into Lex's bedroom.
The bed was empty but not made. There was no sign of
either Lex or Camilla. James crawled gratefully into the
still warm bedclothes, pulled the large leopardskin
covered duvet over his head and went back to sleep. The
digital clock by his side said nine fifty-five.

9

Two minutes to ten and the Duke was sitting on the lavatory. He liked lavatories. They were one of his favourite settings for contemplation and consideration. And this lavatory was in the extremely comfortable and exclusive Stewards' gentlemen's cloakroom at Jockey Club headquarters in Portman Square. All the same, the Duke was not pleased. For today was Friday, October the seventh. His birthday. And as birthdays go it had not got off to a particularly propitious start.

There had been no correspondence whatsoever from his youngest son James. But then that had been only to be expected. James had been much on the Duke's mind of late as he watched with ever growing alarm his son's seemingly determined descent into an abyss of slothfulness, addiction, debt and deceit. When he'd talked to him on the phone the previous evening he'd enjoyed at least the marginal semblance of a civilised conversation. But when he'd rung Loch Tulla again that morning he'd discovered that the boy had skipped class overnight. Run off to Glasgow for yet another riotous jaunt with that fat, corrupt and corrupting bookmaker. The shooting lodge had been left in a state of total chaos and Mr McLavity had been seriously insulted. Something would have to be done.

The Duke's discomfiture had been further added to on stepping out of the door of his Alexander Square London quarters just before nine that morning only to be virtually ambushed by his idiotic eldest son Rowland and a deputation of Rowland's sword-swirling young subaltern cronies up from Aldershot. They had driven all night after a

Torquemada Club dinner in order to present the Duke with a special birthday salute. This they followed up, somewhat illogically to the Duke's way of thinking, with a particularly tuneless rendition of that old Naval anthem *Hearts of Oak*. Extricating himself with some difficulty the Duke beat a hasty if dignified retreat up the Brompton Road before dodging up Cheval Place and on up Ennismore Gardens towards Knightsbridge and the Park. He had intended to walk the rest of the way to Portman Square, strolling through the Park in the pleasant autumn sunshine, but unhappily, no sooner had he crossed Rotten Row than the sun went in behind the clouds, the skies darkened and he found himself drenched by a veritable stinker of a short, sharp October shower. He was able to hail a taxi up by Hyde Park Corner but even so, by the time he arrived at JCGHQ he was uncomfortably cold, wet and shivering, necessitating a stiff drink and immediate retirement to the cloakroom for a restorative wash and brush up.

The Duke shifted his weight around on the well-polished lavatory seat, attempting to find more agreeable purchase, and reflected bitterly on the extraordinary chain of ill-fortune that seemed to have dogged his every movement these past ten days. Ever since he'd seen Louis Weiss. His two-year-old filly had been beaten a short head in the Cheveley Park Stakes . . . by the Canadian-bred. His Nassau Stakes winner had lost a shoe at the start of the Sun Chariot and finished only third. And then there had been Paris. Paris! The Arc de Triomphe! Those twin nightmares guaranteed to bring a flush of loathing into every well-bred Englishman's heart. In this year's happy reunion of the 'Trusthouse Forte Prix de l'Arc de Triomphe' the Duke's Derby runner-up had been practically knocked into the Pelouse by the French jockeys as its Irish-born pilot had attempted to make his challenge up the inside rail coming into the straight. There had been a stewards enquiry but the French, smug to the last after yet another home-trained victory, inscrutably insisted that the

Irish jockey had made his own trouble and stood him
down for seven days for reckless riding.

"Damned French!" the Duke had barked, as he and
Washy and Miles De Berry had stomped away crossly past
the overweening statue of Gladiateur. "What a blasted
shower! Gallic charm? My hat!"

"That's the trouble with the French, Johnny," Washy
had said, struggling manfully to keep up. "They do keep a
grudge."

"What's that got to do with it?" the Duke had replied,
scowling irritably at a coachload of English trippers who
were grinning at him moronically from the traffic jams.

"Well, Johnny . . . you did disqualify their Oaks
favourite just before the start at Epsom," said De Berry.
"And all because the filly was declared to run in blinkers
and then didn't appear to be wearing them on her way
down to the start."

"Absolutely. Rules are rules, Miles. There to be
obeyed."

"I suppose that's what the French feel too, Johnny."

"Blasted French! What a fiasco."

The Duke's angry words seemed to echo around his
brain even now. The final straw of an abjectly humiliating
weekend had come at about three o'clock that morning
when he'd been awoken in his suite at the Crillon by a
telephone call from some whimpering number three at the
British Embassy. Miles De Berry had been arrested in a
bar in Pigalle for being drunk and disorderly and for doing
a full drag impersonation of Madame Mitterrand on the
zinc top bar.

What an Olympian catalogue of disasters! And now his
birthday ruined too. By rights he should still have been
enjoying a quiet but intimate breakfast with his beloved of
the moment, a deliciously blonde and plump ex-interior
decorator who now resided in the comfortably serviced
flat the Duke had bought her at number twenty-eight
Hays Mews. This would've been followed by an excellent
lunch at Scott's and a car ride to Ascot, getting there in

time for the second of the afternoon's six races. Instead he
had been compelled to attend a special Jockey Club
talking to at Portman Square and all because the Tattersalls All Purposes Committee wouldn't change around
their meeting arranged for the following Tuesday.
Though, to be honest, the Duke did admit that this
occasion had been all of his own devising. A sort of
off-the-record ACAS mediation job between the Club,
Racecourse Security Services and legal representatives for
the Lex Parlane connection and Goldline the bookmakers. Goldline's representatives were to offer a compromise
pay-out over their remaining debts incurred from the
Cheltenham betting coup while Parlane's were to be
reprimanded and advised never to take any course of
action which might bring them into this exalted company
again. Then in the afternoon the Scotsman's lawyers were
to be told that there was no longer an official objection to
Parlane applying for a Tattersalls pitch on certain of the
leading southern racecourses. But then that was all part of
a trap being laid and success in that quarter would be
almost as sweet for the Duke as victories in the wretched
Arc de Triomphe or expulsion from native shores of all
American-bred beasts.

He heard a shuffle of feet outside, followed by a gentle
tap tap on the lavatory door. "Er, Johnny?" The familiar
blocked nose and flatulent tones of Washy Cleveland.
"Johnny?"

"Yes."

"Everybody's here. Just waiting for you really." Pause.
Silence. "Johnny?"

"I'm just coming."

"Right ho. Good. I'll, er, pop along." Pause. Silence.
"Good."

The Duke sighed, reached for the lavatory paper and
completed the necessary details.

10

When James awoke the second time the clock had moved on to eleven fifty-seven. His throat was still dry but his head was clearing and his heartbeat had slowed down. A clean-looking silk dressing gown appeared to have been left deliberately over the back of a chair. James put it on. It was several sizes too big for him. Lex's, no doubt. When he put his head rather tentatively around the bedroom door a few moments later the scene was a complete transformation. Everything had been swept, cleaned, tidied and cleared away. Even the carpet had been hoovered. A Tony Bennett album was playing on the stereo and Lex was standing in the kitchen holding an egg whisk and a Pyrex bowl. Aside from the inevitable pair of black shades he looked remarkably fit and well. He was wearing a clean and immaculately ironed blue shirt, a new tie and an immaculately pressed pair of blue suit trousers. His heroic capacity for excess was truly remarkable.

"Good morning," he said cheerfully. "There's a pitcher of Bloody Mary's on the table and a pot of fresh coffee on its way. I'm making brunch. Do you like Eggs Benedict or would the hollandaise sauce be a little too rich for you this morning?"

"Just bacon and eggs will be fine."

"Bacon and poached eggs, no trouble."

James groped his way towards the Bloody Mary and quickly drank two or three glasses. "Where's Camilla?" he asked, opening up the pages of *The Sporting Life*.

"Ah! I took her to the airport early. I bought her a ticket down to London and gave her a few hundred quid for some shopping."

"Terrific."

"Well, she felt she ought to have a new wardrobe for the races tomorrow and the Glasgow stores just weren't good enough."

"Thanks a lot."

"Now don't you worry about a thing, son," said Lex, bringing in a tray filled with two large plates of bacon and poached eggs, a large jug of freshly squeezed orange juice and several racks full of brown wholemeal toast. "She won't desert you, you'll see. It's just my flamboyant personality and charm. It's always a wow with these upper-class girls. I can't help it."

"So it seems."

The Scotsman laughed and poured a huge helping of hollandaise sauce over his eggs. "Believe me, Jimmy, one day you'll get your revenge. And thanks for the poker game by the way. I won a good few quid off your nice young friends. You can take it off the tab. Okay?"

"You still fucked my girlfriend."

"Indeed I did, son. But if there's any woman I can give you in return you only have to ask. And that's a promise."

"I may keep you to that, Lex."

"Do so. Now eat your breakfast and shut up."

James sighed, swallowed a mouthful of bacon and immediately began to cheer up. The bacon was delicious, hot, crisp and salty, and for the first time that morning young Richmond began to realise just how hungry he was. He poured a little hollandaise sauce over his eggs. When he ran his knife very gently over the top of the egg the yolk shot out, warm and yellow but not too runny. It flowed down over the toast and into the sauce and on to the bacon. He helped himself to coffee. It was hot and strong and made with hot milk like a French hotel. It tasted excellent. "Good food," said James, with his mouth full. "Stylish. I wouldn't have put you down as a home caterer."

"Sometimes a maid comes in. Sometimes I depend on the lady I spent the previous night with. But on this occasion that didn't seem to be quite appropriate! All the same a man's got to know how to cook. Food's probably the sixth most important thing in my life."

"What are the other five?"

Lex thought for a moment.

"Money. Horses. Alcohol. Sex and Drugs."

The nineteen-year-old longed to ask him how in the circumstances he ever found time for such immaculate shirt and trouser ironing and other little domestic niceties but, not feeling over-confident in his present mood, he politely desisted.

After they'd finished eating James took a long and refreshing shower while Lex went upstairs to his gold telephones. James had been given the run of Lex's wardrobe and permission to pick out whatever he required. Modestly shunning the more outrageously monogrammed of the twenty or thirty handmade silk shirts, he eventually selected a pale green-and-white striped Pierre Cardin number with corresponding white collar and cuffs. Although the shoulders were ridiculously large on him the general appearance more than satisfied the requisite Lex aura of confidence, wealth and prestige.

Breakfasting, bathing and dressing now over, James's thoughts turned reluctantly and gloomily to Loch Tulla, to his father and his work. When he rang up the shooting lodge he got Mrs McLavity on the line and she was none too pleased with the way he'd left the house on his departure the previous day. On top of that his father had rung and been angry and disappointed to discover that his son was not at home and working hard. James groaned and rang off. When he rang up Dereham Hall he got first the butler and then his father's unctuously smarmy private secretary, Letherby. James was well aware that his father appeared to retain a certain irrational affection for Letherby, a consideration which he could only regard as spectacularly misplaced. With all the odious relish that the goody goody always displays when informing one of his wilder colleagues that he's up for the high jump, Letherby

told James that the Duke was in London on important
Portman Square business but that he'd be back the
following morning and would be expecting a prompt and
apologetic phone call. Then Letherby told him that his
older brother Rowland was down on leave, having just
arrived from London that morning where he'd seen the
Duke. Rowland, said Letherby, was extremely anxious to
have a word with him. James's heart sank even further. As
soon as Rowland got on the telephone he paused for only
the most cursory enquiry after James's health before
launching into his customary peroration on duty, thrift,
responsibility and hard work. Listening to Rowland's
booming bulldog-like tones and reflecting on the piglet-
like nature of his brain and imagination, James was
quickly roused to his usual feelings of depression and
contempt. He held the telephone at arm's length and
then, when Rowland's voice still wouldn't go away, hid it
under a cushion while he went into the kitchen to make
himself a drink. When he returned the line was dead. He
tipped the contents of his pockets on to the living room
floor. Two pounds and twenty-seven pence exactly. And
that's how Lex found him when he returned from the
office upstairs.

"Counting out what you owe me? I like that. It shows
you've got your priorities in the right order."

"I have to go to Queen Street."

"What for?"

"To go back north! To Loch Tulla. My work, Lex. My
bloody exam."

"You can't go today. It's Ayr tomorrow. And Sunday's
the firm's big night. Our annual do at the Bella Vista
Hotel. This year's a Wild West Evening. You're gonna
love that."

"You don't understand."

"Of course I understand. I've got a big day today. My
lawyer's at Portman Square. But I'm not worrying."
James shook his head. "You'll be back at the college soon
enough, son. For now, play. And play hard!"

"But it's my family. The whole bloody mess. It's getting worse, Lex. All the time."

"I'll deal with your family. Every time they ring you can tell them I'm showing you the intricate details of the racing and gambling world. Standing you in good stead for your future." He went to change the record.

"I'm sure my father would be interested to hear about the details of a certain Grand National result." Lex looked up at him sharply. "How did it go with Fat Jimmy last night? Did you sort out the business?"

"McQueen's been talking, I see. It went well enough. The lad in question's shortly going to be enjoying a change of scenery. Spurs probably. About Friday week."

"I just don't know how you do it."

"It's easy. Nothing succeeds like the scent of excess. Confidence is all. Will you stay?"

"I suppose so."

"Good boy. Today we'll take it easy."

"Very likely."

Lex grinned. "Come on. I'll show you some things around the city."

Like many other large and old industrial cities Glasgow's social geography contains a frequent number of quick and sudden changeovers from one area of wealth and prosperity to another contrasting neighbourhood of poverty, dereliction and decline.

Lex walked James down St Vincent Street, turned right into Buchanan Street and then left on Argyle. They crossed St Enoch's, walked over the Victoria Bridge down Gorbals Street and then turned right into Bedford Street.

They were now in a changing landscape of concrete and waste ground bisected by the overhead electric railway cables and bounded by the McAlpine-built Arab mosque on its north side. Just behind them were two crumbling Victorian warehouses. One of them had once been the offices of the Clyde Shipping Company. The other one was a Pakistani clothing manufacturers. About eighty yards in front there were four twenty-three storey blocks

of modern council flats. And about another fifty yards
behind them there was a railway and behind the railway
viaducts they could see the floodlights of a ball park
stadium.

"That's where I used to live," said Lex casually. "For
the first nine years of my life that was home." He sounded
disbelieving. They stood there on the stretch of new
sidewalk, gazing out at the great empty patch of flat grass
between the tower blocks. It was littered with puddles and
piles of gently burning rubbish. A group of hard-nosed
kids formed up around them, attracted by the charismatic
lure of the big man in the black dark glasses. Lex started
handing out five pound notes.

"They ought to put a plaque up there somewhere," he
said. "Like the writers and the politicians." He had a
photograph in his wallet of himself sitting on the bonnet of
his Rolls outside the tenement on the day that the
bulldozers moved in. "McQueen arranged that," he said.
"For the *Citizen*. He's earned his dinners. Wrote a
glowing piece in the *Herald* the following week about the
romantic warmth of Scottish communal working-class
life." He laughed and shook his head. "If that place was
romantic, then so's a hat full of lice. But then it seems to
be a Scottish institution to romanticise misery, violence
and pain."

"The character building values of institutional life,"
said James with a rueful smile.

"A few years ago . . . McQueen tried to get me
involved with some daft scheme. I was meant to be
owning this horse and every time it won half the proceeds
were going to a Presbyterian Boys' Charity down in
Castlemilk. We even laid on a special free day for the
kids. Hamilton Park. Lunch. Meet the stars. Lester.
Willie. Kenny Dalglish. At the last minute the supervisors
of the home rang up and cancelled. They'd had a re-think.
They said they couldn't afford to expose the children to
the immoral vices of gambling and loose sports! Fucking

Scots! They think Hamilton Park's Dodge City. I
should've emigrated like my brother."

"I've never been to Hamilton," said James. "Let alone
Dodge City."

"Let's have lunch."

They slipped back across the river to a smart but discreet
new West End club that Lex had just joined. It was a long,
heavy and alcoholic meal. James tried to tease out a few
more details about the Scotsman's history and early life.
He didn't get far.

"School? My school was in Cleland Street. It's still
there today. A perfect vocational training for life as a
Professional Scotsman. Dull, drunk and guilt-ridden."
James laughed. Lex recalled the waiter. "I think we'd
appreciate a bottle of Dom Perignon with our dessert."

"We had a chaplain at Marlborough who absconded to
Monte Carlo with the entire contents of the organ restora-
tion fund. He took our games master's bored wife along
for company. I liked him. He used to bring a radio into his
lessons during Ascot week and play us Peter Bromley's
commentaries on the big races. He once asked me what
advice I would have given to the Children of Israel before
they set out on their long march across the desert. I said
they ought to have pooled the tribal funds and put them
all on Troy in the '79 Derby! Then they could've gone by
jet!"

Lex roared with approving laughter and leant across
and ruffled James's hair with his right hand, his favourite
gesture. "Good boy! You'll do alright."

The waiter arrived with the Dom Perignon and Lex
luxuriated with spellbound passion over every indefens-
ible bubble. There was crème brulée and peaches with
members of the Scottish Bar. If they knew or understood
black coffee. And there was also a special bottle of
cobweb-encrusted 1985 Armagnac shipped up from deep
in the club cellars. As the afternoon wore on the atmosphere seemed to close in around them. Warm, smoky,

upholstered clubability. Most of the other diners and club members were Park Circus solicitors, accountants and members of the Scottish Bar. If they knew or understood who Lex was or what he did and where he came from they made no acknowledgement. Lex seemed to have the head waiter well in his domain and as long as they stayed seated at the table Cleland Street and Bedford Street and the Castlemilk Boys' Charity receded further and further into the outer darkness.

James began to relax. He decided just to stop thinking about Camilla and his father and his Oxford exam. It was a familiar situation to him. The gradual shedding of onerous responsibility. The unbothered acceptance of whatever came next.

"The good thing about Marlborough," he said, lighting his Havana and leaning back comfortably in the cane back chair, "was that you could always slip away up on to the gallops at Lambourn and Beckhampton. Up on to the downs. I must've been one of the only outside observers to be not that surprised when Enstone Spark won the One Thousand Guineas. I'd actually seen her last piece of serious work before the race. I was meant to be on my first CCF Field Day at the time. No one ever believed I'd have the nerve. I got on at a good price too." A happy, retrospective smile spread slowly across his face. "But then I've always enjoyed . . . outraging the expectations of others. Like Oxford the first time around. I was only sixteen when I took the exam. I should've gone up in October '83. But the idea . . . of just throwing away one's own abilities . . . seemed so much more attractive . . . than just becoming a dull, prosaic workhorse. So I ran away to France. Worked for a while on a stud farm in Normandy. Then I got a job with the British Council in Paris. By the end of nine months . . . I'd got through nearly thirty-nine thousand pounds worth of trust money. Mainly at Longchamp, Auteuil and Saint Cloud."

"A mere bagatelle!"

"Absolutely. My father unfortunately thought otherwise. I was hauled back to England and put to work in the family business for the rest of the summer."

"What's that?"

"Making money, of course. And then my father got on the phone to Christchurch and pulled a few strings. Amazingly they complied. Next week ought to be the start of my second year." He shook his head. "But if I blow this exam a second time around . . . I don't know what."

Lex smiled and squeezed his shoulder. "Isn't it perfect?"

The Mercedes picked them up at four and drove them north again through Kelvingrove Park up to Kelvin Bridge. They pulled up in front of a large, respectable looking double-fronted grey granite house with a winding gravel drive and a neatly clipped high privet hedge.

"What are we doing here?" asked James.

"It's where I used to live," said Lex, telling the driver to wait for ten minutes.

"Again? I thought we'd already been to your place of birth."

"We have. But this is different. I have to leave my ex-wife an alimony cheque. But if I've timed it right she should be out. It's the nanny's day off. She'll be picking our boy up from his grandmother's. We should be safe." He led the way up the drive, casting one anxious look over his shoulder towards the road. Then his key turned quietly in the lock and, like afternoon burglars, the two men found themselves standing alone in the empty silence of the hall. No one came to take their coats. They were adrift amidst the soft and stealthy peace of the white-carpeted house.

The style was expensive, restrained maybe by Lex's current standards but still comfortable nonetheless. Lex disappeared into the breakfast room to make a phone call, so James opened a door and entered what seemed to have been a study. There were boxes of books heaped together on a desk along with a smart looking video recorder, unplugged. The walls were completely bare but on the floor under the desk there seemed to be a box full of photographs. Only all of them had been packed face down, their images turned away from public view.

"I never did pick those up," said Lex appearing at James's shoulder. "I hate removal vans." He walked into the living room. Like every other room in the house it had the typical high ceilings and broad dimensions of every prosperously granite Victorian Scottish home. There were plants and a stereo and a smart television and magazines and novels by Jeffrey Archer and D.H. Lawrence. And there were toys on the floor too. And baby books. And coloured mugs and mobiles and pamphlets on breast feeding and 'The Women's Milk Protest Front.'

"New man, new kid," explained Lex. He was standing by the fireplace. He'd put his envelope, addressed formally to Fiona Louise, on the mantelpiece and he was looking at a photograph of himself holding a small boy up to stroke a horse's mane. The photograph was entitled, 'Lex, Kenny and Sea Pigeon. Malton 1984.'

"Why did you get married?" asked James.

"Why?" Lex sighed. "I don't know . . . I suppose we give marriage a try . . . because we can't believe we won't avoid the same mistakes . . . be more romantic . . . live happily ever after. Also, it seems a good idea at the time. Why not? Why miss out? Have every experience going. At least once. Next, try divorce!"

"What was she like? Fiona?"

"I'll tell you something, Jimmy. Some women . . . openly or secretly, they really like, really want the take-me-and-have-me style of man. They want to be had and possessed. They're usually the kind of women who love to stir, to provoke, tease, taunt and get a reaction. It helps to make them feel that they're manipulating you, that they have the upper hand."

"Sounds like Camilla."

"That's right! Well, I can feel at home with that kind of woman. I can understand them. But Fiona . . . she was so

beautiful . . . but so hard and tight underneath. Outward-
ly . . . she always seemed to be so liberal. Objective and
calm. But under the surface . . . I could feel her twisting
away with disapproval. And then all of a sudden she'd try
to make me choose between her and racing. Like two
fences from home in the Cheltenham Gold Cup. There's
me. Ten grand on the favourite and he's still a length and
a half down. And there's her. 'Lex! You do love me don't
you? You do? I'm not just another fucking horse?' "
There was a long silence. "But I had to have her, Jimmy.
She had the most beautiful eyes and face of any woman I'd
ever seen."

"It can't be easy. Being a woman in love with a
gambler. A racing fanatic. I gather McQueen's gone
through two marriages already. And now the third's on
the rocks."

"That's right, son. Once women start to dislike racing
they go on to hate it. Mind you. Her old man had horses.
He was a big industrialist with a house in Bearsden and a
racing yacht on the Clyde. Never approved of me, of
course. Now I could buy him out five times over."

Outside the weather was getting worse. Grey and wet
with the first intimations of winter in the dwindling light.
The Duke's Indian summer was definitely over. Lex
turned round and smiled lasciviously. "You know just as
we were driving away from the reception I saw this terrific
looking little redhead in black leather hotpants walking
along the pavement towards Milngavie. I almost had to
stop the car and introduce myself!" He paused for a last
look round. "Just don't have children, that's all. They
change your lives. Completely. Let's go."

They left as quietly as they'd come. As the car drove
away towards the Great Western Road, James saw the
back of a tall and elegantly dressed woman with long black
hair and an expensive looking coat. She was walking with
a small child who was on a long pair of reins. The child
was running and scampering along up front pretending to
be a horse and jockey.

The Mercedes took them back towards the river and down into Finnieston. Lex was suddenly fretting about wanting to see Bella and he was privately worried that she might have heard about what he'd been up to with the Honourable Camilla. He wanted some more drugs before he went so they were going to see his coke dealer. The dealer turned out to be just a spotty faced, redheaded teenager who was on the dole and living with his parents in their council estate hutch near the Bilsland Bakery.

The three of them walked down past the Portaster Security Unit and on to the aerial footbridge section of the motorway overlooking Finnieston Quay. Lex paid for seven grammes and tipped the boy extravagantly. After he'd gone Lex gave himself and James a substantial hit off his key ring, having to protect it from the motorway wind with the outstretched arm of his blue Crombie coat. Even so, some of the drug inevitably blew away over the top of the bridge parapet and down towards the EEC timber lorries and the evening commuter cars beneath. James looked at Lex who just shrugged his shoulders indifferently.

"Tight wallet, tight arse, squashed balls," he said, speaking into the wind. "Big men don't count the pennies." James looked down at the speeding traffic, some of it no doubt heading back towards the same destinations that he and Lex and Camilla had passed through in the Rolls almost twenty-four hours earlier.

"I think I'd like to go away again soon," he said, having to talk loudly to make himself heard above the noise.

"Back to Oxford?"

James shook his head. "Abroad."

"That's fair enough." Lex was almost shouting. "Me. I just want more of the same. Only bigger and better."

"I think it's important for someone like me to move around. Travel. Fun too." He sounded very serious about it. "Otherwise . . . I'm frightened that I might just atrophy. Hang about for ever in some racecourse bar."

"Will you just listen to you! Only nineteen and already

a real man of the world." Richmond laughed. "Listen, son. If you want to go, you go. Do it all. All the time." He turned up his coat collar against the rain. "I'm getting out. As soon as I've sold up my shops I'm going to move down south for good." He looked across the river to where the disused cranes of the empty shipyards stood out bleakly against the skyline. "There are too many fucking graveyards in this city." In his overcoat pocket his hand was already flickering over the bag of white powder.

11

The Duke and the others in the end spent an interesting afternoon discussing the Parlane style of business operation. The Goldline affair had been satisfactorily concluded in the morning and a cheque, albeit reluctantly, handed over. After lunch the Scotsman's lawyer presented what he claimed to be an unshakeable case for Parlane's being granted an immediate Tattersalls pitch on most of the leading southern racecourses. The National Association of Bookmakers (Southern Area) had, he said, been unfairly and illegally discriminating against Parlane for many years.

He and the other silver-tongued sharpie went away happy too, smilingly convinced that they'd won their case. After they'd gone the Duke reported to Washy and George Stowell and Christopher Cowdray-Clarke and the other Stewards that from now on a special Racecourse Security Services investigative team would be maintaining a close watch on every aspect of the Lex Parlane Connection's racecourse activities. Every betting movement would be monitored and every sudden and untoward action subjected to the closest scrutiny.

And they'd have him on their doorsteps pretty soon anyway. Down south. The Home Counties. Not that the Duke would ever be seen dead in Weybridge. But at least they might find out just how much truth and substance there really was behind the stories and rumours that the Duke knew had been circulating for many years within the Criminal Investigation Department of the Glasgow City Police Force.

The Duke certainly left the Portman Square offices in a

much happier and more purposeful frame of mind than he'd been in when he arrived there that birthday morning. He and Washy had each placed two hundred and fifty pounds to win – their maximum bet these days – on Lucy Locket, a late developing three-year-old filly of Miles De Berry's who was running in the sixth race, the apprentice race, at Ascot. On their way back from Portman Square the Duke got the taxi driver to pull over by a William Hills betting office in Blenheim Street so that they could listen to the commentary. The rain had been falling pretty steadily throughout the afternoon. Not relishing the prospect of sodden shoes, damp trouser turn-ups and that familiar soggy socks feeling that he always associated with rain in Central London in the rush hour, the Duke picked his way carefully along the wet pavement, endeavouring to avoid the large and polluted puddles of water that lay in wait for the drunk, the dejected and the unwary.

Inside the betting office the lighting was bright, the floor filthy and the atmosphere smoke-filled, warm and steaming like a crowded city bar on a wet Friday lunchtime. There were several minutes yet before the off at Ascot so the two men squeezed their way towards some stools against the wall, finding a small, cramped but empty space between a sullen-looking young West Indian with a betting office pencil in his mouth and a thin tubercular looking man with bloodshot eyes and bad teeth. The tubercular looking man reminded the Duke of a middle-ranking Foreign Office mandarin that he'd once known out in Kenya during his cat hunting days with the Blues and Royals. The mandarin had often been in the habit of using racing and gambling expressions such as, "We're putting the FO's shirt on Kenyatta in the big one.' It wouldn't be such an unlikely twist of fate, supposed the Duke, if this self-same sportsman diplomat had finally been brought to his knees, ill and ill-furnished, in a nicotine-stained betting office off Hanover Square. Gambling was no respecter of persons or social protocol – as the Duke knew well to his paternal cost – and many others equally if not more illustrious had made the same compulsive journey before him. Indeed if the other occupants of that crowded smoke-filled room had but known that the Senior Steward of the Jockey Club and one of his principal confidants were standing in their midst, some of them might have remembered that Senior Stewards of the Jockey Club weren't supposed to bet at all. But then that had never stopped the Duke or any of his celebrated predecessors.

The Duke ran his eyes over the racing pages that had been cut out and pinned to the wall. Another multi-million dollar American-bred two-year-old was due to make its debut the following afternoon. "This could be the best horse I've ever sat on," the jockey was quoted as saying. And that was before it had ever run! Would they never learn? thought the Duke. He moved across to the *Daily Star* which had a full-page profile of Mr Lex Parlane. He was seen relaxing with 'gorgeous *Star* girl Samantha' to whom he was giving the benefit of his 'Bet with the best. Bet Lex' tip of the day at Ascot. He was quoted as saying how much he loved Ascot Races and how it was his favourite racecourse down south. "The punters there all know me," he said, "and they're all my friends. And now that I've bought my beautiful new mansion near Weybridge I shall soon be moving down there for good. And then I can go to Ascot whenever I want!" The Duke winced. What price the Scotsman setting up some promotional public relations company to stage-manage the car park picnics at next year's Royal meeting? he wondered. Then the Extel commentator intervened.

"Under orders Ascot. Off Ascot four forty-nine. Betting on the off. Seven to four number four Lucky Dancer. Two to one number one Crackerjack. Nine to two number eight Lucy Locket. Eight to one number five Chiswick Flyover. And thirty-three to one bar. And they've gone through the first furlong Ascot. And it's Lucky Dancer. Disputing the running with Chiswick Flyover. These two closely followed by Lord Of The Isles. A show Hackney.

Two to one trap one Ahaveen Champion. Nine to four trap four Westpark Mustard. Threes trap three Kylogue Lady. Nine to one trap six Parktown Darkie. Twelve to one trap two Little Bonny. And same price twelve to one trap five Raceway Dan. Two furlongs still to run Ascot. And it's Crackerjack. Moving up strongly on the outside of Lucky Dancer and Lord Of The Isles. Also pressing these three is Lucy Locket. Inside the final furlong. And it's Crackerjack. From Lord Of The Isles. Still finishing fast is Lucy Locket. Nothing to choose between these three. They're well inside the final furlong now at Ascot. And it's Crackerjack. From Lucy Locket, Crackerjack."

"Come on Lucy, darling," whispered the Duke. "You can do it."

"From Lucy Locket. And now it's Lucy Locket who begins to draw clear. Lucy Locket. From Lord Of The Isles. Lucy Locket drawing right away. At the line it's Lucy Locket the winner. Lord Of The Isles second."

"Good old Lucy. I knew she'd do it," exclaimed Washy unconvincingly.

"My God I love racing," said the Duke. And why not too? De Berry's three-year-old filly, by delivering the goods at the more than generous price of nine to two, had just made him more than one thousand pounds richer as he approached his evening celebrations. The fact that he'd just read in the *Daily Star* that Lucy Locket had also been the Lex Parlane 'Bet with the best. Bet Lex' tip of the day did not greatly alter the view that he was by now building up of that man's character, attributes and general personality.

He and Washy talked about their winnings. Washy seemed particularly grateful at the prospect. And then the two of them walked out of the betting office and crossed back over New Bond street to a florist's shop where the Duke bought a large and magnificent bunch of yellow and white flowers. Then, watched enviously by his friend from the pavement, he settled back happily into his taxi cab and rumbled off, a contented man, towards love and a good dinner at number twenty-eight, Hays Mews.

12

Another man riding contentedly in the back of a black
London taxi that evening was Cashel Maguire, a suavely
successful young professional gambler from the Republic
of Ireland. Maguire had been enjoying his day in the
capital city. He'd been taken out to lunch by his Anglo-
Irish stepfather to commemorate the sensational eighty-
eight to one double that he'd recently notched up in the
Cambridgeshire and the Prix de l'Arc de Triomphe,
taking Goldline for one for more than eighty thousand at
the time. And he'd particularly enjoyed sitting in the
Connaught sipping his Puligny Montrachet '78 and
savouring his quails' eggs in pastry, roast woodcock and a
substantial portion of the celebrated Connaught bread-
and-butter pudding.

After lunch they'd adjourned. Maguire's stepfather to
the Garrick for a snooze and Maguire to go shopping.
He'd bought some jewellery for his wife at a shop he knew
in the Burlington Arcade and some cashmere sweaters
and a scarf for himself. He'd then hailed a taxi by the Ritz.
His eventual destination was Heathrow Airport for the six
o'clock flight back to Dublin but first he had one more call
that he wanted to make.

The Daytona Beach Club was a small, modern casino in
the basement of the London Town House Hotel, a tall,
modern and unprepossessing sort of building up at the top
end of Wilton Place. The hotel's chocolate-and-cream
coated and bowler-hatted doorman and its glittering re-
volving front doors couldn't conceal the fact that its main
exit connected guests with the Knightsbridge pavement
almost as summarily as the front door of a back-to-back

terrace in Leeds connects the living room with the street. Inside, all was polished chocolate panelling and polished chrome and fountains and Richard Clayderman piped music. The London Town House was actually owned by Goldline City Leisure Limited, brother company to the bookmaking and betting office business, and in keeping with the horseracing background there was a Newmarket Suite, an Epsom Bar and even a Jockey Club Rooms and Grill which amused Maguire no end. The restaurant prices in both the casino and the hotel were almost as high as the tariff for the Berkeley around the corner but in spite of that and in spite of or perhaps because of the general decor and brassy Fiesta-Club-cum-Dubai-Trust-House ambience there was never any shortage of takers for the hotel's varied and all-night amenities. Conference and convention goers from Basildon and Cheam mixed easily with 'international' business executives from Copenhagen and the Gulf and weary but wealthy young Iranian exiles seeking some respite and refreshment for themselves and their Baker Street ladies during the long and weary hours between lunchtime and drinks.

Maguire asked at the desk for Mr Michael Bolger of Essex Sport Enterprises. The smilingly lipsticked receptionist in open-toed high-heeled shoes and a coffee-coloured pencil-slit skirt, directed him to the lift with instructions to seek the private staff kitchen at the far end of the basement corridor. When Maguire got out of the lift he turned left down a passage of silent pile-carpeted mystery. The doors to several of the gaming rooms were open. It was not yet the hour for evening business to commence but the rooms had been aired and hoovered and the general stink of last night's cigarette smoke and stale alcohol had been largely cleared away. The atmosphere had returned to its normal sleek, plush and green baize velvety expense.

The entrance to the staff kitchen appeared to be through a pair of chocolate panelled and chrome plated double doors of truly Caesar's Palace proportions. Maguire knocked.

The door was opened by Johnny Kinane. Kinane was another Southern Irishman, a big well-manicured bookmaker with straw coloured hair, a beige suit and twinkling light brown eyes. He came forward and welcomed Cashel with open arms. "The boy. How did it go?"

"Excellent lunch. Louis Weiss would've choked if he'd seen it."

"Good man. Come on in." There were two other men present and they both got up when Maguire entered. "Now," said Kinane, ". . .I don't believe you've met Mr Bolger."

"Cash," said Bolger warmly, his identity bracelet clinking through the air. "So glad you could make it." He patted him on the back and ushered him appreciatively towards the centre of the room.

"I hope you've left the cards behind this time," said the other man. "This is Knightsbridge. Not Mississippi."

"He's a joker," said Kinane. "I'm sure you know Michael Garvin."

"We have met," said Maguire, shaking hands.

"You're dead fucking right we have. The Grosvenor House. Stable Lads' Boxing. 1982." Garvin grinned unpleasantly. "My wallet's still burning."

"You won some back," said Maguire.

"True," said Garvin. "In fact I've still got a marker of yours. For three pounds ninety-five."

Maguire frowned. "I don't remember that."

"That's what it cost me in petrol money, chum. To drive out of my way home to get to your place."

"It's a game of chance, Mickey," said Maguire.

"Yeah. Well, I think I'll let you keep it this time. You can buy yourself a drink when I retire." Bolger and Kinane both laughed. Maguire tried a smile. Garvin's dumb North Yorkshire country boy act which he employed so effectively with the public, especially on television, had never fooled anybody in this room. And it

wasn't fooling all that many other members of the betting
and horseracing *cognoscenti* anymore either. Garvin had
never been the champion jockey. But he'd had no need to
be. He was a supreme percentage player. One of the top
money-earning riders in National Hunt history. Only
Michael Garvin was none too particular about the ways
that he earned that money. His face was too square and
pudgy and inclined to the odd red spot to be really pretty.
But Garvin was still unswerving in his efforts to make the
best of himself. The beautifully groomed short-style Vidal
Sassoon haircut and the three and four hundred guinea
Yves St Laurent suits, which Garvin wore as the deserved
attributes of a steeple-chasing box office star were somehow redolent of more than a thousand backhanders and
non-declarable 'presents' and 'drinks' and sealed manilla
envelopes handed over in numerous twilit racecourse car
parks after numerous frostbitten winter afternoons.
Ascot. Bangor-Upon-Dee. Cheltenham. Doncaster. Garvin could go through the alphabet. Nowadays they said
that he'd often just throw a race for the hell of it. Even
when the money was down. Just to show them that he
didn't owe anybody anything.

Maguire sat down at the large kitchen-cum-dining room
refectory table. The table had a polished wooden surface.
Like a butcher's board, thought Maguire. The chairs were
canvas and dark steel, the floor tiles dark red and the wall
tiles white and navy blue like the lighting. The real kitchen
was visible through the other side of a large plate glass but
soundproof window. Maguire could see knives and ladles,
a sharp butcher's saw and a skillet.

The others had all been drinking champagne and there
were several empty and upturned bottles in the ice bucket
on the table in front of them. Mickey Bolger pressed a
button on the table and a red light came on over the
kitchen door. Bolger talked into an intercom like a
managing director addressing his adjoining secretary.
"Another couple of bottles and some more orange juice.
Okay, sweetie?"

"Coming," replied a feminine but invisible voice. Everyone sat there and smiled as if they didn't want to be the first person to say anything. It was like a call back after an audition. They were all meant to be friends but this wasn't quite an ordinary informal situation. As far as Bolger, Garvin and Kinane were concerned Maguire had the part alright but the question was, how to tell him and who? Maguire lit a cigarette. There was a booklet of 'Essex Sport Enterprises' matches on the table in front of him. Who exactly were Essex Sport Enterprises, he wondered? Was it just another one of Michael Bolger's wide range of unorthodox business activities? He looked across at Bolger. He was rumoured to employ methods of persuasion that would definitely not have passed muster according to the TUC guidelines on intimidatory picketing. Just now he was writing cheques out for Garvin and Kinane. He must've been about thirty-five or forty years of age, guessed Maguire. Tall, tanned and fit-looking with broad shoulders, high cheekbones and thick lips. The blue eyes and the lips gave him a large cruel sort of face. He was wearing his tie loose at the neck and the sleeves of his well-tapered shirt were rolled up to just below the elbow. It all added up to the style and appearance of a quietly sartorial plainclothes detective or a successful Football League manager well used to discussing the merits of the 'lads' performances with Jimmy Hill on *Match of The Day*.

Kinane looked up. Their private business was for the moment at an end. "You might almost say that this was Mr Bolger's office, Cashel. He's kindly lent it to us for the afternoon."

"I always do business here when I'm up West," said Bolger, smiling a chunky, self-satisfied smile. "Myself and the manager here, well, we used to have a business of our own in the old days. Down in Tulse Hill." He grinned. "Louis Weiss doesn't know that of course. I like the club though. I like the . . . atmosphere." Maguire looked around at the atmosphere. At the cold bright walls and the uncomfortable chairs and at the scraped and marked surface of the polished table.

"If I'm going to make the six o'clock plane," he said, "I'll have to hurry. If I'm not going to try for it . . . I'll need a good reason to stay."

"Don't worry, Cash," said Kinane. "We won't waste your time."

A girl walked into the room pushing a bar cart stacked high with fresh ice buckets and bottles of champagne, frozen orange juice and a large plate of chicken canapés. The girl was a dead ringer for the receptionist upstairs. Curly black hair and cherry red cheeks with cherry red lipstick to match. She was wearing a tight white shirt and a tight black skirt and her stockings were black and sheer with seams up the back, noticed Maguire.

"You want to be nice to this man, Carol," said Bolger. "All that aristocratic Irish charm. He could do things for you."

"I don't always work here," said Carol to Maguire, smiling. "I've got a very nice flat in Slough. Do you know Slough?"

"No," said Maguire.

"Ain't she something?" said Garvin, slapping Carol's bottom as she passed. "You little gorgeous." Carol returned to the kitchen with her bar cart and the four men picked up their refilled glasses and drank. The champagne was not a label that Maguire would normally have ordered but he drank it just the same.

"Now then, Cashel," said Kinane, leaning back in his chair. "As you already know . . . this venue we are meeting in today is owned by Louis Weiss. These are Goldline premises."

"So?"

"So, Cash, we all know what you think about Louis. And we also know that whatever he had to pay you on your Cambridgeshire job it still wasn't enough."

"Not enough," said Bolger, nodding his head like a benign schoolmaster. "Like any professional today you have to put up with a lot of aggravation. Both from Weiss and from all the other jewboys in the ring. And that's not to mention the fox wallopers over at Portman Square. You feel frustrated? So do we all." Maguire raised an eyebrow.

"As you may know, Cashel, Mr Bolger has invested a great deal of money in the horses . . . over the years."

"I thought he was warned off?"

"Jockey Club rectitude and bookmaker prejudice combined to force Mr Bolger's on and off course business . . . out of business. Since that time he has unsuccessfully pursued every legal route and alleyway open to him. He has even tried to correct the situation by means of a few rousing though legitimate tilts at the ring. Via proxy nominees of course. But sadly these days, no matter how many form books and racing videos, what with the betting tax on the one hand and Racecourse Security Services on the other, the good old fashioned coup is becoming an increasingly hard act for the gambler to pull off. So . . . Mr Bolger has turned to other . . . alternative methods to supplement his income." He paused for a moment to clear his throat. "Over the last twelve months or so . . . Mickey, Mr Bolger and myself have done some very nice business together. Thanks to the little games that Mickey and one or two of the other boys in the weighing room have been pulling on our behalf." Maguire looked across at Garvin. He was reading the City and Financial section of the *Evening Standard*. "We've been doing well enough," Kinane went on, "but somehow there's always been that lingering feeling. Couldn't it be just that . . . little bit better? I mean when you open up your *Sporting Life* next year and you read about a prominent Irish rails layer . . . the biggest bookie in the Republic . . . already quoting a whole set of prices on the 1990 Cheltenham Gold Cup, I want you to be in no doubt. It's not Sean Graham that they're talking about. And it's not Alan Tuthill either. It's Johnny Kinane."

"Vaulting ambition, Johnny. Could cost you dear."

"No chance, Cashel. I never contemplate defeat. And look at young Mickey here. He wants to start training for himself very soon. Out in Hong Kong. But on the flat, not over the jumps. Stands to reason . . . if he's going to give the local boys and the Chinkies a run for their money he'll need every pound note and ten pence piece that he can lay his hands on."

"What about Mr Bolger?" asked Maguire.

"I'm just a cunt," said Bolger softly.

"Exactly," said Kinane. "Now this is what we propose. Mr Bolger will put up the money to make a payroll of up to twenty-five leading National Hunt Jockeys. And I'm talking about the top pilots, Cashel. He and Mickey have been working together on the list for some time. That means we could have a controlling interest in nearly every horse race run over the sticks between the beginning of August and the end of the following May. Just think of it, Cash. We can pull horses, decide who wins what when, organise losing favourites and so on. It'll be like a personal and private betting levy flowing directly from the racecourses into our pockets."

"Easy money, Cashel," said Bolger.

"Mr Bolger will of course also supply the necessary funds to purchase one or two Racecourse Security Services Investigators. And a Steward. Just for insurance."

"A Steward?"

"It can be done," said Bolger.

"We'll be discreet," said Kinane. "We'll only need to pull a race maybe once or twice a week. In a couple of seasons we'll be millionaires. I'm telling you, Cash, it's a bloody cinch."

"We want Ireland as well as England, Cashel," said Bolger. "Johnny helps me to get my money down both in this country and abroad. But I'm told you're the best racing brain in Eire. Help us choose the Irish jockeys. How to approach them and when. If you put in the same basic investment as John you can be on a direct share out of every profit we make."

"Now what do you say?" asked Kinane.

Maguire uncrossed his legs and lit another cigarette. "Are there really up to twenty-five dependably bribeable National Hunt jockeys?" he asked Garvin.

"They can be found," said Garvin, throwing his paper away contemptuously. "Alright, there's the masochists and the *Boy's Own Paper* brigade and our brown-nosed chummies who hope to become a starter's assistant when they retire. But all that most of them have got to look forward to are broken bones, diet pains and an annual Christmas card from Lord Oaksey. Give 'em a few free meals and a pocketful of used tenners and they're anybody's."

"The bigger the scheme . . . ." said Maguire warily, "the bigger the problems. They watch me. Especially in England. And I'm sure they watch you too. Also, how do I know I can trust you?"

"Me?" said Bolger, swallowing three chicken canapés in one mouthful. "Me you don't know. But you might trust Lex Parlane."

"Lexie? What's he got to do with it?"

"Nothing yet," said Kinane. "But we think he'd like to come in."

"Lex can't bear the idea of anything going on that he doesn't know about," said Bolger. "He always wants to be credited as the star attraction. Well, that's alright. He has his own formidable resources as well as a chain of contacts second to none. I sometimes put work his way and him mine. We did a little job together with Mickey just the other day at Newton Abbot."

"Was that the Paddy McLoughlin thing?" asked Maguire. Bolger shook his head.

"I wouldn't touch that bastard," said Garvin without looking up. "I haven't worked with him for more than a year. I only do each way jobs with Terry Nicholson and John Fry."

"Fry? Then it must've been The Bugler?" Garvin said nothing.

"The thing is, Lex is moving south soon," said Bolger.

"I happen to know that his businesses may be involved in a diversification . . . sportswise. And I also happen to know that Lex still has one or two embarrassing moments to gloss over. A few discreet silences to maintain."

"Is that old stuff still true? I thought they were just fairy stories put around by the boys to discredit him."

"Believe me, Cashel, it's true," said Kinane. "Louis Weiss knows that too. That's why Lex loves every chance he can get to hit Goldline's betting offices and shops as hard as Marvin Hagler smacked Hearns and Duran. You see, he's just like you really. And me. And Mr Bolger. And Michael. We all have a shared and mutual interest."

"Have you approached him yet?"

"We're flying up to Glasgow, Sunday. It's his firm's big night. Always a laugh. Why don't you come too?" Maguire hesitated for a moment and then looked around the room at the venal jockey, at the fat and all too easily flattered bookmaker and the relentlessly conniving figure of Mickey Bolger. These men weren't class. If men like these could devise a racket like this one then a man like himself ought to be able to make it pay at least ten times over. "We can put you up here until Sunday," said Bolger. "You'll be assured of every comfort, hospitality . . . and convenience." Kinane was grinning and nudging his head towards Carol in the kitchen. "Be my guest at Ascot. A lot of my golfing and showbusiness friends are going to be there too."

Maguire's first instinct was to shrink at the prospect. Then his mind turned to images of fast money and faster women. Those predictable but deliciously enjoyable accoutrements of the single, high-rolling, self-employed man. He tried to remember. Exactly how much was a one way ticket to Nassau? For Cashel Maguire's fatal flaw was that his shrewd poker player's instinct and calculated charm was almost imbalanced by his patrician disdain for all the more common members of the bookmaking, racing and gambling fraternity.

He looked down at his watch. It was just after half past five.

13

James spent that night in Lex's suite at the Holiday Inn. It was a great improvement on the black leather sofa. He stayed up late studying the *Timeform* for Saturday's Ayr card along with last year's *Timeform Black Books* and the new edition of *Chasers and Hurdlers* which had just been published. On the Saturday morning he was awake early and gave himself a good two hours to eat a substantial breakfast, wash his hair, shave and put on the clean shirt and newly cleaned racing suit that had been especially collected for him by car from Loch Tulla the previous day. James had learned quickly that you must never be late for a racing assignation with Lex Parlane. As he sat in the hotel bar, sipping a vodka martini, eating olives and potato chips and fingering the knot on his grey silk tie he was filled with a sudden overwhelming sense of guilt about his father and his Oxford exam. He got the switchboard to put a call through to Dereham Hall but the line was engaged. They tried again ten minutes later but it was still engaged. Then he saw Lex and McQueen walking in through the hotel foyer and the moment was gone.

The day began on the main forecourt at Glasgow Central. Lex had taken out advertising space on the station's electronic information system and every ten minutes it flashed up his two best selections of the day. A mud-loving two-year-old back to its best distance in the Cornwallis Stakes down at Ascot and one of last season's leading novice hurdlers making his debut over fences at Ayr. At half past ten Lex appeared in person over the tannoy. He sent good luck and best wishes to all his customers, friends and admirers throughout the city and

recommended all southbound Inter City passengers to
'Bet with the best. Bet Lex!' McQueen had arranged for
another photographic team and a special exclusive interview with the *Sunday Times*. Lex was supposed to be
captured informally en route to the Ayr race train. The
station catering manager had even offered the newspaper
a private and restricted corner table in the number one
platform buffet but Lex objected that it hardly did justice
to his lifestyle, habits and tastes. So the interview was
eventually recorded in the nearby though empty Mal-
maison Restaurant of the Central Hotel. Lex told the
interviewer he was a man of the people and the Scottish
punters' choice. He also stressed the importance of times
in flat races and jokingly advised all *Times* readers to steer
clear of female riders, maiden three-year-old fillies and
conditions race form in handicaps. He ended up giving the
interviewer an exclusive antepost tip for the Cesarewitch
and then offered him a cigar.

"No girls in your party?" asked the interviewer, prob-
ing to the last.

"Certainly not," said Lex. "Women and racing don't
mix!" Then the interviewer hastened for the London train
while Lex was meant to be heading for the Ayr special. In
fact, he, James and McQueen hastened round the corner
to the Central car park where the blue Rolls was waiting.
Sitting in the back seat, clean hair and blue eyes gleaming
and all wrapped up in a new fur coat was Camilla. She
smiled vampishly at James.

"Women and racing, eh? I hope Bella's not around."

"You shut your fucking mouth!"

Lex was elated. He'd heard the good news from his
lawyers in London about the Goldline cheque and his
successful Tattersalls application. He'd decided to call off
his campaign to democratise racing. At least for the time
being. Celebration was in order. And over champagne in
the car on their way down to the Clyde Coast he gave the
others the benefit of his private information on the
afternoon's card.

"The Middleham thing's been very well schooled in the first. Donleavy's running too so you might get eleven to ten. Tommy Renton had a double here last year and they say his two-mile novice chaser may be a bit tasty. They've been trying to teach him how to settle all summer and he did used to get a bit low at some of his hurdles. Even so, providing they haven't had too much overnight rain I can't see this lot of rubbish getting near him. Don't have the favourite in the third. The trainer's backing against him. He's won his two round Market Rasen and Worcester but he'll never do the weight against this class. There's a couple of improving novices there from last season. We're meeting the connections over lunch so that should be informative. Our job's in the fifth and the best bet of the day's going to be the Mildmay thing in the Bovis Handicap down at Ascot."

"What about the Cornwallis?" asked James. "The tip on the station?"

"That'll win too. But I'm not sharing my best advice with the hoi-polloi on a bloody railway station!"

Ayr racecourse is not one of the picture postcard tracks of the British Isles. Especially on a wet afternoon when the rain's driving down off the hills and across the rooftops of the squat, grey, Scottish council houses that line the back straight. In the members' restaurant in Western House they were doing their Buchanesque best with brown panelling, deerstalkers, black suits and the fumes of rough malt whisky. Lex's lunchtime connections included an extremely fat man, even fatter then Fat Jimmy, with black sideburns and hair growing out of his nose. There was also a haulage operator from Newcastle in a light blue suit with exceedingly well-cut light grey hair and an enormous gold signet ring on the little finger of his left hand. Lex discussed running plans with these two in tones of strictest confidentiality. Numerous trainers stopped by to offer greetings, advice and latest stable news. Lex was only thrown when a sly-looking little man in a close-fitting suit

and green corduroy tam o'shanter with an orange pom
pom on the top suddenly appeared at his left shoulder.
The man seemed to require some urgent instruction on a
matter of mutual interest.

"Not just now, Willie," said Lex crossly. "Can't you see
I'm eating my chicken vol-au-vent?"

James took a walk before the first. He loved the very
British yet Runyonesque atmosphere of small jump meetings in winter. The local trainers and faces crowding into
their local bars. The small-time hoods and hopefully
villainous looking second division bookies, their tic-tac
operators all grey and ageing or just starting out. It was a
taste of whisky mac and sloe gin and hot roast beef and
horseradish sandwiches. Down in the ring the bookmakers were busy. Hepburn and Bree and Gibbin and
McKenzie and Ricky McCondichie and Dan Flynn and a
Stanley Baxter lookalike called The Braw Wee Punter
with a tartan board and a tartan trilby hat. This was one of
the first really decent days racing of the new National
Hunt season with a lot of promising young horses on view.
Although the crowd was not large by Southern standards
there was quite a lot of flash Glasgow money around and
most of the big firms had representatives in attendance,
handling a lot of office business as well as laying bets on
the track itself. Lex had a pitch in Tattersalls, being as this
was not a Southern ring. It was manned as usual by Willie
Cooper, Maxie Carlisle and Willie 'The Weasel' Wood.
Lex himself was on the rails and gambling in his own right.
Credit clients were being attended to as always by his
number one rails man, Billy 'Two Hats' Mcphee. Billy had
got his nickname from the bewildering facility with which
he was able to lay large bets the one minute and then
disappear to place equally large commissions for the firm
with rival operators the next. He was thirty-five. An
ex-sailor and reformed alcoholic who wore a Kray
Brothers suit with his Boston haircut, he sucked mints
during a race to calm his nerves.

It was Lex, though, who dominated this environment

and he dominated it with the practised ease of a man who has spent his entire professional lifetime perfecting the methods required to become king of his own particular jungle. The men around him like Goldline's Mike Cordrey, sleek in his camel hair overcoat and red polo neck, may have had a certain louche style but by comparison with Lex in his steel black suit, black shades and broad brimmed black fedora they all looked like a convention of used car salesmen from Anniesland gathered round Dutch Schulz. And Lex was as good as his word. All afternoon he layed anything to anyone no matter what amount, what race or what horse, home meeting or away. No computer he, he boasted. No London office boy or deskbound accountant with one eye on the books. He was the natural successor to the late great William Hill. He talked loudly in Cordrey's earshot of the three new yearlings that he'd recently bought at Newmarket sales to be called 'Twisting Louis', 'Lovable Louis' and 'Lou the Knife'. Yet for each race on the card he did three times the business in the ring that he took on the rails, amply bearing out his own determination to get the best possible pitches that he could before he moved down south.

The horses were going down for the first. The Middleham-trained favourite looked keyed up in the preliminaries. He was a neat-looking little four-year-old bay, really bred for the classier purlieus of the flat racing game. He had a look in his eye that suggested to James that he might have his own ideas about the sport. James decided to ignore him and put fifty pounds to win on a four to one shot, the third favourite, a fit-looking ex-flat racer trained by a small-time, Scottish permit holder from Ettrick Bridge.

The favourite went on at the third and jumped reasonably well, but, after an effort coming off the home turn he gave up straight away and his rider pulled him up before the next flight. James's selection lost his position halfway down the back straight but, getting his second wind turning for home he soon began to improve and, leading at the last, ran on well to win by three lengths. James was the first to be buying champagne in the Eglinton Suite bar. The rest of the afternoon went exactly as Lex had predicted.

The Tommy Renton-trained two-mile novice chaser won the second race in a hack canter. Leading from the fifth he jumped boldly all the way and was never in the slightest danger in spite of the ground being much softer than he would have liked. In the third and feature event the favourite drifted before the off. On his previous two outings he'd been allowed to bowl along in front. On this occasion the jockey unaccountably restrained him near the rear of the field and he was never seen in the race with a chance. James put his fifty pounds on an improving eight to one shot, a comparative novice who'd run well to finish fifth in the previous season's Sun Alliance Chase. The six-year-old took time to warm up at his fences but on the second circuit he really came into his own and, brought with a smooth run up the straight, he galloped on strongly to score by a length at the line. Lex was in the bar, grinning.

"What did I tell you," he said, pouring more vintage Bollinger. "That trainer's so bent he's soon going to need physiotherapy just to get up in the morning." He ordered cigars all round. The bar staff were coping manfully with the influx of a large number of singing Geordies, friends and associates of Lex's haulage contractor, happy owner of the winning horse. Camilla was nearly knocked over in the crush.

"It's not always easy . . ." said James politely, ". . . being a woman in a large crowd of men at the races."

"Darling, I'm loving it," she said, holding up a winning ticket from the last race. Lex hugged her and gave her a big kiss. She kissed him back. Then she kissed James. She had one man on each arm and she was wide-eyed and ecstatic and the champagne was beginning to flow out of her ears. If this was horse racing with Lex Parlane then she wanted a season ticket right away.

Straight after the fourth race Lex summoned James to a meeting in the smaller gents lavatory at the bottom of the Club Stand. The job was nigh. As they stood squashed together in the locked cubicle Lex cut two large lines of cocaine out on the down-turned lavatory seat and gave James his instructions.

"The horse's name is Highland Regiment," he said as they both snorted up. "No one knows that yet, not even McQueen. Billy Two Hats is going to come in here in about five minutes time and give you your money. I can't be seen betting because the other boys in the ring would suspect something immediately. So I'll be down on the rails actually trying to lay Highland Regiment. But as far as the rest of the world's concerned it's just another big-priced dog so no one's going to know until we move, especially as Billy's got a firm of faces down there backing all the others. Now the trainer's money's going on off course so we don't go in until we get the first show from the betting offices. Then when Billy gets the signal Billy moves in. And when Billy moves McQueen moves. And when McQueen moves you move!"

"Right!" Lex waited for quiet outside then slipped out of the door and back into the stand. James rebolted the lock and waited nervously for Mcphee. Sure enough, three or four minutes later there was a gentle tap on the door. James slid back the lock and Billy squeezed in.

"Mint?"

"No thanks."

Billy reached into his inside pocket and brought out a large wad of dogeared notes. He counted out five fifties and twenty-five tens and gave them to James.

"Five hundred. OK?"

"Got it. Is this all?"

"It's spread around. Now listen. Your man is Gordon Bell. About five down the line. Next to Dan Flynn. You'll see McQueen. Then you move. Get it all on if you can. Any problems, use your initiative. Record the price and go up to the top of the stand by the clock. Lex'll be waiting."

"Right."

"Follow me out in about two or three minutes. Go straight to Tatts. McQueen should be there by then. Oh by the way, Lex told me to tell you that the Mildmay thing won at Ascot." They heard voices outside. Two men were laughing and talking loudly. They heard them washing their hands. Then there was silence. Billy opened the door a shade to check and then went out. James looked down at his watch. When two minutes were up he flushed the lavatory and walked out nonchalantly to wash his hands. A man was standing at the basin next to him. James saw his face in the mirror. He was about fifty-five, tall and broad-shouldered with a British Warm overcoat and a regimental tie. A look of recognition suddenly flashed across his face. James looked away and nearly giggled. It was an old army and shooting friend of his father's and one of the local stipendiary stewards! On his way back for more port, no doubt.

James walked out through the underpass, past the roll of honour of previous Ayr Gold Cup and Scottish Grand National winners and out into the Tattersalls Enclosure. He found Gordon Bell's pitch almost immediately and he saw McQueen about five pitches away. There were just under ten minutes to go before the off and the prices were going up on the boards. Highland Regiment was a top priced seven to two. Mike Cordrey and Goldline were going no better than threes.

"See that?" said McQueen.

"Seems there's been a leak once again."

"Billy says we still go ahead." He went back up the line to his position. The horses were in the paddock when the first show came through from the offices. Highland Regiment was now five to two. So much for the trainer's money! The signal then came from Billy and James and McQueen moved in fast. As they did so James was suddenly aware of a great rush in the ring as about half a dozen other bookmakers' pitches were also hit simultaneously along with half a dozen big credit layers down the rails. Billy's firm of faces had declared their true colours. One of Bell's settlers recognised James from his fifty pound bets of earlier on in the afternoon but he didn't blanch when James suddenly came out with ten times his original stake money. When they'd all got on they went up to the top of the grandstand and joined Lex on the balcony by the rooftop clock. Standing next to him was Highland Regiment's owner-trainer and the trainer's son who was also his head lad. The trainer was a real Borderer, shy but with a cunning, hungry look, thought James.

The horses were down at the start. Lex had his binoculars on the ring. Highland Regiment had come in to seven to four. There was money for another fancied runner in the race too. Rumour of another job. Down along the rails James saw the man with the close-fitting suit and the green corduroy tam o'shanter with the orange pom pom on the top. He seemed to be very busy with Mike Cordrey.

"Who is that?" James asked McQueen.

"Willie Smith."

"The guy who fucked up on Thursday?"

"That's right."

James trained his own glasses on the start. Highland Regiment was nothing to look at. Light and skinny with lop ears and wistful, put-upon eyes. The race though was ridiculously easy. The two-and-a-half-mile trip on rain-softened ground quickly strung out the mostly mediocre and only partly-fit field. The Irish Amateur Rider had Highland Regiment in the first two throughout. He took a discreet pull halfway down the far side but slipped back through on the inside turning into the straight and plugged on gamely all the way to the line. The winning margin was six lengths. The party on the roof were hoarse with cheering. Cordrey and some of the others on the rails were looking up at them intently. Lex returned their looks with interest. He reckoned he'd taken them for about seventy-five grand.

"It's not what it should have been," he said, putting his binoculars away in their box. "But it'll do!"

Two hours after the last race they were still in the Eglinton Suite bar. The horse racing may have been over but they'd soon found other ways to gamble their money. Lex was two hundred and fifty pounds up in a spoof game with McQueen and the haulage contractor. James had just lost over a hundred pounds playing pitch and toss with Billy Mcphee. It was a new game for James. An extra racecourse diversion introduced by Lex. Billy was now generously refusing to let him continue any further, advising that he and his family had been throwing coins in the streets of Parkhead and the Gorbals since before they'd invented dog racing.

As usual at the end of an epic day at the races James felt as if he could conquer the world and the longer it went on the longer he wanted it to go on. It was like a transatlantic night flight with endless free cocktails. As long as you were cocooned within the warm glow of the aeroplane there seemed no limit to the heights you might achieve when you eventually reached your destination, until finally, the further the journey went the less important the destination seemed to become.

"Terrific day," said James, pressing another glass of champagne into Mcphee's hand. "Great information."

"Information. . ." said Mcphee, ". . . is the curse of every punter."

"It was alright today. We won a fortune. At least I did."

"The more money you have gambling, the more you lose."

"Oh, Christ! Lex! This man is being the spirit of dour Scottishness. Tell him to cheer up for God's sake!"

"Don't mind Billy, son. He's just thinking about Highland Regiment."

"It won, didn't it?"

"It did. But unfortunately there was a premature disclosure of information. It's being attended to."

James shook his head and reached round to see if there

was any more champagne left in the thirty or so used bottles standing on the tables behind them. The racecourse manager appeared at Lex's elbow with a polite request that they should leave. The bar was closed, the last horse box had long since gone, and although the lights may be going on all around the town they were definitely going out on the racecourse! Lex immediately and smilingly agreed, slipping fifty pounds into the manager's top pocket and making concerned enquiries after the health of his wife and children.

"Gentlemen," he said to the others. "To horse! Shawfield Dogs!"

Camilla had to be carried to the car. The excessive alcohol had finally proved too much for her and she'd been 'resting' for more than an hour. Just as he was getting into the Rolls, James realised that he'd left his cigars behind in the bar. He hurried back inside to collect them, stopping on his way back down again for a quick visit to the small gents lavatory at the bottom of the Club Stand. He smiled as he thought of their conspiracies in there earlier in the day and turned round to look at the cubicle where Lex had given him the line of cocaine. The door of the cubicle was slightly ajar and a tightly-trousered leg was sticking out awkwardly. When James got the door properly open he found a man's body slumped untidily across the lavatory seat, his head against the wall. The man was wearing a close-fitting suit and a green corduroy tam o'shanter with an orange pom pom on the top. It was not just another Scottish drunk, it was Willie Smith and his face and body had been badly beaten. He had what looked like razor marks or the marks of a sharp knife or bayonet on both cheeks and there was blood all over his jacket and blood on the cubicle floor. The twisted leg looked unnatural and unhealthy. He was groaning but alive. James backed uncertainly out of the lavatory door and out into the cool evening of the now almost deserted racecourse. He heard a friendly shout from the distant car park and looked across to see Lex

waving at him. He had just been signing a few last
autographs for the racecourse manager and his family.

The evening that followed at Shawfield Dogs was a
strange and unsettling experience. The sight in the members' lavatory had been rather like arranging to meet your
lover in a bar and then walking in to see her kissing
another man in the corner. In the circumstances the
camaraderie expected of James at the dog track, the
endless punting and drunken good humour became harder
and harder to sustain as the evening wore on. And the
attendant events going on around him were certainly
bizarre enough.

Shawfield's thirties-swimming-pool-style front entrance
architecture leads into a small, drab and rundown stadium
with a heavily working-class atmosphere. On the wall
beneath the old fashioned wooden terracing there's a
cartoon of a greyhound relaxing in a beret and shades with
a cigarette holder. By comparison with the cartoon dog
most of the punters are old, tired and ill-looking with
hollow eyes and flat caps. You may see one or two clipped
moustaches and sheepskin coats and smell the odd cheap
panatella from the bookmakers end, but unlike Wimbledon or Slough or even the seediest horse racetrack there's
no accompanying aura of expensive champagne and finest
Havanas to lift the atmosphere. The nearest Shawfield
comes to a restaurant is the Members' Club, a Silver-
Ring-style bar with bare floors and formica-top tables
serving beer, spirits and ham sandwiches.

Lex was sitting with McQueen at a table in the Members' Club drinking whisky and heavy and posing for the
cameras of Scottish Television. With less than a month to
go before the publication of McQueen's book, *Lex Parlane. The Making Of A Scottish Legend*, the Lex publicity
machine was hitting full stride. McQueen, who had been
let off two years' gambling debts by Lex for writing the
book, had made much of Lex's greyhound racing ante-
cedents and the televised Shawfield special had been

arranged accordingly. The two men were to be seen chatting informally about Lex's early days as a raw young street bookie at the flapper tracks of Mount Vernon and Carfin. Lex boasted of the twenty-three grand that he'd lost in his first year to the professional dog backers of the early sixties and went on to tell how he'd recouped his losses three times over when he'd returned a tougher and wiser man to Shawfield and the old Glaswegian White City.

How did he feel about dog racing today? asked McQueen. Now that he was rich and famous?

"I just love it," said Lex. "I come down to Shawfield whenever I can and the punters here all know me and they're all my friends."

James walked outside. The dogs were making their way from the kennels across the sad looking soccer pitch in the centre and up to the traps. The kennel maids and boys wore dirty white coats like butcher's boys and football scarves and hats. The man putting the traps into position had a plastic leather hat and an enormous but mis-shapen belly tumbling down over his trousers like a derailed train over an embankment. The dogs paraded past the stand. A sorry looking crew of Pal and Kennomeat aspirants and potential onion and vegetable bhajis they were too. James looked up at the flashing totalisator board lit up with odds and forecast win dividends and the Jackpot Pool. The two dog appeared to have been dropped in class and seemed to be reasonable value at three to one. When he got to the bookies there was a sudden clamour to get five to two on the two dog and an elderly Jewish bookmaker with red cheeks and horn-rimmed glasses was nearly knocked off his box by the crush. The dogs went into their traps, the floodlights came up and the hare started out on its way. The buzz and zing and smoke of electricity suddenly washed through the stadium as if they were watching an American electrocution. The hare's erratic progress reminded James of a rickety old suburban train moving too fast through a mainline junction. Then the hare passed the traps and they were off. The actual race was over pitifully quickly. The five dog and favourite was baulked badly on the third bend and as they came into the straight there were only two in it. The two dog was greeted by a passionate but finally agonised roar from the crowd as he went down by a head to the four dog, a rank outsider. A crowd of anoraks and jeans and beat up old caps suddenly parted as if by divine command and there was the cashmere coat of Lex Parlane.

"Isn't it a joke?" he said. "I've still got one of the pitches here. The punters don't know that of course but I'm giving this kid from Belfast his first start. And we haven't had a losing night for about two years. It may be chicken feed but these people don't have a fucking clue!"

"I know," said James.

A young boy in a cap was driving a red Massey Ferguson tractor around the track, smoothing down the sand after each race. The starter, middle-aged and cross-looking with glasses and a woolly hat, waved his flag again at the kennel maids like a rather irritable British Railways guard or bus inspector. And so it went on. James had never known much about greyhound racing and after six races he was doing what he always did, losing more and more of his afternoon's racing winnings. He became tired and heavy-eyed. There wasn't even the pleasure of Camilla's sexy and feminine company as Lex had dropped her off at his flat on the way for some much needed recuperation. Finally unable to take any more of Lex's mercilessly sarcastic bonhomie in the Members' Club, James went into another formica-topped bar on his own and ordered a brandy. The floor was full of Cellophane and ash and losing 50p Tote Tickets. A woman next to him was sitting with her back to the window whistling *Moon River* and smoking Park Drive. Behind the counter a girl was selling hot dogs. James drank his brandy, got down from his stool and left. He walked out through the swimming pool entrance, out through the dimly lit car park and out on to Rutherglen Road. The long day and dark night finally began to take on almost hallucinogenic proportions as he waited in the cold by the bus shelters in front of the Italian chip shops and the takeaways where bands of girls and older women were queueing up for their fish suppers and their pies. He saw a drunk lying in a doorway, his leg stretched out awkwardly across the pavement like Willie Smith. The stadium announcer's voice drifted back across to him in the darkness. "Thank you for coming to Shawfield. We hope you enjoyed your evening and we look forward to seeing you again on Thursday next."

14

Draped along the back wall of the Knights Of The Thistle
Banqueting Room in the Bella Vista Hotel was a large and
ornate banner. Scarlet and black lettering on a reversed
scarlet and black background. 'The Lex Parlane Connection. Eleven Years On. And Still Scotland's Number
One.' Lex Parlane sat at the top table, looked out at what
he'd made and saw that it was good.

The more than three hundred and fifty Lex Parlane
Connection employees, guests and their friends arrayed in
front of him were flushed, convivial and happy. They'd
had their pre-dinner drinks, their Potage du Midi au
Stornoway, Filet de Sole Arbroath Bon Pecheur and their
Roast Leg of Prime Aberdeen Angus Scotch Beef served
with Pommes Lyonnaise, Glazed Parsnips and Mange
Tout Peas. And they'd had their thick creamy Atholl
Brose and their selection of fresh fruits and cheeses and
homemade petit fours with their coffee. They'd drunk
Sancerre and a Pouilly Fumé '73 with their soup and fish
and Lynch-Bages '67 with their beef and now their glasses
were filled with the contents of more than thirty cases of
Roederer Cristal Champagne that Lex's Newcastle and
North Eastern Divisional Manager had succeeded in
buying at special discount rates from a wine importing
client of the firm's from Largs whose gambling debts were
legendary.

Lex was adoring every minute. On nights like this every
guest and diner in the room seemed to plug themselves in
to the endless supply of his personality and out it flowed as
warm and bountiful as electricity from the national grid. It
was as if his limitless hospitality could feed and entertain

them all five times over and then still have room left for another three sittings. And for Lex, seeing their expressions of joy and fulfilment was like witnessing the upturned faces of a whole workhouse of Victorian orphans suddenly released into the arms of a rich benefactor with a glittering Christmas tree and a present on it for every one of them.

The keynote theme for the evening was the Wild West of America and as usual Lex was setting the pace. He was dressed in a black frock coat, black trousers, a white shirt, black bootlace tie and a wide-brimmed black felt hat. He was wearing his customary pair of black shades but his hair was slightly longer than usual, curling down over the back of his coat collar. He felt that his general image was in keeping with that of Gary Cooper as Wild Bill Hickock in *The Plainsman*. Most of the other images in the room were equally free with historical accuracy. Camilla was dressed up as a sort of wealthy young rancher's daughter, only with a makeup budget that would have done justice to Britt Ekland or Zsa Zsa Gabor. As Lex and James were engaged elsewhere she was playing coquettishly with one of the firm's younger Assistant Managers, a fresh-faced young fellow from Girvan. The Assistant Manager – The Sundance Kid for the evening – had a wife and a small baby but as often happened on these occasions the baby wasn't well and the wife had been forced to stay at home and look after it, leaving the Assistant Manager to come reluctantly on his own and make the best of a quiet evening. From the way things were going so far he wasn't making too bad a job of it. Reema Donachie, looking like Partick's answer to Mae West, was both teasing and comforting Jack McQueen who himself looked like a Clydeside-Mississippi Gambler with a one-man import concession on Kentucky Straight bourbon. Reema was stroking his fragile pride to his face and then emptying or diluting his glasses of treble Jack Daniels whenever his back was turned.

Then there was Billy Two Hats dressed as a spaghetti Western undertaker and Fat Jimmy as a corrupt town

mayor and about half a dozen members of the Celtic and
Rangers football teams posing as the London and Copland Road's answer to the James-Younger gang. There
were board girls and settlers and shop managers and rails
men and assorted racing correspondents and television
commentators disporting themselves with gusto like a
bunch of whisky-ridden hired hands at a dude ranch
barbecue. There was also the firm's own cabaret act.
Willie Cooper, Maxie Carlisle and Willie 'The Weasel'
Wood. 'The Lex Parlane Wide Boys' re-christened for the
evening 'The Big Sky Country Band'.

Mickey Garvin, sleek in his dinner jacket and cowboy
hat and his 'Who Needs J.R.?' teeshirt, seemed to have
been enjoying the cabaret. Country and Western described him pretty well, thought Lex. A countryman's low
cunning mixed in with the westerner's buccaneering ruthlessness and determined hunger for big money. He'd have
to watch Garvin. He'd had him in his pocket often enough
before now but the trouble was that he kept jumping out.

Garvin was sitting at the same table as Mickey Bolger,
Johnny Kinane and Cashel Maguire. They'd had a summit
meeting with Lex at his head office flat earlier that day.
They'd put certain proposals and Lex had listened politely. He had no intention of giving Kinane or Maguire a full
list of his contacts and associates or of putting a treasure
chest of money at Bolger's disposal. All the same when a
man moved his base of operations from Glasgow to the
south there were inevitably certain expenses that did
occur. New bridgeheads had to be established at every
juncture – Lex had a mind to try the Middle East next –
and certain other matters had to be satisfactorily put to
sleep in his native Scotland. He couldn't afford any
sudden explosions behind his back.

He had an idea that Bolger might try and involve
himself in his business once he moved down to Weybridge. These days he probably needed the money. The
corrupt jockeys ring would be used as a teaser and if Lex
didn't play then he'd be threatened with some kind of

blackmail about his Glasgow past. Well he could handle that alright.

What he'd eventually decided was that for the time being he'd sit back, wait and see what Garvin and Bolger came up with and examine each venture on a circumspect case by case basis. If they made him sufficient profit he'd be in for the next deal. If not he'd back out. They didn't know that of course. Not yet. One thing was certain. Any clumsy encroachments on his territory and there'd be trouble.

Bolger was shouting and grinning at him from across the room. Pouring champagne down the willing throat of a Gants Hill bunny girl with black curly hair and jam roll lips. "Hey Trampas," called Bolger, his eyes glinting with their usual malicious intensity. "Come down here and have a drink!"

"Later, Mickey," said Lex smiling. "Later." Johnny Kinane was waving at him too. He was surrounded by a tide of rippling females and playing a soccer quiz game with Fat Jimmy Docherty. One hundred pounds a point. Cashel Maguire had slipped away from Kinane's side and was sitting on the top table talking to Bella. Lex didn't like Maguire. He couldn't trust anyone who was that suave and Maguire was suave even in a last minute hired out dinner suit. Maguire had a hunger about him too that was somehow unhealthy. Not that Lex minded hunger. He admired and respected it but with Maguire there was no fat man longing to burst out. Only a thin, poker playing snake plotting to consume.

James Richmond was too thin. But with Richmond Lex knew that he was just too neurotic to put on any weight. The boy had a prodigious appetite though. He even read the *Good Food Guide* in times of stress. And why not? Was not a good French menu the stuff that dreams are made of? Lex was confident. In the fullness of time the boy would have a bulging gourmet's belly as handsome and obtrusive as his own. Young Richmond had been sitting at his right hand that evening. Feeling drunk and aggressive and sad and worried about his debts and his work and his family. Lex had attempted to cheer him up by reminding him of all the great days' racing that lay ahead through the coming National Hunt Season. The Mackeson Gold Cup. Kempton on Boxing Day. The Schweppes. And then March. Cheltenham. Another glorious three-day National Hunt Festival. James had pulled out a pair of black shades from his top pocket and put them on. Just like Lex. Big Casino and Little Casino, that's what they'd call themselves. Just like Pat Garrett and Billy the Kid. The boy was looking good that night. Blue-eyed and beautiful. He'd cut his hair slightly shorter than usual and he too was wearing a black frock coat, a soft white shirt and a broad-brimmed black felt hat. The shades completed the image to perfection. Reema Donachie couldn't take her eyes off him. But James, as Lex could see, was totally lost on Bella. And who wouldn't be, he thought to himself proudly?

Amidst this panoply of cinematic images, costumes and American fantasy Bella was draped revealingly in a red silk jersey dress that was more Milan than South Dakota. Bella was about forty-three years of age and what Lex liked to call a big, smelly girl. She was not exactly fat but she was not slim either. She was nearly six feet tall and as befitted her mixed background she had the shape of a classically Italian kind of woman. Big hipped, big breasted and emphatically curvaceous. Like Claudia Cardinale, so Lex said. She drenched you with her every scent, from her Madame Rochas perfume to her warm, ruby red lipstick and the extraordinary mixture of Dunhill, Benson and Hedges and American cigarettes that she half smoked so expansively. For Lex every touch was like the feel of a soft ripe peach, of tight satin and of soft, thick and ticklish pubic hair. She had long brown hair, brown eyes, and even the obligatory husky voice of every true voluptuary.

Bella had once been an actress. In fact back in the mid nineteen-sixties she had been quite a film star. Playing a regular variation on the kind of cool, crisp and sexy English girls that were so fashionably in demand at the time. Sometimes in a black polo neck jersey, sometimes in a pvc mac and knee-length black leather boots, she would usually be found in a series of cinema verité landscapes. Living on a houseboat on the Chelsea Embankment or walking a sheep dog across Hampstead Heath. Cuddling up to Terence Stamp in some Battersea bedsit or doing the shopping with David Hemmings down the Kings Road, her straight hair, fringe, sooty eyes and pale, frosted lips epitomising the brittle modernity of a whole era.

Only Bella didn't quite last the course.

For a while she went out to America as the wife of a brutal and brutally successful young cockney cameraman who built up a flourishing advertising business with offices in Putney making dog food commercials and bigger offices out in Burbank, California, making adverts for jeans and fast food. He used to beat Bella up regularly, breaking her arm three times and her jaw and a leg at least once. He was finally arrested in a bar on Sunset Boulevard for attempting to rape three teenage schoolgirls.

Bella and her career both went into decline after that. She filled out and she dropped out, eventually ending up in a weight loss clinic and a centre for alcoholism. When she came out and returned to England she decided that good health, sanity and a reasonable degree of financial security were preferable to a high pressured life in front of the cameras. So she started looking round for a rich man to marry.

Her second husband was a fat cat international stockbroker who installed her as the mistress of his Knightsbridge and West Sussex houses and made her the holiday-time proprietor of his four children, three dogs, their nanny and the German *au pair* girl. The stockbroker was a rich man alright but he seemed disinterested in sex and Bella was tempted to mistreat him. By now she'd become a beautiful woman again, blossoming for the second time in her life but in a very different way from the fragile girl of the mid-sixties.

The night she met Lex they were staying at a Newbury weekend house party, after the 1982 Hennessy Gold Cup. Lex took the stockbroker for nearly forty thousand pounds in an all-night stud poker game. The following afternoon he took his woman away too.

Bella had few misgivings about leaving. What attracted her to Lex was not just the fact that he protected her but the way that he enjoyed playing with her too, teasing her and enveloping her with his tough, physical sexuality. The toughness came naturally with him, unlike her first husband. It wasn't just a macho playboy act. And she didn't have to listen to any long and tangled tales about his enfeebling public school past either. She knew his reputation with women but it didn't seem to deter her that greatly. At least he never raised a hand to her in violence. And Bella had the confidence and style to be able to give Lex almost everything he wanted or needed. Whether they were striding up Park Lane or sauntering down Buchanan Street, travelling together on the Concorde or squashed on to each other's laps on the Logan-Air shuttle to Teesside, attending a Northern Institute of Directors' lunch in Newcastle or a dinner in the Gimcrack Rooms at York racecourse. She was different from the other bookies' girls, Lex told the *Citizen*. She had a touch of breeding. She had background. Education. And taste. Given half a chance and the right atmosphere she could evoke a nostalgic bygone era of private villas on the Isle of Capri, first-class blue-and-gold wagon lits on the Rome Express and an always reserved suite at the Excelsior Hotel. She did actually have her underwear handmade and specially designed by a generations-old private couturier on the Via Veneto and ever since he'd met her Lex liked to joke that he had to fly her laundry in and out of Prestwick two or three times a week.

Bella laughed a lot and always smiled and listened well whenever she was introduced to one of Lex's new friends or acquaintances. Granted these were not necessarily characteristics that would have immediately endeared her to the accepted canon of feminist thought and belief. But to Lex they mattered a lot. Bella understood about that and some people said that was a source of her power and position. Others said that she was much too soft for their relationship really to last. Others that she always understood precisely in which direction her own best interests lay. Still others said that she and Lex were really true lovers. Like Bugsy Siegel and Virginia Hall.

Tonight she was deftly but definitely putting down Cashel Maguire while flirting with James with her eyes and then turning round every few minutes to smile warmly at Lex. She was feeling in a gratifyingly indulgent mood. On the Friday afternoon Lex had flown her to Paris for the evening and for dinner. Their private and executive Lex Parlane Connection Piper Malibu, in colours of scarlet and black, had taken off again from French soil at just after 4 am. They'd had to leave early on account of Ayr races the following day. On that Saturday night Lex had taken her to his new casino off St Vincent Square and she'd danced riotously on the blackjack table tops, taunting the Greek with occasional fleeting glimpses of her inner thigh. And tonight she'd basked in the reflected glory of Alex John Parlane as he'd made his big speech of address to the assembled company just between the cheese course and the coffee.

The address, as always, was an historic and triumphant moment, like a keynote acceptance speech at an American political convention. Lex told his audience that the sale of the Scottish company would result in a handsome and generous profit share for every one of them. And after he was gone their jobs would still be secure and their futures well cared for by Jimmy Docherty and fellow Glasgow bookie Tony Maclean, who between them would be taking over control of the off course side of the business. Then Lex gave them a foretaste of his exciting new venture down south, the latest glittering shop window in his business empire, which would be added to the ever expanding Tattersalls and credit bookmaking operation. 'Lex Parlane Sports Video International'. He showed them extensive slides of the new company's head offices in Esher and then he showed them trailers of some of the first year's intended products. Internationally marketable high quality video cassettes on the History of Celtic Football Club, of the Scottish National Football Team, the Embassy World Snooker Championships and, as the forerunner and pilot ship, The Life and Big Race Times of Mr Racing himself, Mr Lester Piggott. Only the biggest and best names in sport would be featured and the new company's motto would be one of Lex's own favourite sayings: 'Who needs modesty when you're a genius like I am?''

"People sometimes say that I'm trying to live my life on a short piece of paper," Lex had said to his adoring admirers. "Well I can assure you that's not true. I haven't even half-fulfilled my ambitions. And that's why Louis Weiss is already quaking in his sharp-toed slip-on shoes at his desk in Golden Square. Awaiting my imminent arrival on the London Stock Exchange." Everyone cheered to the rooftops. "My final piece of advice is heartfelt and most sincere. It's the product of everything that I've learned working with you all over these past eleven years. Try and be yourself honestly and stay true and good to those who've been true and good to you. Don't ever cut your cloth to please a newly acquired circle of smart friends. They'll always remind you in the end that you don't belong." There was another resounding cheer and then they all burst into a spontaneous rendition of *For He's a Jolly Good Fellow*. Lex beamed and shone like an illuminated Good Night sign at the climax of a tumultuous firework display.

In private his actual feelings about leaving Glasgow for Surrey and the south were neither romantic nor repentant. But tonight he could afford to smile. It was at times like this, as he stood crouched and private in the gents cloakroom snorting up endless lines of white powder, that he liked to look back over the big moments and turning points in his life and career.

He remembered the day that he'd first walked into the illegal street bookies shop in the room over the bar on Waddell Street. Clutching his father's line, not cocaine but a homemade betting slip, and a faded ten bob note to go with it. All the men in the room had stared hard at the eight-year-old boy who'd stared even harder back. He remembered the details of the room, very far from glamorous by the standards that he'd grown used to today. Bare wooden floorboards, old sagging furniture and a couple of washed-out sporting prints on the walls. One of them the Benny Lynch–Peter Kane fight at Shawfield in 1937 and the other one Steve Donoghue riding Captain Cuttle in the 1922 Derby. And there, lost amidst the cheap smog of their own cigarette smoke were the desperate punters angling to lose their last shilling on a three-legged dog at Powderhall or a dodgy jumper at Haydock Park. And Lex had looked at the punters and he'd looked at the bookie, Lou Corelli, sitting in the back office in his ice cream suit and his little bow tie drinking Scotch and Seven-Up and reading about the teenage Lester Piggott's home life and habits in *Picture Post*. And he'd looked at Corelli's minder counting up the bets and the profits made as the money came in from the district. And he'd thought: I can play this game. One day I'll have ten times Lou Corelli's business. Whatever it takes. It's as easy as Fox and Hounds.

Corelli got to like young Alex. He started giving him commissions for every line of business that he brought in. Pretty soon the boy was skipping school over the lunch break to collect the money and the wagers from the pubs and bars, factories and shops around the neighbourhood. Then he started making his own form book and handicap ratings and pocketing certain of the bets that he considered had no chance and not reporting them to Corelli. When he'd walked out of the Cleland Street School at the age of fifteen he hadn't needed any help or advice from his local Youth Employment Officer.

There'd be other moments that he'd remember too. Like his first year as a rails bookie. A lone operator in his own right around the dog tracks of Northern England. He'd been cleaned out rotten. But he'd come back. First he'd spent three years with old Willie Provan in his small office chain around the western and southern fringes of the city. Willie Provan had taught him half a dozen simple but essential lessons on the process required to turn a pushy young hustler into a real professional operator. He hadn't just taught him how to make a book. He'd taught him the front, side and back ends of the off course bookmaking business, all the minute and tedious details of betting shop management life that the boy had always been too cavalier to take seriously before. He'd also taught him the importance of getting access to the right information, of not wasting too much time and money on loudmouthed tipsters and socialising trainers with nothing to do except drink and talk crap. He'd taught him how to develop his own form book knowledge, how to work out the right line of form in a race and how to be instinctive but not too clever. Who would upset you most if it won and you hadn't backed it? That's what Willie used to say and Lex still adhered to that maxim even now.

When his three years in the offices were up Lex went back to the tracks, taking Willie's business with him to every racecourse and dog stadium north of the Trent and south of the Tay. But aside from Willie the twenty-two-year old had debts of his own to repay, substantial losses that had to be cleared before he could really set out on the road to greatness. Those were bold high tempo days. He once had to leave the engine running on his Rover in the Sedgefield car park while he waited with trepidation at the top of the stands to see if an ex-alcoholic dwarf from Pudsey would deliver the goods in a three-horse frame-up at the end of a bleak November afternoon.

But by the end of the sixties the big ones were beginning

to go in with increasing frequency. When Willie retired in
1969 Lex took over as manager and front man, and when
Provan died three years later he left a more than just
financial legacy to the former bookie's runner less than
half his age who'd brought brass neck and a brilliant
racing mind to assist the older man's thoroughness and
careful mathematical guile.

No one ever quite knew or could say with any unassailable accuracy exactly what happened to Lex in those next
twelve months. He was always racing. He often took
full-page adverts out in the *Citizen* publicising his new
maverick rails betting operation. The adverts were always
entitled 'Lex Parlane. The Flying Scot. Where will he be
tomorrow?' and then there was a photograph to match. In
1973 he suddenly appeared at a Press Conference above a
Greek restaurant in West George Street announcing his
brand new betting office business. Twenty-five shops
opening immediately in the Glasgow and Strathclyde
region. All of them spankingly modern and renovated
with the emphasis on comfort and style. Expensive too.
But wherever the money came from for such a sudden and
dramatic expansion it wasn't from any recognisably ortho-
dox financial institution or source. It frightened some
people. Especially some of that tight little brotherhood of
big credit bookmakers who since the retirement of William Hill and the introduction of betting tax had been used
to keeping things nice and quiet and neat and tidy
amongst themselves. Lex started to notice and look out
for an expression of cringing fear in the eyes and faces of
some of his ulcer-ridden corseted colleagues. A look of
pallid alarm, envisaging their sons' public school fees
going down the drain for another term whenever Lex
appeared at their elbow in his black shades, mocking their
caution, knocking their odds out and slowly but surely
cornering the lion's share of the big players' market. He'd
known then . . . he'd go all the way. Besides how could he
ever possibly have backed out and backed down once the
stories and the legends were launched? As he said in his

first newspaper interview in 1974, he passionately believed that you were what you did, that the only way to
become immortal, to fight death and ignominy was to live
close to the edge. That way, he said, waving his first public
magnum of Bollinger at the news cameras, at least they'd
all know he'd been alive.

He knew he'd been alive alright the day Louis Weiss
had tried to ruin him on Newmarket Heath. It was
Cambridgeshire day and Lex had been saying for weeks
that the ante-post favourite was absurd value at eleven to
two and ought to be more than four times that price. The
horse had been second in the race twelve months previously but it had now gone up nearly a stone in the
weights and changed stables too. The new trainer Lex
described publicly as an ex-Army joke with less idea about
training horses than he had about driving Russian tanks.
Weiss thought otherwise. He was closely involved with the
horse's connections and convinced that it had the class and
courage to win the big race and to put an end to this
excessively visible Scot at the same time. With Lex having
gone on record both in print and on television that the
horse had no chance Goldline threw down the gauntlet.
Weiss got his firm to back the horse with the Lex Parlane
Connection at Lex Parlane prices with every conceivable
penny that they could lay their hands on. And he almost
compelled all of his big credit clients to do the same. Lex
took the bets. Weiss then arranged for a change of pilot on
the favourite and the booking of an ex-American champion jockey and big race expert. Still Lex continued to
take the bets.

The day of the race was misty and cool. The American
jockey gave the favourite a superb ride, bringing it out of
the pack as the field raced down into the dip and then
hitting the front on the hill, but, in the last few hundred
yards Lex's reservations were borne out as the horse hung
fire under pressure and was caught on the line by a
Northern-trained twenty to one shot who'd been a runner-
up three times that season in the Lincoln, Royal Hunt Cup

and Rose of York Handicaps. The Judge called a photograph but the outcome seemed certain. Lex was standing by the winning post on the other side of the course being photographed for an ITV television documentary. Suddenly there was an extra announcement. An objection by the rider of the runner-up to the rider of the winner for 'taking my ground inside the final furlong'. Unbeknown to Lex, Weiss had just urged the American to try and steal the race in the Stewards' room. There now followed, for Lex, an agonising twenty-minute wait as he sweated it out standing with the ITV journalist on the sweetsmelling grass of the heath opposite the sponsor's sign and the creosote-painted Judge's box and the massed, packed stands of the Members and Tattersalls Enclosures. The announcement when it came was the voice of victory. 'Result stands.' Lex Parlane stands against the massed ranks of conventional establishment racecourse opinion. If the result had been overturned he'd have stood to lose more than half a million pounds. Louis Weiss had tried to sever his carotid artery. And he'd failed.

Meanwhile, back in the present at the Bella Vista Hotel, Lex Parlane returned from the cloakroom to the top table and gazed back out enraptured and immobile at the men and women who had looked up to him for their cue in life. Without him, he decided, they'd never really existed.

"Are you a crook?" asked James Richmond loudly, suddenly slumping back down into the seat on his right hand side. Lex laughed hugely and gave him a familial hug. "I mean is it true?" asked the boy who was quite drunk but not irreparably so. "Are you really a gangster?"

"I don't know what you're talking about," said Lex, putting another cigar in the boy's mouth.

"I've heard . . ." said James, his head swinging indiscriminately towards the gathering, " . . .that you've been involved with everything from bank robbery . . . to casino hold-ups . . . to fencing the proceeds of illegal arms sales."

Lex smiled. "The rubbish some people do talk."

"Your very own mafia," said James. "Fixed races . . . bent jockeys . . . bent owners, bookies and trainers."

"I do what I have to do," said Lex, winking conspiratorially. "No more."

"No more?"

"They're just stories, son. Put around by the other bookmakers to get at me. Because they don't like me being so successful."

"What about the violence?"

"Don't you believe all you read in the papers about Glasgow Jimmy. Those are just old wives' tales. Folk stories to scare off the Southerners."

"I'm not talking about 'Glasgow'. Or the papers. I'm talking about Willie Smith."

"A bastard if ever there was one. Got hurt I hear?"

James nodded slowly. "Attacked at the races. Nothing to do with you, I suppose?"

"Don't stir, Jimmy. And don't you ever bother about Willie Smith. He's dross."

"What about the poor old betting public? Your punters. Do you care about them?"

Lex shrugged. "It's a tough game."

"Yeah, yeah, yeah. Tough game, tough city, tough life. I've heard all that before. But what about your average, losing, working-class punter? Do you care about them?"

"We share . . . a common apprehension . . . of the way of the world. Unlike some . . . I reward enterprise. Wit and imagination. They like that."

"I see. And what about some of these other gentlemen here tonight?" James gestured towards Kinane's table. Towards Garvin and Bolger and Cashel Maguire. "Do they represent enterprise? Wit? And imagination?"

"Theirs is a tough game too."

"Fine." He nodded. "Fine." There was a long pause as the two men looked each other in the eye. "Don't you ever get sick of it?" asked James softly. "Racing. Gambling . . . lying. The exhaustive, repetitive monotony of it all. Don't you ever get sick?"

"Do you? You're an addict."

"Oh no."

"Oh yes!"

"No!"

"Yes! I've seen it, Jimmy, and I know. You are a hopeless gambler. In both senses of the word. You need me."

"And don't you need me?"

"Maybe. You're a help, I won't deny. I quite like you too."

"I find your company tolerably entertaining." James gently and accidentally knocked a brandy balloon over with his elbow. The brandy rolled across the table cloth.

"And one day . . ." said Lex.

"One day what?"

"One day when your dad dies you can help me even more."

"Oh yes?"

"Yeah."

"Tell me," said James, leaning forward on to the wet cloth, "tell me honestly. Just once. Are you a crook?"

"Honestly. And just once. No." James sighed and swung round on his chair, his hat falling forward over his eyes. "They're just stories, Jimmy. You can look at my books. I've just been brighter and cleverer than the rest of the gang. Besides. When I go south I'll be going straight. . ."

"Going straight?"

"Going straight into the video and promotional business. Punting will become a less and less major part of my life."

"Fat chance."

"It's true."

"I'm going south tomorrow. Back to the old College. Exam Tuesday. And on Wednesday my father's coming up."

"Give him my best regards."

"What do you think he'll say, Lex? The Duke. What do you think he'll say about my progress in life?"

"I should think he'll commend that fine upstanding friend of yours. That Glaswegian bookmaking fellow. The noble guardian and generous chaperone of your health and business affairs. Mr Glasgow. Mr Scotland. Mr Alex John Parlane."

"Hah! I know what I'd say if I was him."

"And what would that be?"

" 'Jimmy,' I'd say, 'you've got to get shot of that fat crook of a Scotsman. He's a treble-dyed villain and he'll suck you dry. Banish him Jimmy! Banish him!' "

" 'Nonsense,' you'll say. 'Lex is life. Lex is excitement. Lex is the spirit of true adventure. No sooner banish Lex Parlane than banish life itself.' "

"I do. I will. I'm tired!"

"Have some of this," said Lex, pressing a gramme packet of cocaine into the boy's hand.

James looked down at the packet then looked back up at Lex and smiled. "You'll give me a heart attack one day," he said.

"One day."

On his way out to the lavatory James nearly bumped into Bella. He could feel her rustle as she brushed up against him. He grinned and scratched the tip of his nose. She smiled back at him, fractionally raising one eyebrow above the other. When she got back to the table Lex attempted to engage her in a passionate embrace. At the last minute she turned her cheek towards him instead. "What's he like?" she asked.

"Who? The boy?" She nodded. "What do you think?"

"Very young. Upper class. Definitely in love with you. And probably a potential smack addict to boot."

"No way. He just likes the occasional toot like the rest of us." She raised one eyebrow again expertly. "He's an enthusiast. Up for the crack. I think my pretensions to villainy amuse him."

"Why yours so much? They have racecourse villains

down south. At Kempton and Sandown Park. What's wrong with them? Like Garvin and Bolger. Or Kinane over in Ireland. Or if he must spend all his time up in Scotland why not Jack McQueen?"

"McQueen? He's about as witty as a New Year's Eve dance up in Forfar with Kenneth MacKellar and the *White Heather Club*."

"Why you, Lex?"

"You're jealous."

"You think so?"

"He's been brought up in a frigid mausoleum all his life. School the same. No warmth. No fun. I give him a taste of the real world."

"Your world's the real world?"

"It suits you alright."

"I hate the real world."

"I like him. He's young. He enjoys himself. And he's good company."

"Easy to manipulate?"

"Aye. He has a few rich friends." There were candles on the table. Bella's neck seemed soft and smooth and creamy against the candlelight. Lex looked into her eyes and kissed her. "I have to go down south next week," he said. "To see the solicitors. We could go shopping."

"Alright."

"There's no competition, Princess. Honest. Never has been. Never will be."

"Never?"

"Never." They kissed again, their lips tight together. "Mind you, with all these bright young boys and bold lads around tonight it wouldn't surprise me if you were feeling a bit restless yourself. I mean I'm nearly forty-one years of age. I can see my whole life passing in front of my eyes!"

"I'd rather have you than any nineteen-year-old boy. Anytime. Any place."

He gave a sly look. "Suppose I had to go away for a while? For maybe four or five weeks? America or the Middle East? Would you desert me?"

"Desert you?"

"Aye. For another lover. Some Anglo-Scottish big game hunter with a draughty castle up in Argyll. I should think that'd be just about your style. You've played on my team. Now why not try what the other side's like. Your side."

"Never."

"Never?" There was a brief pause. Then Lex's cunning little smile broadened into a wide mischievous grin and he kissed her once more but quite tenderly, not aggressively. "Let's go to bed." He picked up a bottle of the Roederer Cristal champagne.

No two descriptions quite tallied as to exactly what happened next. The most reliable account seemed to come from the hotel's plumply kilted Assistant Catering Manager.

A tough pugnacious-looking man with sandy hair, a blue velvet dinner jacket and a blue cummerbund to match had been standing around in the doorway of the banqueting hall for several minutes. He'd been generally smirking and nodding his head towards the diners in a drunken sycophantic sort of way. Suddenly, just as Lex and Bella had got up to leave, he'd pulled out a gun from the top of his blue cummerbund and launched his way towards the centre of the room, brandishing the gun wildly around his head and screaming abuse at Lex.

"You fat fucking tart, Parlane," he'd shouted, warning away a waiter who'd tried to disarm him. "You stinking thief. You've stitched up every punter in this city. And now you've tried to put my brother away too. Well I've got news for you. There's one or two faces now down south who've got their eye on you. And your friends. They're going to clean you out, pal. Once and for fucking all! They're going to wipe your arse off the Strathclyde map." Then Billy Two Hats tackled him from behind. The man was strong. He lost his gun but he stayed upright. He jumped up on to the top table and flung himself at Lex, kneeing him hard in the groin. Lex swung the champagne bottle at him, cracking him over the bridge of his nose. The man went down. Lex and Billy and Jack McQueen went down after him. The drama shattered the atmosphere in the room and drew everyone's attention to it just as surely as if the man had come into the banqueting hall blowing a whistle and setting off a red flare.

"Just get him out of here," gasped Lex, badly winded. "Get him out of my fucking sight." Billy and McQueen had literally to drag and yank the man from the room like old-fashioned dentists pulling a reluctant and troublesome tooth. McQueen had hold of his legs while Billy had his arms and neck, using his own powerful forearm to gag his mouth in case of further indiscretions. The hotel staff kept out of it. They were quite happy to leave the whole affair to Lex's justice and jurisdiction. Lex was sitting in an armchair. Bella was sitting next to him with a bottle of brandy.

"The Smith Brothers. Bastards. One of them steals my money, the other one performs an uninvited cabaret act at my firm's dinner. How dare they?"

"Ssh! He's gone." Reema and Camilla were standing by the chair looking apprehensive. If Camilla was as apprehensive about Bella as she was about Lex she didn't show it.

"Are you alright, Lexie?" asked Reema.

"I mean how dare they?" muttered Lex to himself. "I'll be taking steps over this one."

Bella stroked his brow gently. "You can go away now," she said to Reema and Camilla.

"It's alright, hen," said Jack McQueen, appearing at Reema's side. "All over."

"Is he gone?" asked Lex.

"Aye," said Billy Two Hats. "Hurt too."

"Bastard. You know what to do."

"Yeah." The two men and the two other women went away, leaving Bella crouching on the floor by Lex's side.

"I thought," she said, "when you left Glasgow . . . we were going to put all this stuff behind us."

"If the Smiths want an old-fashioned carve-up they can have one. They're all trash. I'll drown the bastards. I'll sling them in the Clyde on a dark night. I'll. . ."

"You do and I'll throw you out of my bed." Lex tightened his lips and said nothing. "It's not worth it, Lex. You're ten times the man they are. Ignore them."

"I'm Lex Parlane. I can't afford to ignore anything. Especially not when there's people watching." He looked up at Bolger and Maguire and Kinane. They were all acting as if nothing had happened. But they knew.

Willie Cooper stepped down off the stage and came over to Lex's chair. "Would you prefer something softer from the band, boss?" he asked. "Or something up tempo?"

"Frankie Sinatra. *Strangers In The Night*. Maxie knows the vocal."

"OK, boss." Willie went back up to the stage and rejoined the band and they started playing Frankie Sinatra. Lex took another white packet out of his inside pocket and gave it to Bella along with his credit card. "Cut me out a line, will you?"

"In here?"

"It doesnae matter. Everyone knows and nobody cares." Bella tipped some of the cocaine out of the white packet on to an empty cheese plate. She started to cut out a line with the credit card. "More than that," said Lex. She doubled the amount. The line covered the whole plate. "There's a note already rolled in my other coat pocket," said Lex. Bella found it, took it out and gave it to him. Lex snorted up the line of cocaine. "Help yourself," he said.

"Well, this one didn't last long, did it?" she said, looking at the already dwindling amount of white powder in the little white packet.

"Well, you know how it is. Us country boys. We're just not used to these big city ways."

"You know what I mean. It's addictive. It could kill you."

"It's not addictive and it won't kill me and you sound like you're writing my fucking biography. Posthumously!" Bella didn't laugh. She pushed away the cheese plate and put down the rolled up note. "Now come on. Give me a kiss," said Lex, decisive once again. "A real kiss."

Just as he was succeeding in enfolding her in his loving embrace he caught sight of another disturbance going on in the corner of the room. A new disturbance and a potentially painful and embarrassing one for him personally. It was Camilla Forbes-Sempill, grown drunk and loud and sexy. And she was looking for Lex Parlane.

Earlier that day Lex had warned Camilla that she could only come to the dinner if she promised not to embarrass him in front of Bella. Now suddenly she was getting bored and out of hand. "Where is he?" she cried. "Where is that big fat roughneck sexy man? I want him. Now!" She stood up and kicked off her shoes and lifted her skirt up around her waist. People started to notice her. Bella noticed her.

"What does that drunken little slut want?" she asked. Lex tried to ignore it. He kissed Bella again, gently manoeuvring her round in his arms so that her back was facing firmly against Camilla's end of the room. He kept his own head low. But it didn't work.

"Dolly wants a big Scots dick," came a whining voice above his shoulders. Lex moaned inwardly. He looked up to see James Richmond smiling down at him. Bella hardened in his arms.

"Could she possibly mean you, darling?" she asked.

"Search me," said Lex, his eyes pleading with Richmond. Bella gave a sigh and pushed Lex away.

Richmond saw his moment. "Can I buy you a drink at the bar?" he asked her. "Or perhaps a dance?"

15

James was standing in the window wearing only a shirt and staring out across the grey and black granite rooftops of the city. The room was on the top floor of the hotel and between the television aerials and the high-rise flats he could make out the lights of the night-shifts in the factories along the river. A very pale grey light was just beginning to illuminate the edges of the night sky. In another hour the street lamps would be going out. And a few hours after that James – dressed, packed and hung over – would be on his way to the Central Station for his train south. His return had been decided by a pointed phone call with his father that Sunday lunchtime. So, that was that.

He looked around the room. It was his second modern hotel room of this extended Lex Parlane weekend. The furniture was less lavish than in Lex's suite at the Holiday Inn but still comfortable enough in pine and tartan shades. There was a sitting room and an immaculately clean and well-appointed bathroom. And the bed was large. The one surprising detail was the trio of modern art prints that hung on the walls above the bed. Other than the prints, though, the room had no real character or personality of its own whatsoever. It just did its job. Very adequately. It was centrally heated, still and quiet. No sound from any other part of the hotel, not even a creaking hot water tank or a muffled service lift, could possibly drift in through the air-conditioned double glazing and disturb whatever co-coon of sex and fantasy the occupants of the room themselves decided to invest it with.

Some of Bella's black silk underwear was lying on the

floor at James's feet. He touched the silk with his bare foot. The black underwear fitted in excellently with his general image of Bella's character and role in life.

The ashtray on the bedside table was piled high with her half-smoked cigarettes, their tips smeared liberally with red lipstick. James had long ago tried to convince himself that it was childish to equate cigarette smoking with sexuality but he still experienced a frisson of excitement when extending his cigarette lighter towards the aid of a beautiful woman that he couldn't possibly have felt if he'd just been unwrapping her a Murray Mint or offering her a Galaxy Revels Delight. Both his and Bella's clothes from the Wild West Evening were scattered expansively around the floor and amongst the bed linen. There were bottles and glasses that they'd sent down for from room service. The remains of the gramme packet of cocaine that Lex had given James earlier were smudged across a glass top tray that had ended up lying on the floor underneath a radiator. And over everything there was the strong and heady scent of Bella's impossibly rich and feminine perfume.

At that moment she walked back in from the bathroom. The sight of her naked body was quite sensational. She got back between the sheets, made herself comfortable and poured herself a large Scotch from the bottle on her left hand side.

"Happy?" she asked, smiling.

"Surprised."

"At what?"

"Being here. With you." He paused for a moment. "What do you think he'll say?" (Serves him right was what he actually thought. Now they were even.)

"He'll be too busy drowning, sorry, snorting his sorrows to say anything. Tucked up tight with that blonde slut." James smiled. "I'm sorry. I know she's a friend of yours."

"I don't mind." He put back on his black dark glasses, lit another cigarette and picked up his drink. "Who was that man in the Banqueting Room?"

"Oh, I don't know. Lex says he wants to be a worldwide racing impresario and yet he can't resist a street corner brawl with some bunch of cheap thugs." She reached for her handbag and took out a packet of grass and some cigarette papers and started to roll a joint. James looked up at the Chagall portrait over the bed. It depicted a happy and elated scene of a young man in a red frock coat sitting on his beloved's shoulders and holding a wine glass up in his left hand. The girl was smiling and big-bosomed and wearing a long white dress and purple stockings and in her left hand she was holding up a coloured fan. He looked back at Bella. She seemed to purr and glisten at him appreciatively like some sleekly elegant black cat. But as James had already discovered, feline hauteur and catlike distance were not her only animal qualities. She was extremely affectionate and playful too and then she was less like a cat and more like a large black or brown puppy landing on you triumphantly with her paws on your chest. What was it Lex had said? The price of a weekend at the Albany Four Seasons. And tonight she was playing with him.

"Tell me something." He sat down lightly on the edge of the bed. "How exactly do you . . . fit in with all this?"

She frowned slightly. "How do you mean?"

"With all this. Racing. Gamblers. Lex's world."

"Oh, that's easy." She handed him the joint. "My mother was a kind of lapsed member of the Scottish aristocracy. But my father was Italian. And a compulsive card player. Most of my growing up was spent moving around from one European casino town to another. And wherever they play cards in Europe there's never a racetrack that far away. Baden Baden. Deauville. Cagnes Sur Mer. My mother didn't mind. It was all fun to her. And as for myself and my sisters, well, we absolutely adored it. Now and again my father did make various efforts to enrol us in schools both here and abroad but I was thrown out of all of them. By the time I was seventeen

I had acquired a certain taste for the big risk!" She smiled. "So now you know."

He smiled too and nodded, then returned her the joint and poured them both another drink. "So how did you become an actress?"

"That was my father. He got me a modelling job in Rome. They sent me to England and I went on from there. My first part was in a movie about Casanova being reincarnated in London in the swinging sixties. I was Casanova's best girl. A young English photographer with a flat in World's End. Pure . . . but sexy."

"Good movie?"

"Dreadful. But over the next five years I must've gone around the world and back, oh, at least a dozen times."

"And now you've ended up in Scotland."

"That's right. I love it too. Especially Glasgow."

"Why?"

"It's tough and sexy. Lots of Italians." She winked at him. "I've had a grand time." She leant forward and started stroking his hair seductively.

"What about the children?"

"You know about them?"

"Lex told me."

"Did he?" She held out her empty Scotch glass again, royally. James refilled it. "They've spent most of their lives with my mother in Edinburgh. The court decided that I was not morally suitable to be given custody. The girls seem happy enough though. They were here this summer."

"How does that fit in with Lex's plans?"

"He doesn't mind playing the rich benefactor as long as they're not around that often. Mind you, if we did get married he'd probably see more of his own son."

"Of course. I'd forgotten about him."

"Kenny's a sweet kid. Only two years old and Lex is already taking him to circuses and the cinema and that's not to mention at least half a dozen visits to the racetrack.

He's even opened an account for him with the William Hill Organisation. Fiona nearly killed him." She laughed. "I say it beats the Lloyds Bank young savers scheme every time." She'd been rolling another joint. It was much stronger than the first one and it made her choke. James slapped her on the back and she coughed and they both laughed and she drank a glass of water. Then she rolled back again against the tangled mess that she'd made of the pillows and the heavy pine coloured bedspread.

"Come on," she whispered, her eyes twinkling with pleasure. "Enter a different world."

The sky was getting lighter all the time. Richmond had opened up one of the windows and you could begin to hear the sounds of traffic and railways and milk delivery vans from the new day outside. He was lying on his back and Bella was lying with her head on his chest. Her eyes were shut but she was not asleep. I suppose this is how he does it? he thought. The Big Shot. Jack the Lad. And here I am. Lying in an almost hermetically sealed hotel bedroom. With his woman.

"Bella?" he asked gently. "When Lex moves south down to Surrey . . . will you come too?"

"Of course. Just wait till you see the house."

"It's good, is it?"

"It's completely over the top. But, oh boy, is it comfortable."

"I just can't imagine what he wants to live in Weybridge for, that's all. It's like Beverly Hills without the film stars. Or at least without the good ones."

"You have to remember, Jimmy . . . that to Lex the south of England isn't just the land of self-made ease and plenty. He can get all that up North. It's the final evidence that he's been approved of. His ultimate test of social acceptability."

"Weybridge?"

"Weybridge is just a prelude. He wants the whole Monopoly board. True-born nobility. The aristocracy of wealth and style. That's why he likes you so much."

James shook his head. "Well, he won't find much true-born nobility in St George's Hill. Just bankers and ex-rock stars. And as for money . . . my family aren't even that wealthy any more."

"Lex doesn't understand those things. And even if he did he'd say, 'So what? Who needs to know? They can still wear a better cut of suit than the rest of us.' "

"It always amazes me really. Most upper-class people that I know have little or no imaginative interest in how someone like him lives. They couldn't care less. Oh shit."

"What's the matter?"

"It's the time. I'll have to go soon." He slipped out of bed, hurried across the room to the radiator where he picked up the glass-topped tray and the last remains of Lex's cocaine packet and then hurried back again. He chopped out a line for the two of them. Not like one of Lex's miniature vapour trails but at least enough of the narcotic to help him through the next half-hour. Bella propped herself up and he offered her the tray.

"Do you take a lot of drugs?" she asked.

"I enjoy them. When they're there. Don't you?"

"Yes." She took the line. Then she put the note down on the tray and put the tray back on the floor. "You know Lex sleeps on average four hours out of every twenty-four. Sometimes less. As soon as he opens his eyes in the morning out comes the little white packet and an empty biro stem or a rolled-up note. Added to the alcohol, his weight, the pace of his life . . . he'll kill himself before he's fifty."

There was a long pause.

"I suppose that's the point," said James. "Lex doesn't want to be fifty." Bella sighed and looked severe. "I mean . . . if you're going to be a wild man . . . you can't just do it up to a point, can you? Any more than the man on the flying trapeze. Showmanship. The audience. They all demand . . . all the way."

"A dangerous and romantic theory," she said sensibly.

"Just don't encourage him too much, that's all. Not if you really love him."

"Do you love him?"

"Yes."

"But you don't mind being here? With me?"

"I like handsome young men." She kissed him. "I'm no angel, Jimmy. And I know Lex messes around. He always will. But as long as he doesn't do it right in front of my eyes . . ." she shrugged her shoulders, ". . . I don't mind."

"What about the violence? In his business, I mean? How do you feel about that?"

"How do you feel? You're his friend."

Richmond chose his words very carefully. "I suppose . . . he opens my eyes to the world. And most of the time he's such damned good company that it doesn't seem to matter."

"Exactly. I've known so-called respectable men whose lives, characters and personalities were ten times more violent than his."

"I've met them too."

"And he'd never lift a finger to me. You know my story so you know that matters. But I still love a man who loves women."

"Sounds fair enough."

She kissed him gently on the lips. "We've hardly talked at all about you."

"That's right."

"Why?"

"I'm smart."

"You think so?"

"Oh, yes."

"I feel no guilt, you know? About this."

"Thanks very much." He looked once again around the room. He looked at the Scotch bottle and the free champagne and at Bella's underwear strewn across the floor. Somehow it didn't look quite so good now as it had done an hour or so before. He looked back at Bella.

"Is it that bad?" she asked.

"Well . . . there is a problem."

"What problem?"

"Well . . . there's just a problem, that's all."

"Your father? The exam?"

He shook his head. He wished she wouldn't look so concerned and affectionate. "The problem is . . . that here I am . . . sitting up in bed with this beautiful and mature older woman . . . with whom I am falling passionately in love . . . and yet none of it's real. It's all a game."

"It's always a game, sweetheart."

"Yeah?"

"Listen," she said. "Don't sulk. I can't pretend it's all that likely that this . . . will ever happen again. But I wouldn't have missed out on tonight. Not for the world." She put her arms around him and drew him back round, almost maternally, towards the still perfumed and intoxicating pleasures of her large and naked body.

The station concourse was crowded with tourists and students and senior citizen railcard holders, all with their suitcases on wheels and their zip-up canvas bags and their boxes of Travellers Fare coffee and tea and jumbo ham-and-egg sandwiches. James had a splitting headache and the station announcer's amplified voice was very loud.

It was a cold and windy day and Bella was wearing a suede winter coat with a fur lining and a pair of sheer brown leather boots. She looked marvellous.

Lex turned up on the platform about fifteen minutes before the train was due to depart. He looked rather crumpled and although he tried to be chirpy he was obviously feeling sorry for himself. Bella was clearly determined to make him suffer and he had to caper around in front of her like an anxious dog attempting to retrieve its position with an irate mistress. She let him buy her chocolates and flowers and packets of cigarettes but she made no effort to cover up the situation with Rich-

mond. Rather she lavished every best kiss and smile and
sweet look upon him. James longed to believe that this
display of affection might be all for him alone and not just
a show to catch Lex with. But he wasn't a complete fool.

Lex took James into the gents lavatory of the Central
Hotel and they snorted up several lines of cocaine.

"Camilla's okay," Lex reassured him as they huddled
together in the cubicle. "She'll be down to see you soon.
End of this week probably. And I feel no malice about last
night."

James didn't really care about Camilla just then.
There'd been little time for a shower when he left the
hotel and he still had a marvellously dirty and sexy itch
between his legs. It seemed to him grossly and ridiculously
unfair that he was actually going away at all. The last thing
he wanted now was a romantic farewell at a confounded
railway station. He wanted Bella and lust and love and
miraculous sex and black silk underwear and more sex.

They came out of the lavatory and Lex went to the
bookstall on his behalf. He came back with a handful of
magazines including *Pacemaker* and *Knave, Mayfair, Men
Only, Penthouse* and *Club International* and a copy of the
latest Dick Francis. James did some precautionary antepost business with Lex on the outcome of the Dewhurst
Stakes and on the price of this year's Dewhurst winner for
the next year's 2,000 Guineas.

"Just think," said Lex brightly. "The next time we meet
it'll all be in Weybridge." Bella glowed. Lex put his arm
around her hopefully. They each gave James a hug and a
kiss and waved to him from the platform as the train
pulled out. They could've been his mother and father half
a dozen years before. Except that he'd never really gone
by train to Marlborough. He'd always had to ride there in
the back of his father's stiffly upholstered Daimler, nervously swapping cricket and football stories with the
ageing chauffeur.

He slept for the first two hours of the journey. Dreaming wonderful dreams about luscious Italian women

seducing him in casino bars. Then he woke up just after Carlisle with the sinking realisation that there were now less than twenty-four hours to go before his exam. He hadn't really got enough money for the restaurant car and he supposed he ought to study. He pressed his nose against the windowpane. The dull grey and brown and wet green fell and lakeland landscape looked somehow down and browbeaten too. It was a bleak sky and there was not a human being to be seen, only sheep.

He decided to go to the restaurant car.

16

The Duke was standing in the centre of Peckwater Quad holding his Jack Russell terrier Wallet under one arm. He was wearing an old dun-coloured raincoat and his brown trilby hat. Were it not for the Jack Russell he would have looked less like a weary aristocrat and more like a thirties Scotland Yard detective arriving regretfully but undeniably at some prominent address in Berkeley Square to arrest a charming but murderous toff.

The gravel was damp, the sky muddy and one or two falling leaves were beginning to attach themselves to the Duke's shoes. It was the day before full-term began. There were some trunks already in evidence but on the whole the atmosphere was calm and leisurely. A couple of men strolled past the Duke in a civilised manner, presumably on their way to a late and lingering breakfast in the market. There was hardly any frantic or oppressive sense of intense academic study going on behind closed oak-panelled doors.

Then the Duke heard cries, crashes and general commotion from the direction of the neighbouring quad. Tripe, his other Jack Russell terrier, suddenly darted into view, hurtling full-tilt towards staircase one. Could he possibly know that James was upstairs? wondered the Duke. Pursuing Tripe was the hot and breathless figure of Letherby, the Duke's secretary. Suddenly another breathless figure hove into view from the direction of Oriel Square. Hale, hearty and pink in the face. It was Rowland, his cavalry twills stretching comfortably around the eager motion of his athletic form. He flicked a lock of blond hair out of his eyes and then suddenly caught sight of the perfidious object of Tripe's yapping dementia. It was an aged and petrified-looking black tom cat and Tripe was chasing it in manic circles around the sandwich-like crescents of grass that fringe the centre of Peckwater Quad. The dog was chasing the cat and Letherby was chasing the dog and they were all performing an Indian war dance around the resigned and despondent-looking figure of Rowland's father. The other Jack Russell, Wallet, had been purposefully sedated before the start of the day's business, and he was merely surveying the proceedings from the safety of the Duke's grasp.

"It's alright, Leathers, I'll catch him," bellowed Rowland in a voice loud enough to be heard in Abingdon. The cat, Tripe, Letherby and Rowland now disappeared up staircase two. When they re-appeared five minutes later after more crashing, commotion and general havoc, Rowland was holding Tripe aloft in one hand like a triumphant New Zealand back who has just scored a try between the goalposts at Twickenham. A window was raised three floors up and two more blond young men grinned and shouted down at Rowland.

"Guess what, father?" yelled Rowland. "I caught him in young Charlie Westmoreland's room. You remember Charlie. His brother Tom's in the Irish Guards with Willie McNaught-Davis." There was no sign of the unfortunate cat.

"Let us go up," said the Duke, tight-lipped and signalling Letherby to go on up ahead.

When Letherby knocked on the door of James's first-floor rooms a few moments later James was sprawled contentedly across the carpet studying old copies of *Timeform* Annuals and Black Books with his racing and dog-owning friend Sunny Vengsarkar, who was a prodigious collector of all historic turf memorabilia. The exam now over, James had decided that he might as well sit back, relax and accept whatever destiny his fate might deliver to him. Accordingly he had seen nothing wrong in a little harmless mid-morning party with a few joints, some cocaine and a bottle of his father's good brandy.

"Come in," he shouted, endeavouring to make himself heard above the din of the record player. Letherby opened the door rather gingerly as if the handle might be booby-trapped.

"Ah," he said, reeling from the marijuana fumes. "Lord James. Good morning."

"Letherby? What the hell are you doing here?"

"Sorry. It's er, the Guvnor. Ready?"

"My father?" Letherby nodded. "Oh Christ. He's an hour early." James and Sunny both leapt to their feet at once and immediately tripped over each other and the *Timeform* Annuals. James swept the roaches and the ashtrays into a wastepaper basket and then rushed to open the window just as Sunny was lunging into the bedroom with the cocaine packets and the mirror. Suddenly there seemed to be a vast number of empty bottles on every chair, table and surface in the room. James was caught with two exhausted flagons of Bacardi in his hands just as his brother Rowland entered through the door.

"Oh, God," he said. "Not you too."

"Good morning, brother dear," said Rowland, who was now carrying both Jack Russells under his arms. "Father will be up directly. He's just stopped for a pee." Tripe started barking at the miserable Sunny until Rowland silenced him with a glare that said thumbscrews.

"Was that you making all that frightful row with those bloody dogs?" asked James indignantly.

"I'm surprised you could hear it, old boy. We could hear your jungle music at least a mile away."

"Piss off, Rowland."

"How's the studying going?" asked Rowland, surveying the *Timeform* Annuals. "Working hard?"

"I did the exam yesterday."

"My God. I bet your paper was a stinker."

"Fuck off. You pompous fart."

"Indolence has not improved your language I see."

"Fatuous arsehole."

"I've killed men for less than that. Irishmen. Peasants mostly. Men without the benefit of your general background and education." Rowland was getting serious. As if to emphasise the severity of his feelings he now had his legs planted firmly apart and his jaw was beginning to jut forward uncompromisingly. The effect was only spoiled by the presence of the two Jack Russells, one under each arm. It gave him the appearance of a somewhat ludicrous army officer sheriff quick on the draw and preparing to shoot it out at any moment but with terriers rather than six guns. "Now look here, James," he said. "You've always been an abject little squirt. You are now becoming a perfect disgrace to this family." Then one of the dogs bit him on the finger. Rowland howled. "You blasted hound."

"Well done, Tripe," said James.

"Be quiet the pair of you," spoke a firmly authoritative voice. The Duke had entered quietly behind Rowland and it was now his turn to survey the scene with dismay. "Mr Vengsarkar," he said charmingly. "Good morning."

"Good morning, sir," replied Sunny, shaking hands with his usual courtesy.

"I didn't realise you were reading classics," said the Duke, casting an amused if disparaging eye at the old form books on the floor.

"Ah," said James, uncomfortably aware of the empty bottles that were still in his hands. "We were just looking up the history of past winners of the Dewhurst Stakes. Seeing how many of them had gone on to success in the classics the following year."

"Quite so," said the Duke. "I'm sure all sporting activities are always more enjoyable after a hard morning's academic work."

"You're going to have to excuse me, James," said Sunny, shifting uncomfortably from one foot to the other. "I'm late already."

"Tutorial or lecture?" asked the Duke.

"Neither really. More a kind of lunch. I'm meeting the

proposed trainer of our new greyhound . . ." Sunny dwindled away hopelessly.

"*Our* new greyhound?" James looked ruined.

"Well . . . goodbye, sir." Sunny shook hands again politely and then slipped away gratefully through the door. The Duke sighed, walked slowly into the centre of the room and sniffed the air as he did so. There was something about the smell that reminded him of Miles De Berry though he couldn't quite think why.

"Well, father," said Rowland, who was still holding the dogs. "Shall I tie him down and thrash him for you? I'm sure I can get a birch sent over from the Monday Club."

The Duke sat down wearily in one of the large broad print sofas, unbuttoned his raincoat and handed his trilby to Letherby. "Rowland," he said, taking out a cigarette from the silver box in his inside jacket pocket. "Am I to understand that you have friends in this college?"

"Well . . . friends of friends."

"Then I suggest you take young Letherby away and introduce him. I wish to talk to James. Alone."

"Oh. Right. Right ho, father." Rowland was disappointed. He'd hoped to be a witness at a scene of delicious retribution. "Well come on, Leathers. If we can find Charlie Westmoreland . . . we can have a game of rugger in the library!" Poor Letherby, thought James.

After they'd gone there was an embarrassed silence that went on for several seconds. James tried to break the atmosphere with a touch of levity. "You really shouldn't have arrived early like that, father. Not unannounced. Most unsporting of you." The Duke said nothing. James tried again. "Would you care for a drink? I think I'm all out of sherry. But would a glass of champagne be alright?"

"Sit down, James." James hid the two empty bottles behind the curtain and then sat down reluctantly in the chair opposite the Duke's settee. Now they were literally face to face. "And take off those ridiculous dark glasses." James took them off. "Why?" asked the Duke.

James tried his best to look confused.

"Why what, father?"

"Your irresponsibility, boy, that's what. I spent yesterday morning with Bellingham at Coutts. The full dazzling scale of your indebtedness came as a new and devastating shock to me. Then I had lunch with my old friend Sam Jackley at William Hills. Your gambling bills could now pay many a deserving young man or woman's entire board and tuition fees at this university for at least three years." James looked down at the carpet. There was a long silence. "I have paid both debts, but this is the last time. The absolute . . . and very positive . . . last time. For God's sake, boy, do you want to be a published bankrupt before you're even twenty-one?" James was still looking at the carpet, "You must kick this gambling habit. You must. If you don't it'll destroy you."

"You didn't kick it, did you, father?"

"What do you mean?"

"When you were a young man you used to lose twenty thousand a night playing pontoon and bridge at your club. I remember the stories."

"Then take the advice of one who knows," said the Duke softly. "Gambling . . . will be your downfall. If you let it." James still wouldn't look at him. "Why do you keep doing it?" His voice had picked up again painfully. "For pity's sake, why?"

"The same reasons as you."

"The crack?" His son nodded. The Duke sighed. "I can understand that."

James lit a cigarette. His hand was shaking. "Gambling at a racetrack . . . and the atmosphere involved . . . cigar smoke, crushed grass, fizzing champagne, call it what you will . . . to me has a feeling of illicit pleasure. Of being disapproved of. Forbidden. Well, I adore that feeling. Turning the rules upside down, eh, father? Making each working day a holiday."

"But you don't do any work!"

"Maybe not. But I do love working on the horses.

Trying to figure out the endless permutations of fitness and form and jockeyship and weight. And then the stories and the information. The little snatches of racecourse gossip and rumour that build up and run like forest fires around the enclosures and the bars. And I love the adrenalin, father. I love the adrenalin that flows when I've got five hundred more than I can afford on a five to four on shot in the last race at Windsor on a Monday night. Alright . . . when I lose . . . and lose . . . and lose . . . I feel an utter mocked fool. But when I win . . . and the champagne and the hospitality's flowing . . . it doesn't matter that the rest of the day's been surrounded by frustration and depression and mundanity . . . because I feel magnificent! And the truth is, father . . . the pain I get from losing . . . is so much outweighed by the pleasure that I get when I win.''

The Duke looked distressed, angry and sympathetic all at the same time. "But James, James. You can't afford to lose. Ever. Not on this scale. Losses aren't only lent, you know. They have to be paid for. And if you can't pay for them I have to pay for them. And we are simply not that rich anymore as a family. If I'm to hand over the house, the estates and the business to you and Rowland in reasonably good shape then you simply must change your ways." He got up and walked over to the fireplace. A liberal profusion of James's invitations and club membership cards were on display along the mantelpiece. They included a disturbingly high number of sponsor's invitations to various hospitality tents and luncheon rooms at numerous nationwide racemeetings over the next few months.

"I can understand the attraction of horse racing," said the Duke. "What I cannot understand . . . or forgive . . . is the intolerably rude society that you seem determined to keep."

"Father! Some of the things you've heard . . . may be true. Some I can explain. And don't forget, things always sound worse than they really are. I can't be the first nineteen-year-old to want to . . . sow a few wild oats while I can. Can I?"

"Wild oats, James? You're sure they're not . . . Scots Porridge Oats?"

James frowned. "I'm lost, father."

"Lex Parlane?"

"There is nothing wrong with Lex. He's a friend."

"He's an ill-bred oik."

"Oh, come off it, father. Wrong age. Wrong generation."

"He is also a gangster, a crook and a spiv."

"No he's not."

"Oh yes he is."

"He is not! He's just successful, that's all. The other bookies resent that, father, and that's why they put around these stories to discredit him."

"James . . . Parlane has been involved in acts of violence, bribery and corruption. There is a file on his activities in at least three police forces in England and Scotland. He also has a file at the Jockey Club. Even now, investigators acting under the direct orders of Racecourse Security Services are keeping up the closest scrutiny of his affairs."

"Who?"

"No one you'd know."

"I might."

"They have a man in their London office. And another in the field. And they're both very good." James said nothing. The Duke came over, stood in front of his chair and looked down at him sadly. A tired and disappointed father. But a father nonetheless. "You've got to get shot of him, Jimmy. You must. Otherwise you cheapen our family name and reputation. My reputation. You are special. The second son of an English Duke. You can't just caper around the countryside like the straight man for some blasted Scots comedy act."

"I'll try not to let you down," said James with a sigh, his eyes still fixed on the opposite wall.

"You must. Everyone's still after me, you know. We may have turned down the volume slightly on your Scots friend but the press won't let go that easily. Yesterday I discovered that we've now even got some ghastly little guttersnipe of a provincial journalist on our backs as well. Up in Sheffield, I believe. Thinks he's found another incompetent local Steward up north somewhere. Redcar or Catterick or some such ghastly place." He shook his head sadly as if all Oxford was somehow a party to this conspiracy. "I'm either an incompetent buffoon the one minute or a wicked squire the next. I suppose you agree on both counts."

"No, father. I don't agree. I've always known how much you love racing. I've always known that."

"Let's have lunch," said the Duke. "You do have a jacket and tie?"

"Of course. Hadn't I better find Rowland and Letherby?"

"Bugger Rowland and Letherby."

After lunch James and the Duke took a walk together around Christchurch meadow. The afternoon was mild, damp and windy. The sunlight in the puddles on the piles of cowshit in the centre of the meadow reflected the predominantly russet and yellow colours of the oak and beech trees that grow along the path around the edge.

"I suppose you'd hoped to avoid this meeting," said the Duke.

"I wasn't really avoiding it. I knew it had to come."

"I've talked to Dr Carmichael. Your exam was first class. No problems about staying on from that quarter. He stressed to me repeatedly that Christchurch is not your enemy. Far from it."

"It's not that I don't enjoy the work. I just . . . can't quite see where it's leading to, that's all."

"An Oxford education always leads somewhere. Be it prison or the House of Lords. And sometimes it's a damn close run thing between the two of them." A large black student jogger half-paced effortlessly past the Duke, his tracksuit vermilion and white, his nose buried keenly in a manual on macrobiotic food. "Take advantage of what the university has to offer. Which is not Turf Account-ancy! Have you thought of politics?"

"I hate politicians. They're all smarmy unscrupulous creeps."

"What about the law?"

"Pedants and bores."

"Then what about philosophy or economics?"

"I know my limitations, father. Mind you. Philosophy has its attractions. The logical positivism of the racing analyst in endless competition with the phenomenological uncertainties of the equine mind."

"I presume there are some residual members of the human race for whom you don't feel total contempt?"

James nodded his head emphatically. "Vincent O'Brien."

"He'd done more serious work by the time he was your age than you'll probably achieve in a lifetime."

"I know, father. I'm a hopeless case. If only France didn't have an extradition treaty with England I'd prob-ably just rob a bank and spend the rest of my days propping up the Bar des Anglais at Longchamp race-course."

"No more witty foolishness please. You don't know how much it hurts me."

"I'm sorry." James paused, reached out an arm and touched the Duke gently on the shoulder. "I don't want to hurt you, father. Honestly." They had reached the river. There was the inevitable practising crew skulling heartily upstream. They had just passed a disused Salter's Steamer and were heading at speed towards the Folly Bridge. There was also a man on a bicycle with a megaphone, being chased by a loud dog. James, unathletic to the last, thought the scene looked cold and uninviting. His father was gazing down river past the boat houses and down towards the island and the weir.

"Of course . . . I was bad at your age too," said the Duke. "I remember myself . . . and Tom Rothschild . . . and Monkey Moore-Mainwaring. There were some days . . . and nights . . . that wouldn't bear talking of now." He paused. The rowing crew had stopped too, collapsed, momentarily exhausted over their oars. The man with the megaphone had dismounted from his bicycle and was now delivering some urgent verbal recuperation from the towpath. "Have you got a girl?" asked the Duke.

"No specific girlfriend at the moment. But I did meet this beautiful woman. Only last weekend. I hope she may come up and visit me soon."

"It's good to have a girl. You know the mess my life was in before I met Valerie." They walked on again and the Duke regaled James with splendid tales of the boat burnings and rowing club dinners of his Christchurch roaring boy youth of more than forty-five years before. "I do worry for racing though," said the Duke, as they turned left away from the Thames and carried on up along the footpath along the banks of the River Cherwell. "I worry and I worry and I wonder what the hell I can do about it."

"But it's been a terrific flat season, father. And a marvellously high standard among the three-year-olds."

"Yes, but how many of them are we likely to see next season as four-year-olds? Answer? Bugger all. And what good's that going to be for the breed?" The Duke was off and running. James was well acquainted with the general theme but now the willows and the horse chestnut trees and the little parties of strolling students and tourists were going to get their chance to share in its full import as well. "No wonder we've got so few really decent stallions in this country anymore. The modern owner-breeders are too bloody frightened or too unscrupulous to test their insanely expensive purchases fairly and squarely on the racecourse. And meanwhile this obsessive trend towards the American-bred beast means that the price of an even halfway decent yearling at any sale anywhere in Europe has now become ludicrous beyond belief. And that's beginning to squeeze the boys who really know and love their racing out of the sport altogether."

"But, father . . . surely the fact that nearly all the best of the American-bred horses are trained over here means something? The British racing public witness just about the finest sport anywhere in the world. The Jockey Club must approve of that, surely?"

"Witness it how often? For two-and-a-half minutes round Epsom Downs maybe. But not tried and tested over three seasons of full and rigorous competition. There's nothing sporting about it, Jimmy. These modern boys are shysters."

"Then perhaps it's time for you to change, father. Take them on . . . and beat them at their own game."

The Duke sighed. "Maybe you're right. Though it won't be me who'll do it." He was standing at the edge of the bank flicking the fallen leaves with his foot and examining the little self-operating ferry that connects the Christchurch meadow side of the river with the grounds of St Hilda's and the school playing field beyond the trees. A class of boys and their games masters were engaged in a rugby practice on the playing field. Shrill cries of 'break' and fierce exhortations from the line-out and the scrum punctured the still, damp and late afternoon air at regular intervals. James was thinking about the rugby match and the rowers and the joggers and the walking and bicycling students, their heads filled with serious and sensible thoughts about essay first pages and PPE reading lists and nine o'clock lectures on Hayek and Keynes. And he suddenly wished that if only for his father's sake he could look and act more like one of the team. A paid-up member of the club with his blazer and tie and his subscription and his pewter beer mug that he could put over the mantelpiece of his Oxford college room emblazoned with the inscription: "I am a serious and sensible fellow. I wish to lead a serious and sensible life. I am not a gambler and a wastrel and I am certainly not a drug fiend."

"I dread to think what Rowland will make of being Duke," said the Duke. "He'll probably spend half his time dashing round London nightclubs making a silly ass of himself. And the rest of the year he'll be delivering eccentric nasty speeches to eccentric Tory pressure groups at ghastly Tory dinners. But you. You could do it."

"Do what, father?"

"Take on the shysters and beat them at their own game. If you really loved racing enough you could do it. You know I must make a plan for that place we've got down in Wiltshire. The one near Lockeridge. It's been empty for years. But it's a house. Complete with its own stables. And . . ." he paused significantly, ". . . a whole set of private gallops on the downs. Not so far from your old school."

"I never knew that," said James.

"Beautiful place. It's just been sitting there and going to seed ever since my father died. Seems a shame really. You follow?"

"I don't know what to say."

"Don't say anything now. But think about it. We'll talk again another day."

There were sudden cries of elation from beyond the river. A winning try had been scored and waves of buoyant schoolboyish enthusiasm seemed to ripple out across the pitch, reaching the trees and the bank and the water's edge.

"Get an education first though, Jimmy," said the Duke. "No Scotsmen. And no more betting either. Have a life, of course, by all means. But sensibly."

Sensibly? thought James. How the hell do I do that?

17

The Duke hated winter. He loved June and July. He loved that pleasant early morning feeling when you knew that it was going to be a hot day. On days like that he liked to be out on the gallops before seven watching his horses at exercise. Everything felt fresh and bright and new as if you could start things all over again. Even at the age of sixty-five the Duke always felt that he still had a lot of chances on July mornings. But he hated winter.

Around the end of October he started to shut his eyes and pinch himself and hope and pretend that the winter wasn't coming. If there was a sudden still and mild October afternoon he'd cling on to it with all the nostalgic urgency of a terminally ill man. But in the end November always did come. Suddenly, unreasonably and bleakly grey and miserable. And with the first week of November came the last week of the flat racing season. The last overblown fields of confused and bewildered looking two-year-old maidens blundered round Doncaster racecourse in the frost and dark. The bookmakers set off a few fireworks under their more overdrawn and overplayed clients and icicles started forming on the course commentator's binoculars as he sat alone in his box on the grandstand roof. And then with Cheltenham's Mackeson Gold Cup meeting the jumpers finally moved into the centre of the stage. And as if on cue the Duke – who hated National Hunt Racing and always had – left with his mistress for the first of his several winter holidays in the Caribbean.

Others liked the jumping game. Indeed for the first few weeks of the new season many of the public seemed to adore it and prefer it to the flat, probably because the spectacle was still fresh and invigorating. There were those up and down the country and over in Ireland who were particularly excited about their prospects for the coming months. The plans they'd formulated that autumn gradually took practical shape and the proceeds were steady, unimpeded and most gratifying. The general public, of course, had little idea of the extent to which cynical corruption was beginning to affect the loose ends and tattered edges of their sport. That was because of the care and cunning that Bolger, Garvin, Kinane and Maguire all used in choosing which races to fix, which favourites to stop and which jockey to bribe.

Five racing days out of six Garvin's riding was straight up, ruthless and quite brilliant. By Christmas time there was hardly a week that had gone by without him winning one of the big sponsored steeplechases or hurdle races that are such a regular feature of the National Hunt programme. And then on Boxing Day at Kempton he conjured up a brilliant driving finish from a six-year-old New Zealand-bred gelding with a previously suspect temperament to land the group one King George VI Chase, the only other non-handicap three-mile chase in the calendar to compete in terms of prestige with the Cheltenham Gold Cup. Making up more than fifteen lengths on the leading trio inside the last half-mile, Garvin's positioning at the fences was quite superb.

The King George was in fact the third leg of a treble for Garvin and a great many popular bets were piled on to him to complete his winning streak. The cheers rang out for hours afterwards and as flushed and inebriated punters were fished out from behind the Christmas tree and the grand piano in Kempton's champagne bar, it seemed clear to everyone who'd been there that if this year's big race winner was a real new star in the making, Michael Garvin was the brightest star to be seen in the jockeys' firmament for many a long year.

After racing Mickey Bolger drove them both back down

to the country in Garvin's shiningly new blue BMW.
Bolger owned a modern luxury split-level farmhouse on
the downs near Blewbury and Garvin was his guest for the
week. Garvin looked smug and pleased with himself after
his successful afternoon's work. What was he most looking forward to now? asked Bolger. Over the next few
days? The brace of pheasants in the boot, said Garvin.
The pheasants were a Boxing Day present from Lex
Parlane who'd enjoyed a good morning's shooting at an
Arab-owned estate down in Wiltshire before driving at
one hundred miles per hour up the motorway to Sunbury-
on-Thames for the races.

The following day Garvin went down to Chepstow to
ride the antepost favourite in the Welsh Grand National.
The horse never held a better position than nineteenth in
a field of twenty-three and was pulled up halfway through
the second circuit. Garvin was interviewed by the Stewards afterwards and reported that the horse seemed
distressed and it was his opinion that it couldn't act on the
left-handed track. Mickey Bolger had a good laugh about
that when he read the story in *The Sporting Life* the
following morning.

At the next Haydock meeting in January Garvin rode a
smart young novice chaser called Kill The Blues in a
conditions steeplechase run over two miles. Kill The Blues
had won his two previous races run over two-and-a-half
miles at Kempton and Newbury respectively and it
seemed clear to most observers that his principal asset was
his stamina. But instead of making plenty of use of him
around Haydock's flat galloping track Garvin seemed to
ride him for speed. He had ten lengths to make up on the
leader at the second last fence but was still only beaten by
a length at the line. The general unsaddling enclosure
verdict was that Garvin had just been teaching the horse
how to settle and come from behind. One man was less
convinced.

Graham Mould was a middle-aged racing correspondent on a Sheffield evening paper. He was always coming

up with some new investigative coup on racing's inside villainy. He'd recently drawn himself to the attention of the Duke by touting around some story he'd heard in the bars near Malton about a corrupt and incompetent local stipendiary. Up at Redcar or Catterick Bridge or some such outpost of Siberia, as the Duke would have called it. Well, after the Haydock meeting Mould went home and studied a video of the Kill The Blues race with great care and he also studied a film of the big two-mile handicap hurdle run at Sandown in December, in which Garvin had come late on a well-supported second favourite and just failed to make the frame after being badly baulked on the turn into the home straight. It was Mould's conclusion, which his paper printed in full, that a certain leading Yorkshire-born rider was beginning to write his own form book. With what end in view? he asked. No one took Mould too seriously at the time.

But Mould took himself and his findings seriously enough to write to Racecourse Security Services and the Jockey Club. The RSS official who met him informally in a pub off Portman Square dismissed his ideas as absolute nonsense. The silly complaints of an ignorant punter talking through his pocket. Mould formed the opinion that the Racecourse Security man was trying to steer him away from the whole idea of a Michael Garvin story. Only he wasn't going to be put off that easily. He was the scourge of the corrupt and the weak. And if he couldn't get Garvin he'd get somebody else. Mould's tenacity was to have serious consequences for one or two people.

By the New Year Lex Parlane was firmly established in his St George's Hill mansion and at his new headquarters base of operations in Esher, Surrey. The news, open knowledge for some time now to the élite, of the sale of his Scottish shops and office business to Docherty and Maclean for an undisclosed sum (believed to be at least seven figures) officially broke in November. Any thought, though, that his new involvement in the sports video and entertainment business might lessen his competitive pull against his rivals was quickly dampened by the announcement that he was moving straight into Tattersalls on the southern circuit and not up by the whelks and mussels stall either. At all three United Racecourses tracks for example – Kempton, Sandown and Epsom – he'd be right there by the members rails along with Berners, Rubin, Ted Bassett and all the rest of his old friends and admirers.

Lex wasn't bothered about his Southern rivals. He wasn't that bothered about the story James Richmond had told him in October either. About the Duke and Racecourse Security Services and their special file on his activities. Good luck to them, was his view. He wasn't going to be afraid of ex-traffic cops and elderly private detectives with experience in divorce work. He was fast like a fox. They were clods.

He did think about the Smith brothers, though. He had to find out whether they were acting alone or whether Michael Bolger or even Louis Weiss had been behind the attack at the Bella Vista. Once he knew the position he would act accordingly. Having first lulled his enemies into a state of false relaxation he'd then take them out. That was his way. But he wasn't going to let them spoil the pleasure that he was getting in playing with his new toy.

He'd been keeping a cottage in the grounds of his Weybridge property for over a year. The day that he officially moved into the newly converted main house – formerly known as Timberlane but now re-christened by Lex as Rancho Diablo – was commemorated by a huge photo call for the national press. This was set up by McQueen and carefully stage-managed by Bella and Billy Two Hats.

Lex and Bella together were seen either working, kissing, relaxing or just supervising the removal men in every one of the mansion's ritzily comfortable and expansively renovated rooms. Decorating and design correspondents noted Lex and Bella's every taste in wallpaper, curtains and fittings and some genteel eyebrows were raised on discovering that the turquoise and light blue carpeting of the ground floor rooms was matched by an extensive area of astroturfing in a similar hue which ran from the swimming pool and summer house to the covered verandah and raised Spanish patio beyond.

From this new Surrey hideout Lex made frequent phone calls to young Richmond in Oxford and he was always leaving messages, tips and general information in the Christchurch porter's lodge. He also made several visits to the college in person, mostly to play cards with the latest gaggle of innocent young rich boys that James had managed to assemble for the occasion. He always took James out to lunch or dinner on these occasions, often to the same restaurant that the boy usually visited with his father. Only one of these 'paternal' visits succeeded in causing Richmond any real anxiety and that was in the first week of the Hilary term when a visit from his real father was scheduled for the Wednesday lunchtime following an all-night Lex poker-and-cocaine session which had started out at teatime the previous day. Richmond struggled badly in his attempts to communicate intelligently with the Duke, who generously put it down to the effects of severe scholastic exhaustion.

In truth he had made a very good start to his second undergraduate year. He had an excellent Michaelmas term working steadily and hard and the results were good enough to improve dramatically his reputation with his college tutors. He started to be invited out to their houses in North Oxford for lunch on Sundays and even to college and university dining clubs patronised by dons and other students hitherto unknown to him. In spite of his familiarity with large chauvinistic gatherings in racecourse bars he was easily bored by the restrictively hearty atmosphere of most all-male dining societies and often ended up snorting vast quantities of cocaine both before and during the meal, thus leaving most of his food uneaten while running high-speed rings around many of his more conventional fellow diners whose own sensual pleasures had to wait until a little ritual crockery smashing at the end of the evening.

James still kept up with Camilla. In spite of her dalliance with Lex and with his Bella he couldn't quite resist her. Especially as she was so often around and available. He didn't really respect her, which was no doubt sociologically unsound, but he did desire her. It had something to do with her blonde hair and her pout and her suspendered and gymslipped public schoolgirl image. One night, under Lex's influence, he took her to a charity boxing gala in Shoreditch town hall. Camilla simply adored it. She adored the boxers' muscular bodies and the gangsters in the audience and she kept informing everybody she met very loudly that she wasn't wearing knickers.

But at night and in his dreams James was still haunted by images of the beautiful and experienced Bella. By her brown eyes and hair, her big hips and breasts and her wonderful Rita Hayworth legs. Not that there seemed much likelihood of him ever holding her in his arms again. Camilla had been pretty summarily ejected from Lex's life after her performance at the Wild West Evening and Bella had continued living with him ever since. Living with him, sometimes indeed managing the social side of his life as he'd asked her to and sleeping with him regularly and very happily.

But then one weekend in January James's fantasies came true.

Lex had gone up to Scotland on business and Bella came up to Oxford to visit him for the evening. They drank a lot of whisky and talked a lot and smoked a lot of dope. James charmed Bella with endless stories and jokes that were easier to tell and make good without Lex around. They were meant to go out to dinner and then on to a party in a night club but dinner and the party came and went while they carried on drinking and talking in his rooms. Finally at half-past one in the morning they took the mattress off the single bed and the cushions off the sofa and chairs and lay down on them in front of the fire and made love there rapturously for hours.

The following day they did eventually wander off through the freezing mid-winter fog to some overpriced local restaurant where James attempted to guess Bella's weight in champagne bottles while treating them both lavishly on his brother's gold American Express card which he'd had the good sense to steal on a New Year weekend visit to Dereham Hall. And then at the end of that afternoon Bella got into her car and drove off back to her life with Lex Parlane. In Weybridge.

And Richmond was left on his own once again. For how long this time he just didn't know.

He decided to hang on to Rowland's credit card and even used it to pay off some of his gambling bills – the ones his father didn't know about – and at least in his father's eyes he succeeded in keeping his gambling within reasonable bounds. By a combination of good judgement, moderate luck and judicious borrowing from like-minded friends he was able to maintain regular afternoon visits to various betting offices in the city while also still enjoying his regular all-action Saturdays with Lex at Cheltenham and Newbury, Sandown and Ascot and the rest.

Christmas and January over, Richmond could barely conceal his excitement about the coming March's National Hunt Festival at Cheltenham, now just the length of one Oxford term away. It was at the previous year's meeting that he'd first met Lex Parlane. It had been Champion Hurdle day and he'd caught a train up to Cheltenham from Oxford, changing at Reading. The train arrived late and the town was already clogged with innumerable traffic jams, all of which were made fifty times worse by the driving rain and sleet which was predictably falling on all sides. James got into a taxi with three Londoners, each of them complaining so loudly and miserably about the weather, the town, the racing and life that the eighteen-year-old was forced to enquire why on earth they'd ever bothered to come up there in the first place.

The cab driver eventually escaped from the traffic jams but was then baulked by a red light. Another man suddenly opened the right-hand side rear door of the taxi and jumped in, squeezing his way on to the back seat. He was large. Fat even. Black hat, black suit, black shades and a smart, dark blue belted trenchcoat in a style that was both Marseilles and Chicago. The Londoners didn't recognise the man immediately and they were all indignant.

"They keep complaining," said James to the newcomer. "They don't know why they're here."

"They're here because they're mugs like the rest of us," said the man. "Because they know this is the best three days' racing in the business and because they're dumb enough to think they can win at it. They'd be better off at Sedgefield."

The Londoners recognised him then alright. James too was aware of his nationwide fame and reputation. When he saw that he was smoking a fat cigar and carrying what seemed to be a large Gladstone bag he almost wanted to cry out for joy. Lex laid the Londoners bets in the car on the racing, the angle the rain was falling at and the distance between the lamp posts on the Cheltenham streets. By the time they got to the racecourse two of the Londoners had already lost nearly seven hundred and fifty pounds between them.

The Scotsman seemed to take an instant liking to the young aristocrat, slipping him in discreetly through a private gateway and refusing to accept either cash or a cheque by way of repayment. About ten minutes later, just when he'd expected to be walking around in the rain down below looking for a lager and a cheese sandwich, James found himself sitting in a private luncheon box high up in the grandstand tucking into asparagus soup, boeuf bourgignon and good claret while all-action highlights of past Champion Hurdles played away on the television set in the corner. The forty-eight hours that followed turned into one long orgiastic adventure of gambling, racing, eating, drinking and general excess. James missed the Wednesday night celebrations over Lex's coup in the four-mile National Hunt Chase – the coup on which Goldline had only just paid him even now – because he passed out comatose about two hours beforehand, full to the brim with brandy, vodka and the best champagne. He recovered sufficiently to back the winner of the Gold Cup the following afternoon but was then spirited away up to Glasgow in Lex's private plane for another week of high-flying action at casinos and racetracks on both sides of the border.

He did hesitate briefly before joining Lex's plane at Staverton airport. He could see where it would lead and he was already way out of his depth financially. He had a meeting to go to with his tutors at Christchurch on the Friday morning and a lunch with his father and brother in London on the Monday. But somehow some voice inside of him seemed to keep saying that this could be a decisive moment in his callow young life. The beginning of God-knows-what maybe, but he just knew emphatically that he had to be there. Sharing, consuming and submitting to this extraordinary man's company. The previous three days had been as intoxicating and enjoyable as any benzedrine or cocaine and James was convinced that if he backed down now with excuses and apologies pleading prior commitments, family and work, he'd never see Lex Par-lane again.

He finally got back to Oxford ten days later, after a journey that had taken him via Kelso, Newcastle, St Cloud and Belmont Park, New York. Over the following six months this pattern was repeated many times over, leading in the end to that solemn confrontation with his father at Christchurch in October. And now, with the first anniversary of 'Lexland' only weeks away, James supposed he ought somehow to find the confidence and courage to ward off the Scotsman's wilder plans for celebration and excess. All of them certain to involve – in spite of Lex's legendary reputation for generosity – levels of expenditure astronomically beyond the young man's own legitimate means, especially considering the new budgetary and behavioural restrictions that he was now meant to be operating under.

James had to look ahead too. He'd latterly decided that it might well be worth his while to try and get a decent degree in year three. Could he really sustain any kind of academic effort with Lex at his side, albeit clandestinely, on almost every racing weekend (and weekday too in vacations) throughout the year? Should he think of starting to sever the knot between them now? If he did do well in his finals it might enable him to wangle some kind of benevolent scholarship or grant to some foreign university shore for a year or two. He'd seen Oxford and Cheltenham. And Glasgow. Why not Sidney, Berlin or Santa Monica in a few years time? His weakness shamed him really because he knew that even if he could find the strength of character and personality to stand up to the Scot he wasn't even all that sure that he actually wanted to. And he certainly couldn't bear the idea of missing out on the racing. He'd been thinking about it and dreaming about it and planning for it ever since the last exhausted runner had passed the post in the Cathcart Challenge Steeplechase, now nearly eleven long and hectic months ago. And then there were his antepost investments to consider. Why not just let things slide on forward in their own sweet way and at their own sweet pace? After all, that was what he usually did.

18

Cashel Maguire was having a good winter. No one was better able to disentangle the complex threads of the Irish form book than he. What to many people was an inexplicable fog of unpredictability, perversity and sheer devilment was to Maguire a perfectly decipherable pattern of fitness, readiness, plausibility and 'the knack'. The knack of having just the right four-legged lop-eared friend laid out and waiting for just the right Fairyhouse conditions hurdle race after just the appropriate amount of overnight rain on the suitably misty and Celtic December afternoon. It of course helped that Maguire and his old Clongowes Wood schoolfriend and business partner Connor Delaney, who now trained a thirty-seven horse string just outside Bowlerstown in County Westmeath, were on discreet but first name terms with almost every other National Hunt trainer and jockey in the Republic. As the steady rain that lubricates all Irish steeplechasing fell in incessant droves from October onwards, Maguire made the rounds from Clonmel to Gowran and from Punchestown to Naas, generally applying to this hybrid but irresistible pattern the charm, expertise and intuition that he'd temporarily sold to Bolger and Kinane at their meeting in London at the Daytona Beach Club.

Information could always be prised out while collaboration was always rewarded and payment for services rendered prompt and generous. Maguire became so popular and so dependable amongst the circle of jockeys involved in the ring that they even nicknamed him 'The Tax Rebate Man'. No one in Ireland's racing community really questioned his style or choice of occupation. Amongst his own people his idle brilliance was as well known and as accepted as Lex's flamboyant bravura up in Glasgow. With his tight curly hair and his plump baby-faced good looks he in fact seemed less than his age, which was in reality a good ten years older than his English counterpart James Richmond. Like Richmond his father was a turf aristocrat. Anglo-Irish, a past Steward and a celebrated former skier and pre-war performer on the Cresta Run. Just as young Richmond had many of the potential qualities to become a philandering racecourse swindler, it would have surprised no one meeting them for the first time to discover that it was in fact Maguire, not James, who was the son of a racing Duke.

On Wessels Champion Hurdle day at Leopardstown – an extremely valuable and competitive card – Maguire had to use all his charm and good chappery to look after Michael Garvin, who was over from England for four well-fancied rides. The large modern racetrack at Foxrock on the outskirts of Dublin was packed to capacity with a passionate, vibrant crowd, all of them eager to see many of their home country's most fancied contenders for Cheltenham prizes taking their last public exercise on Irish soil before embarking for the British mainland in three weeks time. It was an extremely cold but dry, clear and sunny day and the going was soft. In the big race itself Garvin rode Shecky Dancer, an attractive looking and improving young five-year-old. A French-bred ex-flat racer who'd won four times on the trot the previous autumn but was as yet untried in the highest class. Garvin dropped Shecky Dancer out at the rear of the field for the first half-mile. Then making rapid headway down the far side he came to challenge in third place as the runners swung left-handed into the straight. He jumped the last flight in the lead and, showing considerable powers of acceleration on the run in, had five lengths to spare at the line. He was receiving weight from all of his older and more experienced rivals and some judges were disinclined to value the form that highly. The race, they said, was run to suit him. At Cheltenham it would be different. At Cheltenham Galtee O'Flynn, the reigning Champion Hurdler and runner-up here, would be meeting Shecky Dancer at level weights and over a course that was much more to his liking than Leopardstown. Nonetheless, Garvin could look forward to his jockey's guaranteed percentage of the winning prize money along with the handsome 'present' that the grateful Birmingham-based owner-trainer-cum-scrap-metal-dealer would be sure to heap on him afterwards. Then, unhappily, the Stewards intervened.

Shecky Dancer, they said, had interfered with the third horse Kilmonaghan on making his challenge going into the last. Whether or not the result was affected Garvin, they claimed, had been guilty of reckless riding and failing to keep his mount on a straight line. Consequently they disqualified Shecky Dancer and placed him only third, moving the novice Kilmonaghan up to second and making Galtee O'Flynn the new and rather fortunate winner. Garvin was given an automatic seven-day suspension.

He was furious. "What do they fucking well think this is?' he said, spitting abuse at Maguire as they stood outside the weighing room door. "The fucking Sussex Stakes? This is jump racing. I pissed on them." He started slagging off his whole afternoon in Ireland. He'd had two losing rides already, he was on a rotten jumper in the fourth race and he didn't know why he'd fucking well bothered to come over there in the first place.

Before the next race, the Arkle Perpetual Challenge Trophy for two-mile novice chasers, Maguire hurried down to the rails to speak to Johnny Kinane. He found him next to the famous Ulsterman, Willie McGrory, the two men positively surrounded by compulsive and fiercely opinionated punters. The volume of betting that takes place at a big Irish Saturday afternoon race meeting like Leopardstown can equal even Cheltenham or Aintree during the Festival weeks. Kinane and McGrory were dispensing their tickets and repartee with all the verve and speed of wide boy market traders moving their goods in haste from the back of a fairground lorry.

Maguire took Kinane on one side for a private word. Garvin's mount in the Arkle was a young horse called Deep Fidelity, a six-year-old Deep Run gelding of exceptional promise who happened to be trained by Connor Delaney. Deep Fidelity, who had fallen when in the lead at the second last flight in the previous year's Waterford Crystal Supreme Novices Hurdle at Cheltenham, was becoming an extremely exasperating horse to follow. In the words of his trainer he had tons of ability but kept on ruining his chances in novice chases through slack jumping. Nonetheless his talking horse status coupled with the stable's general punting reputation guaranteed him favouritism for this particular two-and-a-quarter mile contest. His only real rival in a field of ten seemed to be an honest sort of animal called The Buckaroo, three times a winner that winter but trained over in County Kerry by one of the Irish sport's lesser jumping lights. The Buckaroo was to be ridden by Jayo Donnelly, a real journeyman of a jockey sure to make the running and sure to give his horse every chance to make stamina and sound jumping count over breeding and superior speed. The outcome of Maguire and Kinane's quick consultation was that Deep Fidelity should lose the Arkle Trophy in favour of The Buckaroo. Maguire informed Garvin of their decision while they were standing in the middle of the paddock. Garvin said nothing.

As the horses were being led out on to the track Maguire popped up at Jayo's elbow. "Kick on today, Jayo old boy," said Maguire, smiling. "The favourite's yellow in a fight."

"Is that the truth now?" said Jayo, his red face beaming in the frosty afternoon light.

"It is so. But we haven't got the heart to tell the patriots."

"Well, mine'll go all day," said Jayo happily as he broke away from the lad and cantered off boldly past the stands on his way down to the start. In the race itself both Jayo and Garvin were seen at their best in their own very different ways. Jayo, unknowing and honourable, went on from the start at a cracking gallop and was never headed. Garvin positioned Deep Fidelity just behind another dodgy jumper in the field and at three crucial fences down the far side was mildly but significantly interfered with when that horse screwed to its right on landing. He was also carried slightly wide coming into the straight and still had five lengths to make up on Jayo at the last. His report after the race was that he'd deliberately spared his horse further punishment on the run-in in order to conserve its energies for Cheltenham but that with a clearer round he'd definitely have won.

Kinane and Maguire who had each laid the horse in certain quarters both won a substantial amount of money on the race.

Half an hour later Garvin redeemed himself with the Irish crowd and punters by giving a masterful and completely unprejudiced ride to the other rotten jumper of the afternoon, Bob Beeches, in the Harold Clark Leopardstown Chase. Bob Beeches was a novice up against seasoned handicappers but this time Garvin kept him well-clear of trouble all the way. He was hard pressed by at least three challengers throughout the last half-mile but, summoning up all his qualities of horsemanship, strength and finesse, he just got Bob Beeches home in a pulsatingly whipcracking finish. Everyone agreed that nobody else could possibly have won the race on such a chancy and inexperienced fencer and that the confidence Garvin imparted to his mounts was almost telepathic. And as at Kempton on Boxing Day the champagne corks were still popping and the toasts and plaudits still ringing out around the Leopardstown bars until well into evening drinking hours.

On racedays like this Kinane threw open the doors of his beautiful Palladian mansion in the centre of Phoenix Park and held open house for the evening. He stocked up the bar, got in a firm of caterers and even installed roulette, poker and blackjack games in the various rooms of the house, thus giving everyone present the maximum number of opportunities to win back their losses of the afternoon. Most of the guests were his bigger league clients and friends. Discreet and powerful men with no use for the legal niceties of the betting tax. Kinane was a good host too and usually the drink would be flowing and the cards still turning until well into the following morning.

That night Michael Garvin was the centre of attention, exchanging drinks and conversation with many of the Dublin racing world's leading social lights. Fortunately for them he was in a relatively mellow mood and able to dip into his slim reservoir of charm and recount lurid tales about English racing trainers and their wives. He gave them all tips for the coming month and advised them that his anticipated Gold Cup mount had not been out of its box for over a week. Then he gave autographs for their children while they called for more champagne.

After about an hour Maguire drove Garvin into the centre of the city, up O'Connell Street and out along the Lower Drumcondra Road towards the airport. No money changed hands between them then. That always came later.

"Better see Donnelly's happy," said Garvin as he strolled relaxedly towards security. "Never does us any harm."

"I'll fix Jayo," said Maguire.

There was no racing scheduled for anywhere in Ireland on the following Monday. Just after eleven-thirty on a mild and misty February morning Maguire picked Jayo Donnelly up from the Maddenstown stable and gallops where he'd been riding work and drove him into Dublin for a slap-up lunch. At least that's what he offered him. Maguire suggested Snaffles, Locks or Le Coq Hardi but Jayo Donnelly turned them all down in favour of the thronged tables and homelier atmosphere of Bewley's

Easy Money 183

Oriental Tea Rooms, the steaming-and-stained-glass old tea and coffee emporium on Grafton Street. While Jayo ate his welsh rarebit and his steak and kidney pie in rich gravy and his plate of iced buns with cherries on the top, Maguire sat rather self-consciously over a liver and bacon with onions and looked up his list of future engagements in his Curzon House Club Diary. From time to time he looked around him bemused but amusedly at the old ladies and the young student lovers and at the sprightly ravenous priests keeping their hats on the little wooden hat racks beneath the generations-old plain-back chairs, and then he looked back at Jayo. Big hands, big ears and mouth full.

"This country," he thought to himself. "I could be President of the Republic if only I had a mind to."

A large number of English racing correspondents had come over to Leopardstown that Saturday. Most of them were so drunk by the time the big race came around that they couldn't have told you if they were in Leopardstown, Ireland, or Leopard Rock, Arkansas. Nonetheless, in the days that followed they all dutifully filed their copy listing the supposed Irish 'bankers' that they'd spotted on their high-level scouting mission to the Republic. Most of them overlooked the fact that the horses they named were all the most obvious selections, already well known to the general public and more often than not exactly the kind of horses that don't win at Cheltenham. They also forgot that there are certain wily Irish jockeys and trainers who, after the appropriate amounts of Guinness, Paddy and bubbling champagne, will tip an Englishman almost anything. Including donkeys, dogs and a quick heave into the Liffey.

One man who did complete the trip in a more sober state of mind was Sheffield's Graham Mould. Mould was still smarting from Racecourse Security Services' refusal to take his original Michael Garvin story seriously. This time, still zealous and scoop-hungry, his tiny envious eyes spotted Cashel Maguire ferrying Garvin about all afternoon between the Leopardstown weighing room and the

paddock. Later on he trailed them both back to the party
in Phoenix Park. He stopped his car behind a clump of
rhododendrons, crouched down on the ground behind the
boot and surveyed the scene through a pair of miniature
binoculars. He looked for all the world like a Western spy
peering at a Russian safe house across a stretch of Finnish
no man's land.

At one point he aroused the attention of a party of
returning cross country runners from the fourteenth St
Deirdre and St Kilda's brownie pack who were on their
way back home to Ashtown at the time. One young girl, a
bright young spark, was bold enough to ask him who he
was. "Hey kid," replied Mould, trying to sound like Clint
Eastwood. "Go fuck a duck."

Mould's surveillance concluded at nearby Phoenix Park
racecourse. The bars were open for an evening disco and
for a sizeable cash consideration. Mould managed to
persuade one of the younger drinks waiters to tell him
exactly whose house he'd been watching, what they were
likely to have been up to and just how often those
gentlemen were in the habit of meeting there.

Now anyone who'd ever set foot on a racecourse more
than a dozen or so times or opened up the pages of a
Sporting Life with any regularity would know that Cashel
Maguire was a very big punter. Mould, though, was
determined to have his story and with the jockey *and* the
professional gambler now being discovered in the company of a big rails bookmaker at what amounted to an
unofficial and decidedly illegal gaming party in a Dublin
house he was convinced that he'd found it.

Mould liked racing on the whole. He was even known
to have a bet . . . now and again. His Yorkshire-born
English sub-editor, though – precisely the kind of
bearded, Socialist *Guardian* reader that the Duke and
Washy would've most despised – had a severe view of all
sporting activities, especially racing. He regarded it as a
supreme capitalist conspiracy designed to keep the workers of South Yorkshire in permanent thrall to their feudal

employers. His stark view may have been influenced by
his only known visit to an actual racetrack. In 1982 he'd
attended the Doncaster St Leger meeting in the company
of a Rotherham Miners Outing. He'd drunk more than he
should've done and enjoyed it and he'd shared a swing-
boat at the funfair with an Amazonian miner's wife from
Hemsworth. His day had been ruined though by the
extremely tight-fitting pair of brown Doctor Marten walking shoes that he'd mistakenly purchased from a Barnsley
men's outfitter that morning. From that day onwards
whenever Graham Mould had hurried in to his office with
a piece of scurrilous racing copy he'd seized on it gratefully with the battlecry, "Let us publish and be damned!"

On the Friday after Leopardstown the Sheffield evening
newspaper published a lengthy if generalised article by
Mould associating Michael Garvin with Cashel Maguire
and an as yet unnamed Irish bookie. The article implied
that whatever the Yorkshire jockey's past technical in-
fringements of the rules of racing, his new involvement
with a well known professional gambler could hardly be a
matter of comfort to the Jockey Club, the supposed
guardians of racing's image. The article ended on a
typically unctuous note. "We merely wish to draw Mr
Garvin's attention to the potential embarrassment that
Maguire's interest in him may cause," claimed Mould.
"Rumour-mongers and sensation-seekers always dog the
footsteps of every great sportsman. We at the *Dispatch*
would not wish Mr Garvin to go down in their wake."

Two days after the Sheffield story was printed extracts
of it appeared in the *Sporting Life*. Mould once again took
his tale to Racecourse Security Services but once again
was disappointed. This time he was interviewed in the
lunch room at Kempton races by Rocco Anderson of RSS
and Christopher Cowdray-Clarke, a suave Steward with a
black eyepatch.

Anderson, a Scotsman and former CID Chief Superin-
tendant, was the new strong man in the RSS offices at
Portman Square. Granite-grey and uncompromising he

spoke first, playing the traditionally bluff and no-nonsense
policeman's role. Where was the hard evidence? he asked
Mould. And how would they make it stick? Newspaper
allegations were worthless without proof. And Mould's
only proof was what he thought he'd seen through the
window of a private house while playing at peeping tom in
the road. That and the drunken reminiscences of some
teenage bar boy from the bogs. He couldn't expect them
to take that seriously? That was bollocks. That was a dog's
dinner. And he, Rocco Anderson – Master Mason, Rota-
rian and formerly of the Glasgow Flying Squad – was only
interested in fact. Hard fact.

Then it was Cowdray-Clarke's turn and he took a
predictably more emollient line. The Jockey Club, he
said, were hardly ignorant of jockeys having punters but
as long as they didn't flaunt the situation too obviously
why make a stink? He also pointed out that Garvin, in his
capacity as retained jockey for Captain Roddy Hyde-
Lyne, rode horses for many of the wealthiest and most
prominent members of the Club and Turf aristocracy from
the Royal Family downwards. "You don't expect us to stir
up a hornet's nest there, do you?" he asked. "Not without
real evidence at least."

Mould stamped away afterwards, livid as ever and still
determined to flush out turf corruption wherever he could
find it, including, he decided, "those bungling clubmen at
the top". For if he couldn't catch the Michael Garvins of
the racing world then he'd have to catch the incompetent
officials instead. And he might begin by trying to hunt out
the identity of that corrupt Steward that he'd heard so
much rumour of up in Yorkshire and the North-East. "So
you can stick that on your wind-up gramophone," he
shouted, as he saw the Duke's Bentley glide into the
Kempton car park. "And you know where you can shove
it too."

The Duke and Washy looked on in bewilderment. They
had never met Mould before in their lives. He was a
complete stranger to them. And yet there was something

about his suede zip-up cardigan, his cheap panatella and the way that he effortlessly crashed the gears on his elderly Morris Marina that declared him to them immediately as a racing journalist of the more popular sort.

"Another bloody scribbler," muttered the Duke. "I'd just like to see them ride."

19

Michael Garvin had been warned by his friends in the newspaper world of just what to expect from the Mould article. All the same he was not pleased. Frost and ice had descended on England at the end of February, causing a sudden enforced hold up in the racing programme. For Garvin the break was not a welcome one. Although a part of his great skill as a jockey lay in the extent to which he didn't relish falling off a heavyweight racehorse at forty miles per hour any more often than he needed to, he was a man who had to be kept busy. His mind needed constant thoughts of earnings, profit and investment. Of races to run and races to stitch up. Forced idleness compelled him into acting the role of the traditional country squire at his beautifully situated Georgian manor house just outside the North Yorkshire village of Lastingham. He liked the house. It was his principal symbol of success and he had all the trappings to go with it. But he still found his part a difficult one to sustain for more than one day at a time. Let alone a week.

That morning he and his girlfriend Ingrid had been flicking through the new releases catalogue from their local video dealer for more than an hour. It was still sitting there now on the antique occasional table, clear felt-tip marks in black and red next to *The Bicycle Thieves* and *How to Steal a Million*.

Next to the catalogue were the appropriate copies of the *Sheffield Post Dispatch* and *The Sporting Life*. Garvin looked out of the window. The artificial lake was now all frozen over with ice. He could see the jetty and the bird sanctuary and the grey stone roof of the sixteenth-century dairy in the corner of the summer garden. Then he looked round at his living room. He looked up at the venerable polished oak beam that spanned the ceiling above his head and he looked down at the elegant sage green carpet on the floor. He looked at the cases of Waterford Crystal arrayed along the tops of the polished oak sideboards, at the elegantly faded print on his vast nineteenth-century sofa and at the copies of *Country Life* and the *Shooting Times* sitting neatly around the inglenook fireplace next to the log basket and the two svelte and sleepy looking golden retrievers who were basking contentedly by the heat of the fire. Then he looked back at the newspapers. At Mould's story and at the article on it in *The Sporting Life*. These papers had no place in his sly, well-ordered world, he thought. Their grubby newsprint reminded him of all the ugly things that he'd had to do in order to achieve it. He'd come a long way from the farm worker's prefabricated council house on a pre-war estate near Catterick. And from evenings bottle washing at a Crest Motor Hotel on the M1 in order to supplement his meagre weekly earnings as a teenage stable lad. Garvin was known endlessly to re-run a race in his head if ever he thought that he'd unintentionally given a mount a bad ride. But this was one journey that he didn't intend to retrace. Not ever.

Just then Ingrid came in from the bedroom. Ingrid was a blonde. Blue-eyed, sexy and dumb. Her name may have held out a promise of Oslo and Copenhagen but her voice was all Walsall and Wolverhampton. She'd only recently finished reading a story in *Honey* about an American model and film star being endlessly plagued by nasty cameramen and assorted lewd representatives of the popular press. Consequently the Mould story had started her worrying and in her resulting paranoia she'd been frantically searching through their bathroom and bedroom expecting to find bugs, listening devices and reporters for the *News of the World* awaiting her under her every

Rackhams chaircushion, bath towel and floral print pil-
lowcase.

"You can never be too sure with the press, Michael,"
she said, taking out a light bulb and examining it minutely.
"You just don't understand who you're dealing with.
They're vipers. They've got no morals. They'll stop at
nothing."

"Nobody's been in here except you, me and those two
dogs," said Garvin impatiently. "And there are no bugs
around this house except what we catch off them. This
place is burglar-proof. Pristine, clean and virginal. I've got
the security firm's certificate to prove it. The 'Steal Safe
Guarantee Bond' from Middlesborough. They're the best
security firm in the north-east." Then the telephone rang.
Garvin picked it up quickly. It was Lex Parlane.

"Alright, Mr Scotland," said Garvin. "You've read the
funny pages. From now on I want better insurance. Cash
and otherwise."

"Just hold on one minute, son," said Lex, cool but
businesslike on the other end of the line. "Just what were
you up to in Ireland? Sounds like a Mickey Mouse job to
me."

"It wasn't my idea," said Garvin. "Kinane and
Maguire. They suggested it."

"Not Bolger?"

"They didn't say nowt about him."

"I talked to Bolger the day before you went," said Lex.
"He never mentioned anything for you. Not at Leopardstown."

"Have you talked to him since?"

"He's away on business."

"Yeah. Well, Mickey doesn't always tell, does he? But
you can tell him this from me. I want more protection and
better quality. Otherwise you can forget about this year's
Cheltenham. And Aintree too. Did you hear me?"

"Leave it with me for now," said Lex calmly. "I'll get
back to you. By the way . . . if Haydock's on this weekend

do you want anything on that Devon-trained thing you're riding in the four-year-old hurdle?"

"It's not ready."

"The Lambourn boys seem to fancy theirs." Lex paused. "Quite a bit."

"You can put me down for a monkey."

"You're on." Lex called off abruptly. Half an hour later the doorbell rang. Garvin sent Ingrid into the bedroom and then got up and answered it. It was Michael Bolger.

"You're late," said Garvin.

Bolger grinned. He was dressed up in a pair of shiny black leather riding boots and tight white jodhpurs and his expensive-looking suede and sheepskin jacket was nestling over a finely knit navy blue polo neck jersey. "I thought I'd dress up," said Bolger cheerfully. This is all the rage down my way. It seemed appropriate round here too. A spot of horsey chat on the open road."

"You great waszock," said Garvin. "The gallops are all frozen. We'll walk."

Garvin led the way back down the slippery grey-tile front garden path and out along the lane that led towards the moors. He'd paused to put on a thick green husky, a flat tweed cap and a pair of dark green mud-bespattered wellington boots. He looked confident, purposeful and warm and in spite of his spots like some typical country gentleman conducting a brisk mid-morning perusal of his Saturday coverts. The presence of the upstart by his side seemed to make his image more convincing than usually seemed possible. They passed Bolger's smart red Jaguar which he'd parked rather precipitously on a frost-encrusted bank by the side of a grey stone wall. Bolger looked in enviously at the cosy leather upholstery in chocolate and beige.

After about ten minutes Garvin turned left up a track that led through a narrow gully between a field of kale on one side and a ploughed field on the other. The grass along the side of the track glistened silvery and white and the great clumps of earth in the field were rock solid. At the top of the gully there was a clump of trees and beyond that a flock of freezing sheep and some stone remains from a neolithic barrow. Away to the south you could see clear across the Vale of Pickering to Malton and the Vale of York. To the west were the Hambleton Hills and beyond them the Pennines. To the east was the North Sea.

Garvin dropped down quickly between a row of gorse bushes and down a narrow sheep track into the bottom of another smaller valley. They were in a natural bowl. A bowl of sheep, stone and silence and silver-and-white frosted downland grass. A private secret place unbeknown to the outside world.

Garvin stood foursquare at the bottom of the coomb and waited for Bolger to catch up. Bolger was pink, shivering and badly out of breath.

"It's a good thing you didn't ride," said Garvin. "Your bum would've been sore for weeks."

"Oh fuck," said Bolger. "I've left my fags in the car."

"Listen," said Garvin, changing gear again smoothly. "I've got a plan for Cheltenham. Kenneally's horse. Some Idea."

"That's Renwick's mount surely?"

"He broke a leg yesterday. Slipped over on the ice outside the Malton Stable Lads Club. I've rung Kenneally. I told him I'd ride it at Newbury on Friday if the meeting's on."

"And then?"

"Everybody knows that twelve months ago Some Idea was the punt of the meeting. Aside from Tipperary Jester that is. They know Kenneally. They know that this time it'll go for the two-mile champion chase. I'll get the ride. The public will pile on. And you boys can lay it to the boards."

Bolger looked thoughtful. "It's a good sort. A class horse. I'd fear it normally."

"So?"

"So how will you explain it?"

"Easy. It's got a jumping weakness. It tends to drop its hind legs, especially on a left-handed track. Around Cheltenham the ground that would lose it could be decisive. I wouldn't back it. Even if I wasn't riding." He grinned.

"And yet it won on the track last year. Seems risky to me."

"I'm glad you've noticed. But then I thought that was the whole idea. Big risks for big rewards. Only just at the moment I seem to be running most of them. Like Graham Mould."

"Don't mind him."

"I do mind. But then I'm alright, Mickey. I could retire now and fuck the rest of you. So . . . if you want to keep doing the money I want better protection from rags like that and more of it."

"But we've always been careful. At Sandown and Lingfield it's totally foolproof."

"Fuck Sandown. Fuck Lingfield. Fuck England. I'm talking about this Irish business. That was sprung on me in the paddock. Two minutes before the race. It's not good. You want to keep a check on your blue-eyed boy."

"Kinane?"

"Maguire. He spoke to Kinane before the race and Kinane agreed. I don't know if Parlane was involved. He says he wasn't but I'm not that sure I believe him."

"I'm not sure I do either."

"Well if he's getting greedy you can tell him this . . . I want more money. And I want it now."

"I'll go out to Weybridge on Thursday."

"Do. Cut Lex out if you want. I don't like the bastard. He's only using us as long as it suits him anyway. Any fool can see that."

"So?"

"So . . . if you want . . . we can keep Some Idea to ourselves. You'll have to come through with the money, mind. Kinane knows. He was over at Kenneally's last night. It's up to you what you do with Maguire."

Bolger nodded. "Maguire thinks Lex has got a plan of his own. For Cheltenham. He's heard rumours of it over in Ireland. Most likely it's a hurdler. A novice. But he doesn't yet know which race."

Garvin's face darkened. "I can still deliver your payroll, big man. Just sort out my cover, that's all. No more Mould. Otherwise you can forget about Some Idea for a start off. And most like you can forget about me." Suddenly Garvin zipped his jacket up tightly right up to the neck and pulled the cap down over his eyes. "Come on," he said. "We've got to hurry." He turned briskly and started to walk off along the frozen track up the other side of the valley.

"Where are we going?" called Bolger.

"Lunch with the Captain at Great Cropton," came the reply. "He's got this latest kid over from America. The teenager. He met him out in Keeneland during the sales. They say he can ride a bit. You ought to feel a privileged guest."

"Can't we drive?"

"It's only a five-mile walk across the top."

"But I'm exhausted."

Garvin turned round and smirked at the temporarily wretched-looking gangster. "I tell you what, Mickey. There's an old gibbet on the top of the next hill. You can hang from the cross bar. Take the weight off your legs." He laughed loudly and carried on walking again towards the rim of the bowl. Self-possessed, self-centred and totally self-contained.

A shit like that could get banned from racing, thought Bolger. For life.

20

The café was in a lay-by overlooking the main York to Thirsk road. On one side of the café was a filling station. On the other side was a motel and caravan park. The field opposite had recently been occupied by a travelling circus. Now it was home to Yorkshire's first ever officially licensed snake farm.

The Duke picked up the two toasted cheese sandwiches. Washy had the tray with the cups of tea on it. The two men followed Rocco Anderson to a table in the window. The table was dirty in small incidental ways. Brown coffee stains, trickles of ash and white sugar, a Cellophane wrapper and rings on the tabletop from the last occupant's cup and saucer. A teenage boy was playing the pinball machine in one corner of the room. Two bikers were sitting drinking Cokes on stools at the counter and a bored-looking travelling salesman sat hunched over his steak and chips between the cigarette machine and the fire.   .

It was about half-past five in the afternoon and outside it looked cold and reddish blue in the waning light. Snow and grit from the frosted roads had been trodden into the cafè on the boots of the lorry drivers who parked their rigs outside. There was grit mingled with sugar under Washy's feet.

"I'm sorry about the surroundings, gentlemen," said Anderson. "It's just that you know how Garvin likes his luxuries. I wouldn't trust any hotel, restaurant or smart pub within fifteen square miles of Lastingham. He's got pals in them all. This place may be trash but at least it's anonymous."

"You don't have to apologise, Rocco," said the Duke. "I was on my way north. I had to stop somewhere. And this meeting's important." He sipped at his tea.

"And we've had to put up with far worse bivouacs than this one, eh, Johnny?" said Washy, tucking enthusiastically into his toasted cheese sandwich. "Remember our field days out in Palestine? Not to mention the Irish St Leger."

"A bit different to the West Indies I expect, sir," said Anderson politely.

"You're right there," said the Duke. "Antigua seems a year away already. Did you know that *The Times* and *The Sporting Life* are full of new season stable previews?"

"What's wrong with that?" asked Washy.

"What the hell's it got to do with the press? Running plans are confidential. The business of the owners and their trainer. Not common little scribblers in suits."

"They've got a job to do, Johnny."

"Job my arse. And of course most of the classic hopes seem to be American-breds anyway, as if you wouldn't know it." The Duke shook his head. "I'm going to need this trip up to Scotland. From the end of the month it's going to be hell on turf all over again."

"It already is," muttered Washy.

"Shall we get down to business?" suggested Anderson, his coffee untouched.

"Of course, Rocco," said the Duke. "Fire away."

"Well . . . we think we've managed to put Mould off Garvin at last. But we're worried that he might be tempted into some new general vendetta against officialdom instead."

"Really?"

"Aye. There's been a story going the rounds up north now for many a day." He paused. "About a Steward."

"I've heard the rumours," said the Duke.

"Anything in it?" asked Washy. It was hot in the café and he was beginning to sweat.

"We think not. Nothing worth stirring up any road."

"But now Mould might stir it up for us?"

"He might. Or it might keep him busy and off our backs."

"Let's hope he doesn't find anything," said the Duke.

"Whatever happens," said Anderson, "he mustn't be allowed to foul up this investigation."

"Absolutely," said the Duke. "And Garvin?"

"We've got enough on him now to throw away the key," said Anderson, smiling a wintry smile. "And I'm talking Tower of London."

"That's marvellous," said the Duke.

"As you know our man's made a great many tape recordings. They weren't easy to obtain either. Recorder in the coat pocket jobs. Tape machines sitting in a Kleenex box on the car dashboard, that sort of thing."

"Garvin's lawyer would protest their validity, surely?" objected Washy.

"Maybe. But when we do play them through to him . . . alone . . . in the privacy of our office . . . " he shook his head, "I think they'll be enough to get him out of the saddle. For keeps."

"Your man's done an excellent job, Rocco," said the Duke.

"For a crook," said Washy.

"Set a thief to catch a thief, Washy," said the Duke. "And we must keep him going until at least after Cheltenham."

"He thinks that there could be some fireworks on for the Festival," said Anderson. "Parlane may be in on it too."

"What we really need," said the Duke, "is to try and use Garvin . . . use your man, that is . . . to flush out Parlane's own ring and connections. To try and incriminate Parlane personally. And his henchmen." He suddenly pulled out a diary from his inside jacket pocket and flicked through the pages quickly. "March the twenty-third. Start of the flat. That's when we hit them. It's the perfect symbolic moment."

"Who else is involved?" asked Washy.

"We know a large number of Parlane's contacts and associates but the list seems to get longer each year. We shall be observing him carefully at the Festival meeting and noting any new faces."

"But who do you already know about?" asked Washy.

"Jack McQueen. Journalist."

"He's just a drunken loudmouth," said the Duke.

"Billy Mcphee. Rails man. He's hard. All the on course staff are involved."

Washy looked at the Duke. "And what about James?" he asked. The Duke looked at Rocco. Rocco looked down at the table.

"I'm fairly certain he's no longer involved," said the Duke. "I've spoken to him. I've kept a watch on him this winter . . . and I think he's had the sense to keep clear."

"I'm sure we all hope so, sir," said Rocco.

"Are we sure this is all really worth it?" asked Washy. "All this trouble. The cloak and dagger. The eventual public parade of racing's less savoury elements. Is it really worthwhile?"

"Of course it's worthwhile," said the Duke.

Rocco Anderson was interested. "You think it isn't, Colonel Cleveland?" he asked.

"These men . . . suppose they were boys from the city, or Arabs . . . out to pull off some gigantic stockmarket killing. In bloodstock. You might not like it. But you wouldn't be able to do a thing about it. Their activities would be entirely legal."

"So?"

"So they'd just be trying to make money from gambling. Just like Lex Parlane. Only in his case it's not through stallion syndication fees but through betting on the outcome of a race."

"A bent race."

"Bent maybe. But there have always been bent races. Just as there have always been gamblers. Racing's a natural magnet to men with money and ambition. And when you get those two combined, greed and human weakness always surface . . . in the end. It's the way of the world."

"An edifying philosophy."

"I just cannot see what makes Lex Parlane so much more reprehensible than your detested but legal commercial breeders. That's all."

"No different maybe," said Anderson. "No better either."

"Precisely," said the Duke. "And if I may say so, Washy, you've certainly changed your tune. I seem to remember a certain conversation in Newmarket last October when you described Parlane as the unacceptable face of racing."

"I did say that," agreed Washy. "But I like to think I can change my view according to the realities of the situation. I'm no ostrich."

"And neither am I," said the Duke with feeling. "But it is a part of my job to protect this sport as a sport. For all the decent owners, trainers, jockeys and lads as well as the betting shop public. Louis Weiss is right. We must guarantee them a clean game. If they smell a rat, if general cynicism becomes the order of the day, they'll desert in droves. No more levy and no more racing. In ten years time it'll be as unloved and as untrustworthy as Association Football."

"You're taking it too far, John," said Washy. "A little toleration never hurt anybody."

"You don't tolerate graft and corruption, Washy. You fight it. You destroy it before it destroys you."

"If upsetting the apple cart doesn't destroy you first."

"Oh yes, I know. I know there are other members of the Jockey Club who think like you. When Garvin wins on one of their horses he's their hero of the hour. When he loses, cheat or no cheat, they want him hung, drawn and quartered and his backside nailed up over Newmarket Town Hall. But our duty . . . yours, mine and Rocco's . . . is to find the straight line. And then stick to it. Keep your man on the job until Cheltenham, Rocco. Then we'll move."

"He'll want a lot when it's over, your Grace. You know what kind of man he is."

"He's been well catered for."

"Buying off a crook? Sounds pretty cynical to me."

"I repeat, Washy. Buying off a crook to catch the three or four or maybe even five much bigger crooks swimming in his shadow. And then when we've caught Lex Parlane we can take on the breeding industry."

"I think he may want more than just money, your Grace," said Anderson. "There could be some kind of physical danger involved too."

"You've been in touch with your old colleagues again?"

The RSS man nodded. "The Scottish police can only be of use to us as a long stop. Oh, they know the situation with the Smith Brothers. The Smiths have always been envious of the Lex Parlane Connection and seeing him move out and down south they've been trying to move in to the vacuum. And after what happened at the Bella Vista last October Lex is bound to retaliate eventually. But they'll never get anyone to testify against him. Not up in Glasgow."

"So?"

"So if our man ever gets rumbled he could be in for the same treatment. Like Willie Smith."

"Do as you see fit," said the Duke. "I trust your discretion completely."

"It's amazing really," said Washy, looking out of the window at the snake farm opposite. "How did anything so . . . repellent . . . ever get a public licence?"

"We gave a licence to Garvin," said the Duke. "And one to Lex Parlane."

21

It was a typically quiet and termtime afternoon, an early March afternoon along the prosperously coniferous Surrey–Berkshire borderlands. The private schoolboys were all busily cramming their Latin and Greek for their common entrance. The army cadets were poring over their copies of Fuller's *Decisive Battles of the Western World* and the lunatic murderers were all safely locked up in the Duke of Clarence memorial wards of their local mental hospitals.

And not many fellows were braving the golf links at St George's Hill, Weybridge, either. Although the snow had gone and the temperature was slowly rising again there was still a thick rime of frost clinging to the rough along the edges of the fairways and the usually trim and succulently emerald-coloured greens. The specks of silver and white along the hard pavements looked like the aftermath of a light and dusty snowfall and the white frost, reflecting the brightness of the winter sunshine, set up a hazy glare over the vista of pine trees and locked Volvos and Mercedes and locked-up garage doors and flickering two-way television screens at the top ends of long and silent rhododendron-lined drives.

Here there was a red brick with a white painted Regency porch. There a pink washed façade or a black beamed Tudor with a Lutyens-style three-chimney roof. The houses had names like Windy Ridge Farm, Wildewood, The Carriage Way and Majuba Hill Drive. And there just behind green number seven was the Weybridge Palace Hotel. Lex Parlane's Rancho Diablo. Modest Normandy twin towering mingling in with the massive red brick frontispiece with its Hollywood Gothic oak-panelled front door.

Anyone conducting a particularly close or minute scrutiny of the outer perimeters of Lex's estate would've discovered a few leftover tennis balls from summers gone by lingering lost and unattended to in the leafy ditch between the golf course and the formal, fourteen-foot-high thorn and privet hedge. As for the actual netting on the back garden tennis court, that too needed a little discreet attention. At the moment it was sagging badly like some tired and ageing old dowager bosom at a Torquay Palm Court dance. Other than the state of the tennis courts though, house, drive and gardens were all in perfect condition. There were no leaves in Lex's swimming pool for example. He had it regularly trawled and cleaned throughout the winter in spite of the ice.

Lex had a good view of the pool from the snugly heated sunroom at the rear end of the house. He could see that the astroturf's protective winter covering was still safely in place and from the occasional electrified yelp from the direction of the golf course he could tell that the protective security screen at the bottom of the garden, complete with guard dog warnings and an invisible trip wire, was doing its job as he'd intended it to.

Lex had been listening to *Woman's Hour* on Radio Four. It was not one of his normal after-lunch habits and indeed until McQueen intervened he'd had some difficulty in finding the correct tuning on the brand new quadrophonic music centre that was standing in the corner of the room. The reason for this sudden new enthusiasm was that Lex wanted to listen to himself being interviewed as the programme's main guest of the afternoon. The interview, recorded some two or three days previously, had mainly revolved around McQueen's piece of Lex hagiography, *Lex Parlane. The Making Of A Scottish Legend*, which had been in the bookshops since Christmas. And the Scotsman had, on the whole, been more than satisfied with what he'd heard. He felt that he'd come across nicely as just the right balance between cheekily lovable Scots chappie and shining credit to Weybridge, the south of England and the British economy in general. McQueen looked excessively pleased with himself afterwards, as if it had been his urging alone that had secured the *Woman's Hour* interview along with many other TV appearances besides. Lex was nearly moved to rebuke him for his presumption. But then he decided that he could afford to be magnanimous instead. His only real regret when he switched off the radio was that he'd now have to go back to listening and talking to his three lunchtime guests, Charles St Clair, Jonathan Pointdexter and Mike Delaney-Dalzell.

St Clair was in his late fifties. A suavely affluent Tory junker with houses in Byfleet and Walton-On-Thames. The way that he crinkled his eyes when he smiled patronisingly over the lunch table gave him a false and wholly undeserved impression of agreeably twinkling good humour. In fact he wore his man-of-the-world contempt for all members of the working and lower classes as casually and callously as an Austin Reed yachting club blazer swung over the shoulders on summer Saturday nights outside the Captain's Cabin Club in Runnymede.

As well as his crinkly eyes and his crinkly smile, St Clair had carroty red crinkly hair. And a small mouth filled with too many teeth. His prematurely sunken cheeks gave him the impression of a somewhat cadaverous Packer. A man in a silk-stocking mask. St Clair liked to call himself a 'money lender.' According to his secretary and his closest friends he ran a registered company in Bagshot specialising in 'business finance' and 'professional managerial consultancy'. Whoever he financed and whatever they consulted him about, St Clair spent most of his days at golf course, racetrack and club and he gambled heavily. Lex didn't dislike him for that. He had in fact offered him an account on the St George's Hill fairways only weeks after moving in. He'd spotted him as a hopeless losing punter from the very start and he was quite prepared to extend

him the most generous credit to lose and lose as much as
he liked. If Charles St Clair bankrupted himself with the
Lex Parlane Connection then Lex Parlane would weep no
tears. The only thing that was beginning to worry him was
just how much trouble he might have in eventually parting
the fool from his money. The cheque that was. For the
meantime St Clair had at least been useful in introducing
him to Jonathan Pointdexter. A man of altogether negligi-
ble interest in himself. Except, that, like James Richmond, Pointdexter had a father.

Sir Peter Pointdexter – Slick Pete to his friends – owned
supermarkets. A thrivingly efficient foodbroking and dis-
tribution combine with substantial hotel and catering
interests throughout Australia and the Far East. Not yet a
member of the Jockey Club but close to it, he also owned
a string of flat racehorses with respectably established
Lambourn trainers and this year his company were spon-
soring a new two hundred thousand pound race at Sandown Park on the first Saturday in July. Lex was going to
present the trophy to the winning owner in the unsaddling
enclosure afterwards. For the company the retention of
Lex was just one small but suitably public demonstration
of their go-ahead on-the-ball style in customer relations.
For Lex it was an important totem of his acceptance and
prestige. He would spend the day with Pointdexter senior
and the other directors in their Sandown company box.
Introductions would be made and invitations passed on.
Lex would be passed on. Further up the sphincter of horse
racing's tight little introverted social scale. But then that
had always been his choice. His principal aim and ambition. And for that singular privilege he was now prepared
to tolerate, at least temporarily, not only idiots like
Jonathan and slobs like Delaney-Dalzell but even a buffoon like Charles St Clair, a man with a whole set of
predictably extreme right-wing views on all traditionally
obsessional Conservative Party themes. Views with which
he regularly punctuated his conversation, albeit in a kind
of shorthand code or slang – 'Scargill', 'Blacks', 'Women

and CND' etc – as a kind of shibboleth or rallying cry for his party and his tribe.

As for Pointdexter he had a very high opinion of himself when it came to all matters relating to horseracing. Not that he was any trainer or owner or *Timeform* sage. He was just a fledgling stockbroker with the relatively newish city firm of Bluebell Investment Trusts. Delaney-Dalzell was much the same, only slightly older and richer. Another fattening and prematurely balding ex-public schoolboy he had the advantage of a recently acquired brewery inheritance to feed into the everspiralling over-drafts on his numerous bookmaking accounts. He also said less but swore more often.

As the clock moved on past half-past three DD's lips began to salivate and his cheeks began to glow scarlet and puce in the waning light. DD was getting drunk. So was Pointdexter. St Clair already was drunk. He'd arrived as usual with his own private and personal consignment of alcohol. Four bottles of respectable château-bottled claret which he claimed to carry with him for 'medicinal purposes' as his host's wine always made him drunker and more objectionable than his own. Or so he said. And then there was his much-vaunted reputation as a wine buff to consider. "You see, when you've been used to riding in a Rolls,". he once told Lex, "it's so frightfully difficult to step down into a Rover." In spite of his aversion to the cheaper motor he'd been making the best of his way home today with Lex's liqueurs and in particular with the vintage port, four bottles of which had been decanted ready on the sideboard and three of which were now empty.

"Come along, Lexie," St Clair shouted fraternally. "More porters!" Lex waved McQueen towards the side-board. The journalist lurched to his feet and returned perilously with the fourth decanter. Lex felt that McQueen was beginning to behave stupidly and that perhaps the excitement of Weybridge and the south of England was having a bad effect upon him. Too many

hospitality tents and wine-and-cheese parties. Today he
was playing a role that Lex had himself used on occasion
but just now was getting tired of. The argumentatively
class-conscious Clydesider entertaining three gullible Eng-
lishmen with hoary old tales of street fighting and football
violence from Glasgow's story book past. It was the sort of
thing that young Richmond would've lapped up with
cream and sugar, thought Lex with a smile.

"You can always tell a Glaswegian," McQueen was
saying, his half-Corona sawing romantically through the
air, ". . . from the cries of pain . . . and the clatter of
broken glass." Lex yawned and lit a cigar. Listening to
McQueen's dreary monologue and looking at his and St
Clair's heather mix tartan golfing slacks while regarding
the frost and cold outside his French windows, he reflected that he might just as easily have been in Langside
or Pollockshields as Surrey.

"Quite a character, your Jack," remarked Delaney-
Dalzell from beneath glazed and hooded eyes.

"Oh, he's a character alright," said Lex. "I should get
royalties from his every performance."

"And a notable fighter, I'll be bound," chortled
Jonathan Pointdexter.

Lex nodded. "He holds the Newbury press room record
for getting a drink in the champagne bar on Hennessy day.
Five seconds from doorway to glass. He only has to open
his mouth and they scatter."

McQueen scowled and belched into his port. "Fuck
you, soldier! And no offence to you, sir," he added,
doffing his glass at Pointdexter.

"Fine racecourse Newbury," called St Clair from the
other end of the table. "You meet a better class of
drunkard." He was going into one of his sniffing and
nose-curling routines over the edges of the decanter. He
took a sip of the port, swilling it noisily around his mouth
and gargling with it at the back of his throat.

"Swallow it, Charles," said Lex. "It's not Listerine." St
Clair gagged and then covered up his choking with a

manfully debonair grin and a connoisseur's nod of approval.

"Good brew, old boy," he said and shoved the decanter
up towards Lex's end of the table. The table was from
Maples. It had been polished and laminated a shining nut
brown and the decanter sped across the surface like a
bottle of rye on a Wyoming bar room counter. "Glad to
see they teach you something at these roughneck
schools." Lex was just thinking how he'd like to teach St
Clair how to float face down in a swimming pool with his
hands tied behind his back.

St Clair sat back in his chair with his hands in his
pockets and smiled his most unvulnerable and pleased-
with-himself smile. He looked as if three barrels of Devon
cream had just been poured down his throat through a
funnel. "Tell me something, bookmaker," he said. "What
makes you think that your jumped up self-made little ways
will ever make you acceptable in our neck of the woods?"

Lex glared back at him in silence.

"Ignore him, Lex," said Pointdexter who could see the
warning signs. "He's just trying to needle you."

"And if you know so much about racing," St Clair
continued, "what's going to win this year's Two Thousand
Guineas?"

"What do you think, Charles?" Lex asked quietly.

"Bloody obvious," said St Clair, his expression changing smoothly from smug grin to inscrutable ex-Lloyds
man's stare. "Shirley Grove. Royal trainer. Top-class
two-year-old form, including a victory over the course.
And a perfect classic pedigree to match."

"What do you think?" DD asked Lex.

"Well . . . other than the fact that he's bred to be a
stayer not a Guineas horse, that he doesn't accelerate at
the end of his races and that the owner's already decided
to run him in the Sandown Classic Trial and then the
Derby, I should think he's got a very good chance."

St Clair looked confused. He could see that Delaney-
Dalzell was beginning to smile and the smile enraged him.

"I'll back that horse for Newmarket at any price you care to name," he said, slamming his palm down hard on to the laminated Maples table top.

"You can have five hundred to one with me," said Lex. "How much shall I put you down for? Fifty grand? Oh, but I forgot. You don't carry cash. Do you, Charles?" Delaney-Dalzell roared with laughter.

"He's made a monkey out of you this time, Charlie," said Pointdexter.

"I didn't expect him to just sit there and quote *Time-form* at me, did I?" St Clair reached down on to the floor by his chairleg, hunting angrily for the last dregs of his private wine supply.

McQueen, who had himself finished off the bottle earlier, mistakenly imagined that he had an ally. "I don't think Charles deserves this . . ." he began.

"Shut up, Jack," said Lex. McQueen belched once again and shut up. "There's more coffee and cigars in the library. I'll join you all there in just a moment."

Lex walked alone up the hall towards his office. The house was silent and mainly empty. Most of the staff had been given the afternoon off and those that hadn't were resting in the kitchen.

Bella was away. Lex usually took such opportunities to slip in a dirty afternoon with Camilla at her Battersea flat. But to prevent her from getting too visible again he'd recently paid for her to take a prolonged winter holiday in the Bahamas. He'd needed time anyway. To work out his next move with Bolger and Kinane. And that kind of thing could only be done on your own. But in his heart he knew she'd be back. Sauntering into his bedroom one day at the most embarrassing moment. Hitching her skirt up enticingly and probably holding out an empty cheque book too with that oversexed schoolgirl's smile of hers that he found so irresistible.

Lex's gold telephones had been shipped down from Glasgow along with his cocktail cabinet and his Blooming-dale's desk. He dialled a London number. Twenty-odd miles away in Knightsbridge the phone purred softly in Michael Bolger's casino kitchen-cum-basement office. Bolger answered.

"Alright, Mickey," said Lex. "I've checked out Garvin's story. With Kinane. And Maguire. And it doesn't add up. I think he's getting just a little too crafty for his own good."

"He can't afford to lie to us," said Bolger. "The newspapers are getting beady."

"I know. But it's not Garvin's way to act discreet. The greater the pressure the more flagrant he becomes. I think he's got something up his sleeve for Cheltenham too. Something to embarrass us with. Would you know anything about that, Mickey?"

"No," said Bolger innocently.

"Well, you can keep chucking him money if you want. I'm not giving another cent to your scheme until after the Festival. There may be trouble heading my way too, so I've got to be careful. And Garvin's overpaid as it is. I may still comply with him over one or two one-to-one commissions once the weather thaws. But that's strictly private. We'll discuss the other thing in Cheltenham."

"I hear you've got something for the Festival, Lex," said Bolger. "Something Irish, shall we say? In one of the hurdles?" Lex was silent. "I hope you're going to share that one with us too?"

"We'll discuss it later at the agreed time."

"Lunch. The Queens Hotel. Monday, March the fourteenth."

"That's correct."

"I'm already looking forward to it." Bolger rang off.

Lex looked with pride around his smart new office. Some cuttings from one of that week's Glasgow papers were pinned to the Daylor boarding by the window. The cuttings described how two brothers, William and Robert Smith, had been found tarred and feathered in a private garage on a housing estate near Possil Park. They'd apparently been kidnapped from outside the door of their

Buchanan Street cocktail bar just after a lunchtime meeting with three film producer friends. Later that day the cocktail bar and two wine bars and a nouvelle cuisine restaurant they also owned in the city had been bombed out and badly damaged by fire. Glasgow police were unable to say whether the attacks marked an outbreak of local score-settling gang warfare or whether they were just another random intrusion of outside violence.

Lex nodded to himself with grim satisfaction. And Glasgow was miles better so they said? As far as he was concerned it was just another coat of paint. At least he was satisfied now that the Smiths had been acting alone. They may have used Goldline accounts to get their money down on coups of his that they'd wanted to spoil. But they hadn't been organised by them. Just trying to cash in on his own departure. And Lex was confident that Robert Smith's boast about faces in London storing up trouble for the future was nothing but a boast.

London! It was already getting almost as parochial as Glasgow. Full of lovable cockney wide boys with their sickening rhyming slang. All hoping to get a try out for a TV series.

At least Glasgow had a whiff of America. In many ways Glasgow today reminded Lex of Phoenix, Arizona. The same surface impression of thriving, upwardly mobile new money. But scrape a few inches beneath that surface and nothing much had changed. In Phoenix the cowboys now wore five-thousand-dollar Saks of Fifth Avenue executive suits along with their stetsons as they strolled in the sun up the main drag. But only a mile or so away from the Arizona Stock Exchange men were still strung up by their feet from a mesquite bush and cut with buffalo knives if they'd offended against the vested interests of powerful groups. And in Glasgow the story was just the same. Some of the kids may wear blonde streaks in their hair and drink raspberry chartreuse cocktails in brasseries on Sauchiehall Street but only a short night-time drive away the old methods could still gape at you suddenly down the bottom of a bad, black alley. And for Lex, a hard man who could exist equally successfully in both worlds, that knowledge was both a comfort and a practical advantage.

Now he had a sudden yearning to speak to James Richmond. He'd been trying to contact him for more than three days but all to no avail. Then he had an idea. He rang up the office of a betting shop he knew in the centre of Oxford and described the young man to the woman on the phone. A few moments later a surprised and somewhat embarrassed Richmond came on the line.

"Well, my son. How's it all going?"

"I'm alright. How did you know where to find me?"

"I just used my intuition. Backing dogs at Gosforth on a fog-bound Wednesday afternoon? That's desperate stuff."

"You know how it is."

"Indeed I do. Listen, son. I've got some really terrific plans for Cheltenham. Including a massive touch in the first race. Nobody else has even a clue what the fucking horse is yet. Though they're all sniffing."

"Er . . . about Cheltenham, Lex. I've provisionally booked a few hotels for us to choose from. They're all pretty expensive but I think they should be fun."

"Forget hotels. We're all staying at a friend of mine's place near Stow. A real country house. He used to be a restaurant owner and he's still a terrific cook. We shall want for nothing."

"That sounds wonderful."

"Don't you worry about a thing. All you have to do is be packed and ready a week on Sunday. I'll be there about eleven."

"I can't wait."

"Neither can I. This time it's going to be the big one, son." Then he put the phone down. He was just cutting out a line of cocaine on his desk when he glanced up to see McQueen standing in the doorway and looking at him accusingly. "What is it now, Jack?" asked Lex patiently.

"Don't ever put me down like that again. Not in front of other people. Because I won't take it."

"Listen, Jack. You can dance or cry or sing us a song or just do the fucking washing up if you want. But don't ever tell me what men like Charles St Clair do and do not deserve. Please."

They walked back down the hallway together. Lex paused at the entrance to the library. Delaney-Dalzell was asleep in a chair. Jonathan Pointdexter was trying to read a book about backgammon. And Charles St Clair was sitting with his feet up on the green leather chesterfield and giggling at a picture of Lex riding out with the Kildare Hounds. The whole scene reminded the Scotsman of some of the clichéd old sayings and homely maxims of Willie Provan, the friend and wise guardian of his youth and early days. "You can always get what you want in life," Willie had said. "Providing you're prepared to make the appropriate sacrifice. Only sooner or later . . . you end up wondering whether what you've got . . . is worth the sacrifice you had to make in order to get it."

The only trouble was that Lex had always regarded where he came from with a strict minimum of sentimentality. Except for his fellow bookmaker and brother Willie out in Brisbane his family were all dead or long since lost and ignored in strange foreign towns from Dumfries to Hamilton, Ontario. And any real vestige of authentic nostalgia for his native Glasgow, for Scotland and for his life and times as a fast boy by the Clyde was extremely hard to discern. His one remaining attachment to the land of his birth was as a setting in and scenario for the beginning of a story. His story. A much better than real life adventure too, but quite definitely only the first and shortest part.

Weybridge might well turn out to be a dog. Like Charles St Clair. But that could all change or be attended to. He could make use of them all. A right moment always came up. Then it was on to the next one. And whether triumphant, defeated or just temporarily becalmed, what counted the most was always to move on and move forward. Never to become trapped or hemmed in. Always to be smart.

There was in fact one piece of Glasgow history which Lex had retained in his mind and could still quote from at will. It was the words in the dedication on the statue of Lord Roberts, the crusty old Victorian general commemorated in Kelvingrove Park. "I seem to see the gleam in the near distance," it said, "of the weapons and accoutrements of this army of the future, this Citizen Army, the warder of these islands and the pledge of the peace and of the continued greatness of this Empire."

As an eleven-year-old boy Lex had been none too convinced about the continued greatness of the empire but he had liked the general sentiment. Not that he wanted to be a mere collectivist corporal or private either. He would be an aristocrat and general. And the future that he envisaged and the gleam that he could see was a gleam in the faces of others. Happy, excited, awed and amused by the dominant over-reaching personality of one man. The never ending, ever changing immortality of Alex John Parlane.

22

James Richmond was waiting on the corner of Oriel Square outside the back entrance to Christchurch College, Oxford. Under one arm he was holding a copy of every available Sunday newspaper that he'd been able to lay his hands on in the College JCR, all of them now turned open at their appropriate racing pages. An elderly-looking suitcase complete with faded old labels from Bridge of Orchy, Hendaye and Amelie Les Bains was waiting on the pavement by his side. On top of the suitcase was a pair of binoculars, a complete set of racing form books and a half-empty bottle of Fundador.

It was a dull, dry and bitterly cold day with a threat of snow in the flat, grey sky. The cold wind ripped down Merton Street and sliced along the walls of Oriel Square, burning Richmond's face and ears and numbing his rib cage. A small handful of tourists huddled close to the walls as they made their way quickly from the meadow to the High.

Richmond turned his coat collar up against the wind and lit another cigarette. Considering there was still a full week of the term left to run, a week of collections and internal college exams, his somewhat obviously conspir-atorial gestures allied to his overall appearance and de-meanour may not have done much to deter the suspicions of any watchful don or junior dean. It did however satisfy his own sense of the theatrical. And having looked forward to this moment for so long he was not going to let it be spoilt now by any nosey little library-bound scribe bent on a crackdown.

The blue Rolls glided into the square bang on the first

stroke of eleven. The car smelt of alcohol and perfume. Bella was in the front seat with Lex. James got into the back seat. Bella smiled and kissed him on the cheek. She looked dressed up, made up and powerful. A positive aura of sex and well-being. James looked up in the rear view mirror and saw that following behind them was the white Mercedes driven by Billy Two Hats and carrying Jack McQueen and Reema Donachie.

They stopped for lunch at the Bear in Woodstock. Fires glowed in the dining room and all the bars and Lex glowed with pride as he walked in through the dining room door with a woman on each arm. After lunch they stayed on for several hours in the comfortable lounge, lolling about in their lushly upholstered red velvet chairs and drinking large quantities of armagnac and port in front of a quietly fluttering fire. Bella made James's throat go dry and his heart beat faster every time she crossed and uncrossed her legs. She looked so confident, so warm and so perfectly, physically at ease with herself and her surroundings.

The car journey eventually continued in near darkness. All the way up the A40, through the steadily undulating Cotswold countryside, thoughts of Bella kept crowding into Richmond's mind, competing for his attention with all those form book details about horses and trainers and private information. Once she flicked up the skirt on her smart but severe looking brown tweed suit in order to scratch an itch on her upper thigh. Richmond looked at her knee and her thigh and he looked at her brown leather boots and at the outline of her large maternal bosom beneath her tight white shirt. And then he tried to go back to his horses. But instead of going differentials and weight allowances he could only see images of hips and red lips and thighs and big white breasts. So he tried reading the main news section of *The Sunday Times* instead. In the centre pages there was a detailed story about the shooting of two suspected IRA gunmen by the army in South Down. The story was entitled: "SAS. Did they kill the wrong man?" James was suddenly reminded of a con-

versation that he'd had with his father the previous
weekend. This incident had something to do with his
brother Rowland. Rowland! He'd be sure to be there over
the next few days. Gum boots, tweeds and a game fair
jacket. His official off-duty Cheltenham uniform with a
uniform set of attitudes to match. What a depressing
thought. But then James's father would be equally sure to
be there too.

The boy looked out of the window. They'd turned off
the main road and were driving down narrow country
lanes between dry stone walls. Occasional muffled villages
– Lower Swell, Guiting Power – slipped by in the darkness, the odd light shining in the local manor house or
pub. It was a clear night sky lit up by stars and a full moon
and Richmond could make out the outlines of numerous
old hunters, eventers and ageing point-to-pointers gazing
out quietly over their greystone walls and out at the
surrounding grey and black frostbound countryside. Richmond felt excited, slightly inebriated and generally well
disposed towards the world. In such a generous and
nostalgic mood he always liked to imagine that all of these
horses had some shared and psychic understanding of the
special events that were about to affect members of the
family up at Prestbury Park only ten miles or so away.
Perhaps some of them, nameless and silent old heads that
they were now, had themselves once galloped up that hill
to Cheltenham glory in the days when he was just a child.
He was interrupted from this happy and sentimental
reverie by Lex changing the cassette over on the car
stereo. Frank Sinatra singing with Count Basie was suddenly replaced by Percy Grainger's *In An English Country
Garden*. Lex looked round for approval, his features
twinkling with delight like some demented Master of
Ceremonies on a nationwide mystery coach tour.

"You . . . are ridiculous," said James, settling back
comfortably against his form books.

The car had dropped down into a dip between two
patches of dark and thick-looking woodland. Then all of a

sudden the Rolls swung off to the right through a pair of lodge gates and started to climb up a drive that went up a slight hill through some ornamental parkland planted with oaks and grazed by cows and sheep. At the top of the hill the drive carried on through a grove of saplings and then, just as it was about to join a farm track straight ahead, it dropped downhill quite sharply to the right behind a tall yew hedge, finally swinging round on itself and coming to a halt in a large gravel forecourt in front of a large and beautiful but somewhat sinister-looking old Jacobean house made only slightly less sinister by the lights glowing in the hall and front rooms. To Richmond, seeing the building for the first time, the tall chimneys and the dark stonework and the darkly mullioned windows had a definite aura of the Gunpowder Plot, of necromancy and conspiracy and of mad, murderous, Websterian Dukes with a tendency to lycanthropy and incest. He loved it.

The white Mercedes pulled into the gravel drive only a few seconds behind them. Dogs barked and car doors slammed and then the front door opened and out stepped Daisy. Daisy was a large-bottomed loud-voiced lady in her late fifties. In common with Lex's current girlfriend she had once been an actress. But unlike Bella her mainly theatrical career had revolved around the playing of horsey young *ingenue* roles with names like Binky and Bunty. Tinklingly Home Counties girls the lot of them, but still popular characters in the Hugh and Margaret Williams post-war era. And although her talents might have faded and her career long since changed, Daisy still retained her considerable powers of vocal projection and amplification.

"Lex darling," she cried, fending off the labradors. "You old reprobate." Lex clasped her fondly into his arms. She was clutching a large gin in one hand and a long and aromatic smelling cheroot in the other. Ash from the cheroot sprinkled liberally over Lex's coat collar while splashes of gin hit his shoe.

"Daisy," he cooed. "You know what I think about the

countryside. But seeing you at the end of my road makes any journey worthwhile."

"Aren't you a sweetheart? I know he doesn't mean a word," she added, to no one in particular, "but I still love him for it." She pinched Lex's cheek again affectionately and then swung her eyes round on to the rest of the company. "Bella! Don't you look marvellous."

"Hello, Daisy!" They hugged and kissed. "I've decided. To hell with these men and their racing. I want to hear all your gossip."

"You shall, my dear. You shall. And Reema too. Your hair, darling, looks redder than ever."

"Red for danger, Daisy."

"I know! And here's Billy and Jack. Such big strong men."

"Hello, Duchess."

"Daisy." They both hugged and kissed her on the cheek.

"Oh, gorgeous. And who is this divine looking young man? I want to know all about you." Richmond smiled and took off his dark glasses.

Lex introduced him. "Daisy De Moraville meet James Richmond."

"I'm looking forward to tomorrow night, Daisy," said James politely. "I hear you're a pretty mean hand with the cards."

"What?" she trilled. "Me mean? My dear. With these boys in your house you have to make up your own rules." Everybody laughed. Daisy's eyes seemed to pore over Richmond's body, savouring its every possibility with complete thoroughness. It made Bella feel quite jealous.

"Daisy?" asked Lex patiently. "Can we please go inside. I'm fucking freezing out here."

"But of course. Hugh's waiting in the sitting room with the booze. Ragged! Robin! Do as you're told, you ruffians." The two black labradors were sniffing up skirts. Wet nose, wet mouth, wet tongue. Responding to Daisy's kick they bounded on ahead and the whole party led by

Daisy trooped in through the smoky hall and turned left into an even smokier sitting room. It was a warm, friendly and companionable room. Too friendly for Webster, although there were still a few flickering shadows and dark corners where the lamp light wouldn't reach. Hugh was waiting by the fireplace. He was about forty-five. Still handsome in a seedy, long-haired sort of way. Delightful, charming and, whispered Lex into James's ear, totally ineffectual. Everyone introduced themselves or was introduced for a second time.

"Welcome. Welcome," cried Hugh, his instantly affable personality sliding very pleasantly over them all like some rather sleek lunchtime sherry. "Welcome to Harford and welcome to Festival week. I suppose, Lex, you've brought an entire wine merchant's down with you as usual? Not to mention half the contents of your local butcher's shop?" He turned to Richmond. "You know, he really does seem to think that not only does everybody else drink orange juice but that he's the only man in the country with an appetite."

"Hugh," said Lex. "You are a wet old fart and I love you." The two men hugged and kissed, quite as affectionately as Lex had hugged Daisy earlier.

Daisy was handing round double strength stirrup cup measures of brandy and port spiced with Jamaican rum.

"Here's to some cracking good sport," said Hugh.

"And an excellent binge," said Daisy.

"And confusion to the enemy," added Hugh.

"In some houses, Hugh," said Lex, "I am the enemy."

"You, Lex?" said Hugh tactfully. "Nonsense. You're just a benevolent old softie like me."

"Cheers!"

Glasses were raised and then drained and refilled and then drained once again and then Daisy started off on a full-length tour of the house, showing them all their bedrooms on the way. Lex went out into the kitchen with Hugh. Bella stayed in the sitting room to roll a joint. James stayed with her.

"Hugh and Daisy," said Bella smiling. "Another detachment of Lex's nationwide repertory company of loyal friends and supporters."

"Principal supporting players by the look of it."

"They have a certain style. You either love it or loathe it."

"I like it. Very much." He was standing behind Bella's chair and he could hear Lex in the kitchen. He put his arms around Bella's shoulders. Bella made no acknowledgement.

"Hugh used to run a restaurant in the Cumbrian borders. Daisy owned it but Hugh did the cooking. Lex was in the habit of making frequent late night visits there. Mainly whenever he claimed that Scottish catering standards were going through another abysmal low. Which in Lex's case was pretty regularly. Hugh and Daisy have been friends since Hugh's Dorchester days. She taught him everything he knows about 'the finest of nuances of sauce making and the hotel and catering trade!'" She tore off a piece from an empty cigarette box twisted it round into a roach and slipped it into the end of her marijuana cigarette. "They only moved down to Gloucestershire last year. At the behest of Hugh's cousin. Some bankrupt old foxhunting peer with three divorces, a string of broken vertebrae and a permanently draughty old seventeenth-century house near Broadway. He's paying Hugh and Daisy a great deal of borrowed money to turn it into a discreetly expensive country house hotel."

"How sensible of him."

"The restaurant's already open. I think we're going there tomorrow night."

"Excellent."

Bella had twisted the paper round on the end of the joint and now she put it into her mouth provocatively. "Light me," she said. James found a lighter in his jacket pocket. When Bella handed him the joint a moment or so later he inhaled on it so deeply that it made his eyes water.

He leaned forward and slipped his hands down the inside of Bella's shirt cupping one breast in each hand. He kissed the back of her head, breathing in the smell of her perfume and hair spray. She turned round suddenly and kissed him passionately on the back of the neck. Then she broke away. A sudden gust of cold air shuddered down the chimney and blew more smoke out into the room. "I think Daisy's taken quite a shine to you," said Bella. James smiled. "You'd better watch out. She's a hard woman to hounds."

"Does she mind this?"

"They've got three plants in the conservatory."

"But of course."

"Let's go into the kitchen."

As they crossed the hall they both could hear Reema's voice ringing out ecstatically from an upper landing. "Oh, Daisy. This house is so wonderful. I want to move in now!"

The kitchen was large and furnished with style. More run-down sitting room than fitted pine. Lex and Hugh were running a professional eye over the contents of some delicious-smelling saucepans that were sitting on top of the Aga. "I thought I'd do that old Elizabethan thing with the partridge," Hugh was saying. "The ginger and plum sauce business with the stuffed red cabbage and the bacon." The bookmaker nodded his approval.

"But you must remember," he added, "not to overdo the ginger in the sauce."

Food again, thought Richmond. Where on earth would he be without a sumptuously rich dinner to look forward to each evening? And where would Lex Parlane be for that matter? It was remarkable really just how naturally and easily the Scotsman seemed to blend in to these faded but elegant surroundings. Just as naturally and easily as if he'd been in any Glaswegian bar, betting shop or Tandoori restaurant on Sauchiehall Street. Aga. Gun dogs. Wellington boots. A couple of battered old velvety sofas. Some priceless old Persian rug up one end of the muddy

kitchen floor. And a sixteen-stone Scottish bookmaker
with dark glasses and a fedora.

James went upstairs. His bedroom was on the far side of
the house, overlooking the park. There was a dark, open
stone fireplace with a fire burning in the grate. There were
dark black smudges on the stone over the fire and the
cream-painted walls were stained a kind of sepia brown in
places from years of accumulated smoke and soot. There
was a heavy mahogany dressing table and chest of drawers
and a vast old Victorian armoire which appeared to have
once belonged to a railway hotel in Perth. A lamp had
been switched on by the bed. There were books on the
bedside table and a few paintings and the odd photograph
on the walls. A pre-war racing yacht. Some stallions in
repose. Next to the stallions were a few stuffed fish in a
glass case and a picture of a 1938 shooting party lunching
on an estate up in Fife. The carpet was pale green and
there were floor-length darker green velvet curtains at the
window. James liked the room and he liked the house too.
He decided that he liked it a lot better than a city flat in
Fulham for example. It had a kind of worn, relaxing
charm that had always been slightly missing at his own
family home up in Suffolk. That had been partly due to
the echoing size and chilliness of all the rooms. And partly
caused by the people who lived in them.

James opened the window, stuck his head out and
breathed in the fresh, cold country air. He heard a fox
bark in some distant brake or spinney. Richmond adored
the countryside and he craved the exhilarating, wide open
spaces of Cheltenham racecourse. He'd already decided
that this week was going to be different from the usual
run-of-the-mill Saturday. He wasn't going to let Lex keep
him squashed up in some dreary little Members' bar for
three days on end gazing out at the underpass and the
catering trolleys while drinking bottle after bottle of
grossly overpriced champagne until it might just as well
have been horse piss. This time it would be special. The
beginning and the end of each afternoon. That was the

right and appropriate time for eating and drinking. Victories would of course be celebrated but the rest of the day was to be for the serious business of racing. And what racing! That was why he didn't want it reduced in status to the same level as some dreary little four-year-old hurdle race at Kempton on a wet February afternoon.

He flopped down on to the double bed. It was high and firm and very comfortable with a heavy bedspread and crisp, clean white pillowcases and sheets. He lay there for a moment enjoying the smell of the woodsmoke and the feel of the clean sheets on his hand and cheek. He loved the sense of touch. A Romeo and Juliet cigar rolled between the fingers. Bella's black silk underwear. Clean sheets. The soft and velvety coat of a musclebound racehorse.

He picked up one of the books on the bedside table. *The Three Hostages* by John Buchan. He looked at it for a moment then put it down again and took out the green bound *Chaseform Notebook* from his jacket pocket. He started to read. "Naas. Saturday January the 28th. The Celbridge Handicap Hurdle." Five minutes later Bella came into the room. She'd taken off her boots and stockings and she was holding what was left of James's bottle of Fundador in her right hand. "I'm just reading some form," said James. "I'll be down soon." Bella smiled at him. She kicked the door shut with her foot and turned the lock. Then she walked across the room towards him, got up on top of the bed and stood over him, one strong and classy leg on either side of his waist. She'd pulled her skirt up around her waist and she had a deliciously firm and determined look in her eyes. With one swift gesture she sat down across Richmond's lap, plucked the *Chaseform Notebook* out of his hands and threw it contemptuously across the room. Then she started unbuttoning his trousers.

When James came downstairs again about an hour later most of the others had gone off to play snooker and

billiards with Daisy at the opposite end of the house. Lex
was sitting on his own in the hall. He was reading the
Sunday paper and for once not simply the sporting pages
either. He was also cutting out a trail of white powder on
the hall table.

"Do you want a line?" he asked quietly.

Richmond hesitated for a moment. He felt self-
conscious.

"Er . . . might this not be . . . quite the right place or
time?"

"What for?"

"I was just thinking about Daisy and Hugh. They might
be embarrassed."

"Embarrassed?"

"I mean, I know they smoke dope . . ."

"So?"

"Might they not be quite ready? For cocaine?"

"Who gives a fuck?"

"Well, all I meant was. . ."

"You don't mind accepting a nice fat joint from big fat
Bella? Eh? But not a nice little toot from your old pal
Lexie? Is that the way it goes now?"

"No. That's not the way it goes. I just. . ."

"Seen that?" asked Lex, ignoring his explanation. He
was pointing out a headline in the paper. James looked at
the page. It was another story about the SAS possibly
shooting the wrong man in Northern Ireland. Only this
time there was a picture and a story opposite about his
brother Rowland. He'd been caught off duty and in
evening dress coming out of a night club in Chelsea. A
bedraggled young Countess was kneeling on the pavement
by his side and Rowland was pouring champagne down
her back with great disdain.

"My brother," said James with a sigh.

"I bet the Micks love him," said Lex.

James shook his head. "He's completely mad, you
know. I dread to think what he gets up to out there."

"Well, I wouldn't mention it this week if I were you. At

least not out loud or in any racecourse bar."

"He's bound to be there. I just hope we can avoid him, that's all."

"Everyone who's anyone in racing comes to Cheltenham in Gold Cup week. Trailing a great deal of dross in their wake too."

"You are taking care, I presume?"

"What do you mean?"

"Well, you remember that conversation that we had last autumn? About RSS and the Jockey Club file?" Lex looked back at him impassively. "Well, you've said it yourself. They're all bound to be there this week. Including my father. And if you try anything smart . . . they'll bury you."

Lex smiled. "Now you listen to me, Jimmy. In about four weeks from now you and I are going to be sitting on some foreign beach and soaking up that hot Mediterranean sun. Whistling up the Easter breezes in the company of expatriate bank robbers and flower girls from the native south. All thanks to the profits we're going to make over the next three days. And that's when poor old RSS are going to wake up to discover that the shooting season's over and all they've got to show for it are a couple of turkeys and one big fat Steward's arse. And in a day or so's time you'll appreciate the full import of that last remark."

In the silence that followed both men could make out the sound of Daisy's voice sailing back towards them from the billiard room. She was talking about jockeys. "I don't really hate the little short-arsed bastards," she was saying. "It's just that they're all so mean."

Lex hoovered up his share of the narcotics on the table in front of him and then held his note out to James. "Now then," he said. "Are you going to take that line or not?"

23

Richmond woke with a start. Lex was standing in the doorway of his bedroom fully dressed. The boy looked down at his watch. It was just before six o'clock.

"If you get up now," said Lex, "we can go up to the course and see exercise. Most of the Irish horses arrived by plane yesterday. They'll be out on the track in an hour."

Richmond blinked and scratched his head. He had that familiar dry throat and sand on the eyeballs feeling that was by now customary after a hard evening's drinking with the bookmaker. "I'll meet you downstairs in fifteen minutes."

Down in the kitchen the two labradors, quiet and unthreatening unlike the night before, padded softly across the stone-flagged floor to lick Richmond's hand as he walked into the room. The kitchen was warm and quiet except for the ticking of a clock by the tack room door. Lex had made tea. They stood with their backs to the Aga and warmed up slowly while they drank their tea.

Outside it was almost light. Grey and still very cold but no snow. Lex backed the Mercedes out of the gravel forecourt and they slid off up the drive, turned left through the grove of saplings and eased down through the parkland and out of the lodge gates. Some lights were already on in many of the greystone barns and farm buildings that they passed on their way but the narrow country lanes were still quiet and dark and mostly empty except for one tractor and a dog.

They joined the Broadway to Cheltenham road. It was mainly empty too, although they did pass an attractive young woman on a horse. She smiled pleasantly as they slowed down their speed to pass her. She was wearing a brightly patterned headscarf underneath her riding cap. And she had on lipstick too, even at half-past-six in the morning. James noticed that her legs were long and strong looking.

"I can read your mind," said Lex. James smiled. They both smiled a nice, warm, dirty smile. "Daisy's going to take us to the meet on Thursday. Before racing. Just wait till you see all those women. Sexy? Phew! All that make up with hair nets and whips."

"Tight white breeches and black leather boots?"

"That's it. And you should see the jewellery. I'm telling you. Get 'em drunk and flushed after a good day's chase and they'll fuck the living daylights out of you."

"You think so?"

"I know so. Personal experience."

"Daisy?"

Lex nodded. "I had a little affair with her once. When things were hot up in Glasgow and I had to lie low. She half-killed me." He grinned heartily. For the next ten minutes both men were silent. Then they reached Cleeve Hill.

At the top of Cleeve Hill the whole Cotswold escarpment seems to take a deep breath and then fling itself out to left and right as the land plunges suddenly several hundred feet down to the plain below. To the north the valley sweeps away past Bredon Hill and on up through the Vale of Evesham to Birmingham and the Midlands. To the south-west lies the Vale of Gloucester. And straight ahead lies Cheltenham town and Prestbury Park racecourse, its grandstand, fences and white-painted running rails all clearly if minutely visible like little miniature toys. Beyond Cheltenham you can see the Ridgeway and the Malvern Hills and sometimes you can even see as far as the mountains of Wales.

For James Richmond who was about to attend only his second ever Gold Cup meeting it sent a shiver of eager anticipation right up his spine and right up the nape of his neck. Lex, too, who had seen many days of triumph and even one or two of adversity at Cheltenham races could still not entirely dispel a nerve-tingling sense of excitement and possibility.

They carried on down the hill past the nursing home and the restaurant and the hillside view hotels that would soon be filling up with racing guests and aficionados from all over the country. At Southam they turned off to the right past the Tithe Barn, crossed the disused railway line and then turned left up the narrow lane that leads to the back entrance of the racecourse. Lex pulled over on to an empty expanse of green grass surrounded by muddy gravel paths that twenty-four hours later would become part of the general car parking area for thousands of Rovers, Range Rovers, Jaguars, Rollses and many more modest family tourers and saloon car models by their sides. Lex put a green turf directory onto his lap, took out a bag of white powder from his overcoat pocket and started to cut out two lines of cocaine. This time Richmond didn't hesitate to accept.

When they got out of the car they were on the side of a slight hill. The racecourse was away to their left, the grandstand and attendant buildings at the top of the hill up ahead. They walked down the hill past the chalets and the marquees of the tented village, past the bottom end of the pre-parade ring and the weighing room and out across the paddock, underneath the grandstand and on across the members' lawn. Then they went out through the little pass gate and on to the track itself. They crossed the hurdle race track and the jumps tracks and then carried on walking out into the centre of the course. It was still very cold and the sky looked red-eyed and potato-faced, rather like Richmond always felt after a night on the tiles with Lex. The young man was wearing a new, dark green trenchcoat with a fur lining and a borrowed pair of Hugh's wellington boots. Lex was dressed in his customary dark suit, shades and dark fedora but over the top he was wearing a bulky ankle length brown fur coat. The whole effect made him look rather like Bud Flanagan making an emotional if sinister return to the London Palladium. He had no boots. He was wearing one of his usual pairs of expensive Italian cut black leather shoes. The grass in the centre of the course was thick and tussocky and quite slippery in places from the mud and the early morning frosts. Lex's shoes slipped regularly on the grass becoming progressively more scuffed, wet and covered with mud as the walk carried on.

Across the ditch and out past the helicopter landing pads they reached the two-and-a-half-mile start. Richmond paused for a moment to turn round and look back at the grandstand. Large, modern and functional in mostly pale grey concrete with a concrete awning roof. There was a tier of boxes and entertainment suites up under the roof, a raked seating area and private members' bar beneath the boxes and more bars and a tier of cold grey concrete terracing supported by numerous stout grey concrete pillars beneath that.

It was not what you might call a pretty sight or even outstandingly designed from the horseracing point of view unless you preferred watching your sport through a sheer concrete beam to a pair of binoculars. Yet the unimaginative nature of the grandstand could in no way diminish the majesty of the natural racing amphitheatre that it overlooked. Richmond swung his eyes round from the winning post at the end of the uphill finish, up the long wide straight to the two-mile start and round to the barrelling downhill descent from the farthest point on the course, another hill and the highest of the many undulations and gradients that so starkly characterised this particular track. The whole setting overseen and dominated by the long sweeping line of the Cotswold Hills. It was this spectacular backdrop, free from the sight of any suburban railway stations or gravel pits or dreary rows of birch plantations, which helped to give Cheltenham its unique character and atmosphere. An aura of epic, out in the open, OK Corral confrontations rich in spectacle and excitement.

The fact was that to be a great name in National Hunt racing you had to prove you could win at Cheltenham. And the fact that all the great names had won there – many of them like Arkle, Persian War, Night Nurse and Sea Pigeon running their hearts out at successive Festivals – helped to contribute a timeless sense of history and emotion to each Gold Cup meeting.

Now, at just after seven o'clock on the Monday morning with one day left before the racing began, the place was almost empty. The flags were all in place and the fences newly manicured and trimmed. On each track the top edges of the grass had been cut and the rails repainted. The marquees were all up and ready and the sponsors' logos all clearly in place and readily identifiable for the television cameras. At the moment, though, the only significant gathering of human beings present apart from the Clerk of the Course and his staff were odd groups of about a dozen or so men, mostly Irish trainers and their lads or connections, who were scattered around in the centre of the course watching a small but select detachment of their horses out at exercise. It was towards one such group that Lex was now walking.

In Ireland, where a punt on a horse is still a punt on a horse and not a tax loss or an accountant's cautiously guarded investment, many people's greatest ambition all winter long is to own, train or back an Irish-trained winner at the Cheltenham Festival. And each March a regular cadre of Irish trainers supported by thousands of eager and excited punters make the journey over to sedate Cheltenham in the hope of doing just that.

But whatever the state of their supporters it's mostly only the equine cracks who make the trip. For over the years Irish-bred and Irish-trained animals have indeed lifted a considerable proportion of the generous prize money on offer. So while some trainers may come across with unreasonably high hopes, talking big and probably relishing more the atmosphere and the late-night drinking than any realistic prospects of success, for many of their fellows, men like CP Molloy, Cheltenham is a serious, a deadly serious, business.

Lex introduced James briskly. Standing next to CP were Blazes Heffernan, his assistant trainer, and Tommy O'Shaughnessy, his travelling head lad. Four of CP's string – he had seven declared for the week – were out on the track at that moment. Like all the rest of the Irish horses they lodged in the racecourse stables for the duration of their stay at the Festival and earlier that morning, while Lex and James were sipping tea, bleary-eyed, in Hugh and Daisy's kitchen and while Irish priests, jockeys, gamblers and their like were still waking up and packing their suitcases or just setting off for the airports and the ferry terminals, these four animals, along with a few other choice consignments from the Irish yards, had been walked out of their closely guarded boxes and trotted briskly across to the centre of the racecourse to do a little light, crisp exercise.

While they all waited for the four to canter back James made a quick study of the faces of the three Irishmen.

CP Molloy was a small man. An ex-jockey and an ex-boxer with a tough, wiry-looking body and a crafty little face graced by unfashionably long sideburns and a pair of bright blue lively-looking eyes. He was wearing a thick grey windproof jacket, grey breeches and a small brown trilby hat pulled down over his eyes at a jaunty angle. As a jockey he'd been good and he'd been smart too because he'd saved enough of the money that he'd earned in his riding days to invest it in a stable on his retirement, and although he'd had literally to fight his way up to the top, his record of achievement both on the flat and over the jumps was the envy of many a better-bred gentleman on both sides of the Irish Sea.

Tommy O'Shaughnessy was almost a dead ringer for CP in size, looks and clothing. The two men had a shared passion for the ring. The boxing ring and the betting ring and whenever their horses were off they backed them right up to the hilt. O'Shaughnessy's hard and weather-beaten poker face may have appeared to betray no emotion as he watched his charges at work but behind the dead grey eyes he never missed a trick.

David 'Blazes' Heffernan, tall and dreamy-eyed with a long tweed coat and a flat tweed cap, at first seemed decidedly out of place in this kind of company but once again outward appearances were deceptive. Heffernan, part-English, part-Irish and educated at Harrow, was the youngest son of one of the canniest bloodstock agents in the business and he seemed to have inherited every inch of his father's eye for judging a good horse. He'd been sent to CP to learn how to train the animals once he'd bought them. And to learn how to gamble too.

The ground shook with the low thunder of approaching hooves. The four-strong party of horses had split them-selves up into groups of two and the first two were now moving briskly towards them. One of them was a chest-nut. Still a big baby of a horse bursting with health and vitality but yet to grow into his full frame. His accomplice was a black, mean-eyed, runty sort of animal, nothing much to look at maybe but probably exactly the kind of beast who would go all day in the mud.

The second pair were more interesting. One bay and one brown gelding, both of them looking muscled up, fit and trained to the minute. The brown horse had a smooth flowing action and a particularly intelligent head. He took in his surroundings and the four onlookers with keen interest, without dancing around in a colty manner like the chestnut.

CP, O'Shaughnessy, Heffernan and Lex all seemed especially interested in his condition. Lex was muttering something private in Molloy's ear. The trainer nodded. "He's terrible well," James heard him say. "It almost frightens me. You know?"

"Who is that?" James asked Lex a moment or so later.

"Galway Raider," said Lex quickly. James thought for

a moment. Out of CP's seven declared runners he remembered Galway Raider as having only relatively moderate form to his name, with a recent third at Punchestown over three-and-three-quarter-miles as his most promising effort to date. As far as he could recall the horse was entered for the Kim Muir Memorial Steeplechase on the Tuesday afternoon.

The equine quartet had trotted back towards their trainer who strode out and patted and stroked them all in turn, exchanging brief words with each one of the four work riders. Sitting on top of the brown gelding was the trainer's son, Frankie, formerly one of Ireland's leading young amateur riders and now the top professional in the land. It was a well-known inside fact that on the whole Frankie only ever rode work on one of CP's stable stars.

The horses were blowing and snorting happily, steam rising up from their coats like smoke from a burning grill tray. The brown gelding nuzzled CP's back with his long russet-coloured head. Frankie Molloy was talking to him softly and lovingly under his breath.

"Which horse is that?" James asked Heffernan.

"Galway Raider," said Heffernan disarmingly. Galway Raider started shitting in front of them. They could see his breath on the morning air and they could smell the pungent aroma of horseshit. Further back more horses were making their way out on to the track. Lex had his binoculars trained on them all. He saw two of Connor Delaney's string, Deep Fidelity and the novice hurdler The House Rules, and he could see Delaney with them, but fortunately he couldn't see Cashel Maguire.

"Here comes Big Pat and the Limerick boys," said O'Shaughnessy. The other four scanned the horizon. Big Pat was easy to spot. Padraig Michael McKenna was the original stage Irishman cast in the Brendan Behan mould. An ex-nightclub owner and greyhound trainer turned the most successful current trainer of National Hunt horses in all Ireland. McKenna was indeed a big fat man, fatter than Lex, fat like Fat Jimmy Docherty was fat, but this morning he was jogging along gently by the sides of a strong, keen and bucking little bay horse who, quite unusually for a top National Hunt performer, was an entire colt and not a gelding. The bay colt was Galtee O'Flynn, the Champion Hurdler and a winner at each of the two previous years' Festival meetings, who the following afternoon would be bidding for instant deification and heroic status if he could carry off a share of the Waterford Crystal for the third year running.

The arrival of Big Pat and his entourage meant pressmen, photographers and possibly even a Steward or two. For Lex it was time to move on. He exchanged a few more terse and muffled words with CP and Frankie. This time James could make out only the son's parting comment. "There's really nothing else I fancy," Frankie was saying. "Nothing else at all." CP put one hand reassuringly on the bookmaker's shoulder. Then Lex led Richmond away for a further walk down the far side of the course.

"This big tip for tomorrow," the boy whispered once they'd passed the waterjump and the open ditch and were well out of earshot of CP and company. "Exactly which horse is it?"

Lex looked at him, smiled and winked. "Tomorrow," he said. "You'll know. But I'll tell you this much, Jimmy boy. You've got to hit this one with every dollar, pound, cent and penny you possess." Richmond looked worried. "Don't worry," Lex added. "I'll arrange everything."

They walked on up to the top of the hill and then swung left down the long run towards the turn into the home straight. Lex discussed how you had to make ground up going down the far side and then hold a good position at the hill. "Once they start down the hill," he said, "in a race like the Gold Cup there's often only three or four horses left in it. I can usually name your winner by that stage." He remarked how many fallers there were at the downhill fences and how an enterprising jockey could often kick on at the final bend and outstay his challengers up the long hill to the finish. "Class and courage are not

enough round this place. You've got to be an adventurer
too. A park horse is no good at all unless he's exceptional.
And it's no use banging away each weekend throughout
the winter either. You want an animal from a yard with a
proven record. An animal especially prepared and laid out
for one of these races all season long."

"An animal like Galway Raider?"

"Maybe."

"That wasn't Galway Raider at all, was it?"

"What do you mean?"

"Come on, Lex, I'm not stupid."

"We saw a number of horses. The young chestnut,
that's Ormund. He goes for the National Hunt Chase and
if he gets a clear round he'll win by the length of the
Promenade. Mr Dooley, he's the bay gelding, he goes for
the Sun Alliance. . ."

"Tell me the name, Lex. I'm not going to run off to
Hills and ruin the price."

"You're dead fucking right you're not."

James caught the bookmaker's look and returned it for
a count of five. Then he shrugged his shoulders and turned
away. "Come on," he said. "Let's go home and have
breakfast."

Up by the car park and the concrete grandstand the
racecourse manager and his staff were beginning to arrive.
Busy with their walkie-talkies and their cleaning buggies
and their detailed instructions to the gatemen. For them,
three hundred and sixty two days of careful work and
preparation were now nearly at an end.

As Lex and James walked in through the door at Harford
half an hour later Hugh was just drifting down the stairs,
wrapped in a voluminous dark wool dressing gown complete with gold braid and a monogrammed pocket. It
made him look like a cross between a senior station
master and a postman in Czarist Russia. He was drinking
port from the bottle.

"Well, chaps," he said, wiping his mouth with the back

of his hand. "Breakfast. How does kedgeree and home-made sausages sound?"

"Sounds good to me, pal," said Lex, striding pur-posefully towards the kitchen where he made straight for *The Sporting Life*.

"Thinking of Cheltenham specialists," said James, opening up the refrigerator and taking out a large carton of apple juice. "What about Some Idea for the two-mile championship? He won the Arkle last year. And Kenneally's a trainer with a proven record. Looks like a banker to me."

"We'll have to see about that," demurred the Scots-man. He was reading a piece of publicity about himself and Pointdexter senior and the big race at Sandown Park in July. James took a long drink of apple juice while Lex carried on reading. Hugh shuffled about between them, spooning coffee into an elderly pot and dropping large slabs of butter into a pan of already made kedgeree.

"By the way," said Lex casually. "Your old man's in the paper today."

"Really?" Lex tossed him *The Sporting Life*. On the front page there was a syndicated article by Graham Mould of the *Sheffield Post Dispatch*. It described how the Jockey Club had been alerted by Mould to a case of bribery and corruption involving a lifelong member of the Club on the North Eastern circuit. A Jockey Club state-ment, it said, was eagerly awaited for later that day. Underneath the story there was a rather bad photograph of the Duke, looking haggard and harassed as he walked out of the doors at Portman Square. "The Clubmen," a caption read. "Can they afford to come clean?" James put the paper down slowly.

"I wonder who the hell this is?"

"Some buffoon or other," said Lex.

"My father will be shattered. In his world men just don't do this sort of thing."

"Of course they don't. You know what I think it shows? Just how self-interested this country's become. I mean

. . . when you can't trust a toff, who can you trust?"

"I think I might take a rain check on breakfast, Hugh," said James.

"As you please."

"I'll just take some coffee upstairs. I could do with another hour's sleep."

"Getting all your rest while you can, eh?" said Lex. "And why not too? You've got a big week up ahead." For his own part Lex Parlane looked in no need of rest whatsoever and he smacked his lips most vigorously as the first delicious aromas of frying sausages, kedgeree and percolating coffee drifted back towards him from the Aga.

James went upstairs and walked thoughtfully along the corridor. The door to Lex and Bella's bedroom was open. Bella was putting on her make up and walking up and down holding various clothes up against her body and trying their look out in the full-length mirror.

James slipped inside the room and pushed the door to. Bella saw him and smiled. He blew her a kiss. She was wearing her black underwear. Richmond lay on the bed and gazed at her in rapt fascination. She seemed oblivious and kept stubbing out half-smoked Dunhill cigarettes in an ashtray beside the bed. Richmond leaned forward and tried to run his hand up her leg to the top of her stocking.

"Uh-uh," she said, moving deftly out of the way. "Not now."

"Last night you couldn't resist me." She smiled, raised one eyebrow as usual and stepped into a black, silk petticoat. "You're up early."

"I'm going out."

"Out to lunch?" Bella nodded. "Oh. Where are we off to?"

"I said I'm going out."

"And I'm not invited?"

"That's right."

"Then who are you going with? Not Lex?"

She shook her head. "Reema's coming. And Hugh.

And then we're going to meet an old friend. He owns an art gallery near Bath."

"That will be nice."

"I think so."

"What about me?"

"You can play with your form books, darling." She was laughing at him. "Doubtless you've got plenty to read about."

"Thanks very much."

"And if you get bored I'm sure Daisy will entertain you." She stood there and shook out her hair. It was getting long and curly and she'd added a few ash-blonde streaks to the colour. James adored it.

"Where are you going?" he asked her again.

"I've told you. Out to lunch."

"And then?"

"And then . . . to see a rather beautiful old house and some gardens."

"Near here?"

"Near Bath." He got up and kissed her. She offered him not red lips but one smooth, pale and made-up cheek. He tried to tickle the back of her leg. Just where the top of her black silk stocking met the black suspender belt.

"No!"

"But you look so gorgeous, Bella. Please!"

"I wear nice things," she said, talking slowly and deliberately, "because I like to. Because it pleases me and makes me feel good. I don't just do it for men."

Richmond sighed. In his injured and besotted eyes she'd suddenly become less like a glamorous ex-film star and more like a disapproving school ma'am. "You don't have to give me a lecture, Bella," he said. "I just love you, that's all."

"I'll be back tonight. For dinner."

"With Lex?"

She paused. "Yes."

"I think . . . I'd better go and put a bet on a horse."

The most private telephone in the house was in Hugh's

office, a comfortable ramshackle affair littered with food guides and shotguns, empty French cigarette packets and countless unpaid bills. Hunting through the cupboard beneath Hugh's desk for an Oxford telephone directory James found three bottles of hock together with a half-empty bottle of aquavit. He laughed. It was part of Hugh's private and emergency boozing supply for when Daisy drank him dry. The joke was that in James's guest bathroom there were several bottles of Moët and Chandon nestling behind the lavatory brushes. Part of Daisy's comparable reserves for whenever Hugh got excessive himself. Perfect friends for Lex really.

James was already in pretty deep with Lex for all the Festival races and he didn't want to add to the bill, so he called up Sunny Vengsarkar and arranged for him to use an account they both had with a betting office in Abingdon to put four hundred pounds to win at five to two on Galtee O'Flynn for the Champion Hurdle. He also arranged to meet Sunny on the course at half-past one the following afternoon. Then he rang the Mecca Bookmakers office in London and had another two hundred pounds on at the same price. Finally he rang up his father.

The Duke sounded solemn and tired but he made no mention of the Graham Mould story or the identity of the culprit at the centre of the corrupt Steward scandal. James did a passable imitation of a cheerful young Christchurch undergraduate talking from the call box at the bottom of staircase two. His father sounded too distracted to be unconvinced. The boy chatted away cheerfully about meeting the Duke for lunch in the family box on Gold Cup day and reassured him that for the rest of the week he would be studying hard in his rooms with only periodic visits to the television in the college JCR. The Duke's own visit to Cheltenham was about to begin later that day so for James the imperative matter on at least Tuesday and Wednesday would be to steer well clear of the weighing room and conduct his paddock scrutinies from behind the shoulder of a large and inconspicuous friend.

After he'd rung off the nineteen-year-old caught a sudden glimpse of Daisy wandering loosely and alone around the hall. She was holding a large pitcher of dry martinis in one hand and flicking her riding crop at the pictures with the other. She caught his eye and her face lit up. "Darling," she exclaimed. "How about a little game of strip jack naked in the kitchen?"

24

The Queens Hotel, like all the other hotels, guest houses and tourist board bed-and-breakfasts in Cheltenham, had been filling up with guests all morning. Many of the bookings were standing orders from one year to the next and if you'd tried to make a reservation there and then for the following year's Festival or even for the year after that you'd have been right out of luck. It was the same story throughout the county and throughout the region from Oxford in the south as far north as Birmingham and as far west as the Bristol Channel. From the grandest – or most overpriced – four-poster suite to the meanest B-and-B with cold water, a cold breakfast and two in a single bed, every vacancy was taken and every reservation fully confirmed. Such was the lure of the crack.

Incredibly there were one or two people in the hotel who were not involved with horse racing. Like the middle-aged couple from Edinburgh who were escorting their sixteen-year-old daughter on an official formal interview at the Cheltenham Ladies College. They'd just had coffee in the lounge and were now on their way to have lunch when a large man in a smart black coat, black hat and amazingly for a mid-morning in March shiningly dark black glasses swept across the foyer in front of them. As he did so he brushed the woman's shoulder, knocking her handbag and her Jenner's tartan scarf to the ground. Almost immediately he stopped, bent down gracefully, picked up the handbag and scarf and returned them to the woman with a sweeping bow. "Excuse me, ma'am," he said. "The pace we do live life, eh?" The couple gaped at him in disbelief. He winked at the girl. She could hardly believe her eyes. Such a big, rough, sexy man. Not like the doe-eyed teenaged and honourable wimps who usually came knocking on her mother's door asking for permission to take her out to tea at a close friend's place up in Crieff. Then her chaperones nudged her gently towards the dining room and Lex, whistling cheerfully, went on his way towards the bar.

Michael Bolger, Johnny Kinane and Cashel Maguire were sitting by the fireplace posed beneath a massive oil colour painting of Admiral Sir Charles Napier. Each man was wearing his best suit and had recently cut and washed hair. From what Lex could see they were all drinking fancy and fancy-priced cocktails. He ordered a large bourbon. Without ice.

The room was comfortable and warm. A lot of grey velvet armchairs and potted plants and little tables by the armchairs with drink coasters on them and ashtrays and bowls of olives, peanuts and potato crisps.

"Well done, Lex," said Bolger quietly. "Your idea worked."

"No Garvin stories for almost a week now," said Kinane.

"And there won't be any for at least six months after this," said Bolger.

"The Stewards are upset," said Maguire. "You've shattered their confidence in themselves."

"They'll get over it," said Lex.

"Let's hope they never trace Mould back to you," said Maguire.

"They won't," said Bolger. "They're not that smart."

"And Mould has no idea who gave him the tip-off," said Lex. "As far as he knows it's anonymous sources."

"Lucky him," said Maguire.

Lex nodded. "So," he said, smiling nicely. "How have you been then, Cashel? These past few months. Have you been doing alright?"

"You should know," said Maguire.

"Should I?"

"Mickey asked me to tell you that he's very . . . grateful," said Bolger.

"Where is he today?"

"Southwell, I suppose," said Kinane.

"Don't make me laugh," said the Scot. "He doesn't ride Southwell. It's beneath his dignity. He'll be pulling some trainer's wife in a motel room near York."

"I said that I'd see him for a drink," said Bolger. "Tomorrow night. After racing."

"You'd better be discreet," said Kinane.

"Ah. Now he says it," said Lex.

"What do you mean?"

"I'm not very pleased with Garvin," said Lex. "Or you, Johnny. How could you be so dumb as to let Mould spot you boys together? And in the middle of Dublin too."

"How did I know he was trailing us?" said Kinane. "I mean, I didn't even know that he was in the fucking country."

"If I hadn't got to him . . . and if a certain Lieutenant Colonel hadn't been ripe for the plucking he could have finished us all."

"But you've done private business with Garvin," said Kinane. "How do we know that might not incriminate us three too?"

"Listen, Johnny," said Lex. "They've got nothing on me. At least nothing that they'd ever make stick." He sat back confidently, drained his glass and ordered another.

"Talking discreet," said Maguire. "What's so discreet about this? The four of us together? In the main hotel in Cheltenham? One day before the Festival?"

"The Stewards never come here," said Lex. "It's a Trust House. Not their style. And as for Racecourse Security, they can't afford the prices."

"What about thieves like us?"

Lex shook his head. "They don't stop here so much these days. They're down at the Golden Valley and points west."

"The question now," said Bolger, "is whether the scheme carries on. And whether we give Mickey the extra money that he's asking for."

"I'm not happy with Garvin," said Lex.

"Why not?" asked Kinane.

"I don't trust him, that's why."

"But he runs a good set up," said Maguire.

"The best. When it works," said Bolger.

"Why not invest it in the flat instead?" suggested Lex. "They're off again in ten days time. Just as many jockeys for sale. And no jumps to contend with either."

"But you already have people for that, surely?" said Bolger.

"I do. But I can always use more. And I don't like jockeys who cheat me."

"Hold on, Lexie," said Kinane. "Garvin's done quite alright as far as we're concerned. And I'd like it to stay that way."

"Besides," said Maguire, "Irish jumping goes on all year round. Why should we spoil our profits just because you've got a prejudice in favour of flat racing?"

"Then carry on on your own if you want. But without my money."

"Garvin could be a menace," said Bolger quickly. "I have to admit that I don't like him that much myself."

"But you're stuck with him. Eh, Mickey?" said Lex.

"We're stuck with him together."

"Are we now? You know what I'd like to know most? Just what he's pulling this week. And I don't mean women."

"You've heard his stable tips," said Kinane.

"And his news about the Gold Cup favourite."

"But what's he pulling?"

"Why ask us?" asked Maguire.

"Bolger knows. Don't you, Mickey?"

"I don't know what you're talking about."

"Grow up, Mickey. I know all about your nice little Garvin games. Like Tommy Kenneally and friends. So when I ask you a straight question don't fart in my bedclothes. Alright?"

Bolger frowned. When he spoke it was through clenched teeth. "I do not regard myself as wedded insolubly to any business partnership with Michael Garvin."

"I'll bet you don't."

"There are other ways to consider."

"Other ways to do what?"

"Other ways to make money from racing."

Maguire laughed. "What are you going to do, Michael? Sell off a few fraudulent Barking yacht marinas and buy an Epsom-based two-year-old colt? I can just see it now. *The Sporting Life*. Tuesday, July the twenty-third. 'Stewards enquire into gambled-on winner of last night's Windsor seller.' "

"There are other ways."

"To do what?"

"Stop horses. Lex knows what I mean. Don't you, Lex?"

"Doping?" asked Lex. Bolger smiled a knowing little smile. "Hah! I thought that's what it was."

"Oh, no," said Kinane. "I don't believe it. We've got a grand scheme going with the jockeys and now you want to throw it all in to get yourselves involved in some daft old business with laxatives and a syringe. Look at the gangs who've tried it and failed. It doesn't work anymore. Not in 1985. Whatever you come up with, the vets and the scientists, they always come up with something better. I'm telling you it's worse than the dogs. Let's keep things going as they are." His face looked flushed and pink from anxiety and he gulped down the remains of his cocktail, sloshing lime juice and gin round his lips. Then, in an effort to regain his composure, he clicked his fingers suavely at the waiter.

"You're right about the doping, Johnny," said Lex. "I did try it on. In the old days. And it's a mug's game. The boys with the chemistry sets, they always catch up with you far too fast. But then that's the same with this jockeys' ring. You see, exploiting greed is a fallible business. You constantly need new systems. And new people. Or sooner or later the Stewards will tumble to your picnic."

"Doping yes," said Kinane. "That's scientists. But Garvin no. The Stewards just aren't that smart."

"Not smart," said Bolger.

"They've never bothered me," said Maguire.

"Don't worry," said Lex. "They will."

"Still ahead of the field, eh, Lex?" smiled Maguire.

Lex nodded. "Still Scotland's number one."

"So what have you got to tell us?" asked Bolger.

"You've heard."

"What's that?"

"Kilmonaghan."

"More than that, Lex," said Bolger.

"Much more," said Maguire.

"We can read about that in the papers," said Kinane.

"He's the best young prospect to come out of Ireland since Arkle," said Lex.

"Come off it, boy," said Kinane. "I've been hearing that story every year since the great one died. And they've all been the purest moonshine."

"This time it's true," said Lex. "I was over in Cork last Thursday night. After Limerick races. I stayed on with Joe Carmody."

"So?"

"Carmody says it's in a class of its own."

Maguire said nothing. Kinane sighed and lit another cigarette.

"It's in the first race tomorrow, right?" asked Bolger.

"The Waterford Crystal Supreme Novices Hurdle."

"What about the English runners?"

"They're not in his league. You know the form. Still only a novice and yet he ran second in the Wessels Champion Hurdle. Accept the facts, Mickey."

"How many other Irish horses are declared for that race?" Bolger asked Kinane.

"Three, I think," said Kinane. "Fandango's Revenge.

Big Pat's thing. And Mylerstown."

"Mylerstown?"

"That's CP Molloy's horse."

"You can forget about that one," said Maguire. "He's got a weak heart. CP told me himself."

"Why's Delaney not running?"

"Because he knows that he can't beat Kilmonaghan," said Lex. "So take the tip and get on. And if you can all get better than evens hit it with every dollar, pound, cent and penny you possess."

"Let's hope you're right," said Bolger.

"Let's hope Garvin doesn't go and pull a fast one and embarrass us all," said Lex.

"I'll deal with Garvin," said Bolger. "And for now we'll keep playing his game. I say 'we'. But what about you? Eh, 'Lexie'?"

"Yes," said Kinane. "What about you? Are you still in our scheme or not?"

"And if not, are you going to rot it up for the rest of us?" asked Maguire.

"I've given you Kilmonaghan," said Lex, importantly. "I'll decide about the rest at the end of the week. I'm still considering my next move."

"I've always got mine worked out," said Maguire. "And right now I'm one step ahead."

"That's nice for you, Cashel," said Lex. "I'm hungry." He got up. He could see the teenage schoolgirl lingering provocatively in the doorway to the bar. He looked across the room and caught her eye.

"Let's eat," said Maguire.

"Good idea," said Kinane. "In a week like this you need all your dinners."

"I always think," began Bolger as the others got up too, "that the charm of the Cheltenham Festival. . ."

"Is the unexpected result?" finished Lex.

"That sort of thing," said Bolger.

Lex smiled.

25

By teatime the atmosphere at the Queens was very much like that of a conference centre hotel during a seaside political convention. The tearooms, bars, foyers and suites were all alive with anecdote, rumour and gossip.

Cashel Maguire met an old acquaintance from the Irish Turf Club smoking a cigar in the lift. "Looking forward to the races, eh, Cash?" asked the man.

"Nothing else like it," said Maguire.

"I hear the Brits might be feeling a touch offended over all our successes of the past few years," said the man.

"Oh, really?"

The man nodded. "I hear that they might get nasty too. Especially if the good boys give 'em half a chance."

"Excessive use of the whip? That sort of caper?"

"Not necessarily. More where the money goes. And whose money it is. Do you follow?"

"Not necessarily," said Maguire. But he was thinking hard as he walked down the corridor to his room.

Downstairs a big London bookmaking firm were holding a reception in the Gold Cup room. The racing press were there in force doing their best to drink up the company's entire lifelong budget in champagne, wine and the stronger spirits. Amongst the other hundred and fifty or so guests present were about fifty betting shop managers and their wives. Many of them had once run small businesses of their own, family concerns which had only recently been forced into the arms of their big city neighbours. They accepted the hospitality and enjoyed it but in the back of their minds were constant worries about coronaries and takeovers, unbalanced books and unbalanced head office managers. Their honest endeavour to earn an honest living was little different from the struggle of any other small operator fighting to survive and they could have done without the razor-edged amputation at the knee style of their new management school bosses. They could also have done without the flash, wide boy, wide suit image of men like Lex Parlane. But then there was no Lex Parlane invited to this gathering.

The company bosses were getting particularly anxious about three things. One of them was the general press and drinking situation. Another was the fact that they'd invited a string of celebrities – actors, footballers, snooker players and alcoholic comedians and the like – and so far less than a third of them had showed. Most of them owed big money to the firm and these kind of events were a minimal repayment demanded in return for their continuing freedom to bet. Goldline Investments would have to see about that.

The third worry was that they'd hired a team of personality dancing girls to entertain the guests and although they were more than an hour into the bash there was still no sign of any dancing. Louis Weiss didn't like it. He felt that it was bad economics. They only had the room for another fifty minutes and at the prices these girls were being paid he wanted flashing legs and sequinned tits all around the cheese display and the asparagus rolls. Not that any of it was to Weiss's liking. The whole room smelled wrong. Too cheap and common. Too much face powder and acrid sweat. But it was an annual firm occasion which as yet Weiss had been unable to convince the board to cancel. Mike Cordrey handed him another Perrier water and an egg and cress sandwich. A well-known racing journalist stumbled past winking frantically at the two of them and trying to communicate in tac-tac to his girlfriend who was trapped behind a wall of cockney settlers across the other side of the room. Louis Weiss looked at the journalist. He was a disgusting sight. He had a bad case of dandruff and he'd also been eating a plateful of sausage rolls. Flakes of pastry from the rolls had spilt down his suit and his shirt front, mingling in with the flakes of dandruff from his scalp.

Another man reeled out of the crowd. Weiss recognised him immediately as that John Kinane, the Irish bookie. He didn't like Kinane. He didn't like his stout fellow grin or his business attitude and he didn't like the Jameson smell on his breath either. Weiss was sitting in a chair on a dais by the stage and even sitting down he was still several inches taller than Kinane. That gave him some form of comfort at least.

"Well, well, Louis," said Kinane. "I didn't think you'd even be here. I didn't think you could stand the heat. Not real racing."

"I don't see any racing," said Weiss.

"You may think you're cock of the dungheap now, Louis. But next March you could be freezing it out up in Sedgefield and I could be giving the party."

"Was he invited?" Weiss asked Cordrey.

"Don't worry, Louis," said Kinane, pulling out a bundle of new notes from his best suit pocket. "I can afford your prices. And here's a grand here that says your profits will be down ten points by Thursday night."

"I don't lay bets," said Weiss contemptuously. "If you want to make a proper transaction you can see my man on the course. Tomorrow." Suddenly an insistent percussion beat started grinding its way into Weiss's inner ear. The dancing had begun. Kinane swung round with all the other heads, hoping to catch a generous glimpse of breast and leg and gyrating hips and thighs. Weiss got up and walked away.

He'd only trailed up to Cheltenham that week as a result of the Duke's persuasion. Just to attend some vile Jockey Club function the following day. A sickly luncheon in the tented village under the guise of selling racing to the advertising industry as a commercial enterprise.

He'd had a rotten year. Especially the last six months.

He'd been patient. He'd played the Duke's game and he'd always kept quiet when the Jockey Club had asked him to. He'd even been prepared to tolerate that loudmouthed Scot betting on the Members' rails at Ascot. But when the man bought a house only a mile or so away from his own luxury Barratt's property then his patience finally ran out. He knew RSS had files. Well, he kept files of his own. On characters like Parlane, Kinane and Mr Cashel Maguire. And if the Stewards didn't agree on a concerted plan of action by the end of this week then he'd take his files to the police.

A voice called out to him from the floor.

"Come on, Louis," it cried. "Come on in and join us. The pressboys want a snap." Weiss turned round and his mouth dropped open. It was him. The man himself. That Scotsman. Alex John Parlane. And he was dancing with the cabaret girls. He was dancing with the Jack of Diamonds Personality Team Dancing Girls. At the Gold-line Investments party.

In fact for such a heavily-built man he was gliding with surprising grace around the dance floor. Johnny Kinane was stumbling drunkenly around behind him. Mike Cordrey and the heavies made to move in but Weiss waved them back with his hand. He wasn't going to give the Scotsman that much status and satisfaction. Lex started singing.

> *Chicago, Chicago*
> *It's my kind of town.*

Kinane started singing too and it was horrible. Weiss's lip curled. What he liked was a nice barbershop quartet.

26

The path was lined by emptying offices and closing shops. Boots, Littlewoods and WH Smith's. People with Marks and Spencer shopping bags and anoraks. Fold-away plastic macs and limited savings in a post office account. Lex Parlane walked on past these people like a fox through a chicken run. He could hear the loud thrum of a jukebox from the open doors of a pub. A boy standing by a news stand beneath the trees sold him an evening paper with tomorrow's declared runners in it. It had been raining and although the rain had stopped now the pavements beneath his feet were still wet and lined with wet leaves. He could see the wet and soggy newsprint of other discarded racing papers lying in the gutter.

An elderly country bus accelerated away through the lights and on up Portland Street. As he carried on out of the main shopping area of the town and up the hill towards the racecourse Lex gazed in at the windows of the big old Georgian double-fronted houses along the Evesham Road. Too late for tea. Just right for sherry. But too quiet and too safe to hear his passing foot fall upon the street outside.

This had been a fine old start to the week, eh, Lexie? Upstaging Weiss at his own party. Bolger and his two pantomime Micks completely hooked. And Charles St Clair would be here tomorrow too. Much more to be coined from that source. And then, to cap it all, fucking a sixteen-year-old schoolgirl in the ladies lavvie at the Queens. Only a quick ten-minute job maybe. But she'd been juicily keen and worthwhile, that was for sure. And all the while Bolger and Kinane had been sitting there and fussing over Michael Garvin, Kilmonaghan and Lex's top tip for the week. They were still only starting on their melon and prawn cocktails when he came back to order. That was Lex Parlane for you.

He turned right up by the roundabout opposite the course, walked a little way along the road and then turned right again into the grounds of a now mostly deserted boys' private school. The majority of the inmates had been sensibly sent away on a Combined Schools Rugby tour to Wales for the length of the race meeting. These dark and empty redbrick buildings, so far undisturbed by either racing enthusiasts or officials, suited Lex's purposes ideally.

But now someone was walking towards him from out of the shadows. A tall-looking boy in a denim jacket and a flat cap. As the boy got closer Lex could see his face. Young, wide-eyed and nervous-looking. Lex recognised him from the previous April's Epsom spring meeting. "Good evening, son," said the bookmaker. "Go buy yourself a shave." He slipped a fiver into the stable boy's top pocket. The stable boy paused for a moment and then walked on quickly and sheepishly out of the grounds.

Lex found Billy Two Hats and James Richmond round by the back of the bicycle sheds at the rear end of the covered playground. They were smoking cigarettes in silence. "Everything go okay?" Lex asked Billy.

"Fine," said Billy. "All the lads have been paid and I've recorded all their news and views. It's much as we thought." Lex nodded. "That boy you passed was the last one tonight."

"Good work, Billy."

"Cigarette?" asked Richmond. Lex shook his head.

"I'll have a line instead." He took out a torch from his overcoat pocket along with his cocaine packet and his credit card. Then he started chopping out a big line of cocaine on a pocket mirror which he rested on the saddle of some teenage schoolboy's padlocked bike.

"I never realised you had so many people on the payroll," said Richmond. "As well as hotels and pubs we've been into about half a dozen stables. Just walked up the drive and banged on the front door."

"They're only small fry," said Billy. "Permit holders and amateurs."

"I wouldn't go up to the front door of one of your top drawer boys," said Lex. "Jockeys either. I have other ways of dealing with them." He cleaned up his line with a flourish. "Cheltenham's when I give 'em all their annual bonus. Like a Christmas box. Cheltenham for the jumpers. Royal Ascot for the flat. I use this spot for some of the kids who are staying in the hostel by the racecourse stables. It's nearby but anonymous. I mean, what diseased mind would imagine a racketeer paying off informants behind the bicycle sheds in a prep school playground?" They all laughed demonically. "Not that it's really corrupt, mind. Louis Weiss and company, they're all at it too. Only with them it's always mysteriously referred to by our polite journalistic friends as 'the bookmakers' information system'. Well, I'm telling you, son, if you don't give old Louis what he's asking for he rings up the Abbey National and gets 'em to foreclose on your mortgage. You follow my meaning?"

Richmond nodded. "He's not a nice man."

"Not a nice man."

"And he doesn't have your dress sense either." The boy flicked Lex's two-tone blue and gold orchid pattern tie with his finger and thumb.

"Enough of that, you cheeky young ponce." He gave him the cocaine packet.

"Jack's down in the press box, Lex," said Billy. "He's meant to be finishing his copy but he's been at the bottle too. Do you think we should fetch him out?"

"I think for sure we should fetch him out. Who's driving?"

"Willie Cooper. He's in the car park now."

"Alright. Go and get Willie and tell him to bring the car

round by the front entrance to the racecourse in about ten minutes time. Jimmy and I'll go down and fetch Jacko."

"OK, Lexie."

Lex and Richmond walked out of the school grounds, across the road and into the racecourse through the car park nearest the road. A few self-conscious looking workmen were still lurking around by the Tattersalls entrance but no one attempted to stop them walking through. They walked up the steps to the press box and stood outside the glass-plated window looking in. There was no sign of Jack McQueen. Only one man was present in the room and he was sitting on his own by the far window looking out over the racecourse. On the table in front of him was the card for tomorrow's racing, a large pad of white paper and several boxes of crayons. By his side was an ice bucket with a half-empty bottle of vintage champagne.

Lex and James recognised the man immediately. It was the doyen of all television racing commentators. The undisputed and unrivalled voice of racing for more than thirty years. He was painstakingly filling out a colour chart for himself for all the runners in the following days' televised races so that he could go back and memorise them later in the privacy of his hotel room. Lex took a hip flask out of his overcoat pocket and held it up to the window in a silent toast. But the man never looked round.

The other two walked back down the steps, through the underpass and out across the members' lawn. It was 7 pm and the lawn and concrete stands and terracing were all but empty once again, as they had been at seven that morning. James Richmond paused for a moment to lean on the running rail opposite the winning post. The running rails glowed bright and phosphorescently white in the enveloping darkness.

"Had a good day with the girls?" asked Lex.

"A not unenjoyable one. I spent most of the morning playing bicycle pursuit races with Daisy round the kitchen table. I was quite glad to get away, though. Excited too."

"I thought you'd find it interesting. Seeing how that side of the business works. It's educative."

"Eye-opening."

"A broadening experience. Did you see Bella?"

"She swanned out the front door without me."

Lex nodded. "She was off to lunch with this art dealer geyser that she knows down in Bath. An old friend of hers and Hugh's."

"So she told me."

"I don't really mind. It gets her out from under my feet. She understands when I'm busy."

"That's good."

They started to walk back towards the gate. They saw a car nudging forward towards them just beyond the Tatter-salls entrance. A drunken head leaned out of the non-driver's window. "Come on, Parlane, you big fat bas-tard," it shouted. "I want my tea." Lex didn't laugh.

"You know, Jack," called James. "You're worse than some crop-haired guardsman propping up the bar in the buffet car on the nine forty-five out of Euston."

"James?" called a voice, quiet but authoritative. "Is that you?" The two men swung round. Or to be more precise James's head jerked round suddenly and nervously. Lex turned round more slowly. Casually even.

A tall and distinguished-looking man had stepped for-ward by the Prestbury Suite rear entrance. He had a trim moustache and an aquiline nose and he was wearing an old dun-coloured raincoat and a brown trilby hat. Another younger and more clipped-looking man stepped forward by his side. He was wearing gumboots, tweeds and a game fair jacket. A third man who was holding two bulging briefcases, one in each hand, hovered uncertainly in the background.

"Well, well, well," said the younger man in a voice at once both bland and smarmy. "The Scholar Gypsy. Playing truant once again."

"Shut up, Rowland," said the Duke.

"Father," gasped James, the word expiring out of his mouth like life out of a dying body.

"Good evening, sir," said Lex, stepping forward smartly. "We haven't yet met, I believe. My name's Lex Parlane."

"Good evening," said the Duke politely, though refusing the proffered handshake. Rowland said nothing while Letherby just continued to hover. James Richmond felt as if he'd blundered unthinkingly into a woodshed and now several hundredweight of freshly cut logs were about to come crashing to the ground all around him.

"What fine weather it looks like being," said Lex. "A touch of rain maybe but then what's Cheltenham without the rain, eh, sir? Not heavy enough to worry about, I say."

The Duke ignored these specious remarks. He had his eyes on his son. James was beginning to feel sick. That awful and depressing mixture of numbness, distress and irritation when you've just been forced to witness the real pain that your thoughtless actions have caused to someone else for whom you have affection. He had to lie. "I got invited, father," he began. "This afternoon. To a friend's house party. Near Stow."

"How incredibly convenient," said Rowland.

"Damn classy," said Lex. "And you should taste the food, sir. Are you in some local pub?"

"Do you ever do anything you say you're going to do?" asked Rowland. He was looking at James.

"Always changes his mind at the last minute," said Lex, shaking his head cheerfully. "He's lost so many bets that way."

The Duke turned his gaze on to Lex. He looked him up and down and he looked him in the eye, but when he spoke it was to utter no barked command or Jockey Club order. He addressed him quietly but firmly in the tired but dignified tones of an elderly parent sorely tried. "You have your hooks into my son, sir," he said. "Do not attempt to deny it." Lex didn't. He just waited calmly for

whatever was coming next. "You are a vainglorious bully.
A fraud. And a thief. And I intend to do everything in my
power to get you thrown off the track." Lex said nothing.
He didn't speak. He didn't move. And behind the darkness of his darkened glasses he didn't even blink. "As to
the nature of your . . . friendship . . . with my son. If, as
he insists . . . it is not entirely propelled by commercial
interests . . . if you have any real grain of care or
consideration . . . for his future welfare and his happiness
. . . then I beg of you . . . please . . . do not encourage
him to gamble any further."

"If you've got the right information," said Lex, in a flat
and level voice, "it's not really a gamble. Is it?"

"I'm too cautious to be a real gambler, father," said
James quickly.

"Takes after you, no doubt, sir," said Lex. "Caution
. . . always made good losers."

"You pleb, Parlane," began Rowland. He wanted to
say more but at that moment someone banged loudly on
the car horn of the waiting white Mercedes. They all
swung round. Lex made a cooling down gesture with his
hand and the noise stopped. "Do yourself a favour,
bookmaker," said Rowland. "Stick to dog racing and all
the rest of that Brighton Rock caper. It's more your
style."

"I like your style, sir," said Lex, the crafty animation
returning to his eyes. "A first-rate military mind mas-
querading as a gay boys' tailor's dummy beneath a flat tin
hat. I bet those Micks were fooled."

"You disgust me," said Rowland. "And so do you,
James. Come along, father, let's go home."

For about the twentieth time that day the Duke ignored
him. "I'm staying at your aunt's near Bledington," he
said to James.

"I thought you would be."

"Tomorrow and Wednesday I have engagements. But
we shall expect you for lunch in the box on Thursday. At
twelve for twelve-thirty. Alone."

"Thank you."

"Do you want me to send a car?"

"No need for that, sir, but thanks," said Lex. "I've arranged transport for us all for all three days. Rather more stylish than by motor vehicle. Quicker too. First call's tomorrow at eleven. Eh, boys?" These last two words were shouted at his men in the white Mercedes and accompanied by a broad grin and a thumbs-up sign for victory. For a second time someone banged happily on the car horn. The Duke wasn't rattled though. He simply turned on his heel and walked away. In the opposite direction. Leaving Letherby and Rowland – and James and Lex's eyes – to follow on behind.

27

The first helicopter breasted the top of Cleeve Hill just after half-past eleven. There were three of them and they were travelling in convoy. Lex, Bella and James were riding in the first craft. Reema, Daisy, Hugh and Jack McQueen were in the second, while the third carried Charles St Clair, Jonathan Pointdexter and Mike Delaney-Dalzell, these last three having driven up from London to Harford together earlier that morning. The Weybridge lunch party, it seemed, had been quietly forgotten.

The helicopters had come up from Staverton Airport landing and taking off again in a field behind Harford Farm. Lex's flight briefing to the pilots had been a simple one. An exhilaratingly whirlwind tour of the plateaus and hillsides of North Gloucestershire culminating in a full-length circuit of the racetrack before sweeping down to land in the centre of the course. He'd also given each passenger a stereo headset to fit into their earphones, complete with a tape of carefully selected Cheltenham Festival theme music. The tape began with the theme tune from *Superman*, followed by the helicopter overture from *The Towering Inferno*. Then came Elgar's *Pomp and Circumstance March, Number Three in C Minor* and the final climax was Wagner's *Ride of The Valkyries* which exploded into Richmond's ears just as the wireless masts of Cheltenham Common, three hundred and thirty-odd feet up above the racecourse sailed dramatically into view.

Outside the day was cold but dry, though overcast. The overnight sleet had disappeared and for once, incredibly for Cheltenham race week, it was not raining. As Richmond sat there in the helicopter in the grip of Wagner's music and the bookmaker's cocaine, he could look down out of his window to see the ground rushing away beneath him. Not the paddy fields of South East Asia but the pinched looking brown and grey and dull-green checker-board of English fields and villages and leafless woods. The adrenalin beginning to flow through his veins was irresistible. He felt completely elated. There was no longer any time for regret or concern about his father. Here they were lunging at speed towards a venue of unavoidable risk, excitement and uncertainty. The horses were imminent. Decisive battle with the bookmakers was about to begin. And at long last the Cheltenham National Hunt Festival was getting underway.

The three helicopters landed in close proximity and then the whole party walked across from the centre of the course towards the grandstand. Large groups of people were already inspecting the last fence and the last hurdle. Daisy recognised several prominent American foxhunting millionairesses, their horses trained by nice respectable young Lambourn trainers and somehow doomed, so Lex said, to finish either ninth or be pulled up.

The official going was good to soft but the turf felt thick and springy underfoot. It would be hard to make excuses for any beaten animal on ground such as this. They walked across the racetracks and up into the grandstand and then out along the overhead walkway and down towards the paddock and the pre-parade.

The bars and stands in the various enclosures were only just beginning to fill up. Down in the tented village, though, the chalets and marquees were already packed with eager business parties expansively awaydaying it from London and seeking to quench till sufficiency and beyond the gasping thirsts and pregnant stomachs of their gladhanding guests.

One or two enterprising racing columnists – men like Bunter Shreeve-Snelling who contributed a monumental three paragraphs a day to one of the cheaper and more popular rags – were cleverly doing the rounds of more than one lunch tent at once, thus guzzling three servings of lobster, roast beef au jus and Bollinger where those without press cards had to make do with one. Richmond recognised that celebrated television pundit, the book-making expert from York, today looking positively restrained in a ratcatcher and norfolk jacket. He was tucking away into a nasty paper plateful of chilli con carne and rice while gazing in hopefully through the pink-beribboned doorway of the Turf Club tent.

Along the edges of the tented village were a line of trade stands where a wide variety of salesmen and women were hawking all manner of goods from saddles to shooting sticks and from hip flasks to Barbour jackets. There were bundles of birch twigs (for jumps that is), tinted-up prints of Arkle and Red Rum and generally rather florid-looking landscapes of either contemplative or action-packed horsey scenes. A sharp-looking man in a black bowler hat sold Lex twelve tickets for a raffle in aid of the British Field Sports Society.

Overlooking the unsaddling enclosure was a small wooden booth in which all the cups and trophies and Waterford glass for the week's racing were on display. Nearby was the statue of Arkle. An Irish priest in a smart little beret and a black Crombie overcoat was standing next to the statue and reading out a solemn prayer of hope and benediction for the Irish horses running at the Festival. A partly bewildered, partly enthralled crowd of all nationalities stood in a group by his side, mostly silent and reverential until all joining with him in a resoundingly emphatic chorus of 'Amens' at the end of his prayer as he offered up a final plea for the safety and salvation of all those men and horses who were about to take part.

Back up in the grandstand in the Gold Miller bar, large queues of hungry diners were starting to form up for crab claws and crayfish and fresh salmon with mayonnaise. In the background television highlights of past Festival races competed for their attention with various clattering and intrusive homemade videos recommending all manner of items such as lawn mowers, picnic tables, horse feed and 'Elasta Glide' double glazing.

"Ready Park Trailer Homes welcome you to the National Hunt Festival and look forward to entertaining patrons in chalet number 14 x 279 in the bottom left hand corner of the tented village."

Amongst the crowd now there were dozens of celebrated faces waiting in line for Lex's greetings and recognition. And none of them more prominent than the Irish. Faces wild-eyed, elfin and handsome. Faces bucolic, red-nosed, cherubic and curly-haired. A touch of William Bendix mixed in with W B Yeats. Bold bad boys though, the lot of them, in caramel coats and big-brimmed hats with beautiful bright-eyed women by their sides. All of the girls in their nice saved-up winter clothes and their best coats, their faces brightened up by a Max Factor smile.

These were old racing and poker and backgammon playing cronies from Dublin and Galway, Limerick and Cork. Farmers from Kerry and County Sligo. Club owners, businessmen and entrepreneurs from the Liffey to the Shannon and America too.

These were the men like Foxy Doogan and Ciaran Antoon. Dirty Billy Rafferty and his brothers Patsy, Michael, Declan and Frank from the Mile High Mountain. Kevin O'Hagen. Joe Dan Carmody. And Fennessy Conroy from the North.

Also up there in the mêlée of the bar were Danny McFarlane, the big wine importing client of the firm from Largs and the man who'd arranged the champagne concession at the Bella Vista, and Eddie Carntyne, the glitteringly silver-grey haulage contractor from the North East. McFarlane, like Lex, had a whole wardrobe of monogrammed shirts and suits. And he also had a grey wool coat with a blue velvet collar that was not quite Harrods. Motherwell snooker promoter, Tony Capaldi, was there along with his brother Michael, who exported ice cream cones to Pakistan, and two of Michael's young investment broker friends, Alan Furness and Willie 'The Dog' Burns. Furness and Burns were a pair of right rich young long-haired gentlemen who between them owned two of the most fancied horses running at the meeting, both of them handled by an up-and-coming Southern stable.

Further down the line there was Brian Turner and his partner, Colin Wade from Manchester. Self-styled Carpet Kings of The North. Brash and heavy men with feathered trilby hats and loud brown-and-white large check bold patterned suits that made them both look like a cross between Josiah Bounderby and Liberace. Turner's half-caste brother Gino Garvey, a nightclub comedian from Birmingham, smoked small flat cigars like chocolate cigarettes and wore a long leather overcoat trimmed with fur, the hemline reaching to the ground.

But the Turners and Wade and even Carntyne and the Capaldis were Mister Milk Toast and the Water Babies compared with the Chappell family. Billy Chappell, former British and European Middleweight Boxing Champion from Balham in South London, and his four sons, Chas, Tommy, Albie and Duane. They'd all had a whale of a time in their morning dress in the Royal Enclosure at Ascot the previous summer and now they were intent on enjoying Cheltenham too. It's true that their lips did seem to move when they smiled but that didn't fool anybody and they each had a stare that could block up an artery.

The talk throughout amongst all of these gatherings was of course about horses and tips and bets struck, but there was also a buzz of excited speculation about the terse Jockey Club statement at the top of the front page of that day's copy of *The Sporting Life*.

"In connection with certain allegations originally made in a Sheffield newspaper," it said, "an internal Club enquiry had established that a case did exist under Jockey Club rules against a certain member of the Club who had been acting on the North Eastern Circuit. The individual concerned had offered to resign from the Club forthwith. His resignation had been accepted and he would henceforth hold no further official position of any kind under the rules of racing. No further statement," it said, "would be issued."

No further statement maybe, but that couldn't stop all the rumour, the gossip, the guesswork and the intense speculation. And that speculation was music to Lex's ears. Inside *The Sporting Life* there was another article about some of the biggest gamblers on the modern racing scene and the article included a grinning photograph of Lex taken after last year's Festival coup over Tipperary Jester. "Lex Parlane," read the caption underneath the photograph. "A man who is proud to declare himself one of racing's true democrats."

"Marvellous value this seafood," came a thick Irish voice at his back. Lex turned round. It was Johnny Kinane, looking plump and healthy. He was just dipping brown bread and butter into a large pool of pink seafood sauce which was nestling on the edges of his plate of cold salmon. "I just can't believe it," he went on, speaking with his mouth very full. "It's by far the best buy on the racecourse."

"I know," said Lex, dusting mayonnaise-stained lettuce pieces from his coat collar. "I intend to eat some myself." He despatched Richmond towards the bar with a clutch of twenty-pound notes and sent the loyal Reema towards the fish queue. At that moment a rerun of the Wessels Champion Hurdle started up on the television set above his head and Cashel Maguire popped up at his elbow. Maguire looked sharp and slim in a light-brown camel-hair coat worn with a red check scarf and newly bought brown leather shoes to match.

"You can forget Shecky Dancer," said Maguire as they re-watched the Wessels together. "Galtee's nailed on."

"I know," said Lex. "Where's Bolger?"

"Back at the hotel," replied Maguire.

"They really won't let him in then?"

Maguire shook his head. "Warned off means warned off."

"Pathetic," said the Scotsman. "And him a grown man too."

"It's the gatemen, you see," said Kinane. "They've all got his image imprinted on their minds like a pre-war fifty-pound note."

"Lucky old them," said Lex.

"We've seen Garvin," said Maguire. "Down by the weighing room."

"Michael's seeing him tonight, I believe," added Kinane. I guessed he might be, thought Lex.

"He's got an agent with him today," said Maguire. "Arranging his commissions and organising outside rides."

"Nice work if you could get it," said Kinane.

"Forget agents," said Lex. "Agents are pimps. Are you all set up for Kilmonaghan?"

"I'm down for twelve grand," said Kinane. Maguire said nothing. "According to Hills it'll open up at two's. But the weight of offcourse money should soon push it through evens to odds on."

"Then here's to celebration." Reema and Richmond had returned with the seafood and the champagne and for the first time that week the champagne corks started popping. Lex did his best to make sure that the various elements in his party were all introduced to one another. Duke's son to boxing champion, female equestrian to club owner and stockbroker gambler to rails bookie and so on. He knew how to play them all off against each other and it had been his experience that there was nothing his more upper-class clients liked better than a little first name chatter with the low life. As soon as he was sure that all was well he excused himself politely and went off upstairs with Bella. They'd been invited for a private drink in Camilla's father's box.

James Richmond found himself left with Charles St Clair and his friends. He was actually none-too-delighted about these three late additions to the party. St Clair he already knew about. The other two he took an instant dislike to. Jonathan Pointdexter had in fact met James the previous summer at Royal Ascot where he'd developed an irritating habit of banging him over the head with a rolled up newspaper whenever he'd wanted to attract his attention. He'd also kept bragging on all week long about his various punting successes without ever demonstrating the extent of these financial coups by offering to buy anyone even so much as one half-glass of lukewarm lager. And from the look of him Delaney-Dalzell would be scarcely much better. Yet Lex was effusively charming to both these men and especially to Charles St Clair whose facial expressions conjured up in Richmond's mind the image of an overgrown monkey with lockjaw.

What an old pike the bookmaker was, thought the boy. He had plans for these three alright. Richmond could tell from the gleam in his eyes. A golden gleam matched by the glint from the newly-capped tooth in his bottom front row.

Jonathan Pointdexter was staying with family for the week but St Clair and DD were in at a hotel in Stow. They'd got the last room in the house, so it seemed, and they were going to have to share a double bed.

"You know what I'm worried about most?" St Clair was chortling, to anyone who cared to listen.

"What are you worried about most, Charles?" asked Pointdexter.

"A jolly good rogering up the back way from old Grizwold here. Aren't I, Grizwold?"

Delaney-Dalzell scowled unpleasantly. "Fuck your own sticky little arse, Charles."

"Oh, come along, Grizwold, don't be a Grizwold." Then his eyes lighted delightedly on Kinane and Cashel Maguire. "And come on, you criminals. I want to know exactly what's going on here today. All the tips. Kilmonaghan, I believe?"

What followed was less a question-and-answer session

than a series of statements by St Clair which didn't really
need any answer or at least took no notice of one when
they got it.

"What about White's Club?"

"A nice young horse but. . ."

"Out of his depth. And doesn't act on this ground, I
believe. Is the trainer in form?"

"He never does that well at this. . ."

"Ask Roddy Hyde-Lyne. Hyde-Lyne would know. I'd
ask Roddy Hyde-Lyne."

"He's not keen on the. . ."

"Last race. Irish. Good form or not?"

"They don't look that strong though. . ."

"They don't win that race. Irishmen never. They don't
ever win that race." His curiosity at least temporarily
satisfied, St Clair looked around for his private hotline to
the rails. "And where the hell is our Scotsman? Where is
that blasted Scot?"

"He's drinking upstairs," replied James. St Clair poked
him suddenly in the ribs with a long and bony finger.
"And hey. What's all this Steward with his pants down
nonsense? Will we be allowed to know who?"

"I doubt it," said James. "He'll be under the carpet, not
on it."

"Quite right too," called Maguire, but St Clair had
already stopped listening. "Where *is* that blasted Scot?"

"Do you see that girl?" asked Delaney-Dalzell. He was
pointing out a fragile young blonde who was standing next
to Duane Chappell. She had on high heels and fishnet
stockings and a very thin white frilly dress and she was
holding what seemed to be a white lace parasol in one
hand. Her costume would've been more in keeping with
Goodwood than Cheltenham, though even there it would
hardly have been approved of. "I'd like to fuck that girl
and then throw up all over her," said DD.

"Go and tell her boyfriend, Mike," said James mali-
ciously. "I'm sure he'd be interested to know."

What on earth did Lex see in these people, he wondered, as he escaped gratefully up the brown-carpeted staircase towards Camilla's father's box on the top floor. But the company there was equally varied.

In keeping with his status as a still-swinging peer, Lord Kinglass had assembled a motley collection for lunch. There were a number of pop stars present as well as various of Lex's Irish connections, several prominent daily gossip columnists and a large gathering of Camilla's young friends from Gloucestershire and London. All in all there were about fifty people squashed into a space that would-'ve been tight for twenty-five. As usual the hirsute peer, his spectacles already steaming up thanks to alcohol and sexual titillation, greeted James like a long lost son, thrusting large glasses of Pol Roger into his hands from the outset. James gulped the champagne down breathless-ly, grabbed a plate of cold hors d'oeuvres from a nearby waitress and then endeavoured to survey the scene more closely.

Camilla was deep in conversation with lots of Lucys, Arabellas and Annabels. Marks, Willies and Toms. Some of the girls wore their brother's grey or brown trilby hats along with their own long coats, their dark blue corduroy trousers and their flat-soled shoes. One bored-looking button-nosed blonde was shivering visibly in some thin-looking velveteen knickerbockers. Amongst the more conventional, though not necessarily older, married women there were plenty of regulation Hermès scarves matching up with their handbags, blue tights and small black leather gold-buckled shoes. Reema was there, talk-ing avidly to two blond and aesthetic young rowing men from Goring and Henley-on-Thames. And there too in the corner of the room was Bella with Lex Parlane, Bella looking beautiful in a long purple and black check skirt worn with her black lacy stockings and a pair of low-key, low-heel black Pinet shoes. Earlier she and Camilla had exchanged transparently combative pleasantries with each other while Bella kept a firm eye on Lex and Lex talked betting with Camilla's father. Now she was being very charming to Sunny Vengsarkar and also to several other of Richmond's richer young Christchurch friends, all of whom seemed keenly interested in whatever she had to say. And all of whom had only recently opened credit accounts up with the Lex Parlane Connection.

And then the door of the box opened once again and in came Billy Chappell and his son Duane. They too were both greeted with warm and fraternal kinship by their aristocratic host.

And so it went on.

28

Down in the ring the pitches were filling up fast. All of the big city boys were out in force, their ranks swelled by a number of additions from Ireland and the North. Nearly all the bookies had put on their best or most expensive-looking suits and coats and signet-rings for the day, testifying to their readiness to repel the punters' invasion. One man, a prominent London face with long fair hair and a wispy moustache, had bought himself a new calf-length camel hair coat replete with a large and floppy-looking belt which Lex thought made him look like a gay bear in a bath rug.

Rails bookmakers are not allowed to advertise their prices on a board in England as they are in Ireland. They have to shout their odds at a stentorian bellow, especially if they're going to compete with their rivals on the boxes in Tatts. Lex was well equipped by nature for this particular kind of shouting match and at Cheltenham he also had the advantage of a prime rails pitch, bang there between William Hills and his most dedicated and detested rivals, Mike Cordrey and Goldline Investments. And like all these other firms Lex accepted cash bets at ten pounds minimum a time as well as all his credit wagers.

At just after five-past one, still more than an hour before the first race, Willie The Weasel Wood opened up the shining silvery clasp on the black and well-polished Lex Parlane Connection satchel. And there it was. Deep, gaping and ready for business. Maxie Carlisle had the ledger and the pencils in his hands and a pocketful of betting tickets which he passed to his boss.

Willie The Weasel looked up at the grey and sunless sky and whispered into Lex's ear. Lex looked up for himself and then looked back round again at the early inquisitive punters who were beginning to mill around at his feet. He grinned.

"Alright, gentlemen," he roared, the granite in his voice cutting out the competition at a stroke. "Let's see a bit of the action. What time's the rain going to fall at Prestbury Park today? I'll lay six to four the fourth race. That's five-past four. The Waterford Crystal Stayers. Seven to two it's during the Champion Hurdle. And ten to one it comes before the first. Now come on, gentlemen. Let's see the colour of your money. I'll lay six to four the rain dance."

A normally timid and pink-faced man hurried up towards him as if mesmerised. He pushed four ten-pound notes into the bookmaker's massive hand. "Forty pounds please. The fourth race. To win . . . only."

"To win only?" cried Lex to the gallery. "As if it could be each way, sir." The men on either side of him laughed cruelly and the pink-faced man blushed even pinker. "Sixty pounds to forty, down to the gentleman. Thank you, sir." Lex handed him a ticket, his first of the meeting. The Festival takings had begun.

While Lex was striking his first bet of the day on the racecourse, Billy Two Hats Mcphee was standing at the window of a thirty-pounds-a-day hotel room in the King's Cross district of London and reflecting on the work already done. There were two single beds in the room separated by a bedside table and a radio and television console. The curtains, chair covers and bedspreads were all of a tartan pattern, in keeping with the tastes of the Coventry-based Scottish owners of the hotel chain. At half-past ten that morning, before Lex and his party had even taken off from Harford, there'd been six open suitcases sitting on the top of those bedspreads, three suitcases on each single bed. Inside each case had been neat bundles of money. Mixtures of one, five, ten, twenty and fifty-pound notes, all wrapped up in last week's copies of *The Sporting Life*.

The men had been shown up into the room by the paid-off management in groups of five at a time. Billy had given each of them their stash, their district of London and a route and timing schedule from shop to shop. Now he and Willie Cooper would handle the telephone commissions. The London-based ones that was. There'd be others from six other cities, including two in the Irish Republic. After they'd got it all on, Billy would report back to Lex at Cheltenham via the office blower. Then he'd ring the hotel room service and order himself a Coca Cola and a cheese sandwich for his lunch. Finally, with a new packet of Polo mints bought especially for the occasion, he'd settle himself down on the tartan upholstered sofa, switch on the television set and prepare, not for the first or for the last time in his life, to have his nerves frayed and shredded to the roots by the result of a four-minute horse race.

Meanwhile back at the racecourse the clock was ticking on towards a quarter-past one. And down amongst the larger marquees and the hospitality tents the Jockey Club's 'Racing and Advertising Industry Talk-In' was long since over. Representatives of about half a dozen London-based companies selected rather randomly by the Club's Administration and Finance Committee had been invited to make presentations for a brand new horseracing account and to recommend, in Lord Stowell's words, "How Horse Racing might be best sold to the public over the last fifteen years of the twentieth century."

The ad men had digested the Levy Board–Jockey Club pitch and then fired maximum customer potential target questions at them for the next couple of hours. One or two smarter and younger members of the Club had been wheeled in especially to take the flak. Men with Sandhurst–Cambridge scholarships and high passing out marks from the Royal Agricultural College at Cirencester.

The Duke had detested the whole spectacle. He had far

graver matters on his mind anyway and the sight of
George Stowell ingratiating himself all morning with some
George Best lookalike with a sunray suntan was absolute-
ly repellent to him.

Now at last it was all over. And the Duke and Dickie
Frampton-Mansell – ex-Hussars, a Hunt Master and number two on the Disciplinary Committee – found themselves backed up defensively against one wall of the
marquee, a glass of pink gin or something stronger in each
hand. In front of them the projector and the screens had
been packed up, boxed and moved away. The tables had
been rearranged for drinking over and the chefs were
sharpening their knives behind the carvery. The guests
however were still present and would unfortunately continue to be so throughout the afternoon. The Duke looked
around at them. Smoothly philishaved men with well-
coiffeured hair and credit cards, discussing lunch and the
racing and maximum potential targets (still) and lunch and
other lunches on other London days in Charlotte Street
and Soho.

"I've found a really *simpatico* little Italian place," said
one. "Just behind Marshall Street baths. Marvellous
homemade pasta."

"You can't go far wrong with Geccone's," said another
man. "I've said it all before and I'll say it again. They do a
very decent kebab."

A number of journalists were present too, including the
dandruff-afflicted correspondent from Louis Weiss's reception the previous afternoon. Once again his plate was
full and the Duke eyed him with especial disgust. He
thought he was just another common little Wardour Street
bum boy. "See how they run, Dickie," he said, angling his
nose towards the journalist. "A typical example of your
advertising breed."

"I think you're wrong there, Johnny," said Frampton-
Mansell. "I think he's a scribbler actually. On the *Life* . . .
actually."

"Is he really?" said the Duke. "You amaze me. I

thought he was an oil-slick. Like that frightful little
smarting arse Weiss."

"Weiss!"

The two turf aristocrats scanned the horizon seeking out
the whereabouts of the miniature sodomite who annoyed
them both so greatly. They eventually spotted him hovering in the doorway to the tent, hair slicked back, shoes
slicked up and with a small and ineffectual-looking whisky
glass bobbing up and down in his rat-like paw.

Weiss was having a miserable time. He had just been
remonstrating with one of the Jockey Club's principal
guests. A Junior Minister of State at the Home Office, the
government department officially responsible to Parlia-
ment for the proper workings of the racing industry. Weiss
had been trying to convince him of the need for a
crackdown on both turf corruption and Jockey Club
ineptitude. Otherwise, he said, bookmaking's image and
reputation would be in tatters. And then if they ever got
another Labour government they'd all be ripe for the
storming of the Bastille and the bloody guillotine. And all
because the Jockey Club had about as much idea about
public relations and image building as Enid Blyton and
her blasted golliwogs.

But it was all to no avail. The Minister could detect the
whiff of controversy in the air as clearly as he could smell
microwave Roast Lamb and Mint Sauce from the carvery.
And controversy it was political duty to avoid at all costs.
For, as Weiss well knew, no Conservative Home Secretary was ever going to get himself too heavily involved with
the Top Men of the Jockey Club who preferred to keep all
politicians – even those of their own tribe – at a good
arm's length. If the Jockey Club vouched that they, not
the Levy Board, not the Racehorse Owners Association
and certainly not hostile opposition sub-committees, knew
what was best for horse racing then Tory Cabinet Minis-
ters would be only too happy to shut up and leave well
alone. That's because they all lacked spine, thought
Weiss. Or lacked bottom, as the Clubmen themselves
would say.

Weiss sighed, stroked his wide pattern silver-and-turquoise Burton's tie and plucked a sausage roll from a passing tray. He could see some foxy-faced man with a Guard's tie and a mulberry-coloured birthmark glaring at him fiercely from across the other side of the room. Weiss had a sudden fantasy about sitting having afternoon tea with the Prime Minister in the back drawing room at number ten Downing Street. She wouldn't compromise. She'd understand about his fearsome reputation for business efficiency. And she certainly wouldn't shake in her shoes every time one of these damned patronising gymkhana-and-shooting-stick types started talking to her.

Actually Weiss did know that he was quite highly thought of by Conservative Central Office and a prospective Parliamentary candidacy had even been mentioned by one or two high-ups in the know. Weiss hoped it would be somewhere local. Somewhere like Esher. Or Epsom and Ewell. Weiss liked Epsom. He remembered being wheeled across the downs in his pushchair by his mother and sister when he was just a baby. All three of them relishing the clean air and blue skies of Surrey after the terror of the ghetto back in Warsaw. Even today, Derby Day was the only racing occasion that Louis Weiss actually enjoyed. He liked the jockeys who came over from America. They seemed to have so much better manners than their English counterparts. And he liked the whelks and mussels. The taste of salt and fish and pale ale. Real England. That's what he called it in his speeches. Real Elgar's England. And that's what Louis Weiss loved.

A gap appeared in the crowd in front of him and Weiss caught the Duke's eye. The Duke was trying not to notice him but Weiss was determined to hang on and he could be every bit as tenacious as one of the Duke's own Jack Russell terriers.

"Ah, Louis," said the Senior Steward, looking up and smiling spontaneously as the bookmaker elbowed Frampton-Mansell to one side. "Didn't see you there."

"When are you seeing Mould, your Grace?"

"Later today."

"And then?"

"An extremely painful interview with a lifelong friend."

"And then?"

"We're allowing *The Times* man to do a sort of article in tomorrow's edition. No names."

"That's a mistake."

"Thank you for your advice."

"What about the Scotsman?"

"I've been reading Racecourse Security Services' reports. I'm having copies made and sent on to the Disciplinary Committee. They meet next week."

Weiss shook his head. "Also a mistake. What do you have to wait until then for? There's no telling what damage Parlane might do in the meantime. These three days are crucial to my business."

"Thank you for the advice, Louis."

"Can I see the reports?"

"I'm sure Disciplinary can handle it. RSS have given them every possible assistance."

"And after next week? What happens then?"

"I've no doubt the Disciplinary Stewards will notify the subjects and then set up a full Portman Square enquiry. Date and timing to be announced." Weiss had his mouth open again but the Duke cut him off. "But we must be delicate, Louis. And we must be organised." He dropped his voice to a mumble. "The fact of the matter is that there's a lot of . . . covert evidence. Especially against Garvin. And he's bound to be well spoken for."

"But this involves me too, you know."

"Not any more, I think."

"Now look here. I've done what you wanted me to. All bloody winter long. But when the public finally read about bookmakers like Lex Parlane and the full extent of his criminal activities the backlash against firms like mine could be considerable. So I'm warning you . . . if you let this man get away . . . I'll pull out our company sponsorship at a stroke."

"Excuse me, Louis. I'm due at the Royal Box." He turned away.

"I'll even democratise racing myself. Single-handed." But without looking round the Duke squeezed his way past the bum boys and the advertising accounts directors and past the advertising accounts directors' flashily expensive-looking wives – or girlfriends – and on out into the comparatively sweet-smelling air of the members' lawn.

"I've just been looking back over the form for Thursday," said Frampton-Mansell as they strode across the grass. "Wide open Gold Cup. I just can't make my mind up at all. This pair up from Lambourn, well, they look indivisible on paper."

"We must hurry," said the Duke. They reached the staircase. Frampton-Mansell nodded at a familiar-faced detective. Whenever royalty had a tip for a big race the detective was always in the know and the Master of Foxhounds had a regular arrangement with him.

"My God, I'm excited," said Frampton-Mansell, running one hand through his hair. "This could be one of the most memorable Festival meetings for years."

"I do hope you're wrong, Dickie," said the Duke. "I do so hope that you're wrong." A crisp knock, another security guard and the door to the Royal Box was open.

29

Outside all the talk and debate was now beginning to focus around the first race of the day and the sense of excited expectation snaking around the bars and up the staircases and out across the lawns towards the ring gave off an audible hissing sound like a lighted fuse proceeding down a trail of gunpowder.

The Waterford Crystal Supreme Novices Hurdle is a championship race run over two miles for young novice hurdlers who may go on to make the grade in the championship proper in a few years time or who may become top-class two-mile steeplechasers instead. And this year there were nineteen runners.

A large section of the crowd were craning their necks to get a better look at them in the pre-parade and especially in the saddling up boxes at the top and bottom end of the ring. As the clock ticked on towards five minutes to two most of the runners were then led by their stable lads and girls out of the pre-parade and into the main paddock area proper, its tiered gallery at the top end lined with spectators more than fifteen and twenty lines deep.

James and Sunny looked up at the first show of odds that were displayed next to the runners and riders board. Number eight, Kilmonaghan, was the five to four on favourite. Second best at seven to two was White's Club, the top young Lambourn-trained two-mile novice hurdler. Then came another Irish challenger, Fandango's Revenge, with the Northern-trained Just Jimmy, both bracketed on the five to one mark. Then they went eight to one Cabinteely (Big Pat McKenna's representative), ten to one two more English-trained runners, Suicide Pact and

The Old Country, twelve to one Mylerstown, who was trained by CP Molloy, and sixteen to one bar.

James looked up at the number board. Mylerstown was number eleven. And in the morning papers number eleven was down to be ridden by its part-owner Dr Eamon Sheedy, a chartered accountant from Baltimore and a full seven-pound claiming Amateur Rider who had never yet ridden a winner round any recognised racecourse. Up on the racecourse number board though there was a change of jockey. Mylerstown was now down to be ridden by young Frankie Molloy, the trainer's son. And, as James well knew, 'Boots' Molloy didn't need to be claiming any seven-pound allowances either. James and Sunny looked back at their copies of *The Sporting Life*. Kilmonaghan's form was well known and seemed outstanding. Fandango's Revenge had won three novice hurdle races in Ireland that winter and also run second under a big weight in a handicap at Fairyhouse in February. White's Club had won his only two races at Ascot and Newbury. Just Jimmy had won four off the reel but all of them at hayseed tracks like Hexham, Catterick and Market Rasen. Cabinteely had only run once over hurdles but had been unbeaten in his three Irish bumper races before that. As for Mylerstown there was a story that he'd once nearly died of a heart condition as a three-year-old but he'd recovered well enough from it now, so it seemed. He'd won twice and been placed three times that season, last time out running on under gentle handling over two-and-a-quarter miles at Leopardstown at the beginning of March.

Most of the field had now arrived in the paddock and the buzz of conversation and the blocked nose announcements over the public address system were punctuated by the regular clatter of horses' hooves on the paddock tarmac. Nearly all the runners looked well and beautifully turned out, though the favourite Kilmonaghan had a slightly subdued air about him, thought James. One horse was still being attended to in the saddling up boxes. He was snorting and kicking out boldly with his near hind leg.

James couldn't yet see his number cloth because the stable lads' backs were in the way. Then at the last minute he saw the tall, grey-suited figure of Blazes Heffernan whip the rug off the horse's back. And there he was. Number eleven. Mylerstown. The Galway Raider of yesterday morning being led last of all into the parade ring. His hind quarters gleamed and he danced keenly on his toes as he saw the crowd, sensed the atmosphere and watched the diminutive figures of nineteen jockeys spilling out into the ring from the weighing room. A vivid and colourful splash of golds and blacks and scarlet and emerald checks and royal blue with burgundy cross belts. The two young men looked up once again at the odds board. Kilmonaghan had gone out to evens. Mylerstown had shortened suddenly to eight to one.

"I think this is it," said James. A hand bell was rung in the parade ring.

"Jockeys please mount," came a voice. "Jockeys please mount."

"Can we get on?" asked Sunny. "We've got to get on."

"No need to," said James with a smile. "Lex is fixing everything."

"Let's put some cash on it too," said Sunny. "We might as well."

"Why not," said James.

And so the two of them started walking, then walking faster and then running towards the ring, dodging, brushing and pushing their way past the huge crowd that was by now beginning to wheel uncertainly between the bars, the paddock, the bookmakers and the stands.

Down in the Tattersalls enclosure the action was fast, furious and building towards a climax. Clamouring punters, arms outstretched, were forcing great wads and fistfuls of money up into the bookmakers' hands. James fought his way up to a board near the rails. Mylerstown had come in a further two points to a top priced six to one.

Along the rails the big boys were competing for the biggest money. And there was Lex Parlane. Coat open,

head held high and shouting the odds across the ring. "I'll
lay six to one White's Club. Six to one this five-year-old.
Even money Kilmonaghan. Evens this favourite."

Then came the Ulsterman Willie McGrory's deep
gravel-voiced bark as he laid into the supposed favourite.
"Alright, gentlemen. Are you ready? I'll lay six to four
Kilmonaghan. Six to four this talking horse." A new rush
of the innocent pushed their way towards him. On his box
in the ring Jack D'Angelo went to two's but then a torrent
of mostly English money brought the favourite's price
tumbling back to evens.

Men with the off course blower connection were talking
back feverishly at the big layers. Another flurry of tic-tac
activity further down the line and the prices changed yet
again. Five to one Mylerstown. Five to one. James
and Sunny had a hundred apiece on in cash. Some
of the cash-only bookmakers had already gone nine
to two. James watched the bets being laid. Ninety
pounds to twenty. Four and a half hundred to one. Five
hundred and forty pounds to one hundred and twenty,
ticket number eighty-six. Eighteen thousand pounds to
four.

The horses were coming out on to the course. The two
young Oxford undergraduates fought their way back out
from the ring, struggling with the rest of the crowd
through the narrow and stomach-crushing defile that led
from the Tattersalls enclosure into Members.

As they walked across the lawn they saw the runners
cantering down past them towards the start. They saw
Kilmonaghan go by, followed by Fandango's Revenge and
White's Club. But their eyes were fixed on the brown and
yellow checks and the cream-coloured cap of number
eleven, Mylerstown. He was cantering down a little too
freely for James's liking. Frankie Molloy would have to do
something about that once the race began. That would be
essential.

They found a place on the lawn behind the named
members' benches and focused their binoculars on the

start. Nobody was sitting on any of the benches just now, but when the five-and-a-half-foot Sunny attempted to stand on one of them for a moment to make a final check on the blinkers and overweight details on the main runners and riders board opposite the winning post a fat tweed-skirted woman in a Will Scarlet jerkin and a Lincoln-green cap started banging him crossly about the shoulder and bottom with her rolled up umbrella. "I say. You. You! Get down. Get down at once."

"Madam. Please. Desist," replied the Indian as he jumped down nimbly to the ground. "Your attentions are entirely unwelcome."

"They're all the same these Arabs," muttered one military-looking man whose shoulders and back were not so much ramrod as reinforced cement. "Take 'em to one race meeting and they think they own the lot."

Sunny smiled patiently at James and relayed the final odds on the race. "Five to four Kilmonaghan. Nine to two Mylerstown. Eleven to two Fandango's Revenge. Eight to one White's Club. And ten to one bar."

A second or so later Will Scarlet and the Colonel were elbowed further back as Lex and Willie the Weasel Wood arrived at Richmond's shoulder. "I told you yesterday you'd find out in time," said Lex grinning. "I've put you down for a grand. It's spread all around. Top priced fourteen to one."

"Fuck." James Richmond shivered suddenly as he thought of just what he might do with fourteen thousand pounds.

"Taj Mahal's got five hundred pound on at twelves with William Hills." Sunny grinned too. He was well used by now to the Scotsman's customary cheerful abuse.

"But what about Kilmonaghan?" asked James.

"It's over the top. And that's official. It had a very hard race at Leopardstown and it's only running here because the owners want to. They think that he'll finish in the first four but they don't expect to win. Not even Cashel Maguire knew that."

"But what about Kinane? And St Clair? All the people who've backed it?"

"I've covered their losses." James was staring at him. "Look, son. I needed their accounts to help get my money down. But I couldn't afford to tell them. Arseholes like St Clair would've bragged about it from Park Lane to Ullapool." James shook his head. He was not exactly shocked. In fact he was quite impressed in a way. But even so he was still glad that he wasn't Charles St Clair. "Besides," said Lex, "why should they complain? They usually owe me money. Today they might just break even."

Down at the start there was a slight delay. One of the horses, an outsider, had unshipped his jockey and was currently facing in the opposite direction about twenty-five yards behind the others. James looked round. He couldn't believe how calm and sanguine Lex and Sunny both looked. For his own part he could feel and hear his heart pounding as he held his binoculars up to his eyes. His hands and arms were trembling too. He looked back over his shoulder. Every place and vantage point on the racecourse seemed crammed to capacity. Even the course enclosure on the opposite side of the track was packed. Up in the grandstand the top tier of reserved seats were all taken and the richer racegoers were lining the balconies of their boxes, binoculars in hand. He looked up at the grandstand roof. In the old days the racecourse commentator used to have to climb up an outside ladder to get to his commentary box. Right up and out on a limb. Richmond knew how he felt.

More than half-a-mile away the loose horse had been remounted. Soon the starter would be calling them in.

"How much do you stand to win?" James whispered in Lex's ear.

The bookmaker breathed his reply very softly. "There's a lot of people involved. Off course mainly. In London. Glasgow. And Dublin. Between us . . . and if Billy's done his job as he should . . . we'll take out at least half a million."

"Half a million? Pounds?"

Lex nodded. "And then there's our friends on the course. As soon as I knew that we'd got the good prices I showed them the right way to go."

"How many people?"

"About . . . two hundred and fifty."

"Oh my God."

The course commentator's voice broke in. "They're under starters orders." James felt the muscles in his stomach begin to tighten and stretch. His heart had stopped pounding and he'd now entered a kind of fluttering no-man's-land of uncertainty. The commentator again: "And they're off. And as they run towards the first it's Cabinteely who's the early leader. Followed by Just Jimmy, Laurentian, Patient Scenario and Revoke. In behind these five comes Araminsky followed by Fandango's Revenge, Kilmonaghan and My Romeo." (A brief pause). "And they're all safely over the first. And as they run down now towards flight number two it's still Cabinteely making it from Just Jimmy. Revoke going up on the outside. Then comes Patient Scenario, Laurentian, Araminsky and Fandango's Revenge. And they're followed by White's Club, Kilmonaghan, Cameron Tartan and My Romeo. And then a slight gap back to Lady Fingers, Suicide Pact, Bankers Order and The Old Country. Day By Day on the inside. Mylerstown on the outer. And bringing up the rear at this stage Our Kid and The Battler. Over flight number two. And it's. . ."

And as they swung away left past the stands on the first circuit Cabinteely looked well and full of running in the lead. Fandango's Revenge had moved up a place or two on the inside rail while Kilmonaghan was near the middle of the field tracking the English champion jockey on White's Club. Mylerstown had certainly settled alright. But as they started out down into the country towards the third flight of hurdles he had only two horses behind him.

It was this point in a race which Richmond found indescribably nerve-racking yet exciting. As the horses streamed away from the grandstand and down the far side of the course you knew that there was no way you could re-wind the tape and bring them all back to the start, get your money back and change your mind or your selection. You'd played your cards and from now on the result was out of your hands.

When the going is good at Cheltenham a race like the Waterford Crystal Supreme Novices takes approximately three minutes and fifty-five seconds to run. After about one minute and fifty seconds and five flights of hurdles the now eighteen runners were approaching the farthest point on the course. Just Jimmy had just taken a heavy fall at the fourth and Kilmonaghan was making ground. Back to the commentator.

"And as they run towards the top of the hill with one more flight left to jump on the far side of the course it's still Cabinteely who's made all the running from Revoke, Fandango's Revenge. Right there on the inside is Kilmonaghan and just behind Kilmonaghan comes White's Club and The Old Country. And then all in a bunch and tracking this leading group are Cameron Tartan, Araminsky, Bankers Order, My Romeo and Suicide Pact."

At the top of the hill Frankie Molloy was still only fourteenth in a field of eighteen. Then at long last he started to make his move and they all lost him for a moment as horse and rider moved up on the outside of their field on the side farthest away from the grandstand. The course commentator lost him too. But then suddenly, as the roars of the crowd started to build and as the leaders began to pick up pace and thunder down the hill towards the second last hurdle, he picked him up.

"And as they come down now towards the penultimate flight in the Waterford Crystal Supreme Novices Hurdle it's Fandango's Revenge who shows fractionally ahead from Cabinteely and Kilmonaghan" – (a big cheer from the crowd) – "with White's Club just in behind those three. And also making significant headway now on the outside of the field is number eleven, Mylerstown" – (an even bigger cheer from Lex and James and Sunny) – "And these five have suddenly drawn some three or four lengths clear of their nearest pursuer who is in fact Cameron Tartan."

"Come on, Frankie. You can do it," roared Sunny.

"Go on, Frankie. Go on, my son," yelled Lex.

"Come on Mylerstown," cried Richmond. "Come on you beautiful, beautiful creature. You can do it. Come on."

"Over the second last . . . and a bad mistake there by Fandango's Revenge who has in fact unseated his rider" – (a gasp from the grandstand) – "and also interfered quite badly with Cabinteely. And as they run round the turn into the home straight with just one flight of hurdles left to jump it's Kilmonaghan who strikes the front. Kilmonaghan. From White's Club. Kilmonaghan in the centre of the course. White's Club on his inside. And these two being challenged strongly now over on the stands side rail by Mylerstown. Over the last. . ."

Over the last! And what a tremendous leap young Frankie conjured up from the five-year-old. With just one crack of the whip before take off, Mylerstown really reached for the obstacle, landed running and then put back his ears and powered his way up the Cheltenham hill, showing a magnificent galloping surge of acceleration. White's Club tried to come back at him on the run-in but the Deep Run gelding would not be denied and with Frankie Molloy pumping away, hands and heels in perfect rhythm, he crossed the line three lengths to the good. White's Club was second, the tiring Kilmonaghan another two-and-a-half lengths back in third and the luckless Cabinteely a further six lengths away back in fourth.

As Mylerstown swept through his final triumphant fifty yards his sixteen-year-old stable lad, Dandy MacNama, hurled his saddle cloth and blanket up high into the air where, for the briefest fraction of a second, they brushed against the broadest of Lex's broad-rimmed black fedoras which he too had flung passionately towards the sky. And from the chorus of ecstatic cheering that rang out around the stands the English spectators were left in no doubt that however many punts had gone down on Kilmonaghan they themselves had been wrongfooted once again by the Irish insiders in the know.

James and Sunny were hoarse from cheering and weak from nerves. Lex had recovered his hat and was still punching it in the air in jubilation. The three of them started running towards the unsaddling enclosure. The doors and passageways from the Members' were ludicrously narrow and cramped and the rush of outgoing racegoers trying to reach the celebrations struggled, squashed and tumbled their way through like an escaping army or cavalry pile-up herded into some narrow defile.

Beyond the stands the race was on to get a good position by the top end of the paddock to see the winner's return and the presentation. James and Sunny started running down the terracing towards the bottom of the gallery but Lex was already heading for the owners, trainers and officials entrance in the middle. "Come on," he shouted. "This way."

"We can't go in there."

"Yes we can. I'm an owner. I bought a half-share over breakfast." So in they went. And out there in the middle of the paddock a crowd of almost fifty people had already materialised as if from nowhere as one leading Irish racing personality after another made their appearance. All of them, it seemed, a part of Lex's two or three hundred 'close friends' who had at the last been put right about the favourite. And at the centre of it all was the proud and smiling figure of CP Molloy. Men rushed up to congratulate him and shake his hand and slap him on the back. CP smiled and glowed and accepted their praise gladly. The press tried to swamp him but the boys warded them off. James and Sunny found themselves swirling around in this milling crowd of suits and hats and dark blue and green coats and cigars and shamrocks. Then the cheering started up again in earnest and James looked up to see the first four horses coming back in again at the bottom end of the unsaddling enclosure. Frankie Molloy was waving his whip in the air and grinning from ear to ear. James could see the hills behind the horses. The sun was coming out. He looked back around at the huge crowd gathered on the terraces and now all starting to roar their applause for the winner. He could see the looks of identification and admiration in their eyes and for one brief moment he felt as if they were applauding him as well as the horse.

"You know," he said to Sunny, "I think this is the most exciting day of my life."

Dandy MacNama was nearly in tears as he led Mylerstown back to the number one spot. Someone had put a shamrock behind the horse's ears and on one side of him was a goat called Rusty. Rusty had been his constant companion ever since his heart attack of two years before and he wouldn't even go outside his box now without him. That was how a goat came to be honoured in the unsaddling enclosure at the Cheltenham Festival.

"Can you imagine this happening at Royal Ascot?" said Cashel Maguire who had slipped in to shake Lex's hand. Maguire bore no malice. Unlike Bolger and Kinane his professional gambler's instinct had warned him that Kilmonaghan was no good thing and when he'd seen which way the money was going he'd helped himself to three thousand pounds each way on Mylerstown at twelve to one. Kinane too had spotted the trend in the market and had been careful to lay off his bets, but even so he was mad as hell at Lex and while the Scotsman was grinning spontaneously for the cameras and applauding Dr Sheedy and CP and Frankie as they collected their winners' trophies from the wife of the managing director of Waterford Glass, Kinane was already heading towards the telephone boxes for a private and confidential call to Michael Bolger in the Queens Hotel.

Charles St Clair, though, like Pointdexter and Delaney-Dalzell, had been too busy talking and drinking in the Golden Miller bar to even notice the drift in Kilmonaghan's price. Later, standing out on the lawn, he caught a glimpse of Lex's face and he saw the fedora flying into the air as Mylerstown passed the winning post in first place. And immediately he began to feel like a cuckolded husband. Even when he got down to the paddock the gateman wouldn't let him in because he wasn't wearing the correct badge. "What do you mean 'owner'?" he screamed. "Do you think they're all owners? Only yester-day morning I was playing golf with a past secretary to the Jockey Club."

"I don't care if you're the Aga Khan's brother, sir," replied the gateman firmly. "You can't go in there without the proper badge."

"Then fuck off, you indescribable little shit!"

At that point St Clair was forcibly moved away by angry officials. He finally caught up with Lex and his party back up in the Mill House bar. "You bastard. You tipped me the wrong horse."

"Cool it, Charles," said Lex, as he saw the banker's thunderous expression. "I saved your money for you."

"But what about my share of the bloody profits?"

"Let's say I'll knock it off the tab."

"You arse-greasing bastard."

"Sure, sure. I'm a big bad bully and you're a poor wee lamb. Now get yourself a drink and shut up." And with that he turned away. And St Clair could find no one else satisfactory to complain to. Not DD who was drunk and didn't care and not even Jonathan Pointdexter who was already claiming to have backed the winner himself with his local publican at Compton Abdale some three or four weeks before everybody else.

After about fifteen minutes in the Mill House bar Lex took himself and Bella and James and Sunny and Hugh and Daisy and CP Molloy and Foxy Doogan and Ciaran Antoon and about half the members of the Chappell family and only about forty others back up to Camilla's father's box on the top floor. Lord Kinglass had just broken out some vintage Krug as his contribution to the celebrations. For some reason the Junior Minister of State at the Home Office was up there too and Lex made sure that he shook his hand and got a picture of himself doing it for one of the more society-conscious Sunday newspapers. There were so many people present by now that the party quickly overflowed into the corridor, drawing rumbles of protest from one bookmaking magnate who was attempting to entertain in the suite next door.

"Probably backed a loser," trilled Kinglass with glee. "The horrid old stinker."

30

The rest of the afternoon unfolded quickly. It was dramatic, exciting and sometimes brutal. In the second race, the
Arkle Trophy, Connor Delaney's Deep Fidelity was the
subject of another substantial gamble, backed from eight
to one down to eleven to two. He was still cruising on the
bridle when he took a crashing fall at the third last fence.
His jockey, Billy Hannafin this time not Michael Garvin,
went to hospital with three cracked ribs, concussion and a
broken collar bone. Deep Fidelity broke a shoulder and
had to be destroyed. Richmond had his binoculars on the
incident. He saw the flags go up and the screens come
round and the vet's wagon and trailer speed towards the
fence. He saw Deep Fidelity's rear legs kicking up feebly
in the air as the horse tried to lift himself up from the
ground. Then they pulled the screens right around and
shot him. The trainer had tears streaming down his face as
he walked back down the hill with the horse's number
cloth in his hand. Less than a month before he'd seen
Deep Fidelity put deliberately wrong at a lot of his fences
at Leopardstown in order to make a killing. Now the
gelding had made a real mistake and paid for it with his
life.

Ironically the principal beneficiary of Billy Hannafin's
misfortune was Michael Garvin. Hannafin was the established jockey of Galtee O'Flynn and once the extent of his
injuries became apparent a great deal of wheeling and
dealing began in the weighing room to decide who would
take his place. In the event it was Michael Garvin who got
the ride. He had to get off Shecky Dancer to take it and
that horse's owner-trainer was absolutely furious but as

Garvin pointed out he had no contractual obligations to ride for him and was free to take whatever big race rides he wished. And Big Pat McKenna was in no mood to be sentimental. With the English and the Irish champion jockeys both booked up on stable-retained mounts he wanted the best possible service he could get, both for the sake of his horse and for its owners. They certainly got their money's worth.

The first half of the Champion Hurdle was run at a snail's pace. By the time they'd jumped the first three flights Michael Garvin had already decided that he was sitting on a stayer not a speed merchant and he knew that if he sat there and suffered much longer he'd be slaughtered for pace in the closing stages. So halfway down the far side he moved his horse up into the lead and then quickened the gallop appreciably. At the top of the hill he poached an even bigger advantage and as he kicked on for home down the long run towards the straight he was as much as five lengths to the good.

It was thrilling but also alarming to watch from the stands. Had he gone too soon? Had he played his hand too early? The doubters seemed to have it when three other horses closed up on his heels as they turned around the bend and made for home and two of them touched down in front over the last flight. But Garvin had one more ace up his sleeve. He'd actually been allowing Galtee O'Flynn a slight breather. Inside the last two furlongs of a Champion Hurdle. About three or four strides after the last he rousted the champion up once again for one last, supreme effort. And as Shecky Dancer and the other two park course specialists began to tie up on the long Cheltenham hill and as the crowds roared and roared from the grandstand, Garvin lifted, carried and bullied his mount up that hill and back into the lead. There was only a neck to spare at the line.

Michael Garvin really got to the bottom of Galtee O'Flynn that day and the champion was never the same horse again. But as Pat McKenna remarked afterwards, having won two Champion Hurdles Galtee was fully entitled to remain in his box and his paddock now for the rest of his natural life.

An even bigger cavalcade of friends, admirers and supporters threatened to engulf Big Pat and Galtee O'Flynn than had swamped little CP Molloy and Mylerstown. Two of the stable's biggest gambling owners attempted to chair Pat around the winner's enclosure on their shoulders but he was a very heavy man and the attempt nearly ended in disaster with Pat and his bearers almost crashing into the presentation party, shattering the Waterford Glass trophy and burying at least one small bowler-hatted Steward in six feet of well-mown turf. But in the end order was at least partially restored and good humour maintained by one fellow shouting out to his pals as the Queen Mother lifted up the trophy: "Can you tell me, boys? How are the English horses doing at the other meeting?"

Michael Garvin was a hero now too and not a villain as he had been half an hour before. The Duke and Frampton-Mansell and Christopher Cowdray-Clarke and the other Stewards may all have shaken their heads in dismay at his 'disloyalty' and at his ruthless eye for the main chance but they, none of them, could deny the brilliance of his victory.

Just over half an hour later the sly, stocky Yorkshireman was back in the winner's enclosure and giving a repeat performance for the television cameras of his canny but grinningly unemotional little north countryman act. He'd just won the twenty-five furlong Waterford Crystal Stayers Hurdle for his governor Roddy Hyde-Lyne. His mount – form choice of the race with long distance victories to her credit already that season at Ascot twice and Haydock – started a remarkably generous priced seven to one third favourite, thanks to another ludicrously typical Festival plunge, this time on another CP Molloy-trained animal who'd trotted up in two two-and-a-half-

mile races over in Ireland but had never yet been tried
over this extra distance.

Like the emotional sucker that he knew himself to be
James Richmond couldn't resist joining in on the gamble
and his two bets of first six hundred pounds and then
another two hundred pounds to win at fours and three to
one respectively probably did their bit in assisting this
precocious creature to go off at the ridiculously short price
of nine to four. He held a good position for the first two
miles but then once the pace hotted up on the final circuit
he went rapidly backwards and eventually trailed in a well
beaten ninth of twenty-one.

Even so Richmond had still won over fourteen
thousand pounds on the day so far, thanks to his Galtee
O'Flynn bets on top of Mylerstown. He'd collected a lot of
petty cash from Lex and his pockets were bulging. In the
circumstances it was hard to keep his vow of not repairing
to the bar until the race was over. By now, with four races
down on the card and two still to go, the air outside was
thick with the hot smell of cigar smoke and the rancid
aroma of burger grease from the kiosk parked by the
Tattersalls stand. And still there on the lawns and in the
bars was all the social mix of the racecourse with conversations to match.

"Of course . . . you know why the Irish always win
everything?" said one army man to his friend in the
gents.

"No," said his friend. "Why's that?"

"B and F old chap. Bog and Fog."

"Bog?"

"And Fog. Bog to run on. Fog to run in." The army
man whinnied with pleasure. His friend laughed too but
rather weakly.

A few feet away a man with a medallion around his
neck and an imitation sheepskin coat was discussing a
trainer with another man who was wearing flappingly wide
flared trousers.

"The question is whether the fucking trainer's trying or

not. He's such a bastard, how do we know?"

"They all try here," said the other man wearily. "It's Cheltenham. They all want to win."

"Yes, but you can't tell me that it's straight. I've heard them talking. In pubs. They're all bent."

A group of young upper-class women were hovering around outside the weighing room door and staring in longingly at the jockeys as they came and went. "God, Sara, they're all so fanciable," said one girl. "I mean just look at those muscles. They're sort of rippling. And yet pert."

Elsewhere two middle-aged thrusters in elderly trilbies and elderly green puffajackets were watching an interview with the Prince of Wales on a television set in a bar. "Well, of course, I'm particularly fond of all horsing activities . . . actually," said the Prince to the interviewer.

One of the thrusters leaned across confidentially to his chum. "You know," he said. "The really capital thing is to ride out hard on a Saturday . . . until the best hounds bloody well drop . . ."

"And then?"

"And then to go out again on a Monday and knock hell out of somebody else's country."

"I say. You're right you know." They chuckled and ordered more gin.

Richmond lost another three thousand pounds, to Lex this time, on the fifth race of the day, the Kim Muir Memorial Steeplechase in which the real Galway Raider was an unlucky faller at the last. Richmond's selection was a young Northern-trained novice who was taking on the older horses for the first time in his career. The novice ran well for much of the race until his jumping let him down in the last half-mile. He managed to hold on to third place on the run in but at odds like a hundred to thirty he had not been worth backing each way.

As James walked away out of the ring he could see hundreds of losing betting tickets lying on the ground all around him. Useless small pieces of coloured paper scattered like confetti at a wedding. He knew that he ought not to bet on the last race of the afternoon, the Cheltenham Grand Steeplechase. He didn't really need to. He'd won quite enough money already from his earlier betting coups and now his luck and his judgement were beginning to desert him. But he also knew that he wouldn't be able to resist it. He was like a man walking out to sea along a long wall. He knew that he ought to turn back but he was gripped, drawn and hypnotised as if by some distantly beckoning harbour light.

He walked up the rails and placed a thousand pounds each way with William Hills on a locally-trained eight to one shot, a course specialist who'd finished second in the Grand Annual the previous year. Then he and Sunny walked out down to the second last fence to watch the action from a closer vantage point. It proved to be an instructive experience.

Like anyone who's ever got up on the back of an even halfway decent horse and experienced that sudden sense of power beneath one, Richmond understood that even when you pop them over a few quite small and inauspicious looking obstacles it can suddenly seem an awfully long way down to the ground, especially if you're perched up there rather insecurely on your inadequately sized saddle and hanging on desperately to a handful of mane as you prepare to fly through thin air. Richmond hadn't ridden seriously himself for years now, but in his youth he had once been regarded as a reasonably proficient teenage horseman and one with a touch of real flat racing style to go with it. Of course he'd been thoroughly schooled by his mother round the usual gymkhana and ponyclub circuit and he had even been out hunting with her a few times. The contrast though between that experience and his first sight of professional jockeys riding and jumping at speed in a proper steeplechase had been a sight and a sound that he'd never forget. And as he stood there by the second last fence that Cheltenham Tuesday afternoon the whole experience came flooding vividly back to him.

There were eighteen runners in that year's Grand
Annual Chase and as they started down the hill towards
the second last fence at least ten of them were in there
with a winning chance. The leaders had been bunching up
together for some time and there was little room for
manoeuvre and little daylight for an uncertain jumper.

Richmond and Sunny could hear the hooves rattling
before they could really see them and just from the sound
of the hooves you could guess that they were moving at a
cracking gallop. The sound effects climaxed as they flew
over the actual fence. A sound like flames ripping through
a barn. Snapping birch and twig and brushing gorse and
turf divots flying and the yells and curses of the jockeys.
One of the front runners pecked badly on landing and the
jockey was ejected violently from the saddle. Straight
over the top between the horse's ears he went. Crashing
down on to the grass, face first. As the horse righted itself,
it cannoned into James's selection which was moving up
nicely in behind. The other jockey had no chance whatsoever of staying in the saddle and he tumbled out heavily
to his right. He rolled over against the running rail and lay
there in a heap. Winded and badly shaken. While the race
carried on with both loose horses still in contention, the
ambulance men rushed across to the two prostrate jockeys. The first one down was in great distress. When the
ambulance men lifted his head up slightly James and
Sunny could see blood pouring down his face from a deep
cut over his right eye. The blood was mixing in quickly
with the pink and white colours of his racing silks. He was
groaning too and clasping his left shoulder. Away to their
left, James and Sunny could hear the crowd cheering as
the race reached its climax. Their own wagers had gone
down and they would miss the finish but that was unim-
portant. What they would remember would be the sight
and sound of smashing bone and cracking rib, of torn
tissue and burst blood vessels and of air rushing out of
your body as the earth comes up to club you in the solar
plexus.

Over the last few days James had heard a lot from Lex about bent jockeys and bribes and corrupt betting rings and the rest. In the circumstances, considering the hazardous nature of their profession and the meagre rewards on offer it was hardly surprising if riders were always to be found who would accept a bent penny as some mitigation for a harsh life.

But as the Cheltenham first day drew to a close James preferred to think about all those other pilots who, whether they were riding at Cheltenham in March in front of forty thousand people or at Plumpton on a wet Monday in November in front of six hundred, had never taken Lex's shilling or Michael Bolger's or Kinane's or Cashel Maguire's. Of course Lex would say that it was only a matter of time, that in racing as in life everyone had their price. But as far as Richmond was concerned when it came to the Corruption Stakes most of those small, hard men in the weighing room couldn't begin to hold a candle to the likes of Lex Parlane. But then that was something that no moron in a betting shop would ever understand.

By the end of that afternoon James had nine thousand pounds left of the more than fourteen grand that he'd won on Mylerstown and Galtee O'Flynn. When he got back to the grandstand he discovered that Lex had left Camilla with Lord Kinglass, the Junior Minister of State and CP Molloy up in the peer's box on the top floor and was himself now down in the ground floor Members' bar overlooking the underpass and the catering trolleys. A number of James's Christchurch friends could be seen in there too, working out their afternoon's debts to Lex on the back pages of their *Timeform* Racecards. In most cases Lex was generous with credit but the bills were still mounting.

Bella was there, being mainly ignored by her bookmaker lover who was busy getting into the spoofgames and the pitch and toss. So James entertained her instead. He devoted to her all of his charm and all his attention and other than offering to put bets on for her on the following afternoon's races he banished all mention of horse racing from their conversation. For Bella this was quite a dispensation. These big three-day race meetings were a real marathon endurance test for a woman like her and in spite of her love for Lex and her joy at his victory she was more than grateful to have just one hour's break not devoted to the subject of betting.

For the first time James began to unbend with her, letting his guard drop and telling her all kinds of details about his childhood and his school, his father's gambling habits and his mother's affairs with jockeys, stable lads, Swiss ski instructors and many other diminutive sexual athletes.

He recounted the details of his mother's death. A head-on collision with a Chevrolet convertible driven by a waterbed salesman from Chantilly. Poetic justice, the Duke had said. In spite of her beauty and her sexual attraction the quality that James's mother had most prized in herself had been her ruthlessness. But, he confessed to Bella, he could never fall in love with a woman like that. He dreamed of warmth and softness and femininity and . . .

"Gimme a drink for fuck's sake." The intrusive voice of Jack McQueen. A sharp reminder that the rest of the crew were all still around. McQueen had been sick in the lavatory opposite the bar and he was now being looked after by the kindly and generous Reema whom McQueen was shouting at bitterly for being quite drunk herself.

Daisy De Moraville was still loyally singing Lex's praises, even though he'd been curt and off-hand to a point with her and Hugh all afternoon, preferring the company of Lord Kinglass and the Chappell family. Hugh had actually left before the last to drive the fifteen or so miles to his restaurant near Broadway and prepare for the unenviable task of cooking dinner for Lex and at least twenty-five members of the immediate entourage. All party to the glorious coup and celebration that would now be known for evermore as 'Mylerstown'. Without Hugh,

Daisy was bravely putting up with Charles St Clair who, vastly impressed by the money won on Mylerstown, was now trying to assiduously worm his way back into Lex's good books and winning ways. Delaney-Dalzell was drunk in charge of a bottle of sloe gin and Jonathan Pointdexter had gone for a run around the course, only no one was watching. Lex was still gambling hard in the corner of the bar.

Finally and as darkness closed in, the heroes and villains from Ireland and Glasgow, from London and Newcastle and from Birmingham and the North, all gradually slumped, stumbled or bullishly held their heads high and walked away. To hotels and pubs and private homes. To receptions and parties and dinner parties. To a night of wild consumption for all.

The Duke and the rest of the Stewards, Michael Garvin and the jockeys and Louis Weiss and all the other bookmakers had long since scurried off home.

And at half-past seven, more than two hours after the last race had ended, after the pitch and toss school and after forty-six consecutive rounds of spoof, Lex and Bella and James Richmond walked back across the racetrack towards their helicopter.

31

Lex had always known that there'd be trouble at the poker game. Even before the attempted Mylerstown coup he could feel the Bolger and Kinane situation coming to a head. And after that coup had succeeded confrontation became inevitable. All that mattered now therefore was to plan and calculate how he'd deal with the situation once it arrived. Which certainly didn't prevent him from looking forward to his game of cards.

The Tuesday night poker game was a regular feature of Lex's Cheltenham Festival week. And for the last two years that game had been held at Harford Farm. The poker players sat around the table in the hall. The light down low over the table and the firelight flickering around the dark, mahogany-panelled walls cast alternate shadows and shafts of light across the players' faces and across their hands of cards.

Hugh wouldn't play. As soon as he got back from the restaurant he picked up a bottle of port and went off up to bed. Lex could tell that he'd offended him over dinner. Hadn't praised him enough for the quality of his cooking. Hugh was touchy like that but right now Lex had other things on his mind.

For the first couple of hours Lex played with Daisy and James and Jack McQueen and Willie The Weasel Wood and one of the young Christchurch boys from the race-course that afternoon. McQueen lost fifteen hundred pounds and then folded suddenly and dramatically. Then Kinane arrived with Bolger and Cashel Maguire. Maguire was as cool as a pitcher of New Orleans iced tea and the crisp, terse and economical style with which he cut, shuffled and dealt the cards had James Richmond gasping with admiration.

Time was when some of the biggest poker games outside of Las Vegas used to take place at Cheltenham during the Festival week. Those were the days when Cashel Maguire used to win thousands of pounds off his more impulsive and muzzle-headed fellow countrymen. Sitting in state in the back room of the Queens Hotel and trading shot after shot until well after breakfast time. Tonight he had only Lex and Michael Bolger to beat.

James's young Christchurch friend capitulated quickly, endorsing a cheque over to Lex from Hoare's which was in fact a payment for the sale of some family shares by his father's stockbroker down in London the previous week. The money had been intended to pay a University battels bill. Now it was paying a gambling bill. James went to two thousand down and threw in the towel. There was no point in him even attempting to compete with people like this. Daisy, who was quite capable of holding her own against the men, threw in her hand to console him. When Billy Two Hats arrived back from London the final make-up of the table was complete.

Bella had disappeared but the other women sat around the edges looking on and occasionally waiting on the men like half-bored but still available whores in some Storyville bordello.

Kinane was the first one to crack. When he'd arrived at the beginning of the night he, like Bolger and Cashel Maguire, had been the very picture of good-natured affability and charm. This was, after all, an habitual and longstanding engagement and sportsmanlike protocol demanded at least an outward display of gentlemanly good manners and style. But as the night wore on Kinane's betting became wilder and more reckless and his bluffing progressively more incredible. It seemed to be the atmosphere of the house that got to him. The dog hairs in his whisky and the firelight in his eyes and the fadedly comfortable but not at all ritzy old furniture. That and the

imperturbable poker face of Lex Parlane. He finally went
out at half-past five in the morning, hopelessly overstak-
ing against a Lex hand of aces and eights. Within the next
hour Willie The Weasel and Billy Mcphee had dropped
out too, leaving Bolger, Lex and Cashel Maguire.
Maguire was still the big winner. Bolger didn't seem to
mind this. Nor was he perturbed by Kinane's behaviour.
He drank only tonic water and kept a strict record of all
his bets, losses and profits made in a small red notebook
by his side. Just after half-past seven Lex challenged him
to cut cards with him for five thousand pounds a time.
They cut three times and each time the Scotsman won.
Then Lex turned to Maguire. Maguire won the first cut
and then immediately doubled the stakes. Lex complied.
Maguire won again. And again. And then Lex won two
cuts in a row. Maguire suggested raising the wager once
more. To twenty-five thousand pounds. Lex complied and
Maguire won. They cut again. Still the Irishman came out
ahead. In not quite two-and-a-half minutes Lex lost more
than one hundred and twenty-five thousand pounds. And
that's when Bolger's composure really snapped. He knew
that Lex had been slipping out to the lavatory and snorting
cocaine up all night long and the habit really annoyed him.
On top of that he hadn't been offered any. What finally
got to him though was the conviction that Lex was almost
deliberately losing money in order to flaunt his successes
of the afternoon.

He stood up and hurled a handful of poker chips across
the table. "Why don't you quit for fuck's sake? Can't you
see when you're beat?"

"You know what I think, pal?" said Lex, still smiling.
"I think you should apologise to this lady." He was
nodding at Daisy.

"Apologise? What for?"

"For intruding your cheap and common personality into
her house. If it was up to me . . . I'd have made you eat in
the kitchen."

"You wanker, Parlane," said Bolger.

"Forget it, Michael," said Maguire.

"You fucking Scots wanker."

"I said forget it. I'm off." Maguire got coolly to his feet and started to collect his winnings.

"Scotsmen?" yelled Bolger. "I've had 'em. And they're not worth a dead rat's bollocks." At that point he pulled out a gun. It seemed such a theatrical and unlikely gesture that the others all looked at him for a moment only half seriously as if this must be some kind of cockney joke.

"Put the gun away, Michael," said Lex calmly. "You'll do yourself a mischief."

"I'm not fooled by your Scots hard man act, Parlane," said Bolger, his shoulders back and both feet firmly apart. He looked like Ron Atkinson playing Steve McQueen. "You. Jock Stein. Andy Stewart. And Laurie fucking McMenemy.."

"Laurie McMenemy's a Geordie, Michael."

"And don't interrupt! You Picts. You're all bastards. Insular. Boring. And paranoid bastards. And drunks. Drunken bastards. Someone should blow you all away."

Then Billy Mcphee chopped him from behind. The way he'd been taught by his martial arts instructor in the Royal Navy. The gun went off but the bullet hit the ceiling, narrowly missing a priceless chandelier and then ricocheting off through the hall window. Bolger was a big man but Billy was a fit man and he quickly wrestled Bolger to the ground. Forcing a knee into Bolger's back he put a lock on one arm and yanked the other arm right up behind the Londoner's neck. It was all like a re-run of Robert Smith and the Bella Vista ballroom and Willie The Weasel's wiry and athletic form was quite enough to deter Johnny Kinane from getting involved. As for Cashel Maguire he just stood there and lit a cigarette.

Lex got up and walked slowly around the table. Bolger was looking down at the floor until Billy yanked him up by the hair. "You stupid man," said Lex. "Did you really think you could nuzzle your way into my world? Insinuate your dirty little hands into my action?" Bolger said nothing. "What on earth would I want with a gimp like you? I tried to warn you. But you wouldn't listen. So yesterday I had to teach you a lesson on the track. And now you're squealing like a sick dog."

Bolger whispered his reply. "You're finished. Cunt."

Lex shook his head, picked up an unopened bottle of port and broke the bottle over the end of the table. He considered Bolger's face for a moment and then swung the jagged bottle through the air as if he was going to smash it over Bolger's nose. At the last moment he arrested the blow just glancing the bottle against Bolger's forehead. Then he smiled, tipped the bottle up and poured what remained of the contents over Bolger's head. He waited until the last trickle had dripped down over Bolger's collar, jacket and tie. Then he looked up at Billy. "Take him away, Billy," he said.

Half an hour later Lex and James were strolling together outside. They were walking down a long and grassy ride with a stream on one side and a steep bank on the other. The bank was covered with bracken and underbrush and up above the bracken there was a line of beech trees and beyond the beech trees a large coppice of oak and pine. A number of small but tricky looking obstacles lined the path ahead of them. Miniature jumping fences that had been built there by Daisy to give her eventers a little early season practice. The fences were spaced out neatly at regular intervals.

It was a damp, chill and overcast morning with patches of mist and fog still lingering around amongst the willow trees and alder bushes by the water's edge. Occasional somnambulant cows lumbered out of the mist like black-and-white apparitions in some Scandinavian film.

As Lex and James walked along by the river and down this grassy ride they carefully circumvented the natural fences and discussed the other kind of hazards that Lex still had to overcome if he was to secure respectability and a big future for himself down south.

"How did you like yesterday?" he asked.

"It was unforgettable."

"Really. Well I think I'm getting too old for it, Jimmy. It's not that I can't handle it. I just don't need it anymore. You know? That's why these video jobs are so important."

"How's that?"

"Diversifies my business. Gives me a greater aura of respectability."

"How do you measure respectability?"

"Flat racing," said Lex emphatically. "Owning good horses and meeting rich owners. That and attracting a few more nice rich southern clients for the firm."

"Men like St Clair?"

"Maybe not him so much. But Pointdexter's father, he could be useful."

"Portman Square are still watching."

"I know that, son. But I've still got a timetable. I've got a plan. Yesterday was all a part of that plan. And now with the legitimate investment that I'm beginning to pick up . . ." he nodded his head, ". . . I'll soon be able to cut out the funny stuff for keeps." A plump pheasant shot up suddenly in front of him. Lex jumped back nervously. The pheasant flew away over their heads and on up the bank towards the trees. Lex looked down at his feet. The grass in the field was soaking wet and as usual Lex was wearing shoes not wellington boots. His shoes were already muddy and wet right through. "The question now," he said anxiously, "is what to do about Bolger and Johnny Kinane?"

At that moment he cut a rather woeful figure. Standing there at eight in the morning. In a damp Gloucestershire field in his city suit and shoes with only James and the cows for an audience. For almost the first time in their relationship James felt that he held the upper hand in terms of confidence, initiative and drive. He felt surprisingly awake and alert in spite of having been up now for twenty-four action-packed hours. Whereas Lex was beginning to exhibit all the symptoms of a typical cocaine-induced depression. The natural let down after the intense euphoria and adrenalin high of the races and the poker game of the previous night and day was combining with the intense lack of sleep and never ending ingestion of narcotics to make the bookmaker seem subdued, doubtful and suddenly and rather pathetically out of place and out of time. Richmond had to take up the reins from his flagging friend.

"You've got to neutralise Bolger," he told Lex confidently. "And Maguire. And Johnny Kinane. After yesterday and especially after what happened last night they'll be out to get you and soon."

"I think they'll maybe wait until the end of this week," said Lex. "They've got a job of their own to pull first. It's today too."

"With Michael Garvin?"

"That's right. Some Idea. In the Queen Mother Champion Chase."

"Well, that's as maybe. But if they go to the Jockey Club now you could be ruined. Discredit them first and you discredit their story."

"Now that's what I like to hear. Cigar?"

"No, thank you." Lex lit one up for himself. "Now how about this? There's a lot of Irishmen at the racetrack, right?"

"Most certainly."

"A lot of rich Irish punters and bookmakers with money to burn?"

"Quite indubitably."

"Well suppose it was found that some of those highrolling boyos were passing on funds from the racetrack . . . to the IRA?"

"Brilliant."

"You'll have to fit up the evidence first. Say maybe in their luggage in their hotel rooms."

"Then tip off the local police?"

"That's right. And what with royalty around in the

area, before you know where you are you'll have the
anti-terrorist squad down on their necks like dogs after
cats up a tree."

"But Bolger's not Irish?"

"The police won't know that at first. And even if they
clear themselves later, suspicion will always remain."

"And by then I'll be out of the woods?"

"Precisely."

"Jimmy. You've given me new heart." Lex hugged the
boy warmly to his chest and ruffled one hand through his
hair.

"But you'll have to find someone to handle the break
in," said James. "At the hotel."

"That I can arrange," said Lex. "I'll call up the
Chappells straight away. As soon as we get back to the
farm. I thought they might just come in handy."

A young bullock trotted towards them out of the trees
and stood there just in front of Lex, apparently staring at
his dark black glasses with great curiosity. Lex stared back
at him uneasily for several seconds. "Take 'em to Mis-
souri, Matt," he mumbled.

32

When they got to the racecourse there was a distinctive atmosphere of hangovers and sore heads, of ashen faces and shattered wallets. The rain started falling around lunchtime and the crowds clung to the bars. Lex and James found a quiet corner in the Mill House bar and drank several large Bloody Marys. Then they had a bottle of champagne with some orange juice and a hot roast beef sandwich with mustard and horseradish sauce. Then they went down to the large gents cloakroom by the main entrance. They each went into a cubicle, adjoining cubicles. Lex took a gramme packet of cocaine out of his overcoat pocket and tipped half the contents out on to a small glass mirror which he placed on the downturned lavatory seat. Then he cut out two lines, snorted up his own line and slipped the mirror and an empty biro stem under the gap at the bottom of the wall and into James's cubicle next door. Only the first time he got things the wrong way round. James was in the cubicle to his right. Lex pushed the mirror to his left into a cubicle which was currently being occupied by a rather bad-tempered old flat racing trainer from Findon. The trainer was surprised to look down at his trouser legs and suddenly see a small mirror gliding across the floor towards him. Fortunately he was ignorant of the substances involved because a moment or so later the mirror disappeared again yanked back by Lex with a rolled-up newspaper, like a cardboard mouse on a string. "Bloody lavatory cowboys," barked the trainer crossly as he pulled up his trousers and pressed the flush. "Worse than Piccadilly Circus." Then he went away.

The danger over, Lex pushed the mirror back under the wall to his right into James's cubicle. After they'd both finished Lex waited for a decent interval then flushed the lavatory and walked out of the cloakroom on his own. Three or four minutes later James followed.

Back up in the Mill House bar Charles St Clair was waiting for them along with the rest of Lex's crowd. St Clair was still complaining about losing money but he was spending it too, anxious not to lose face with Lex in case there was a betting coup afoot for a second day running. As a result of the Mylerstown race Lex's photograph was back in all the papers as well as in *The Sporting Life*. Jack McQueen had fixed it so that the Junior Minister of State at the Home Office figured prominently too, along with Camilla's father. McQueen was congratulating himself on another piece of successful media manipulation. He was also apologising for being so drunk the previous day.

"It's working on your own that does it," he said to James. "All your energy goes inside. You become moody. And introspective. And that's when you turn to the bevvy."

"Especially at the races, eh, Jack?" said Lex.

"I know," said McQueen. "But I try. Honestly. I really do try."

"You do alright," said Lex.

"It's just that I've reached a certain stage in my life. A time of transition." He was gazing into his champagne glass and caressing the glass stem meaningfully. "And I can begin to feel things slipping by me. Bit . . . by miserable bit."

Reema kissed him and squeezed his arm. "Well, you can't slip away from me, you old bastard."

"We should all be aware of our own mortality though," said McQueen. "You especially, Lex."

"Do me a favour, Jack," said Lex. "That's one thing I don't think about." Billy and Duane Chappell had arrived. Punctual for the twelve-thirty appointment that Lex had made on the telephone from Harford earlier that morning. Lex bought each of them a drink and then they went off for a long and confidential walk around the racetrack. After they'd gone James went off to have lunch with Bella and Sunny Vengsarkar in the Prestbury Suite. James was paying. As they were waiting for their table to be cleared Bella slipped her hand into his and kissed him lightly on the cheek.

"Well, hotshot," she said. "Still up?"

"Still up."

"How much did you win?"

"By the end of the day?"

"By the end of the day."

He lied. "About ten grand."

"Don't lose it all, Jimmy. Please. You don't have to be like the others." She reached out a hand and touched him gently on the face. She ran her fingers down his arm and brushed them softly against the back of his hand.

"Let's have a drink again later. After the last."

"I'd like that."

"We can go back to the house if you want. We don't have to stick around here and play games."

"Alright." She kissed him again. "Be lucky. Mister Man."

"I am lucky."

It was a long lunch and they all had time to glance through their *Timeform* racecards while they ate and talked. But not for the first time James found it hard to concentrate his mind on the subject of training records and jumping performances over a distance of ground. He was thinking about Michael Bolger and Lex and the plan. But he was also thinking about just how nice it would be to be lying in bed with Bella right now back in her bedroom at Harford Farm. Enjoying at leisure the fabulous pleasures of her soft and voluptuous body.

One thing was certain. Bella would be an expensive woman to maintain. Not easy while you were losing almost a thousand a week on the horses. In his more suspicious moments he still couldn't quite work it out in his mind that Bella might be genuinely fond of him and was not just being used by Lex to keep him and his friends betting with the Lex Parlane Connection. What a show it would be all the same if he could suddenly prove to his father, to the world and to himself that he'd given up gambling and horse racing too to devote himself to the love of a good woman. But what would Lex have to say about that?

Perhaps he ought to try and become a don. Nice easy life. Good food. Long holidays. Not enough money, though. Perhaps he ought to try producing blue videos or importing cheap jeans. Not enough class. Then perhaps he ought to go and buy a dilapidated old Georgian mansion in the West of Ireland and breed racehorses. Ah! Racing again.

"I'm sorry to interrupt you, my friend," said Sunny, interrupting him charmingly. "But you do still owe me a monkey. From Galtee O'Flynn."

"The bill's already paid, Sunny," replied James, returning to his racecard decisively. "After Ormund wins the National Hunt Chase we'll be flying down for dinner in Mayfair."

He propped his folded copy of *The Sporting Life* up against the wine bottles. Next to his *Timeform* and the *Chaseform* Notebook. On the back page of the *Life* there was a small but sinister story about the well-being of the antepost favourite for the 2,000 Guineas. Rumours from Ireland suggested a training problem, said the story. And the American-bred colt had been taken out of the ante-post lists by Mecca and William Hills.

Next to the story was another half-page article on the corrupt Steward scandal, accompanied by a tight-lipped picture of the Duke and his senior men standing inscrutably in the winner's enclosure at Cheltenham the previous day.

The juxtaposition was particularly appropriate. For while James and Bella and Sunny were up in the Prestbury Suite and while Lex and the Chappells were taking their

anti-clockwise turn around the racetrack, the Duke and
Washy Cleveland were sitting in an old-fashioned Land
Rover parked out in the centre of the course. They were
each wearing a mac and a trilby hat and Washy's hat was
turned up at the front as usual. From their position by the
top of the hill they could look down out of their Land
Rover towards the home straight and the stands. They
might have been two old irregular tank commanders out
in the Western desert, waiting to pounce on a detachment
of German outriders amidst the sands of Wadi Halfa. But
there was no sand or sun here. Only streaming rain
thumping down loudly against the Land Rover windows
and roof, each drop rapidly turning the ground outside
from soft to bottomless.

"Why, Washy?" asked the Duke.

Washy sighed. His face was screwed up and he was
sweating badly. "I was under a lot of pressure, Johnny,"
he replied. "According to Sandhurst . . . my boy's a
complete duffer. The bank want me to sell the farm.
They're calling in my debts, you see. And I think Frances
. . . has been seeing another man. I thought if I could
raise some extra cash . . . make our life . . . a little more
attractive . . . I might be able to persuade her to stay."

"You could've asked a friend, Washy. We've all had
. . . those sort of problems."

Washy shook his head. "You can't mention that sort of
thing. At least I can't."

The Duke took off his hat and ran a hand through his
hair. "It couldn't have happened at a worse time. Everything was building up nicely, as you know. The RSS file.
Anderson. We were only waiting for the flat. It seemed
the perfect moment to strike. And now? Bang! When we
do make our move it'll just seem like revenge. Make
Parlane the sympathetic one."

"I don't know how they found out, Johnny. Honestly I
don't."

"Someone's always looking for dirt in our game,
Washy. Didn't you take precautions?"

"I never saw or met anyone. It was always by phone. They embarrassed me at home once or twice. When they wanted something done . . . a sudden improvement in form . . . no enquiries on a beaten favourite . . . I collected my . . . remuneration . . . from phone boxes. Station waiting rooms. That sort of thing." He sighed. "None of it big league stuff though. None of it Lex Parlane standard. Just a handful of Northern trainers. And jockeys. One or two well-known names. But small-timers mainly. They've been at it for years. I was their latest . . . victim."

"We'll deal with them later."

"I just needed the money, that's all. Of course I knew about Mould. But he never had any evidence. Someone . . . malevolent . . . must've tipped him off later on."

"We think Parlane was behind it. To divert attention from Garvin and the two Irishmen."

"And to think I was in favour of letting him off."

"Our case . . . will be directed primarily against Garvin and Parlane himself. Though we hope to get the Irishmen too."

"I'm sure you'll do better without me."

The Duke shook his head. "I'd rather have done it with you, Washy. I'm no politician. I need allies. You see our Guineas favourite's already on the easy list? And the season's not even begun." He punched the windscreen with his fist. "These bloody American-bred beasts. Their owners aren't interested in horse racing. Just hide and seek."

"I wish we were away at some point to point," said Washy quietly.

"I wish I was back in Antigua," said the Duke.

"Damned Cheltenham," muttered Washy.

"Damned Irish," said the Duke.

"Actually . . . they did give me a tip for today. If you're interested?"

The Duke didn't reply.

* * *

The first race of the afternoon was run in a downpour. Connor Delaney's The House Rules, a heavy ground specialist, was backed down to five to two favourite and succeeded in landing the odds by a couple of lengths from a less well fancied Irish runner ridden by Frankie Molloy. There were only four in it throughout the last half-mile and The House Rules turned into the home straight at least three lengths clear. Only then he shied away from the stands as he began to hear the cheers of the crowd and his jockey had to employ quite forceful methods of persuasion to get him back on a straight line up the run in. There was a Stewards' Enquiry afterwards and the jockey was fined by the Duke and the others and sent on to Portman Square for excessive use of the whip. This decision was as applauded in some quarters as it was resented in others. It's never an edifying spectacle watching any racehorse being beaten like a carpet in front of the public gallery. But this horse was carrying a great deal of public money and the jockey was under considerable pressure to get a result. If he'd failed to give his mount a really vigorous ride then his job could've been on the line.

The next race was the Queen Mother Champion Chase run over two miles. There were only seven runners, two of them having dropped out during the morning due to the heavy rain and the marked change in the going. The previous year's winner was out of the race with an overreach and the two market leaders were I've Been To Ballyporeen, trained by Big Pat McKenna, and Some Idea, trained by Tommy Kenneally up at Malton. I've Been To Ballyporeen, owned by a Cork businessman with emotional ties with the States, was a talented but lightly raced horse who was prone to breaking blood vessels during his races. Some Idea was a brilliant young front running steeplechaser who had a habit of taking frightening liberties with his fences but who had still scored an impressive ten-length victory in the Arkle Trophy twelve months before. And with his regular jockey sidelined by injury, Michael Garvin had been booked for the ride. His second big substitute mount of the week. The first show of betting on the race went six to four on Some Idea and six to four against the Irish challenger.

Lex Parlane described the race as a farce. Johnny Kinane could be seen laying fistfuls of money on Some Idea at well over the odds and in full view of the Jockey Club's ring inspectors. Lex went no better than the average odds, attempting to discourage all betting on the horse. And he was careful to place no wagers either for himself or for the Lex Parlane Connection on any other runner in the race, other than the normal laying off of firm liabilities.

I've Been To Ballyporeen made the early running, closely followed by Aussolas who was ridden by Jayo Donnelly. Although the less well backed of the two Irish representatives, Aussolas had some distinctly useful form in the mud but most of it was over hurdles. He hadn't run over fences for at least two seasons. Michael Garvin seemed to drop Some Idea in behind these two but as they started out down the far side he was already nearly ten lengths adrift. I've Been To Ballyporeen made a bad mistake at the first open ditch and then fell at the next fence. By that time Aussolas, who was skipping through the puddles of water like an aquaplane, held an almost unassailable advantage. Some Idea, who appeared to resent not being given his head, started making mistakes as Garvin had predicted he would and hard though Garvin tried to drive him as they ran down the hill towards the straight he was never going to close the gap in time. Aussolas crossed the line six lengths to the good. His starting price was fourteen to one. There was a stunned silence from the crowd, followed by an immediate announcement of a Stewards' Enquiry.

Garvin told the Stewards that he'd been under express instructions to conserve the horse's stamina in the heavy ground and that was why he'd ridden it from behind and not employed the usual front running tactics. Kenneally could only echo his jockey's story and claim that the changed going had forced the seven-year-old into a string of untimely mistakes. He was actually livid at losing such a valuable and prestigious prize but he'd been bought off by Garvin and Kinane in advance and there was nothing he could do about it afterwards other than walk away quickly from the circle of eager pressmen, his lips pursed tightly together and his hat pulled down low over his eyes. The Stewards decided that they couldn't accept either Garvin's or Kenneally's explanations and as with the first race the case was sent on to Portman Square.

The Duke was overjoyed. Any extra evidence on Garvin was always a bonus and as for Kinane he'd played right into their hands.

Lex was contemptuous in the bar.

"Can you believe it?" he said to James. "They've practically done our job for us. The Racecourse Security boys were all out in force with their pocket Kodaks. They'll all be busted wide open."

"What about Bolger?"

"Oh, he'll get his money. But that's the last stunt that he'll pull with Garvin for a while. Your old man'll see to that even if we don't."

"Do we still go ahead with the plan?"

"Of course we do. Tomorrow morning. I don't just want them down, Jimmy. I want them out for the fucking count."

"Suppose they incriminate you?"

"They can't. I stayed well clear in the ring. My books'll show that too. Kinane's are going to read like his own death warrant."

"What a foolish man."

"He's just a greedy mug. It's the pressure that's got to him. He just had to show off. Just had to be a big shot. He couldn't stand the knowledge that he's always going to live in my shadow." Lex picked up a bottle of champagne dismissively and walked off on his own towards a television set.

The third race was the Joe Coral Golden Hurdle Final

and it was won by a thirty-three to one shot trained by a local permit holder from Eastleach. Forty minutes later the permit holder notched up a sensational double by sending out the sixty-six to one winner of the Sun Alliance Steeplechase, a race in which CP Molloy's Mr Dooley finished a well beaten third. In the fifth race, the National Hunt Steeplechase, CP Molloy saddled Ormund, the handsome chestnut that James had seen working on the course that Monday morning. Ormund had only ever run three times over fences and he had only completed the course on two of those occasions. And yet such was the strength of his home reputation that he was backed down to fifteen to eight favourite. Over four miles and twenty-four fences and against twenty-seven amateur ridden opponents.

Ormund unseated his rider at the fifth fence.

By the end of the afternoon everybody was getting increasingly drunk and bad-tempered. Lex's mood of derision for his opponents seemed to have worn off on the whole company. He himself became almost wilfully callous and less generous, snubbing his old friends in almost exact proportion to the degree with which they loved him. Daisy and Hugh had arranged an elaborate race week dinner party for him later that night at Harford. Another special menu had been prepared and the guest list was thick with prominent flat racing personalities. All of them friends of Daisy's and all of them charmed, coaxed and persuaded into sitting down to dinner with the Scots bookmaker. Lex decided to skip the dinner and drive off to Oxford to play darts in a pub instead. He took with him McQueen, Charles St Clair and James Richmond.

Bella had already gone back to the farm and James had been trying to escape back there too for hours. But then he had too much to drink and took too many drugs and in the end he found himself not for the first time being dragged off into the darkness by Lex towards an evening that he couldn't afford and for which he had no appetite.

And by the end of that night he had four thousand pounds left out of his original fourteen grand.

Sometimes Richmond hated himself.

33

That Wednesday night Johnny Kinane threw a party in the Golden Valley. Supposedly just to entertain clients and friends but actually to gloat over his swindling triumph with Some Idea. Michael Garvin did not attend. The party climaxed with Kinane being dunked by Fennessy Conroy and the Rafferty Brothers in a bathtub full of Veuve Cliquot.

Kinane had rung up a nightclub he knew in Mayfair and ordered a couple of hookers to be sent up directly by chauffeur-driven limousine. Only then he passed out before he could get back to the Queens Hotel and avail himself of their services. So Cashel Maguire stepped in instead. Maguire didn't usually go for hookers. Not that he had anything against them. He just didn't see why he should pay for the pleasure. But that night he'd just won a twenty-five thousand pound pot in a poker game with the boys. So for once he decided to relax and indulge himself.

There was one young blonde with a trim firm figure and a lot of lipstick and one slightly older redhead who looked like she'd seen a lot of nights.

It was just before seven and the threesome were curled up happily asleep together in Maguire's bed at the Queens. Maguire was sleeping on his side with his head up against the blonde. The redhead was sleeping spoons up against his back. The police came in simultaneously through the door and the bedroom window. A split second beforehand the redhead had woken up with a racking smoker's cough. Her eye make-up felt tired and heavy and she still had her black-and-white polka dot bra on from the night before. As she reached round to loosen the clip on her bra the police came in. They all had guns.

"Freeze," said the first detective.

"Darling," said the redhead. "If you're that desperate you can have it for free."

Then the blonde woke up and started screaming. Maguire opened his eyes and his heart shot through his mouth. "Who the fuck are you?"

"Cashel Maguire?"

He nodded.

"You're under arrest."

"What for?"

"Conspiracy to cause explosions. Suspected membership of an illegal organisation." The detective had a broad Gloucestershire accent and as well as a gun he had a badge and a warrant in his other hand and he waved them around under Maguire's nose like an American cop in a TV show. "It's the Prevention of Terrorism Act, old son. We've got you."

"But I'm not a terrorist."

"You're Irish, aren't you?"

Kinane was asleep in a linen cupboard on the top floor of the hotel. He'd eventually got back from the Golden Valley but then he'd passed out again before he could make it to his bed. He awoke to the sounds of muttering voices and footsteps in the corridor outside. When he took a peep around the linen cupboard door he saw uniformed policemen talking with dressing-gowned guests and more big men with anoraks and dogs on their way down the back stairs.

Kinane looked down at himself to discover that he was wearing nothing but a pair of bright red elasticated boxer shorts with Father Christmases on them. His head hurt badly and he couldn't for the life of him remember how he'd managed to end up in the linen cupboard.

The sight of policemen always alarmed Kinane and, dressed in his current state, he felt that things might not look good for him. Were they after him for the Some Idea race? A repeat of the Gay Future raid of ten years before?

He had a naturally guilty conscience. A product of his Catholic childhood. He decided that he'd try to make a break for it.

He slipped out of the linen cupboard, made a dash for the back stairs and came out through a fire door on to the roof. A new day was breaking over Cheltenham. Pink, grey and shivering. And with only his pants on Kinane was freezing. He made a bolt for the fire escape that led towards the garden. The fire escape was slippery after all the rain and Kinane bounced and slithered towards the bottom. In his yuletide underpants he looked like some plump Santa Claus sliding down an incommodious chimney. Unfortunately the police and their dogs were waiting for him at the bottom and Kinane fell into their hands as easily as a fat apple into a sack. They considerately provided him with a blanket and then he and Maguire were both driven off to Cheltenham Police Station and locked into separate interview rooms.

Maguire was seething. He wanted a lawyer. And he wanted to know the exact basis of these preposterous charges that he was being held under. Two hours later detectives from the Anti-Terrorist Squad arrived from London. They ignored his first request. Then they produced various papers, documents and Provisional Sinn Fein propaganda leaflets which they claimed to have found in his suitcases and in the bottom drawer of his chest of drawers at the Queens. Some of the leaflets were about Provisional housing policy in the North and Provisional Sinn Fein gains on the newly elected Ulster local councils. Others were about NORAID and IRA connections with Republican sympathisers and other Irish groups in the USA. There was a piece of plain notepaper with a typed list on it of prominent Irish gamblers and bookmakers with differing sums of money typed in on the paper next to their names. And there were substantial amounts of hard cash, all of it actually a part of Maguire's winnings from the poker games at the Golden Valley and Harford Farm.

"You've been passing the cap around, haven't you?"
said one of the detectives. "At the races?"

"What are you talking about?"

"For NORAID. For your Yank friends?"

"Are you kidding? My uncle's a former Chief Justice of
the Special Criminal Court in Dublin."

"That proves nothing," said the detective. "You Micks.
You're all the same. You're all republicans at heart. You
hate us British."

"Can you wonder why?" asked Maguire.

It wasn't until gone lunchtime, by which time most of
Cheltenham was on its way to the races, that Maguire got
his lawyer. Sent up from London by his stepfather. And
when Maguire discovered that Kinane but only Kinane
had been arrested too he started to think. Someone had
fitted them up alright. And his first guess was Michael
Bolger. Then he thought again.

Kinane was enjoying himself. He'd been given trousers,
socks and a shirt and he was entertaining his captors with
jokes, tips and typical stories of the Irishman abroad.
He'd already convinced himself that these charges –
albeit false ones – would make him famous. Get him
into the Irish Racing Annual at last. For whereas
the corrupt jockeys ring perforce compelled all of its
members into secrecy, the publicity surrounding
these charges was bound to make him into a national
celebrity.

The London police hardly thought he looked terrorist
material. But he was Irish, much more broadly so than
Maguire. And a catch was a catch.

The seriousness of Johnny Kinane's predicament had
yet to sink in on him. As for Maguire, he didn't take to
confinement. The police station he found vulgar and dirty.
Dreary yellow paint and old-fashioned wooden tables and
chairs. The rooms smelled of cheap cigarette smoke,
disinfectant and bad food. Bad, cheap food for cheap,
ugly people. When his stepfather's lawyer confirmed that
he was to be charged on two counts under the Prevention

of Terrorism Act he was dismayed to think that he might be in for a long stay.

So far no one had been found who could testify to their sobriety at the time of the poker game at the Golden Valley. And thus prove that the money had been won in fair play. And as for the Harford crowd they'd denied that there'd even been a game. Maguire started to rage. Then he laughed. He'd been given a paper to read by the police and he'd just seen the date. Thursday, the seventeenth of March. St Patrick's Day. That was the luck of the Irish. But he'd be revenged. He'd be revenged for the events of this day. He'd get bail and get out and then he'd go back to Ireland. And then they'd see.

Michael Bolger avoided the swoop at the Queens. After his humiliating experience at Harford Farm he'd driven back to Blewbury alone. He'd watched the Wednesday racing on the television set in the privacy of his own house. And then he'd called up his contact in London. To discuss the events of Tuesday, including the Mylerstown race and the poker game, as well as Some Idea's performance in the Queen Mother Champion Chase.

Wednesday night he spent at a dinner party in Gloucestershire given by a wealthy ex-Amateur Rider turned racing correspondent. The former five-times winner of the Bollinger Trophy was a man with close contacts with the Jockey Club and several Jockey Club members were present at the dinner. Bolger chatted with them relaxedly, cheated successfully at backgammon and bridge and impressed everyone present as 'a bit of a character' but 'a good sort at heart'.

Early on Thursday morning he drove up to Cheltenham. He had another important meeting to go to after breakfast and he wanted to check out of the hotel first. He parked his car behind the Town Hall and then walked up through Imperial Gardens. Halfway across the gardens he became aware of a great deal of commotion going on outside the entrance to the Queens. He could see police cars and vans, uniformed policemen and men with walkie-talkie sets in their hands. He slipped behind a shrub next to the pavement and took out a pair of binoculars from the pocket of his sheepskin coat. A man was being led out of the hotel in handcuffs. With the aid of the binoculars Bolger recognised Cashel Maguire. Ten minutes later Kinane followed. Kinane had a blanket round his shoulders but he was wearing neither trousers nor shoes.

Bolger slipped back to his car. There was a call box near the Town Hall. He made an urgent phone call, then he got into his red Jaguar and drove off at speed in the direction of Stow-On-The-Wold. It was just after half-past seven.

34

The Duke's sister Helena was a widow, having lost her husband at about the same time as the Duchess met her death in the car crash. A brisk and sprightly fifty-five-year-old she now managed her own dairy farm just outside the village of Bledington.

It was a typically solid and late seventeenth-century Cotswold stone farmhouse. Nothing like Dereham Hall, but comfortable nonetheless and much the same size as Harford Farm though without the dark and dimly lit Jacobean corners of Hugh and Daisy's house. The atmosphere at Helena's farm was altogether plainer, bluffer and more conventional.

Thursday morning the farm was a hive of activity and not all of it concerned heifers, milk yields and calving dates. The first car pulled into the farmyard just after five past eight. The man was greeted by the Duke and by the farm manager who took him off to breakfast in the back kitchen. Rocco Anderson arrived just after nine. With him were two plain clothes detectives. One from Gloucestershire and one from London. The three of them went into the back kitchen.

At about half-past ten the three Stewards of the Jockey Club Disciplinary Committee arrived. Dickie Frampton-Mansell, Lord George Stowell and Christopher Cowdray-Clarke, still with his black eyepatch. The sun was shining but the morning was cold and damp and the Stewards had to pick their way carefully through the farmyard, avoiding all the puddles and the cowshit as well as two boundingly black-and-white dalmatian dogs. They were shown into Helena's office where the Duke joined them for coffee.

Letherby was there to take notes. Rowland tried to join in but the Duke threw him out.

To begin with their conversation was about the racing and Helena's trout streams and their respective prospects for the start of the flat. But it was a phoney war. The Duke liked Frampton-Mansell. He was an amiable sort of companion and now that Washy Cleveland's disgrace was an accepted fact their friendship was likely to grow stronger. Stowell and Cowdray-Clarke, though, were not his friends.

Lord George Stowell or 'Stowell the know-all' as the Duke always called him, liked to believe that he, not the Duke, should have been the Senior Steward. He had a long nose, a brisk crisp manner and simply loved the sound of his own voice. He was always much in evidence on governing bodies, scholarship award schemes and Home Office judgement panels considering compulsory training orders for wayward youth. If there was ever to be a single paid, racing supremo, as various odd Government reports and advisory committees would occasionally recommend, then Stowell was absolutely convinced that his mixture of brains, brio and worldly understanding would make him the obvious and ideal candidate for the job.

Cowdray-Clarke was sitting on Stowell's right. Aged fifty and smooth as a pebble, Cowdray-Clarke was a Merchant Banker. He owned it along with numerous others under various different names and pseudonyms and combinations of names and pseudonyms. In racing matters Cowdray-Clarke was ruthlessly establishment, in business affairs relentlessly pragmatic. Indeed one of his many roles was that of a leading financial adviser to the Thoroughbred Breeder's Association, a role he clearly revelled in as it gave him frequent opportunities to suavely bully the Duke on his generally retrograde and old-fashioned attitudes, especially in regard to syndicate ownership and the influence of American-bred bloodstock. Cowdray-Clarke, who never bothered to open his mouth very much when he talked, could produce a tough Old

Etonian drawl when required and used it to some effect when dealing with jockeys and other delinquents. He wore smartly cut suits and a lot of hair oil and his hair was slicked up slightly at the back. By recreation he was a practised shot and he pursued people with the same minute determination as partridge or snipe.

After about half an hour Rocco Anderson came into the office and joined them. He had three large manilla files in his hands, together with three edited cassette tape recordings. He gave the files and the cassettes to Letherby and Letherby handed out a file and a cassette to each member of the Disciplinary Committee. The Duke's copies were already on the table in front of him.

"There it is, gentlemen," said Rocco. "The finished product. I got the last tape recording yesterday morning. My report's at the back."

"Well done, Anderson," said Stowell, blandly. "Very good work."

"It includes all the events of the last two days. Though after this morning we may not need them."

"What's happening in the kitchen, Rocco?" asked the Duke.

"I think we've managed to convince the London police that he's been working for us. They accept anyway that he's an extremely unlikely candidate for terrorist fund raising."

"And yet they found all this evidence?"

"So it seems," said Rocco. "In their luggage at the Queens. Lists, leaflets, fingerprints, the lot. I don't believe it myself. I think somebody's stitched them all up."

"Any idea who might have done it?" asked Cowdray-Clarke.

"I could make an inspired guess."

"The Scotsman again, eh?" said Frampton-Mansell. "A falling out among thieves."

"Tell that to the Anti-Terrorist Squad," said Rocco. "In the current atmosphere anything with suspicious Irish overtones is being pushed home to the limit. Kinane and

Maguire are both almost certainly innocent . . . but they'll both almost certainly be convicted."

"They'll be mad for the Scotsman's blood then, I should think," said Cowdray-Clarke.

"They'll have to get out of jail first," said Rocco. "Lex has done a great job. He thinks he's wiped out the enemy in one decisive act. He just didn't reckon on one of them working for us."

"We'll let Maguire and Kinane take their chance in the courts," said the Duke.

"Knowing they've been framed?" queried Frampton-Mansell.

"They'll have to prove that for themselves. We owe them no favours. And it narrows our case most effectively. Garvin. And Lex Parlane."

"What about Washy Cleveland?" asked Stowell. Everyone was silent.

"A separate matter," said the Duke quietly.

"My men up in Yorkshire know who to deal with there," said Rocco. "We'll release their names to the press next Wednesday. At the same time as we give them Garvin's. And Lex Parlane's."

"Garvin must be shitting himself," said Stowell.

"He'll probably win the Gold Cup today," said Frampton-Mansell. "He's got a great chance. He'll probably do the Gold Cup–Champion Hurdle double." The Duke coughed. Frampton-Mansell shut up.

"It's going to be a bloody long enquiry," said Stowell frowning.

"Two days, I should think," said the Duke. "But that's up to you to decide." He got up and walked away across the room to the window. At that moment and in that room he suddenly looked old and tired and rather frail. "From now on it's out of my hands."

"How long shall we give them?" asked Cowdray-Clarke. "Six years? Ten? Life?"

"Garvin out for life, I should say," said Rocco. "Or at least forced to retire."

"And Parlane?"

"Six," said Stowell. "Or maybe ten."

"That's up to you," said the Duke. "You're the committee."

"Seen the *Life* today, Johnny?" asked Frampton-Mansell. "You were right about the Guineas favourite. He's out for the season. It's official."

"I know," said the Duke.

"I heard from Tom Hastings," said Stowell, "that they'd already fixed up a stallion syndication deal way back in January. For thirty-five million dollars."

"I heard that too," said the Duke.

"No good fuming, Johnny," said Cowdray-Clarke. "These days it's the way of the world."

"Somebody else said that," said the Duke.

"Take 'em on if you're mad enough, Johnny," said Stowell. "But don't expect us to all rush to your side. It's not on."

"And it may just rebound on your own head, John," said Cowdray-Clarke. "You're still quite a target yourself. At the hall."

"What do you mean?"

"The gramophone. The early morning serenade for your stallions. It's too eccentric."

"What do you call it these days, Johnny?" asked Stowell. "Music while you work?" Stowell and Cowdray-Clarke both laughed.

"Don't worry, George," said the Duke. "I won't embarrass you. I shan't take on anyone anymore." Stowell and Cowdray-Clarke exchanged interested glances.

"Cheerier matters, eh chaps?" said Frampton-Mansell. "What are you going to give us all for lunch today, Johnny? In the box?"

Meanwhile down in the back kitchen Michael Bolger drank another coffee and reflected happily on the fact that he had no more unsavoury meetings to go to with Garvin, Kinane and Cashel Maguire.

The Lex Parlane Connection tip of the day stared up at him from the pile of racing pages on the table. Bolger smiled. Not long now before the Michael Bolger Connection, trading under the old name of Essex Sport Enterprises, would be back on the rails. And what price then even so much as a racecourse cloakroom attendant's job for the big Scot?

What a day to look forward to.

35

Once again Richmond had a thumping hangover. The night of darts and pool in Oxford had led on to a hair-raising drive down to the Quat' Saisons in Great Milton for a long, late and sumptuously expensive dinner. They'd eventually got back to bed at Harford at half-past five that morning and then they were up again three hours later.

Lex was in a triumphant and magnanimous mood. His news so far was of a successful operation at the Queens. Which was all thanks to Duane Chappell's expert bit of B-and-E at the hotel while everyone had been up at the racetrack the previous afternoon. Most of the 'evidence' had been flown over from Belfast to Birmingham on the afternoon flight. Courtesy of an Armagh butcher's family who owed Lex a few favours. What Lex didn't yet know was that Michael Bolger had not been amongst the men arrested.

Lex and James started Gold Cup morning at the promised meet of the local hounds on the lawn at Harford Farm. The whole party was in attendance. Daisy was riding. So was Camilla. Lex, Bella and Richmond were all very much on foot.

Out in the countryside, especially in the county Gloucestershire countryside, fox hunting is still very much part of the National Hunt racing scene. Lex relished the racing and he relished the atmosphere at Harford Farm. In spite of his cavalier manner he liked both the company and the hospitality to be found under Hugh and Daisy's roof and he was quite prepared to tolerate the fox hunting side of things as a necessary adjunct to the Festival's social week.

He'd even made a few concessions to country clothing.
As he helped Hugh and Daisy greet their guests on the
lawn he was wearing not his usual black suit, black shades
and broad-brimmed black fedora but a pair of Lee
Trevino-style worsted check golfing trousers along with a
bright red polo neck jersey and a Pebble Beach golf club
cap.

The clothes were a mistake though in more than one
way. Not only were they the kind of things Lex would
have laughed at if he'd seen them being worn by
McQueen or Charles St Clair. The shedding of his traditional image, albeit for a joke, seemed subtly to underline
his already diminishing power and influence. Yet Lex was
too busy being a star turn to notice.

During his foray on to the Oxford pool tables the night
before he'd won nearly one thousand pounds off a man in
a pub in Headington. The man turned out to be an
economics don. A hard-nosed 'New Right' theorist from
Magdalen College. The don had been unable to pay his
debts so Lex had taken possession of his car instead. A
well-worn bottle green Range Rover ideally suited to
country pursuits. For the meet Lex had stocked up the
boot of the Range Rover like a cocktail bar and he
supplemented Hugh's stirrup cups by handing out bourbon and tequila highballs to any hunt member who wished
to imbibe.

The hunt members were much as James remembered
them from childhood. The women had hairnets and whips
alright, but they weren't quite up to Lex's advance billing.
Stony-faced and hard or horsey-looking types but without
much in the way of either make-up or jewellery. There
was the expected complement of young pony club daugh-
ters. Bored or aloof or shy-looking blondes who might end
the day with a bloody little fox's paw nestling in the pocket
of their elegant black Harry Hall riding jackets.

"And did you see Mr Fox, darling?"

"No, mummy. The huntsman shot him in a drain."

It was an early start because of the racing and the

hounds moved off from Harford Farm at approximately nine-thirty. The sun was out but there were grey and white clouds in the sky and the clouds looked heavy with further rain. The fields, lanes and bridlepaths between Harford and Winchcombe were sodden with mud and puddles of muddy water.

'Foxington', the hunt correspondent of the local newspaper, was following the field on his bicycle. He would later report that 'hounds found by Captain Warmsley's pheasant osiers and ran hard across country by Williamson's covert and Lansdowne Bottom before cutting back sharply towards the Bourton road where they killed their fox in a drainage culvert by Wickhams. A second fox found by the railway end of Whipps Spinney proved a more redoubtable opponent. Working his way across country he – Reynard, that notable fighter – led hounds a merry chase on a five mile point from Throwers Gap to the Warrens at Down Spinney before finally being called to account in the back garden of the old vicarage on the edges of the Cutsdean road. Amongst those riding were the Honourable Mrs Charlotte Smyth-Marsham, Major Willeys, Sir Guy and Lady Fielden, Mr Roger Jaggett, the Honourable Camilla Forbes-Sempill, the Honourable Daisy De Moraville, Mr Billy Arkell' etc. etc.

The majority of the hunt followers followed the field by car. Lex didn't set off with the first detachment. He and Bella and James and McQueen went back inside to have breakfast. Once again Hugh generously did the cooking. Reema was not around. She disapproved of fox hunting. Billy Mcphee was in London.

After a couple of hours Lex took his new Range Rover off the lawn and drove himself and Bella and James and McQueen out to meet the field near the proposed location of the last draw of the morning. James got out of the car ahead of the others. He still needed fresh air for his hangover. He walked back over two fields and then up by the side of a fallow field to the top of a slight hillside looking down over a valley through which flowed a slow and sluggish tributary of the River Windrush.

The grass in the field was wet. There were ponies grazing in the field and he could see cows in the distance and rooks nesting in the tops of the trees opposite. It was a gentle scene. Then came the hunt.

The grazing ponies all seemed to look up and cock their ears simultaneously. The birds flew away noisily from the tops of the trees. And then the first pony ran towards the fence at the edge of the field. Then the others followed. A moment or so later James heard the sound of approaching hooves. Then he heard the horn.

The leading hounds charged through the farmyard at the bottom of the valley about one hundred yards away and below him. They hurtled on up the tarmac road past a pair of farmworkers cottages and disappeared as the road turned into a dark belt of coniferous woodland. After about a five-second gap a redcoated rider in a hard black hat came charging through the farmyard after them. Five seconds after him came two more redcoated huntsmen and then about another five-second gap after them came a party of about half a dozen of the more energetic and hard riding hunt members. Daisy was in that group. Gradually over the next five minutes the remainder of the field, or what was left of them, passed eagerly and not so eagerly through the farmyard. Last of all came the gate-shutters. They were both women.

The birds continued to flee the woods, wheeling and screeching and cawing their way upwards into the sky. Just when the whole hunt seemed to have passed away out of sight and out of earshot into the next parish, the baying of the hounds started up again, getting louder and nearer. Either the fox had doubled back down the stream through the valley or the hounds had picked up another scent.

The baying of the hounds was a chilling sound. Insistent, repetitive and melancholy. The kind of sound that could grind into your mind and drive you crazy with exhaustion and desperation.

After about another five minutes the field emerged

from the conifers and ploughed on up a grassy hillside across the other side of the valley. At the top of the hill the leading riders took a four-foot thorn hedge in good order and then had to swing sharply to their right as the hounds dropped downhill again into a thicket of scrub oak which led back down to the stream and the tarmac road. At the bottom, by the road, they were lost from view but you could see the stragglers still spread out across the hillside opposite.

As Richmond stood still by the edge of his field he could hear the baying building up again and then the first hounds breasted the hill. For one moment they looked like rather lovable lop-eared pets bounding after a tennis ball or stick. Then he noticed that they seemed to be heading straight for him. A ferocious-looking huntsman and his whipper-in appeared over the brow of the hill. The whipper-in was flailing his long and bloodcurdling looking instrument of chastisement around his head and the huntsman's face was twisted with apoplectic rage as he yelled and cursed into the air.

Richmond froze to the spot. Had he been mistaken for a detested anti or hunt saboteur? Would he now be tied up by his toes from a beech tree in some sinister forest glade and thrashed within an inch of his life by an irate hunt master? But mercifully the huntsman and the whipper-in galloped straight past without looking at him. The objects of their wrath it seemed were canine not human. The enthusiastic but stupid foxhounds who had lost the fox's scent and bounded straight on into a field of newly-planted spring wheat in the middle of which stood a large, white, hand-painted sign declaiming: 'Riders Keep Out. This Means You.'

After much lashing, verbal and physical, the two riders managed to corral their pack and herd them back towards a derelict greystone barn at the far end of the fallow field. The rest of the hunt had kept to the safer course of the tarmac road along the valley.

The sound of dogs, hooves, horns and hunters passed

away for a second time. In the valley below, Richmond could see the cars, vans and Land Rovers of the assorted hunt followers as they sped on after the redcoated brigade in pursuit of the next scene of action. He eventually caught up with the field again along another sunken valley path about half a mile further on. Lex's Range Rover was parked by the top end of the track. The keys were still in the ignition but there was no sign of Lex himself or Bella. To the right of the track was a spinney of thick oak and horse chestnut trees. To the left was a gently sloping patch of bracken and fern and beyond that another birch plantation. In amongst the bracken and fern was a hive of earths and old rabbit warrens. The fox was believed to have gone to ground in one of these earths and the two hunt terriers, fierce, scarred and muddy-nosed little dogs, were waiting for their chance in the huntsman's saddle bags.

Many of the field had now trotted off home and there were only about half a dozen riders remaining. Most of them had dismounted and were helping out the huntsman with the digging. Some of the remaining hunt followers were helping out too. They were trying to stop off one of the exits from the main earth while digging open the maze of tunnels so that they could put the dogs down and successfully 'call Reynard to his final account'.

The path was bathed in sunshine and it was getting warmer. There were one or two new green buds on the trees in amongst the black and grey boughs and after the rain you could smell the coumarin scent of the grass and the wet bracken and the strong odour of sweating horses' flesh and foxes. The horses cropped gently at the bracken while the dogs padded around by the whipper-in's wagon, wagging their tails and sniffing and licking at the horses' hooves. And all the time the men dug on into the warren. It was a pretty sight. As long as you were able to forget what its true purpose really was.

A tender-looking man in a black riding coat came along the track past Richmond, leading his mount by the rein.

The horse wasn't lame but his rider definitely was. One of the hunt servants looked round as the man approached.

"What the buggering fuck happened to you, then?" he asked.

"Took a bit of a tumble actually," said the man. "Hurt my wrist actually."

The whipper-in spat into the bracken. "Where's old Didger, then?" he asked.

"I haven't the faintest idea," said the man as he carried on past.

It was gone eleven-thirty by now and Richmond decided that he might as well leave. He didn't really want to see or hear the fox meeting its end. He rather hoped it might have got away. Slipped out of its earth by another entrance and be perhaps a field or so on now by Deadmanbury Wood.

He looked around for the Range Rover, only to see it just disappearing up the track in a cloud of exhaust fumes and spraying mud. Well, that was nice. It would be at least a five-mile walk back to Harford. Fortunately he then spotted Daisy who had just boxed her horse up and was about to drive back there herself. For once Daisy seemed more preoccupied with the condition of the suspensory ligaments of her seven-year-old gelding than with any thoughts of pouncing on the young man's body.

Lex's Range Rover was parked in the drive outside the house. When James walked in through the front door the hall was a dramatic sight. Lex's belongings were scattered all over the table, carpet and floor. Shirts, trousers, jackets. Broad-brimmed black fedoras. Gucci shoes. Bottles of aftershave lotion and shampoo. Form books. Newspapers. The lot. Bella was upstairs kneeling on the landing floor. She had her face pressed up against the banister and she was crying her eyes out. Daisy had gone to the stables. James went upstairs.

"Bella?" He sat down gently. "What on earth's the matter?"

"Everything's the matter."

"What happened?" She shook her head. She was sobbing violently. "Did you come back alone?" She wouldn't look at him. "Bella? Did you come back alone?"

"I went for a walk . . . in the wood. And I passed a path. A grassy ride I hadn't noticed before . . ." She shut her eyes. "An innocent pretty looking path leading into the wood." She opened her eyes. "And guess what I saw at the bottom of that path?"

"Lex?" She nodded.

"With your blonde slut. He was lying on the ground. With those ghastly trousers round his ankles. She was lying underneath him. In her half-dressed riding gear. And they weren't digging for foxes either."

"Oh."

"I thought it was all over. 'A one night stand,' he said. But there he was. Big fat bum waving through the air like a full moon. I'm surprised he wasn't afraid of being bitten."

"Or scratching his arse on a blackberry bush." He tried to comfort her. She shook him away. He tried to make her laugh. "And in all that mud too? He's going to ruin his new trousers. Which is perhaps just as well."

"It's not funny, Jimmy."

"You're laughing."

"Yes, but I'm bloody upset too. And bloody angry." She hurled another shoe down over the banister.

"I know, Bella. I'm sorry."

"You men. I'm sick of you. You're all so childish. Lying. Drinking. Spending money. Showing off. You're not adults at all. You want a nanny or a mistress or a little sister. You don't know what it's like to know and love a real woman. You're all just children."

"It is childish, I agree."

"And you're just as bad. You invite me to meet you for a drink after the racing's over but then as soon as your friend wants company your own personality melts away like a snowflake in August. Can't you ever stand up to him?"

"It's not easy."

"Of course it's not easy because you're all cowards, that's why. You don't deserve us. Any of you." There was a long silence. The silence was eventually broken by the sound of helicopters landing on the lawn outside, ready to take them to the races.

"I'm sorry . . . about last night, Bella. I regret it bitterly. And I apologise."

"Thank you."

"I'm sorry about this morning too."

She lifted her head up slowly and looked at him. "Of course I know what he's like. But why her all the time? She's got a face like a vole and a body like a bicycle frame."

"Perhaps he's taking lessons. In show jumping I mean. Perhaps she's teaching him how to three day event."

"Lex can't ride."

"But what about the picture? Of the Kildare Hounds?"

"That's just a fake."

"A fake?"

"He paid some photographer in Shannon Airport to set it up for him. He couldn't ride a donkey on a beach."

"I don't know. Lex Parlane and Harvey Smith. They speak of them in the same breath." She had to laugh at that. But she was still crying. James put an arm around her shoulder.

"I do love him you know," she said. "I really do." She had one of his wide pattern ties in her hands. "I do love him."

"I think he knows that."

"Do you? Do you really think so?" James nodded. "You know what the psychologists would say?"

"What?"

"That deep down . . . men who gamble . . . they want to lose. They want to be punished."

"That's rubbish."

"Of course it is. It's the women who live with them. They take the punishment."

They heard the sound of Daisy's voice coming from the kitchen downstairs. Then they heard men's voices joking and talking loudly.

"Are you there sweetheart," called Lex from the kitchen. "The Master asked me in for a drink. It was really class. You should've been there." Then they heard him walking through from the kitchen to the hall. Then there was silence. "Bella?"

36

Lex loved Bella in his way. But he had to keep
gambling that love. Risking it on the edge as he sought
continual instant gratification from every moment of the
day and night.

Whatever he said to her in the half hour that they
spent together in their bedroom after he'd walked into the
hall at Harford, he somehow managed to persuade her to
put her make-up on and her best clothes and get into the
helicopter with him and James and Jack McQueen and fly
off to Cheltenham for the third day running.

When they got to the racecourse he was in his most
charming and attentive mood. Cracking jokes, kissing
Bella fondly and often and buying champagne once again
for all the company. Bella put up with it and smiled a bit
and drank her champagne.

James Richmond, though, could see big, dark thunder
clouds hanging over them all.

Thursday was the big day. The climax of the three-day
meeting and the day when everything that had gone on
before built up to its final showpiece crescendo. National
Hunt Racing's premier classic race. The Tote Cheltenham
Gold Cup.

The ring seemed to be even more awash with punters'
money than on the first two days. The tents and marquees
were even more crammed and packed with lunch guests
and badge holders, cronies and freeloaders and with more
than one hour still to go before the big race the drinkers in
the grandstand bars were hemmed in as tightly as sardines
in a tin. Even the helicopters wheeling and landing and
taking off again in the centre of the course seemed to

generate a greater air of urgency and of serious intensity
than on the earlier days. And all of Dublin, all of
Birmingham, Bristol and the West of England and almost
half of London – including the City – seemed to have been
given the day off.

The sun was still shining but the ground remained heavy
after the drenching of the previous day and hail and sleet
were forecast for the weekend. Each of the day's six races
would be a severe test of stamina. None more so than the
three-and-a-quarter miles of the Gold Cup itself. The
ground would be all against the favourite, Fort Reunion,
who'd won the previous year's race on good to fast going.
Fort Reunion, an ex-American hunterchaser and three
times a winner that winter, was trained in Upper Lambourn by Jack Denning, a seventy-one-year-old veteran of
the sport who'd saddled three Gold Cup winners, not to
mention three runners-up as well.

The principal Irish challenger, Ace In The Hole, was
trained by Connor Delaney. Ace In The Hole seemed to
be another talking horse. His reputation had preceded
him around England and Ireland for three seasons now
but he'd never yet delivered the goods on the big occasion.

Other English challengers included Fort Reunion's old
Lambourn-trained rival Frolic, a winner of both the
Hennessey and the Whitbread Gold Cups but never yet a
winner round Cheltenham. Michael Garvin was riding his
King George VI chase winner, the New Zealand-bred
gelding Captain Dandy, who'd only run once since Kempton, falling at the second last fence in a three-mile limited
handicap run at Newbury in February.

The season's top staying novice, Lucifer, was a runner
too. He'd won the Lambert and Butler Final at Ascot but
then bypassed the Sun Alliance to have a crack at the big
one. And another challenger over from Ireland was
Rocky Boreen, trained down in County Waterford by
Danno 'The Gasman' Hughes. Two years before, Rocky
Boreen, who revelled in heavy going, had run out a

ten-length winner of the Sun Alliance Chase and he'd been among the antepost favourites for the following season's Gold Cup only to be found lame in his box on the morning of the race. This winter Rocky Boreen's Gold Cup preparation had been unorthodox to say the least. He'd won two races in the autumn, one bumper and one hurdle race and then been put away until January when he'd run fifth in the Thyestes Chase at Gowran Park. That was followed by a gentle second over two miles at Naas at the beginning of March.

Danno Hughes was a gambler alright and it was clear to all the boys with eyes to see it that Rocky Boreen had been trained for one race all year. And the ground had come right in his favour. On the morning of the race the dogs were barking for him. Thirteen to two from twelve to one. Lex laid him to lose sixty five thousand pounds in little more than half an hour. And the money kept coming.

After he'd had a drink with Lex and Bella, James went into the gents cloakroom by the Annual Members' bar, combed his hair again and smartened himself up. Then he went off to his father's box in the older part of the grandstand. On his way down the stairs he bumped into an Oxford bookie that he knew. The bookie wanted paying on a debt. James gave him five hundred pounds in cash towards the debt and then placed another bet on a horse called Bandit in the first race of the afternoon, the *Daily Express* Triumph Hurdle. Lex had been given a tip for Bandit. It was owned by Alan Furness and Willie 'The Dog' Burns and trained down at Epsom by Burns' younger brother, an ex-dogs bookie from Perry Barr and a man whose talent with a chemistry set was well known. Bandit's current price was fourteen to one. James had a grand each way.

The Duke was not Lord Kinglass and there were just twelve guests for lunch in his box. When James arrived a uniformed waitress gave him a glass of dry sherry and he was pecked on the cheek by his aunt who was scrutinising her racecard through her new pair of glasses. Aunt Helena was just as he remembered her. One of the elderly overcoat-and-Robin-Hood-hat brigade. At least one Duchess was present and the inevitable batch of Colonels' wives. The men all had hard bowler hats and old-fashioned suits with old-fashioned trouser turn-ups and shoes with big toecaps that shone in the light. James recognised Dickie Frampton-Mansell, but Lord Stowell and Christopher Cowdray-Clarke were not present.The average age must have been at least fifty-five.

James was asked questions about Oxford and rowing and whether he'd thought about the army as a career, all of which he fielded politely out of consideration to his father. It wasn't done for the Duke to bring his mistress to these occasions, so Helena was playing hostess for him instead. James glanced up to see her standing down the other end of the box, legs characteristically apart and giving orders to the staff. She was quite like his mother in a way. She still had a terrific figure and she could be charmed but it was not easy work. James made a brave fist of it throughout the soup course.

Helena's friends talked about holidays in South Africa and interfering Bishops and the need for the immediate introduction of compulsory dog training classes in towns and cities throughout the land. Then one of them started a subtle disquisition on the mysteries of the female mind. "The thing is, Helena," opined the Countess, a Rob Roy lookalike with a small black moustache, "that women have so much smaller brains than men."

"Speak for yourself, Tory," replied Helena, bridling at last. "Speak wholly and entirely for yourself."

"Oh, I don't know," came a voice. "I quite agree with Tory. That's the sort of line we want to hear. Eh, men?" It was Rowland. Newly arrived from the Turf Club tent. James felt his heart begin to plummet through the floor. And he thought he heard his father groan too. But to the rest of the box Rowland was an attraction. Not a long-haired gambler or academic like James, but a dashing

young military man. Prince Andrew taking time off from
his young ladies to lunch with the old folks upstairs. And
he was greeted with appreciative coos by the women and
familiar nods and grins by the men. James decided to
leave Rowland to it and moved down the table to be
nearer to the Duke. So far his father had said little to him
other than one casual greeting when he'd walked in
through the door.

"What do you fancy in the big one, dad?" he asked.

The Duke frowned. "Old Fort Reunion's a champion,"
he said. "Jack Denning won't hear of defeat."

"Old's the word though," said James. "Lucifer's young
and on the upgrade. Sure to go well."

"You don't think a novice'll win the Gold Cup?"

"No, I don't. I fancy Rocky Boreen."

"The Irishman?"

"He smells right," said James. "I think he's been
prepared for this race all winter?"

"He could be a major threat," agreed the Duke.

"Frolic'll win," shouted Rowland, from the other end
of the table. "He's the form horse."

"Never won on the course," said the Duke.

"And never will," said James.

"Frolic will win," repeated Rowland.

"Balls," said the Duke.

After the filet de boeuf en crôute with carrots,
mushrooms, peas and new potatoes, James went out on to
the balcony. The electronic information system down by
the winning post was flashing up the first show of odds on
the first race of the day, the *Daily Express* Triumph
Hurdle. Romany Bay was the nine to two favourite. Then
they went ten to one the field. Rowland had followed
James outside and the two brothers stood together on the
balcony looking at the crowd milling around on the lawn
below. A band was playing by the paddock and strains of
the *Londonderry Air* drifted back towards them.

"They're playing your tune," said James. Rowland said

nothing. A Cessna light aircraft chugged across the sky. It was trailing a huge banner and the banner was clearly visible from the racetrack. 'Bet with the best,' it said. 'Bet Lex.' James smiled.

Rowland was fuming. "Bloody Irish," he said. "If only they'd stick to horse breeding they'd save themselves and all the rest of us a great deal of trouble."

"Lex is Scottish," said James. "Not Irish."

"Same thing," said Rowland.

"Really?"

"I know you think I'm just a blinkered blimp," said Rowland. "But I have some respect for your Irishman. They've given me a good tip for today. Blarney Fox. Fourth race. It was the trainer who told me himself."

"Who's that?"

"CP Molloy. Small chap but a very decent sort of fellow. He had a winner here on Tuesday in the first."

"I know," said James.

"The whole section's going in hard. Some three or four thousand pounds." Rowland smiled proudly. "I've given all the money to Molloy. He's going to see we get it on and get a price. Success is assured."

"How do you know that?"

"I assessed Molloy's character at a stroke. An honest little man. Admires the role we're playing out in Ulster. So he thought he'd try and give us all a cheer."

"I'd better put some money on myself."

"I should think you've gambled quite enough for one week."

"Not quite."

"You realise the trouble you've caused?" Rowland's horses' head tie was bouncing out of place inside his tweed suit jacket. "Father's had enough on his plate without you adding to his worries."

"Of course. Washy Cleveland."

"A good man brought low by swine."

"Oh, so that's what it was. Nothing to do with money then?"

"Why don't I push you off this balcony?"

"It was my idea first."

"Cut it out, boys!" The Duke was standing there beside them. He put his hands on the balcony rail and looked down distastefully at a fat redheaded man in a teeshirt and jeans who was sitting on the ground on the Members' lawn drinking beer from the can. "I saw you in the papers today, Rowland," said the Duke. "Did you have to climb right over that marquee?"

"It was damned good fun," said Rowland defensively. "Except the whole bang shoot nearly collapsed under our weight. Just imagine. All those grubby little nouveaus eating scampi in a basket because the bride's Jewish father was too mean to make it salmon. And Rory and I nearly wrapped 'em all up like a snot into a handkerchief."

"Fetch me another drink please, Rowland," said the Duke.

"Actually I was just about to tell. . ."

"Fetch me another drink. There's a good chap."

"Oh. Yes. Sorry, father. I could do with a top up myself." Rowland went inside.

"What are you doing next week, Jimmy?" asked the Duke.

"Well . . . term finishes this weekend. I thought I might as well go up to Doncaster. See the start of the flat."

"Don't bother. Doncaster's not a racecourse. It's a National Car Park."

"But I've never seen a Lincoln."

"Two bit handicap. Wait for Newmarket. In my day no flat racing trainer worth his salt would've been seen dead with a runner before the Craven."

"I like Newmarket."

"Do you really? I thought this was your favourite stamping ground?"

"It is. But I like Newmarket too. You've taught me how to appreciate it, father."

"I'm glad to hear it."

"The sense of history. The Rowley Mile. I even think

the bleakness can be beautiful. And the racing's superb."

"Of course it is, Jimmy. Flat racing. The real thing."

"But I have been invited to Doncaster."

"You can't go."

"It is the vacation, father."

"He won't feel much like it himself."

"Who do you mean?"

"Lex Parlane." The Duke dropped his voice to a murmur. "This is by the way of an unofficial warning. Because next week . . . the proverbial shit is going to hit the fan. And I want you to keep well out of it."

"Well out of what?"

"You'll see. You're coming to a meeting at Alexander Square. Tuesday morning. Nine o'clock sharp. And don't be late."

"What for?"

"To thrash out your future once and for all. I'm getting Brewis in from the Nat West trust department. He looks after your money. If you're ever going to handle a trainer's life we've got to get you fixed up with an Assistant's job as soon as you leave Oxford. Abroad first maybe. Australia. Or even California."

James hardly knew what to say. "You're no longer angry then? That I'm here this week?"

The Duke shook his head. "I can't go on playing the gruff Victorian forever. Let's just think about the future."

"Oh yes, father. I'll drink to that." A waitress had come out on to the balcony carrying a tray with several new glasses of claret on it. James and the Duke each took a glass. Rowland was busy talking guns inside. Down by the paddock the band struck up a new tune. Gershwin's *Let's Call The Whole Thing Off*.

"I'm getting out of racing," said the Duke on cue. "I'm stepping down from the Senior Stewardship. A year early."

"Because of Washy?"

"That mainly. But this whole corruption business has left a nasty taste in my mouth. Then when you discover that a majority of your colleagues are sniggering and conspiring behind your back . . . and that your best friend's a crook . . . what's the point in carrying on?" James was silent. "But you must carry on. Racing will always have its share of ill-mannered louts. Not all of them from the Silver Ring either." He was looking at the redheaded fat man who was now rolling cans across the lawn but he was thinking about Rowland too. "But it will still be men like us who run this game, Jimmy. You were born into that tradition. But you must make a choice. Either to be part of it . . . or to be excluded from it for a very long time." James sighed. "Just don't let one youthful indiscretion follow you around for the rest of your life. Because that would be a tragedy."

The boy looked up. "I know what to do," he said quietly.

"Good. I'm having a drink with Jack Denning after the last. Why don't you come too? Some of the finest jump horses of the last thirty years have passed through that stable. You'd love the atmosphere. He'll tell you all about Arkle and Mill House."

"I'd like that, father . . . but there's something that I must do first."

"Well you won't want to do it round here."

"Why's that?"

"Rowland's got the box after racing. A party for his Aldershot friends. They'll do even worse things for your blood pressure than they do to mine."

"Come along, Johnny," called the moustachioed Countess. "We want a tip for the first."

"Oh, don't ask him," retorted Helena. "He's the worst bloody tipster in the world." The women all laughed. Very loud and very shrill. James could see his father wince. Just like when his mother was alive. The Duke turned and walked inside the box, his eyes pleading with his son to follow.

James quickly turned his binoculars on to the odds show by the winning post. Romany Bay was still the nine to two favourite. Bandit had come in a few points to eight to one. He swung his binoculars on round to the ring. He picked up Lex immediately. Standing out on his pitch between Goldline and William Hills. Head held high, shades glinting and granite voice roaring out the odds across the ring. "I'll lay five to one Romany Bay. Five to one this Gipsy."

James went inside after his father.

37

The *Daily Express* Triumph Hurdle had a field of more than thirty and the run to the first was like a cavalry charge. There were two fallers at the first flight and two more at the second which would be the last flight on the second circuit. One of the two second flight fallers, who were both brought down by loose horses, was the favourite Romany Bay, a beautiful looking chestnut ex-flat racer who was undefeated in four races over hurdles.

As the field cleared away past the hurdle and set off on the left-handed turn towards the far side of the course it became apparent to the crowd in the grandstand that Romany Bay had shattered a bone in his off fore. If Romany Bay had been a champion flat racer, an entire colt with a million dollar future at stud, his life might've been saved. But Romany Bay was a gelding. So they shot him. And they had to do it quickly too, in the two minutes remaining before the rest of the field came round again to jump the last flight.

The horse was standing up well enough on its other three legs but its crippled fourth leg hung there pathetically in the air. The wagon raced towards the scene and the green screen came around. The jockey was still standing by the horse and the horse was looking round at the sky and the grandstand opposite and at the crowd in the silver ring. The jockey and the vet had to collapse the horse gently on to the grass ready for the bullet. The dull report of the shot echoed across the track towards the boxes and the Members' Enclosure. The vet's men worked quickly, hauling Romany Bay's carcass off the track and away from the hurdle and up into the waiting blood wagon. Just as they got it off the track the leaders in the race swung round to their left into the home straight, less than one hundred yards away, and began to bear down on the last flight.

There were about a dozen horses in the leading group. Bandit, who had held a good position all the way, stopped like a shot duck as they ran towards the last where his seemingly less well fancied stable companion Foxtrot Charlie came with a storming late run on the outside to take the lead off the Irish pair, Thieving Dago and Delaney's Bar. Running on strongly up the hill he scored a one-and-a-half-length sixty-six to one victory. The result was greeted with stunned silence by the crowd in the stands but Foxtrot Charlie was given a hero's welcome as he returned to the unsaddling enclosure where his owners turned out to be none other than Alan Furness and Willie 'The Dog' Burns, who had done a Lex with Mylerstown and bought a two-thirds share the night before. And from their broad grins and whoops of joy you could tell that in spite of their tip for Bandit they'd backed the outsider of their two horses and confidently expected it to win the race too.

"Tell us the truth, Alan," said the TV interviewer in the paddock. "Did you put us all away?"

"Yeah," sniggered the shoulder-haired broker, resplendent in an auburn-coloured, double-breasted corduroy coat with an auburn fur collar to match. "I put you all away."

"Bastard," said Lex, who was following the interview on a TV set in the bar. "They've just cost me ten grand."

"That must call for the Smith Brothers' treatment," muttered James.

"No need," said Lex. "Furness will get his. That horse'll never pass a dope test."

"You reckon?"

"I reckon there were so many narcotics stuffed up that horse's bum it's a miracle if it wasn't hallucinating during the race. They should've brought joss sticks into the unsaddling enclosure."

"What about poor Romany Bay?" asked Reema.

"It wouldn't have won anyway," said Lex. "It could never beat a cheat like that."

"I meant the fact that it's dead."

"Tough break." Lex broke away towards the bar.

Bella shook her head. "So that's the price the horse has to pay for your gamble."

"That's right," said McQueen. "And shooting it's the kindest thing to do. No use getting sentimental. It's the way of the world."

"Don't tell me," said Bella. "No one ever said life was fair. Especially not for horses."

"Precisely," said Charles St Clair. "You can't afford to take these things personally. I had five hundred pounds on the bloody thing's neck and yet it let me down and died. But I'm not crying. Am I, old girl?" He took a nip from his hip flask and then passed it to Jonathan Pointdexter who passed it on to DD who passed it back again. They ignored Bella.

"Hey Charlie," called DD. "What odds will you give me on Ratcatcher completing the course in the next?"

"Fifty to one."

"I'll have a score. Three times."

"You're on."

"You make me sick," said Bella. "You boast of your callousness . . . your self interest. You make it a kind of virtue. As if you're all the sensible men of the world and we're all the fools."

"That's right."

"Absolutely."

"What else do you expect?"

"From you . . . nothing." Bella turned on her heel and walked out of the bar.

"Someone not doing his business in the sack I'd say," said DD.

"These women," said Pointdexter. "You've got to

screw them regularly. If you want to keep them quiet."

The second race was the Christie's Foxhunters' Steeple-chase for hunter chasers and Amateur Riders over the Gold Cup distance. There were nine runners. The favourite, Sonny's Rambler, was a top point-to-pointer in the West Country with a brilliant reputation between the flags. But he was still something of an unknown quantity on a real racecourse. His two main opponents were Flurry Knox, a now veteran-age Irish hunter chaser and The Gamekeeper, a tough and wiry ex-handicapper from the North. The best jockey in the race was undoubtedly Tomsey Lehane, the Irish Amateur champion who was on board Flurry Knox.

According to some experienced professional gamblers it's a dangerous habit to start betting on these Amateur Rider races. Lex had five hundred pounds on The Gamekeeper at fives. Just for an interest. James couldn't imagine Sonny's Rambler having the experience to cope with the Cheltenham fences and he saw a big tip for The Gamekeeper in *Timeform* which rated it ten points clear. The Gamekeeper had the services of Mr Valentine Witts, a four-pound claiming gentleman farmer and newly elected member of the Jockey Club. James put all his remaining Lex credit, two thousand pounds, to win only on The Gamekeeper.

Flurry Knox and Tomsey Lehane scorned reservations about the heavy going and took the field along at a cracking gallop. Coming to the downhill fence on the first circuit one young English Amateur attempted to come up on Tomsey's inside. Tomsey cut him off as they went into the fence, sending the horse into the wing and the jockey over the rail. Fortunately both horse and rider escaped serious injury.

With a mile left to run Flurry Knox was still going strongly in the lead. Then, at the final open ditch on the far side, he pitched too steeply on landing. And fell. A shocked cry that could be heard by the drivers on the Bishops Cleeve road rang out from the Irish crowd in the stands.

As they started down the hill for the second time The Gamekeeper was the new leader but Sonny's Rambler, galvanised at last by his hitherto sleeping jockey, was going ominously well in second place. Going to the third last fence Sonny's Rambler stumbled on a patch of loose ground and his jockey, taken unawares, lost his balance and slipped out of the saddle on the flat.

"Come on The Gamekeeper. Go on my son," roared Lex and James from the lawn.

The Gamekeeper rounded the home turn four lengths in front. The horse still seemed to be going well within himself. His nearest pursuer, Waddling Joe, ridden by Captain Anthony Wagsby-Welling, a sometime officer in the Royal Artillery, had seemed to be dead on its feet at the top of the hill. But now Waddling Joe, given unattractive but strenuous looking support, was beginning to make ground and although The Gamekeeper looked full of running Mr Witts seemed glued to the saddle and was making no effort to kick on to the line.

Running to the last Waddling Joe drew level. The Gamekeeper made the better jump and landed fractionally in the lead but then the assistance that the horse got from his rider was farcical to behold. Mr Witts seemed to be flinging his reins up into the air as if he was trying to drive away a wasp. Captain Wagsby-Welling on the other hand gave his mount no quarter, hurling himself up and down in the saddle like some grotesque parody of the sexual act while applying his stick to Waddling Joe's hind quarters like Wackford Squeers after Smike in full cry.

Waddling Joe got the verdict by a head and there were jeers and boos from the crowd. More surprisingly, in view of the trouble of the previous day, there was no announcement of a Stewards' Enquiry concerning excessive use of the whip.

"And now the prize for the winning jockeys," called one Dublin voice. "A complete set of riding lessons." Everybody laughed. As the horses trotted back towards the unsaddling enclosure James got a closer look at Mr

Valentine Witts. He turned out to be none other than the same black-coated gentleman that he'd seen making a painful exit from the hunt that morning.

"Licensed buffoons," said Lex. "They shouldn't be allowed."

A small sandy-haired man in a deerstalker hat turned round and offered a rebuke. "Actually he's got a very bad wrist," said the man. "Very delicate, I believe."

"I know," said James.

"Then he shouldn't be riding," said Lex. "Fucking Amateurs. They do all your money. They take up two whole races on the Festival programme and then they ride like a jelly just out of the mould and we're supposed to call them all sportsmen and thank them for the effort. Someone should help them over a cliff."

The sandy-haired man turned away crossly to his friends. "Gamblers," he was saying. "No basic love of the sport."

"And that's not true," added Lex.

"I'm broke," said James.

"The fourteen grand?"

"All gone."

"You've got plenty antepost on the big one."

"I need cash." Lex took a huge roll of twenty and fifty-pound notes out of his back trouser pocket, peeled off a handful and shoved them into Richmond's hand. Richmond counted the number. There was five hundred pounds.

"I need credit too."

"Credit?" James nodded. "How much?"

"Two thousand?"

"Make it five if you want."

The boy's fingers were itching around the edges of his *Sporting Life*. He'd had four-and-a-half months to work out his selection for the Cheltenham Gold Cup. Of the ten runners about to go to post he had antepost bets on three of them and useless vouchers on at least three others who were now non-runners. Yet even at this late stage he just couldn't make up his mind. He was determined to back the winner. He was determined to get out of debt once and for all. And he couldn't resist gambling on one other horse. He looked up at Lex. "Can we make it ten?"

"What are you going to back?"

"Rocky Boreen. Everything about it's right. I can shut my eyes and see it galloping up that hill and past the winning post. I know it, Lex. In my veins. Fifteen years of following this race meeting. It's not Fort Reunion. And it's not Frolic or Ace In The Hole. Rocky Boreen's going to win the Gold Cup."

"And that's your best bet of the week?" Richmond nodded. "Ten then. I'll put it with Mecca and Ward Hill."

"Alright."

"And all to win?"

"All to win."

"Cheer up. If you win you can take us out to dinner. In Las Vegas." Lex laughed. "I'll tell you something funny. You were right all along. I was talking to Fennessy Conroy before the last. And he said to me that some of the boys . . . " his voice had dropped down to a whisper ". . . do pass around a hat for the Provos."

"Like who?"

"Like CP. Old CP Molloy."

"You're kidding?" Lex shook his head.

"He's got another touch in the fifth race today. A Republic Bank of Ireland job. It's in the paper." He ruffled the boy's hair. "I'm going to go to work."

James's mind was reeling. Of course. Blarney Fox. His brother Rowland, the English SAS Major, had been made an unwitting accomplice to an IRA sting. An ingenious ruse to raise money to kill men like Rowland with. James started to laugh out loud. He had to have a piece of that action. Then he noticed that people were looking at him suspiciously. He tried to compose himself. First he needed the Irish Racing Gods to smile on his fortunes. On Rocky Boreen. He had to win that race. Everything depended on it.

He stood there on the lawn in his suit with his rolled up copy of *The Sporting Life* in his hand. Then he put on his dark glasses and walked towards the ring.

38

The Duke had been looking at the Gold Cup runners in the paddock. And thinking about a bet. He was meant to have given up betting. He'd backed White's Club on the first day and The Gamekeeper in the Foxhunters' and they'd both lost him money. But instinct led him to believe that his son James could well be right and that Rocky Boreen was indeed the horse to be on in the big race itself. So as he was walking back towards the box he turned left by the stairs and cut round by the Tote windows overlooking the racetrack and the lawn.

There were huge queues of people waiting in line for each of the eight or so windows in front of him but back in the paddock the runners were still walking round and the Duke had to have this bet. He calculated that he still had about fifteen minutes before the start of the race. He joined one of the queues for a five-pound window. The one-pound windows were next door. The punters around him were not big punters. Tote punters rarely are. Duchesses and housewives, retired officers and bank clerks handing over their fifty pence pieces warily and all determined not to lose. As the Duke stood patiently in the queue someone tapped him on the shoulder. He turned round. It was Lex Parlane.

The two men talked, standing there together in the Tote queue with the waiting punters shuffling slowly forward all around them. The English aristocrat and the Scots bookie.

Lex smiled confidently. He had a sharp and glinting look. "Do you want a tip?" he asked.

The Duke shook his head. "I can read the formbook, thank you. And weigh up the hunches."

"Betting on the Tote . . . is losing money. Whatever odds they give you, I'll go two points better."

"Are you offering me an account?"

"I've had the aristocracy. Some of them charming. Some of them needed a few reminders with the bills."

"We don't have your modern self-made business rigour."

Lex smiled. "I like that." The queue moved forward.

"I hear they had some trouble at the Queens," said the Duke. "Friends of yours?"

"I hold no brief for terrorists," said Lex. "The worst of all crimes in my book I hope they all go down."

"All?"

"Bolger, Kinane and Maguire."

"I heard of no Bolger," said the Duke.

"Londoner. London or Essex. Fat. Cocky. A big fat thug."

The Duke smiled. "Oh, Michael Bolger?" Lex nodded. "Oh, no, Michael Bolger has been working for us." Lex looked puzzled. "That's right. For what . . . nearly five months now." Suddenly Lex looked worried. "We know everything."

The bookmaker's smile froze. His eyes flickered behind his dark black glasses and a muscle twitched involuntarily in his cheek. He spoke quickly. "Witnesses? Corroborative evidence? You haven't got any."

"Oh yes, we have." Again the queue moved forward. The Duke was nearly halfway down the line. "You see, Bolger made recordings of all your conversations. And we have the tapes. The Daytona Beach Club. Your house. Garvin's. Even the Queens Hotel last Monday. We've got the lot."

All colour drained from Lex's face. "I'll deny everything."

"It's on the record. You're finished."

"You're bluffing."

"I'm afraid not." A punter was complaining. He'd been given the wrong tickets. The Duke looked back towards the track. No sign yet of the horses.

"Never mind them," said Lex, his voice rising. "I want to know how you stitched this up."

"We always knew that Garvin was a villain," said the Duke calmly. "But we never had the evidence against you. That's where Bolger came in. He was a bookmaker. He'd been warned off. And he was worried that by the time he got back on to the rails you'd have taken all his custom."

"Too bloody right."

"We used Bolger to set up the ring with the jockeys. Garvin we knew would be unable to resist it. And Kinane. And Maguire. You were the gamble."

"I was?"

"We banked on your vanity. That it would be too great to prevent you from getting involved. We were proved right." The queue had started moving once again. The Duke edged forward. In the background the racecourse commentator announced that the runners were about to leave the paddock. The Duke was excited.

Lex wasn't thinking about the horses. He was looking disbelievingly at the Senior Steward. "But Bolger should've been arrested? With the others?"

"He didn't stay at the Queens last night. He only got back there this morning. In time to see two men being arrested. Maguire. And Johnny Kinane."

"But the police must be looking for him? Surely they must?"

The Duke shook his head. "The police have been appraised of the situation by RSS. They're pressing no charges. It was a good try. You've done for Kinane and Maguire. The police want heads and we won't intervene. But you and Garvin are done for."

"But Garvin was never that big in my plans," cried the bookie. "Garvin was Bolger's boy."

"So you both thought," said the Duke. "Too late now." He moved forward again.

"But Bolger's a crook anyway!" Lex was shouting now.

"He's been warned off. I've never been to Portman Square in my life."

"Last October?"

"That was different and you know it." Astonished punters gaped at the two men. Spectators waiting for the big race pricked up their ears and craned their necks in an effort to get a glimpse of the confrontation.

"But unlike you, Bolger is also discreet. In return for his help we let him back on the track this winter."

"He's acceptable but I'm not?"

"That's right."

"You people amaze me."

"You've been playing the wrong end of the market, my friend. You should be in bloodstock." He pointed to the article in *The Sporting Life* about the premature retirement of the Guineas favourite. "They make fortunes every year."

"And they're the right kind of chap, I suppose?"

"Unfortunately yes." The Duke had reached the window. He took out his money.

"I'll fight you," shouted Lex. "All the way. I'll take the whole damn Jockey Club to the High Court."

"You can try. Number five please. To win. Ten times." The Duke handed ten five-pound notes over to the lady behind the Tote window. She gave him his ten Tote tickets. "Thank you." He moved away quickly from the queue. "The amazing thing is," he said to Lex, "we're not quite as stupid as we look. Good afternoon." And with that he lifted his hat and slipped away quietly into the crowd. Out of the action and out of the limelight for good.

Lex was left standing on the grass. He was rooted to the spot. "I can still take your son down with me," he shouted. "You'd better remember that." People were still looking at him but the Duke had disappeared amongst the crowd. Lex Parlane could suddenly see ruin staring him in the face.

The Gold Cup runners were starting to parade up the course about twenty-five feet away. Some of the horses

were jogging and jinking nervously before the huge
crowd. One or two of them looked surprisingly rough and
pitponyish for a Gold Cup field. The current champion
though, Jack Denning's Fort Reunion, looked magnificent. He walked near the head of the parade looking as if
he owned the place, as if the Gold Cup was his by right
and as if any claimant or pretender would have to fight all
the way to take it off him. Fort Reunion inspired Lex.

James Richmond was standing right up by the rail
looking at the parade. Lex came up behind him. "What
are you on?" Lex asked him.

Richmond looked round, his face incredulous. "Rocky
Boreen. You did put it on?"

Lex nodded. "Ten grand. To win at five to one."

"What about you?"

"I've laid it. All day. If it wins I'll lose a quarter of a
million on the race."

"I see. My victory, your loss?"

Lex nodded. "And it's the same the other way."

"Other liabilities?"

"Lucifer's my next biggest loser. I've taken nearly
twenty-five thousand on the horse. Most of it here."

"What about your own bet?"

"Fort Reunion. I've been backing it all winter long.
Captain Dandy's next best. But the Fort'll win. First dual
Gold Cup winner since L'Escargot."

"I hope you're wrong."

For Richmond it was a thrilling sight seeing these
twelve horses, nearly all of them top flight chasers,
parading together before the start. Not hiding from each
other any longer in small out-of-the-way contests at small
provincial tracks. They could see each other face to face
at last.

And they were not to be confused with flat racers
either. Delicate, light and highly strung creatures who
waited for their races like excitable athletes at the start of
an Olympic final. Jumpers were more like professional
heavyweight boxers, poised tense but menacing in their

corners at the outset of a championship fight. Did they recognise each other, James wondered? Or even communicate by word or look? Did they share their jockeys' general sentiments like 'Good luck pal' or 'Move over, grandad, I'm coming through'? How much of the atmosphere was in the mind of the onlooker? How much was generated by the horses themselves?

Lex was thinking different thoughts. As the field cantered back towards the start he was looking at the crowd all around him. Clutching their betting slips and their Tote tickets. He shouldn't be rubbing shoulders with these people. He should be on high. Up in the stands or in a private box. These people were losers. If not now, the next race. If not today, tomorrow or next week. He shouldn't be here.

He thought he saw Michael Bolger grinning at him from the ring. Then he heard the commentator's voice. "They're under starters orders."

The crowd gasped with excitement. Too late now to move away.

"Can you hold the baby?" a woman asked her husband who was standing nervously by Richmond's side. "I want to have a pee."

"What, now?"

"Well, what's wrong with now?"

"Oh nothing. It's only five seconds before the start of the most exciting jump race of the year and with a little bit of luck you'll miss the whole thing and then you'll only have to wait another twelve months before it comes round again." Then a real row developed.

James turned his binoculars onto the start. Lex wasn't watching.

"And they're off. And as they run towards the first, it's Too Many Crooks the early leader. Too Many Crooks from Vulelek's Pride, Fortria's Lady, Fort Reunion and Rocky Boreen. Over the first. And a bad mistake there by Ace In The Hole" – ominous sounds from the crowd. The Ace would be up to his usual tricks – "but they're all safely over it. And as they run down now towards fence number two it's still Too Many Crooks making it. The thirty-three to one outsider from Vulelek's Pride, Rocky Boreen and last year's winner Fort Reunion. And a marvellous jump there by Fort Reunion which carries him right up to dispute the running as they go out away from the stands towards the far side on this the first circuit. Too Many Crooks. Fort Reunion. Vulelek's Pride and Fortria's Lady. These four some two or three lengths clear of Rocky Boreen with Ace In The Hole tucked in on the inside rail and closely followed by Frolic, King's Banner and the novice Lucifer. Bringing up the rear at this stage are Michael Garvin and Captain Dandy.''

As they went down the far side the sun went in behind the clouds and a chill wind started drifting across the course from the North East. The field stayed tightly together as they raced down the hill for the first time past the blank patch of grass where the house used to be. Some of the cattle grazing in the field beyond the track started lolloping along in a bunch as the Gold Cup runners swept past.

They came into the straight to jump the fences in front of the stands for the second time and the leaders were still the same. Just as they took what would be the last fence the next time around a deep volley of thunder rattled out over the Cotswolds and a sheet of white lightning lit up the sky. The lightning seemed to frighten the outsider Too Many Crooks, who dropped his jockey out of his saddle and then galloped on alone up the hill past the winning post and on towards the racecourse stables and home.

Rain was falling as they started out down the far side of the course for the second time. The rain quickly turned to hail. Heavy hailstones bouncing off the heads of the crowd. The runners started spreading out. Michael Garvin had suddenly moved Captain Dandy right up from last to nearly first and as they took the water jump he was showing fractionally in the lead with the Irishman Ace In The Hole on his outer, Rocky Boreen going beautifully

just in behind them in third and Fort Reunion, who'd
been taking a slight breather, a few lengths behind them
in fourth. The novice Lucifer, in spite of making a
string of mistakes, was still bang in contention in fifth
but Frolic, who appeared once again to be exhibiting his
traditional hatred of Cheltenham, was six lengths adrift.
Vulelek's Pride and Fortria's Lady were another four
lengths behind Frolic and King's Banner had been
pulled up.

Then Frolic began to make ground. Vulelek's Pride was
pulled up too at the fifteenth and Ace In The Hole took
the fence before the final open ditch by the roots and paid
the penalty. As the horses reached the top of the hill the
rain on the far side of the course had become a thick and
impenetrable mist. There were only five horses still left in
the race now with a serious chance.

As they came out of the mist and raced down the hill in
the still pouring rain Rocky Boreen was right there in
second on the inside rail. James Richmond wondered how
many of the non-racing world knew or had any idea of the
poetry and emotion involved in the contest that was
building to its climax right now. Out there at this hour on
the rainswept green stretches of Prestbury Park. He felt as
if he wanted this moment to last and last. He wanted to be
able to carry it around with him for the next twelve
months for his own private use and joy and encouragement. Then it happened.

"As they make the long run towards the third last fence
in the Tote Cheltenham Gold Cup it's Captain Dandy still
showing just in the lead. But Rocky Boreen looks full of
running on the inside with Fort Reunion and Lucifer just
behind these two and Frolic still trying to close. And as
they jump the third last . . . and Captain Dandy's down!
And he's brought down Rocky Boreen!" Richmond's
binoculars fell with a sickening thump against his chest.
Cries of horror and anguish resounded from the grandstand for what seemed like the umpteenth time that week.
But the race carried on. "And that leaves Fort Reunion

with a clear lead. Lucifer is over in second and Frolic is still making ground up in third. And as they run round the turn into the home straight with just two left to jump in the Gold Cup it's Fort Reunion being pressed now by Lucifer. Fort Reunion in the centre of the course and Lucifer with the sheepskin noseband over on the stand side. Fort Reunion's over that one in the lead and now Frolic is putting in a challenge too. And it's a wide open race as they run to the last."

"Come on The Fort. You can do it," yelled Lex.

"And as they come to jump it, it's Lucifer who's taken up the running. Lucifer from Fort Reunion but a terrible mistake there by Lucifer and a brilliant recovery by his jockey. And they're on the run in now and it's Lucifer being pressed by Fort Reunion. Lucifer from Fort Reunion . . ."

"Go on The Fort, go on my son," roared Lex.

". . . Frolic putting in a run but as they race up towards the line it's still Lucifer from Fort Reunion. Lucifer. Fort Reunion. At the line Lucifer's the winner. Fort Reunion is second and Frolic is third. And that's the one two three in the Tote Cheltenham Gold Cup. And so the official result is first number. . ."

The cheers and yells peaked and died like a firework display as the horses pulled up by the racecourse stables and as the jockeys patted them down the shoulder and shook hands with one another in the saddle.

James Richmond felt sick and numb and stupid. He'd just lost the biggest bet of his life. Two days before, his biggest ever bet had been the thousand pounds on Mylerstown winning him fourteen grand. Then they'd known the trainer and the jockey. They'd had the information. They'd known that it was going to be the big time touch. Now, forty-eight hours later, he'd put ten times that amount on a horse where he had none of that private knowledge and in one of the most competitive horse races, jumping or flat, of the whole year.

"The Fort should've won," said Lex. "It's just that he

was in front too soon. On this ground he had to be held up for a late run. He's got the speed but he hates the ground."

"We've both lost," said James.

"But The Fort should've won! If only the others hadn't fallen. Or if Lucifer had fallen. But this result!" He shook his head. "There's no way he should have lost that race."

"It's cost me everything."

"I know," said Lex. "I've been keeping a tab." His voice had hardened suddenly and unkindly. "So now you'd better work out how you're going to pay the bill. Hadn't you?"

"I suppose I had." The boy turned away into the crowd. Lex went in the opposite direction towards the paddock.

The rain was still bucketing down over the heads of the crowd and the Stewards and the Queen Mother and the presentation party in the unsaddling enclosure. Lucifer, the seven-year-old novice trained up in Yorkshire by one of jump racing's formidable band of lady trainers, was given a generous reception. The cameras whirred and flashed and Lucifer's owner, a handsome and expensively dressed woman in sopping wet furs and a wet felt hat, fondled his ears lovingly and stepped forward to take the Gold Cup trophy from the Queen Mother herself. Everyone, it seemed, was happy in spite of the rain. It had been a terrific race and a novice winning the Cheltenham Gold Cup was a victory for sport over business. For boldness and daring over caution and greed. So while everyone smiled and shook each other by the hand and went off to have drinks with the directors of the Steeplechase Company Lex Parlane met Michael Garvin by the weighing room steps.

Garvin had just got out of the ambulance that had brought him back after his fall at the third last fence. He looked exhausted. He was covered with mud like a facepack and the rain was dripping down over his eyes and ears, ruining the smart Vidal Sassoon haircut. When he saw Lex he scowled. "What do you want?"

"You and me," said Lex softly. "Our names are to be inextricably linked. Our destinies forever paired by history."

"What the fuck are you talking about?"

"Bolger's been working for Racecourse Security. He's made tape recordings of all your conversations. Mine too."

Garvin looked ill. "How do you know?"

"His Grace the Duke. He told me himself. Kinane and Maguire are already tucked up. You and I get the high jump. Portman Square. Our official letters are probably already in the post."

"They can't do that. Not now. Only one more season and I'd have retired voluntary. They can't do it." Garvin sat down suddenly and heavily on the weighing room steps. And began to cry. He sat on the steps leading up to the ultra-modern one-storey weighing room building and blubbered and cried his eyes out like a child outside the Headmaster's study. Other jockeys, trainers, officials, valets and spectators all stood and stared at him alike. In utter and complete astonishment.

"Pull yourself together," said Lex, handing him a monogrammed silk handkerchief. "And ring your lawyer after racing. I'll call you myself next week." Then he walked away.

"They're under starter's orders. And they're off."

39

Three races left on Gold Cup afternoon. Only three out of eighteen to go. And only three more chances to bet. The atmosphere in the ring now was getting down to serious diehard stuff. The getting out stakes were underway.

Richmond was ten thousand pounds out of pocket. And he'd spent all of Lex's five hundred pounds worth of cash too, giving fifty to Bella, one hundred and fifty to the bar girls, one hundred pounds to the Oxford bookie and another two hundred to William Hills. Could he somehow win ten and a half thousand pounds on the next three races? Not without capital to bet with. He couldn't ask Lex anymore. He couldn't get credit with any other rails firm and he couldn't ask Rowland or his father.

He started touring the racecourse urgently, looking for potential sources of revenue. He found Sunny Vengsarkar by the evil-smelling Hog Roast behind the paddock. Sunny had an Oxford friend with him. A rich boy called Jeremy whose parents owned a stud near Newbury. Jeremy was the original fat bespectacled schoolboy who wanted friends and would gladly buy them if necessary. James borrowed two hundred pounds from him in cash. Then he went away to look at the form for the Ritz Club Chase.

Ballyconran was the much-tipped favourite but an Irish horse hadn't won this race for years. This time James decided he'd ignore Irish tips. He put his two hundred pounds to win on Army and Navy ridden by Michael Garvin and trained by Captain Roddy Hyde-Lyne. Army and Navy was a consistent handicap chaser and Grand

National prospect with a record of achievement over the Cheltenham fences.

The race was won easily by Ballyconran who led after the first circuit and jumped his rivals into the ground, finishing ten lengths clear. Army and Navy finished fifth, beaten twenty-one lengths.

Only two races left to go.

James was getting desperate. He went back into the ring. Things were getting sleazy. The rain had stopped but the sun was only pretending. And the big bookmakers were fighting the confused punters to a standstill. They were like Wimbledon champions coming back in the fifth set after being two sets down. Punters looked ill and tired and wan. Heart bypass surgery would soon be necessary. Men fingered their copies of *The Sporting Life* and *Timeform* racecards hopelessly. Seasoned racing correspondents stood holding *The Times* racing page the wrong way up and worrying at their trilby hats. And hanging over them all as the air got sharper and the light began to fade were the suffocating fumes from the hamburger stand at the back of Tatts.

The County Hurdle was one of the biggest betting races of the meeting. Twenty-one runners and a plethora of tips and the ring was as thick with flying bankrolls and wads of money as for the first race on day one.

The logical bet seemed to be Union Castle, a tough and genuine little hurdler who'd run second in the Schweppes Gold Trophy. But James had backed a logical choice in the Ritz Club Chase. For this race his nose told him that he wanted a gamble. And as he watched the betting on the rails and with the bookies' pitches in Tattersalls he found it. CP Molloy's Blarney Fox. Of course. How could he forget? Lex and Rowland's touch. And hopefully the best and most profitable joke of the week.

Blarney Fox had five noughts to his name in the formbook but he'd been a good four-year-old the season before and he was mysteriously tipped by three correspondents, including the Dublin correspondent, in *The Sport-*

ing Life. His estimated starting price in the morning paper was twenty-five to one. His first price on the boards was ten to one. James had to get some money to back Blarney Fox.

He found Camilla walking away from one of the Tattersalls pitches. Lex had given her fifty pounds in cash to bet with at the start of the day. She'd backed the winners of the Gold Cup and the Foxhunters' and now she'd put her last ten pounds each way on a horse called Royal Santino in the County Hurdle. Royal Santino was a novice but an improving one who got into the handicap on bottom weight. It was a smart bet. Camilla had always had an eye for the horses.

"You've been neglecting Dolly," she said when she saw him.

"You've been alright, it seems."

"That's my affair."

"Camilla. I don't care what you do. But could you lend me some money? Please."

"Why should I lend you money?"

"You'll get it back at the end of the afternoon I promise. When a bookie pays me. I'm just temporarily stuck for cash."

"How much?"

"Fifty."

"Fifty?" James nodded. "Will you be nice to me then?"

"Aren't I always?"

"Nicer than you are to that Italian woman?"

"She's only half-Italian. And half-Scottish."

"You know what I mean."

James needed the money very badly. He smiled. "Much nicer."

Camilla gave a sigh. "Twenty pounds and that's the lot."

He needed more. "I'll take you out to dinner if I win. In London."

"Promise?"

"Promise."

She sighed again. "Oh, alright." She gave him another three ten pound notes. "But that's it."

"Good girl, Bella. I mean sorry . . . Camilla." Camilla glared at him and walked away. "See you after the last," he mumbled insincerely.

Blarney Fox was being backed right enough. It was already into eights from ten to one. James managed to get the ever-considerate Hugh to lend him another fifty pounds and he put the whole hundred on to win with Jack D'Angelo at eight to one. He also managed to persuade the Tote's antepost representative, an old schoolfriend, to lay him another two hundred pounds worth of credit at sevens. There was a further rush of money for the horse as the runners cantered down. Some of the bookies even began to take Blarney Fox out of their lists.

James watched the race from the ring. Next to Berners and Rubin and Ted Bassett and Jack D'Angelo. D'Angelo kept laying bets throughout the race as the lead changed hands five times. Some of the losing bookies started packing up their pitches before the race was over. Some of them drank tea from paper cups or took pills for their duodenal ulcers. Others, the big boys, looked on. Cool, impassive and unperturbed by anything to do with money. They had money. Other people lost it. All around them was the ragged litter of their trade. Discarded betting sheets. Pens and chalk. Losing tickets. Cigarette packets and thermos flasks and one or two empty champagne bottles and glasses down among the umbrellas and the full satchels. For a one pound note one young black kid down on his luck shined Jack Rubin's shoes as he stood there in his nice warm coat on his upturned crate in the cold late afternoon air.

The gaggle of regular losers stood around the bookies trying to look like they were part of the scene. Like they always stood there. Like they hadn't lost. Oh no. They were never losers. They were insiders. They knew trainers and jockeys. By their first names. Met them in the clubs and bars only racing people knew. Yes, they'd just lost another monkey on the last but that money didn't count. Not to them. Jack and Les and Teddy. They understood. They knew that they were real racing men. Real men.

Blarney Fox brought like Mylerstown on the wide outside by Frankie Molloy, came with a beautifully timed late run to take up the lead before the last and win going away by two-and-a-half-lengths. Royal Santino was a fast finishing third. Blarney Fox was returned at five to one. It was CP Molloy's second winner of the meeting and Frankie's third, putting Frankie in the lead for the top jockeys trophy. It was Ireland's second winner of the day and their sixth of the meeting.

James had won twenty-two hundred pounds, eight hundred of it in cash. He didn't quite know how much Rowland had won but one thing was certain. It would be a lot less than CP Molloy and the rebels. But that was Rowland's problem. Blarney Fox had given him the necessary pocket money for the eighteenth and final race of the meeting. The Cathcart Challenge Cup.

The Cathcart had a field of only seven. Usually it was a gift for the favourite. This year that was Jack Denning's Hypnotist, a horse just short of the top class who'd been second three times at Cheltenham but never won there. His opponents looked moderate. I've Been To Ballyporeen was making his second attempt in two days to win a race at the Festival but confidence in his chance was not improved by the trainer's declaration that he was only turning out for expenses. Also in the field was the now fourteen-year-old one-time two-mile champion chase winner, Dessie's Image, still trained by Big Pat McKenna but nowadays seen mostly point-to-point racing down in County Tipperary.

Hypnotist's opening price was eleven to ten. He was likely to shade evens or odds on pretty soon as desperate punters piled on the cash to try and get out and cover their losses. Twenty-two hundred pounds would not be enough to get back much of Richmond's ten grand. He had to borrow once again. He started searching frantically across the lawns and through the crowds in the bars, looking for anyone who could lend him some more money. An inglorious collection from Sunny and Sunny's friend and Hugh and Jack McQueen yielded another couple of hundred but that would still be useless at odds of eleven to ten.

He found Bella in a little group with Reema and Daisy, the three of them alone by the open air champagne bar on the lawn. They all looked bored and tired and unhappy. He tried to talk to Bella on her own.

"I need your help."

"Ours? Darling. You boys are having lots of fun without us."

"I'm not joking, Bella. Please help me."

"How?"

"I need to borrow some money. It's my last chance. *The* last chance. The last chance of the meeting."

"I said you didn't have to be like the others, Jimmy."

"But I've got to try and win some of it back, Bella. I've got to try and halve my debts. My father'll have a heart attack."

"You'll only get deeper in debt."

"No I won't. I know the winner. Hypnotist. But he'll soon be odds on. I need real money to back it with. Otherwise the price won't be worth it."

"Forget it. Give up. You never win."

"I can win on this race."

"No."

"If you lend me the money I can win on this race."

"No, Jimmy. I won't do it."

"I've got to have a bet."

"Then put it on another horse."

"What's the good of that? Hypnotist's going to win. Not another horse."

"An outsider, Jimmy. Bigger odds." She looked him in the eye. "Bigger gamble."

He thought for a minute. "Maybe you're right." The horses were going down. He saw Hypnotist canter past.

Followed by Dessie's Image. "I'll be back later on."

He ran towards the ring and started dashing up and down amongst the crowd and down the line of pitches. Hypnotist was as short as six to five on in places. He couldn't put twenty-two hundred pounds on a six to five on shot. It was a drop in the ocean. But at least it would be a winner. And to go out on a winning note. That would make him feel good. But suppose it didn't win? Then it would've been the worst betting value in the world. He stood there and agonised over his decision. The runners were now all down at the post.

He looked back at the odds. Hypnotist had hardened again to thirteen to eight on. I've Been To Ballyporeen was a seven to two shot. And Dessie's Image was at seven to one. He walked towards Jack D'Angelo. He ignored Lex. He took out the sum total of cash that he had in his pocket. The eight hundred pounds from Blarney Fox plus the two hundred pounds worth of stake money that he'd managed to raise in the bar. And he put it all on Dessie's Image. To win. At seven to one. Then he went back across to the Tote representative and asked for his entire winnings less tax, approximately fifteen hundred pounds to be placed on the same horse at the same price. And then he walked away out of the ring. He couldn't bear to watch the race at close quarters so he walked out of the Tattersalls enclosure and down behind the stands, behind the now mostly deserted paddock and the paddock terracing. He heard the course commentator's voice.

"They're under starter's orders. And they're off."

There was a giant-sized video screen down by the new Tote building and a large group of punters were watching the race on the screen rather than from the lawn or on the terracing in the stands. The real horses galloped past them in the flesh only about fifty yards away to their right but they were glued to the kingsize Race Course Technical Services versions performing on the video screen. James watched with them. It was getting very cold. The sun had finally given up and the sky was still grey and black in places from the hailstorm. A few drops of rain started to fall.

It was a good race. Dessie's Image was tucked in behind until the top of the hill on the second circuit where his jockey kicked him on into the lead. He went three or four lengths clear running down the hill and seemed to have the other horses beaten as he made the home turn. Then he hit the second last hard and I've Been To Ballyporeen and Hypnotist moved up to challenge as they raced towards the last. Hypnotist landed in front at the last to a huge roar from the favourite backers in the crowd and started to go away up the hill, but then the gutsy old fourteen-year-old Dessie's Image, a real Cheltenham type right down to the tips of his horseshoes, crossed over to the stands side and suddenly started to run again. And with Tomsey Lehane going at it like a true Gaelic Football hero he battled back in front to win by a length at the line.

Richmond was shaking. He'd won about seventeen-and-a-half thousand pounds. Wiping out his debt to Lex with something to spare. It was more even than the fourteen grand that he'd won on Mylerstown on Tuesday and then nearly lost again twice over the next two days. That was racing. He couldn't take a strain like this again though. Not for a long time.

All the same that lucky but desperate victory in the last made him feel bold and sweet and confident about the future. He'd come back. Survived. Got out. And if he could win like this today, gambling on the horses, he could win some other way too. In the future.

Richmond went to find Lex Parlane.

40

The festival was over. And almost from the moment that the Cathcart runners passed the winning post half of the crowd began to leave. Exhausted, punchdrunk, hungover and gambled out.

The bookies in the ring began to pay out their final debts of the week to the last queues of shivering punters. And then they packed their bags. To them and to racing's regular gamblers Cheltenham was already just another meeting. A profit or a loss to be written off accordingly. Tomorrow there was Lingfield and a big jackpot to chase and then there would be Harringay dogs. Every race, it seemed, came just the same. The Tote Cheltenham Gold Cup or the Lingfield seller. And now it was back to the seller.

The rest of the crowd stuck to the bars. As the helicopters started spluttering into the centre of the course, picking up clients and wheeling away again into the sky and as people started scrambling into their cars for the long jam home, the tills and cash registers in the bars continued to clatter and ring with the rattle of fast money. It was as if nobody, not even the winners, wanted to go home with money in their pockets. They wanted to divest themselves of everything they had. And so to one more round.

Lex's gang were all down on the lawn by the outdoor champagne bar. Old betting tickets and empty bottles and plastic glasses and discarded *Sporting Life* pages rolling around at their feet. The war was over and the troops were about to go their own very separate ways but there was still a definite feeling of acrimony and serious friction in the air.

"I just can't believe it," St Clair was saying. "You've got me up here for three bloody days. You've given me all the bum steers. I'm more than forty grand out of pocket and it's all down to you."

"Ain't life grand," said Lex.

"That's the Festival, Charlie," said Pointdexter.

"Festival? It's a bloody graveyard."

"Buy another bottle, Charlie," said DD.

"I've had a very good week," said Pointdexter, looking smug. "And substantially up on betting. You should've been in on our Lloyds syndicate. Fourteen wagers. Fourteen winning bets."

"Arrant drivel," retorted St Clair.

"Just fuck off, Jonathan," said DD.

"I don't believe you either," said Lex. "But you can have another drink." He splashed more champagne into Pointdexter's glass.

"Lex? Please," implored Hugh wearily. "About dinner. You must tell me. Are you still coming or not? And if so how many?"

"Not now, Hugh," said the bookmaker.

"But I must know."

"Piss off. Stop bothering me. You can all piss off if you want."

"Not me, darling," said Daisy, still wearing her indefatigable smile. "You can pretend all you like."

"Pretend what?"

"To be a nasty fat Scotsman. I'll still love you."

"Will you really? I can't think why."

"Let's pick up some whores," said DD.

"Let's go home," said St Clair.

"Let's go to a casino," said Jonathan Pointdexter.

"Boys," said Lex, an arm around DD and Pointdexter's shoulders. "Your pleasure is my desire."

Bella and Reema Donachie had been drinking together all afternoon. Bella didn't look that drunk. She was too tensed up inside. Reema was roaring drunk and getting louder all the time. She was kissing strange men and dancing on the lawn and spilling champagne down her coat. Jack McQueen didn't like it. The sight of two grown women out of control and unashamed seemed to threaten him. He started shouting.

"You fucking tarts. You're both behaving like tarts."

"Don't shout at us," yelled Reema. "Women are allowed to get drunk too, you know."

"Aren't they, Lex?" fired Bella. "Or don't you approve of that? Are we supposed to just stay quiet and polite in our corner? Chatting to the girls about knitting and babies and recipes and periods while you boys all play with your toy trains."

"Do you like her?" Lex asked a man. "She's got a loud voice, don't you think?"

"I need it to compete with you."

"Then don't bother." He turned away to play spoof with Charles St Clair.

Bella looked up at James Richmond. "To think," she said. "I know just where he'll be each day throughout the year. Propping up some nasty little racecourse bar until seven or eight o'clock at night. Surrounded by that."

"Stout fellow, Charlie," came Lex's voice. "It's time you had a winner. Let me buy some more shampoo."

Bella carried on. "No change. No variation. No surprises." She shook her head. "I can't take it any longer."

James looked at Lex. He did seem to be surrounded by an ever-increasing rabble of tawdry and second-rate people. There were still one or two attractive and excited faces. Like Sunny Vengsarkar and Lord Kinglass, who had each won one thousand pounds on the County Hurdle and were very drunk and still fabulously in awe of the bookmaker's company and couldn't quite resist him. But James watched him hurting Bella and Reema and lifelong friends like Hugh and Daisy and he couldn't bear it.

Of course he didn't know about the Scotsman's conversation with his father. All he could see was a man who seemed suddenly and drastically reduced in scale and status. Bella was right. A friend was anyone who'd agree with him. Anyone who'd say yes. Anyone who'd drive away that night in the dark to play snooker or pool or darts or poker and say, 'Sure, Lex. You're the greatest. Anything you say. We'll stay up all night if you want and all tomorrow night too."

"Take me somewhere," said Bella to James, her voice trembling and her eyes searching his for encouragement. "If you want."

"Are you sure?"

She nodded. "I'm sure."

James pushed his way towards the bookie. He undid the buttons on his overcoat, took out all the cash from his inside pocket and pushed a brick square of it into Lex's hand. He'd even got D'Angelo's boy to wrap it all up in neat elastic bands. Then he gave him the cheque.

"The cheque's made out to you," he said. "From the Tote. Ten and a half thousand pounds."

"Thanks very much."

"And there's five grand cash. That should cover what I owe you."

"Cover it and more."

"Did you win on the day?" Lex shrugged. "On the week?"

"I won on Mylerstown. That'll do."

"Mylerstown. It seems a year away already."

"There's always another day."

"Not for me. You can close my account." The book-maker raised an eyebrow. "I'm through."

"You've lost your appetite, haven't you?" Lex smiled. "It had to happen. But you'll get it back."

"I'm going now," said James.

"Fine."

"And I'm taking your woman with me too."

"You think?"

"Watch me."

"I will." James took Bella gently but firmly by the hand. She took one more long and painful look at Lex Parlane. He was still smiling. He held his arm up towards her in a last valedictory gesture. Bella hesitated for a moment. Then she and Richmond turned and walked away. Bella was crying.

"Nobody walks out of my world, pal," Lex shouted after them.

"There's just one more thing I have to do before we leave," said James. "I have to go and say goodbye to my father."

"Alright."

They walked out through the ground floor part of the grandstand, turned right past the binocular van and the paddock and the closing-up Bank of Ireland kiosk, went in underneath the Royal Box and then carried on up the stairs and along the corridor to the Duke's box.

The scene inside was chaotic. Rowland's party for his army and shooting friends was well under way. There was no sign of the Duke or Frampton-Mansell or Helena or the Countess or any of the old-timers. All of them, it seemed, had made good their escape. The room was filled with chaps in green tweed jackets and green corduroy trousers and black shoes. Lots of viyella check shirts and ties with horses' heads and foxes on them. Girls squeaking and braying and pelting their boyfriends with the leftover bread rolls. Two men were standing on chairs in the centre of the room. One of them was blowing a hunting horn. The other one was Rowland and he was singing a song about culling Paddies to the tune of *A Hunting We Will Go*.

Another little porky-faced man in a three-piece check suit was lying on the floor full length with a champagne bottle in each hand. "Filthy rich," he moaned. "Filthy rich. We are filthy, filthy rich. Clarissa. I love you. The chocolate eclairs. Please."

Bella was staring at them all in horrified amazement. It was the same kind of look she gave Charles St Clair, DD, and Jonathan Pointdexter.

"They're not my friends," said James.

"I know," she said.

In the kitchen and serving area of the box next door plates filled with custards and cakes and wobbling pink jellies were sitting waiting neatly on the table. Rowland was going to have a food fight. In teams. James caught a glimpse of Camilla posed on the balcony and chatting silkily with Christopher Cowdray-Clarke and George Stowell. She'd transferred her affections soon enough.

Having failed to catch his father James wanted to leave quickly. Then Rowland saw him. "Brother dear," he bellowed. "Welcome. Welcome. Get yourself a drink."

"No thanks, Rowland. Another time."

"What about Blarney Fox, eh? That made the bookies squeal."

"It surely did."

"One thing I couldn't understand though. I thought it opened up at fourteen to one. And yet the Irish said they couldn't get our money on at better odds than sevens."

"Never mind, Rowland," said James. "I'm sure it's all gone to a good cause."

Outside dusk was spreading. Tractors were beginning to pull the stuck Daimlers and Bentleys out of the mud in the bottom car park. As James and Bella walked up past the Arkle statue towards the taxi rank in the top car park they passed the saddling up boxes and the pre-parade. Two men had set up the three card trick on an upturned box outside the parade. There were only about half a dozen men standing watching but already a flurry of notes had changed hands. Inside one of the saddling up boxes a last, late departing horse was being wrapped up warmly by his lad as a prelude to being led away back to the racecourse stables. The lad was hugging the horse and whispering to it affectionately.

"I never want to lose touch with that sight and that feeling," said James emphatically. "I love horses. And horse racing. In spite of the gambling. It's all so beautiful."

"I know," said Bella. She was holding on to him very tightly. "I love it too. I really do."

41

Down by the winning post the electronic information system flashed up its final message of the week. 'Have a safe journey home. See you next year.'

The few remaining racing correspondents still left on the course seemed determined to ignore at least the first part of that advice. Having tossed off their final copy of the week, read it through and then thrown two-thirds of it in the wastepaper basket, they had now settled down for one last serious drinking session in the press box. All except for Graham Mould, that was. He sat alone at the table in the window working diligently on the content of his latest investigative coup to be entitled: 'Excessive use of the whip. Jockey Club dither. A new furore?'

The Irish were all leaving town. CP Molloy and Big Pat McKenna. Connor Delaney. The Rafferty Brothers. Doogan and Carmody. Conroy and Antoon. Fixing up to meet again at Fairyhouse on Easter Monday and at Punchestown in May. Only Johnny Kinane and Cashel Maguire still sat, waiting for bail, locked up in their interview rooms at the police station two miles away.

Michael Garvin had set off home for Yorkshire straight after the last. To call up his lawyer and compose his retirement letter for *The Sporting Life*.

Michael Bolger was already back in London. Checking on the catering arrangements for the celebratory dinner party that he was planning to throw in the Daytona Beach Club that night. October the fifth. That was the date that Rocco Anderson had given him for his return. Seven months to go.

Louis Weiss would be an honoured guest at Bolger's party. After Mylerstown, the Goldline chairman had gone back to Chertsey in a state of shock. He'd taken off his sharp grey suit and his trim black shoes and he'd put on the nice blue polo neck jersey that Val Doonican had given him that Christmas and then he'd locked himself up in his den to worry. Now he was happy again. At long last the Jockey Club's cumbersome system of justice was cranking into action. And at least Bolger was a man you could deal with.

All the racketeers were on the road. The Chappell family. McFarlane. Turner and Wade. The Capaldis. Gino Garvey. Alan Furness and Willie 'The Dog' Burns. Billy Chappell had enjoyed it all so much that he was planning to enrol Duane in their local riding school in Selsdon. He wanted to see him winning the Foxhunters' Chase in four years time. Everyone, it seemed, had new schemes to think up, new faces to mull over, new races to cook.

Lex was scheming. He went into the last cubicle along in the ground floor gents cloakroom. He tipped a whole packet of cocaine out on to the glass mirror which he'd placed on the downturned lavatory seat. He looked at it for a moment. Then he snorted up the whole gramme. Then he packed away his mirror and his biro stem back into his overcoat pocket, screwed up the paper packet and threw it down the lavatory. He pressed the flush and walked out.

A young man bumped up against him as he walked out of the cloakroom door. "Easy, pal," said Lex.

"Mind where you're going, fat man," said the kid. Lex looked at him. He remembered that face. It was the young Belfast bookie that he'd been giving a start to at Shawfield dogs. The kid had the look alright. A real hoodlum's look.

"You'll do alright, son," he said. The kid scowled and walked out. Lex walked back on to the lawn. He was grinning now. As the cocaine began to race around his mind and body his spirits lifted once again. And his brain sharpened. That Belfast kid had given him the inspiration that he needed.

He'd always known that it would come to this one day. But he could take it. He'd tell them. Where would horse racing be without men like him? Without his colour, his personality and bravura. His fourteen-carat million-dollar style. 'Lex Parlane: Last of the bad men.' Racing needed him as much as it needed betting levy, TV and sponsorship. He was the necessary other side of the coin that had all those bland and clean-cut gentlemanly heroes emblazoned on the opposite face. But if the Jockey Club were determined to have their ritual he'd go through with it. In his way. In full view of the cameras. He'd give them the best star turn gangster they'd ever seen. And if it did go against him, so what? Not the end of his career. Not by a long shot. Just the beginning of the next and newest phase in the one and only career. Being Lex Parlane. His life's work.

And while he was taking the clubmen through the courts he'd still have his income to count on from the Sports Video and Promotional business. He'd get rid of Jack McQueen. He'd need a new man in the press room. Then he'd keep Cooper and Wood and Maxie Carlisle here in England and he'd take Billy Mcphee with him to America. To see the boys from New Jersey. And Las Vegas. Last stop . . . Keeneland, Kentucky. The death of the Lex Parlane Connection and the birth of Lex Parlane Bloodstock Worldwide.

He was sorry, though, about James Richmond. He knew that the boy was disappointed in him. And Bella too. But what could he offer them earlier that afternoon? As a prospective bankrupt and warned off bookie? Now things would be different. He knew that the boy wanted Bella but Bella loved Lex in her heart. He'd get her back one day. The boy too. Once he'd paid off his debts and served his period of obligatory good behaviour in the eyes of his family, he'd be back. His dad might set him up as a trainer one fine day. Then he'd need Lex. He'd need him as his racing manager. That's how it would be.

Lex Parlane looked around the lawn. It was dark. The figures were lit by the lights that had been switched on in the grandstand bars. He could see St Clair and Pointdexter and Delaney-Dalzell still arguing in a corner. He could see McQueen lying face down on the grass. There was no sign of Reema or Hugh or Daisy De Moraville. And the rest of the faces he didn't recognise.

He started to walk across the racetrack and out across the centre of the course towards his still waiting helicopter. He saw a discarded evening paper lying on the turf at his feet. He thought he'd better pick it up. It might have the form in it for tomorrow's declared runners.

As he walked towards the helicopter his lips parted and he started to sing.

> *There may be trouble ahead.*
> *But while there's moonlight*
> *and music and love and romance . . .*
> *Let's face the music and dance.*

The public relations man from the helicopter hiring company was still waiting by his caravan. He greeted Lex obsequiously. Lex got into the helicopter. Alone. The helicopter's take-off lights came on. The engine cut into action. The blades started up.

> *Before the fiddlers have fled.*
> (Lex liked that line.)
> *Before they ask us to pay the bill.*
> *And while we still have a chance.*
> *Let's face the music and dance.*

The helicopter climbed into the darkness. Lex didn't look back. He took another packet of cocaine out of his overcoat pocket. Up, up he went. Up into the dark night sky.

DAVID BRIERLEY

SKORPION'S DEATH

Cody is unique. Recruited by the ISS, trained by the CIA, and now she hunts on her own. Very much on her own.

Her quarry is a pilot, Borries. Hired by an unknown organisation for an undercover job in Tunisia, he's gone missing and his wife wants him back.

Cody finds Borries, at an army garrison deep in the Sahara, but by then it is almost too late. By then the organisation has a name: Skorpion. And Skorpion has a secret, a secret so deadly it will torture and kill to protect it. And Skorpion has Cody in its pincers . . .

'Tough, staccato, sardonically witty'
The New Yorker

'Fine unflagging stuff'
Observer

CORONET BOOKS

E.M. CORDER

THE DEER HUNTER

He was a young steelworker from a sad little hill town in
Pennsylvania. Nothing had prepared him for war in the
jungles of Asia . . . nothing except the hellish heat of the
blast furnaces . . . gut-searing boilermakers . . . the
trailer life . . . and the strength of his passion for hunting
the great deer of the Alleghenies.
The deer hunter was young, but he had steady nerves, the
grace of a cat, and the high mountain passes in his heart.
He would need all of them to survive.

A deeply moving story of courage and friendship set
against the terrifying odds of war.

'One of the most powerful films of war yet made . . . the
Deer Hunter will come back time and again to haunt even
the sternest mind'
Daily Mail

CORONET BOOKS

BRYAN FORBES

THE REWRITE MAN

'A marvellously readable, funny and poignant story . . .
Bryan Forbes has created some splendidly living
characters, sparkling dialogue and a truly touching novel
of obsession and jealousy'
Sunday Express

Harvey Burgess is a Hollywood scriptwriter suffering a
bad case of professional burn-up. Hoping to rekindle the
spark, he answers the SOS of a director stranded in the
South of France with a stalled film about the French
Revolution. It should have been child's play for a pro like
Harvey, but then he hadn't budgeted for his obsession
with the mysterious protegée of the director, the very
young, the very beautiful Laura . . .

'Bryan Forbes has written a very good book indeed, based
on all his experience of the film business . . . it's a long
time since I felt such enthusiasm for my bedside reading'
The Mail on Sunday

PATRICK HARPUR

THE SERPENT'S CIRCLE

What if the Thirteenth Century heretics and greatest rivals
to the Roman Catholic Church, *The Cathars*, had not
been destroyed but had calculated revenge for over 700
years?

What if that revenge was about to take shape in the
blackest contest ever between good and evil?

And what if only a boy with second sight and a scholarly
Italian Priest could prevent the heretics' supernatural
power from toppling Christendom?

The Serpent's Circle is a thriller which relentlessly weaves
a spell of awesome force and intensity.

CORONET BOOKS

THOMAS HARRIS

BLACK SUNDAY

. . . it would be the bloodiest Sunday America would ever see.

And it was all in the mind of one man. The terrorists had him in the palm of their hand. He was the puppet, the girl controlled the strings, and behind her the devil himself must have been unravelling the ball. For this man, this lover of the free, open sky, where his hot-air balloon floated carelessly like a huge, soft bird, had been chosen to deliver death to 80,000 innocent people . . .

The Arabs set it up; now the Israelis had to shoot it down. And quickly. But David Kabakov didn't even know where to start. How could he, an Israeli, get anywhere with some information but no real leads? What could *he* have known about the observation balloon, the biggest flying fragmentation bomb of all time? The bomb which was being primed for the terrible day when it would hang over the biggest football crowd of the season. The day of horror and devastation . . .

CORONET BOOKS

ALSO AVAILABLE FROM CORONET